D0567395

THEY
WHISPER

THEY
WHISPER

a novel

■

ROBERT OLEN BUTLER

[signature]

HENRY HOLT AND COMPANY
NEW YORK

Henry Holt and Company, Inc.
Publishers since 1866
115 West 18th Street
New York, New York 10011

Henry Holt® is a registered
trademark of Henry Holt and Company, Inc.

Published in Canada by Fitzhenry & Whiteside Ltd.,
195 Allstate Parkway, Markham, Ontario L3R 4T8.

Portions of this novel have appeared in somewhat
different form in *Harper's Magazine, The Missouri
Review,* and *The Virginia Quarterly Review.*

Library of Congress Cataloging-in-Publication Data
Butler, Robert Olen.
They whisper: a novel/Robert Olen Butler—1st ed.
p.   cm.
ISBN 0-8050-1985-5
1. Men—United States—Sexual behavior—Fiction.
2. Man-woman relationships—United States—Fiction.
I. Title.
PS3552.U8278T47   1994   93-38261
813′.54—dc20   CIP

Henry Holt books are available for special promotions and
premiums. For details contact: Director, Special Markets.

First Edition—1994

Designed by Paula R. Szafranski

Printed in the United States of America
All first editions are printed on acid-free paper. ∞

1   3   5   7   9   10   8   6   4   2

For Ron David,
who heard every word

THEY
WHISPER

E ven before I knew there was another part of girls that would one day whisper to me, that would call me over and over, there was the machine in my uncle's shoe store and there was Karen Granger and she was on my mind all the time and I somehow knew that I had to get her to put her feet in the machine. My uncle's was the last shoe store in Wabash, Illinois, to put in an X-ray machine to check the fit, and as soon as it was ready, I went to Karen and brought her to the shop. She had on her black Mary Janes and white lace anklets and she went up on the step and put her feet in the slots and my heart was beating furiously as I stepped up beside her, for there were two view ports and together we looked at the bones in her feet. I lifted my arm and I put it around her, cupping her far shoulder in my hand. "Wiggle your toes," I said.

She did, and to this day, though I am now thirty-five years

old, there have been few moments in my life as intimate as the sight of Karen Granger's actual bones, her actual articulated bones with their shape visible to me, the shape that had been secret even when she stood barefoot in the grass of her front yard bossing me and giving me an excuse to keep my eyes cast down. She wiggled her toes in the green glow of the X ray and she let me keep my arm around her and she began to hum softly.

As I remember her now, it seems true, that the intimacy of the moment with Karen Granger in 1955, in the tenth year of my life, was rarely matched in all that has happened since. For here she is, humming inside me though twenty-five years have passed. Though it is 1980, a new decade. Though things have taken a drastic turn in my life in the past few weeks that should make me think of two other women before anyone else. But it is Karen Granger instead. She came to me yesterday morning with a newspaper article on X rays and health and I let the paper fall from my hand by my canvas chair on the beach here in Puerto Vallarta, even as a parasailor lifted from the sand down the way and rose on his tether into the morning air; she came briefly with that and then, much more strongly, an hour later, with the smell of shoe leather in a shop in the hotel, with that and a glimpse of the bare feet of a slim blond woman wearing a towel knotted at her hip slipping past me without a glance. I can't remember what song it was that Karen hummed as I pressed her against me, though trying to remember it distracted me in the Mexican shoe shop. I did not look again at the blond woman but fixed on the buckle of a sandal in my hand and I tried to make the humming shape itself into a tune.

And now, of course, I understand that it's not the tune I really want to know. I want to know *why* she hummed. Did she know her bones were beautiful to me? Did she feel the same intimacy? Did she wait for me to ask to put my own feet in the machine? This is the thought that bothers me. I wish now, wish devoutly, that I had whispered to her, "My turn," and I had put my feet in the machine and she had seen my bones.

But it's not just her, a ten-year-old girl I never touched again. I'm wrong; they haven't been rare at all, those moments of intimacy with the surprise of what they include and the surprise of what they don't. I sat on the beach yesterday and the man clung to his sail and lifted high over Banderas Bay and the water was the color of the South China Sea, the color of a jade dragon on a pedestal sitting in the slant of early-evening sun in the Saigon Museum, and a paddle fan whisked overhead and the shadow of a woman I had never seen before darkened the jade—even as a cloud darkened the bay before me—and on that evening in Saigon I saw only a brief flash of her eyes, she bowed her head at once and her waist-deep straight black hair fell over her face, the closing of a curtain, and she was gone and I would never see her again and I did not move for a long while, I could not move from a deep sense of her, and she came to me yesterday morning, too, even though a woman I love very much, more perhaps than any other, lay sleeping at that moment in our hotel room. She and I had touched at last and I had left her sleeping, her breath soft beneath the spill of her hair, and I came down to the beach to read my newspaper, and I have to try to understand all of this. I remain forever in this place inside me where a smell of leather or a glimpse of a lovely elbow or shoulder or earlobe or some movement of air or cast of light thrills me in ways that I cannot put into the safe terms of the mind. I can't analyze these things in ways that separate them from the ravishment of my senses, because that is how I live, and all the rest—the labels for my feelings, the ways of understanding through my head—all these come later and are grave distortions. Lies, really. I don't mean to justify anything harmful that I feel or do. I am ready to be profoundly sorry. But more important than anything for me now is to tell the truth about my life in this body of mine, and I have to tell it in the ways that it really happens, through my senses.

Like the smell of Ivory soap. Only a few weeks ago I washed my hands in a black onyx lavatory off the executive office of some guy selling radar detectors to the world. He sat in a leather chair and beyond him the roofs of mid-Manhattan steamed in the cold and I excused myself and I went into the hard little room and I stood leaning against the basin for a time. It was the sinuousness of the steam that I was avoiding. That and the image it brought of the woman who had showed me to this office. She had an adhesive bandage in the hollow of her throat and I wondered what kind of wound was there, I wanted to gently remove the bandage and kiss her there. I wanted to move inside her like that steam. And that was all I could hold in my mind as I listened to the radar man explain his product to me so that I could explain it to others. So I stepped into the lavatory to clear my head and then I washed my hands and it was with a bar of Ivory and I lifted the soap to my face and the smell was a Saigon smell.

I worked in Saigon city hall, and around the corner in the shade of a tamarind tree was the massage parlor called Kim Ngan Hoa. Honeysuckle. The Army taught me Vietnamese for a year before I went over and I was musical as a boy so I learned it well, the trills and falls of the tones of the words, and the best thing about the language was that the women loved me for it. For all the life I'd led before going to Vietnam, I'd been stricken with the awkwardness of the desire I'd felt for women, a desire that came upon me for countless reasons— because a woman was smart or funny or strong or unutterably brown-eyed or whatever—and I could never find the words to speak of my ardor. But now I suddenly found the words possible in Vietnamese. I learned a new language and renamed the world and I found that I could speak things that I never could before and just the speaking of them made the woman I desired want to be with me, want to touch me in return. So for two hours in the middle of the day I would go to Honeysuckle and there was a large, dim concrete room in the back with the steam and the showers, and the soap was Ivory. I would stand in the hot water and then sit on a bench in the steam and all of this was imprinted with the smell of Ivory. Just outside the door was a basin where the women went to rinse their mouths and hike their throats and spit after the blow jobs in the wooden stalls. I would sit and listen to the women speaking, though if they knew I was there, they wouldn't talk as freely but would call to me in Vietnamese as I sat in the steam: "Are you ready yet, Mr. I? The honeysuckle flowers are all waiting in the garden for you."

My favorite was Miss Hue. Her mother, Mrs. Hong, ran the place and had lost her husband, Hue's father, the previous year. He was a lieutenant and died near the part of the Cambodian border called the Parrot's Beak. The first time I saw Hue was in July. The rainy season was in full swing and I was a little delayed getting to the massage parlor and I just beat a squall. I stepped in and the rain started to blow through the door behind me and Hue rose from the chair in the corridor before the stalls. She was wearing loose black satin pantaloons and a white blouse with a bow at the throat. She smiled at me with a little dip of the head and her eyes had so much French in them—like her mother's—that they were very nearly Western. I looked at Mrs. Hong, who was sitting beside her, and even before I could ask about this new young woman, she said, "My daughter Hue. She can go with you."

Hue dipped her head again and led me to the end stall. I stepped in and there was the high table and a wooden chair wedged next to it at the foot. I sat on the chair and took off my shoes and I was startled when I looked up because she was still there. All the women at the parlor left while you undressed. They'd go out and sit along the wall and paint their toenails and talk about the mangoes at the market or a pop singer or the rain and they'd wait for you while you made yourself naked as if you both weren't really doing this at all. For me this was the sad part of the place. Not one of them knew how close I felt to them when they came into me and I was naked. I'd shower and sit in the steam and come back or I'd call one of them in at once, and whoever I'd choose would come in full of schoolgirl slaps and giggles and she'd say, "How you've grown, Mr. I" or "Mr. I is always ready for me" and she'd touch me as if I were a piece of fruit at the market. I could put that aside, though. I could always focus on something about their faces or their hands, something that maybe no one had ever noticed before. Miss Chien had a middle knuckle that rose high above the others and had a hollow that I once kissed and Miss Trang had a little notch in the upper curve of her ear and there was something like that for each of them and that's what I focused on intently as I filled and yearned within their mouths.

But Hue did not leave the stall. She stood there watching me undress and she touched the bow at her throat over and over, her finger plucking softly at it for a moment and then withdrawing and then returning right away. She watched and I was soon dressed only in my shorts and she still did not avert her eyes. Her hand fell from her bow and did not rise again and she smiled at me, at my hesitation, I think. I did not hesitate from shyness. It was as if I was bending near her ready to tell her a secret. I had to bring my mouth close to her ear and speak very low and she was straining now, ready to listen, and I hesitated only because it was that moment of faint trembling before a secret is spoken. What is that trembling? I'm not sure. But it's always here. Then you whisper this hidden thing. And Hue waited, her hands still, her bow untouched.

And she did not take me from her when I came. And she did not go out of the stall to the little basin by the steam room, but she turned her face and laid her head there beside the part of me that she seemed so glad to know about. I draped her long black hair over my chest and put my hand gently on her upturned ear and followed its whorls with my fingertip. And a little later I sat in the steam with a bar of soap in my hand and I listened and she never did rinse her mouth and she never did speak of the market or the weather. And in the Republic of Vietnam, in 1969, in the twenty-fourth year of my life, this seemed to me on some scale like something you could even call love.

And it isn't lost on me that I closed myself off in that black onyx room and I leaned into whatever was blowing through me and the woman who appeared was a woman I saw ten or twelve times in my life and never took to a restaurant, never slept a night with, never shed a tear with, never argued with, never taught how to say my name properly but let her call me Mr. I like all the rest of the honeysuckle flowers, a woman I laughed out loud with only once, brought a flower to once, kissed on the mouth myself, suddenly, in the sunlight just one fine little confused time, and I certainly never married her, certainly never walked through a door into an apartment with her and settled in and figured that this might well be the rest of my life. But I thought of her even though Ivory soap should have made me think of Fiona, as well.

Pronounced with a lift of the voice, the sound of "I" means "love" in Vietnamese. My name, Ira Holloway, only made the Vietnamese roll their eyes in despair. But when I spelled out my first name to the women at the massage parlor, they seized on the first letter and it was my Vietnamese name and they draped themselves over my shoulders and they were thrilled that I spoke their language so well and they kissed me on the cheek with noisy kisses and I said to them in Vietnamese that they were each as beautiful as a fairy princess, a very special, rather old-fashioned compliment, and they kissed the cheeks of Mr. Love until they were wet.

It was the soap, of course. I was closed in the radar man's lavatory and the smell was more strongly connected to Hue than Fiona. But it shouldn't have been that way. The first bath Fiona and I took together, in a big wooden tub sitting on the kitchen floor in her fifth-floor walk-up east of Avenue C, we floated a bar of Ivory between us and I never once thought of Hue then. Fiona leaned her head back and let her hair fall out of the tub behind her, the hair that was the same color, I noticed at that moment, the same exact pale tea rose red color of her nipples which suddenly appeared, shedding water, as she leaned back. I floated the bar of Ivory between her breasts and it passed quietly between them and foundered there just below her throat and she looked down and laughed.

I can remember Fiona laughing and her laughter seems miraculous to me now, knowing the pain she was hiding. We sat in the tub and all that would happen between us did not yet exist and I simply floated the soap between her breasts and she laughed. We had met the week before on the street. It was Eighth Street and Sixth Avenue and some guy was selling incense in front of Crazy Eddie's Electronics and I was only a few months back from Vietnam and the incense pulled me to it, though idly at that moment. I glanced at the wisp of smoke as I passed and I realized I could not smell it, I could smell only bus exhaust, and when I looked up, this woman came around the corner and she had a wide, thin mouth and it was stretched as far as it would go, smiling, and she was looking straight at me. It twisted me around to her, even as I kept moving. She slowed and also turned to me and she did not quite stop either but it must have occurred to her what I was responding to.

"This happens to me a lot," she said.

"What?" I said.

"I come around the corner and I've just smiled at somebody out of sight but the smile stays on my face and it looks like I'm smiling at the next person. Am I making sense?"

"Yes. The smile wasn't for me." By now the gap between us was maybe ten feet and we were walking backward away from each other. Since she was still moving, I decided this was all that was going to happen, though by now I was very conscious of her, of the hiddenness of the shapes and smells and colors of her beneath the midi skirt and bulky sweater she wore. But I turned away. The smile wasn't for me, after all. And I went around that same corner and I wondered who it was she smiled at. A little old man with a dustpan and a short-handled broom was hunched over the curb before a florist and there was no other man on the block ahead of me and I felt the release of a knot of jealousy in my chest. I didn't know it was there until it had unlooped and fallen away and it surprised me that I could feel like that over somebody who had slipped past me so quickly. But I was sure the smile was for the little old man and I was glad about that. Then I heard her voice just behind me. "Excuse me."

I stopped and turned around. She drew near but remained just beyond arm's length.

She said, "I didn't want to give you the wrong impression. It's not that you aren't worth smiling at, too." She said this with an earnestness that surprised me. She was watching me closely to see that I was okay.

"I understand," I said.

"Are you sure?"

"I'm sure. Thanks."

"Good." She nodded sharply, like that was an end to it, but she still seemed worried about me. The corners of her mouth were turned down.

"So," I said. "Let's have one, then."

"Pardon?"

"A smile. If I'm worth a smile, give me one now, please, so I can make my appointment." For I was in fact heading to a job interview.

"I'm sorry," she said. "Of course." And her lovely wide mouth opened in a brilliantly asymmetrical smile, lifted much too high on one side but not in a way that seemed the least bit ironic. The smile made me stagger back and it was so odd and beautiful that it seemed a complete thing in itself, requiring no further action on my part. It was final and even at that moment I expected it to be one of those things I would always remember. I dragged myself away from it, moved off, but her voice stopped me once more.

"Have I really made you late?"

I was walking backward again, though now she was keeping up with me. "Yes," I said without thinking and when I saw the pinch of guilt in her face, I realized how abrupt I'd been sounding all along, which wasn't what I meant at all, not at all, and I said, still abrupt, unable to soften any of this, "No. Not yet."

She brightened. "Then since I've already made a pretty big fool of myself anyway I might as well tell you this one thing. You have yourself smiled at me no less than three times since this conversation began and with each one, your eyes went soft and that meant you didn't have the slightest thought that I was crazy or stupid and under the circumstances that's a remarkable thing for you to be able to feel and then to show me just with your eyes." She ran out of breath at the end of this declaration, all done in a rush so as not to make me late, and she went "Whew" and began to turn away and I knew I had to stop her.

"Let me call you," I said, and she looked into my eyes once again, searching, I suppose, for more of whatever she'd already seen there and then she smiled a slow, faint smile and nodded and that's when I got Fiona Price's phone number and my future was sorted out in some drastic way with nothing more than the faint swish of the old man's broom in the background. She recited the number to me and repeated it twice so she knew I had it right and her voice sounds clearly in my head, even at this moment, and I can smell her near me, citrus, ripe fruit on a windowsill, and when I say that my future was sorted out, that doesn't mean in an understandable pattern, necessarily. Otherwise I'd have no compulsion to speak now. Maybe I wouldn't even have this compulsion to remember. But maybe

I would. All the women I've loved in all the ways that surprise me even now: *they* compel me, as they always have.

Not that I had much early experience with them, not directly. But I had always dreamed tumescent dreams about them, found myself inside them in my mind over and over, and the dreams always carried voices, I could give the girls voices that spoke clearly to me, and I think that was how I first came to understand something about the love of a woman. I was sixteen or so and too skinny to be noticed by girls the way I wanted. I knew the janitor at Wabash Senior High was a drunk and he did his drinking early, passing out from about six to nine. Then he'd miraculously revive and do his cleaning, but for those three hours the school was unlocked, unguarded, and uninhabited. I sat in a stall in the boys' room one morning between classes and I saw all the writing on the walls, and I think my idea started out much more simply than it ended up. I just wanted to know the words that girls spoke secretly, to each other. I had that faint trembling in me the rest of the day, and that night, about seven, I came back to school and slipped in and I went to the main girls' rest room by the front office.

I opened the door and stepped in and it was dark. There was no reason for that to surprise me, but it did. I had never been inside a girl and this felt suddenly like a dream of that, of moving through a door into unexpected darkness and you can't see a thing, not even the hand in front of your face, though I raised both of them now and felt the air against my palms like the thick soft hair of the girl who sat in front of me in social studies class, who always lifted her face and shook her hair in pleasure whenever she answered a question correctly. She had a plain face, with tortoiseshell glasses and no chin, and she often answered correctly, so her lush hair would fall on my desk, and whenever she raised her hand to answer I would put my own hands, palms up, on the desktop ready for her soft touch. The more I touched her hair, I found, the prettier her face seemed to me. Her glasses magnified her eyes and I realized with a shock one day after touching her hair that they were the green of bluegrass and they seemed very beautiful.

But I stood there in the dark in the girls' room and I could scarcely draw a breath. I found the light switch and turned it on. I flinched in disappointment. The place looked like the boys' room. The same scab red tiles, the same dim mirrors, the same mole gray stalls, though I think I was a little grateful for all of this. If the place had been more personal, had reflected our differences, I would have been caught that first night, for I would never have left. I did take one quick peek in the trash can, but it, too, was bland and sexless, with crumpled paper towels and a Coke bottle.

So I went to the row of stalls and faced the first door and I was cracking my knuckles furiously, I realized. I clenched my fists to get hold of myself and I pushed open the door and stepped in. I looked first at the walls and nothing was there. No words at all. I looked closer and there weren't even places where words had been scrubbed off. The girls had all been silent in this stall. Then I grew conscious of the bowl. As brutally similar as it was to ones we used on the other side, I felt a difference. I've felt it since, often, when a beautiful woman has just left a room. There's some sense of her that remains, a residue. And you have to understand that I was sixteen and I was downright balletic inside with desire for girls and yet I had never touched one, really, certainly nothing private on one, and so I extended my hand and ran my fore-finger along the inner rim of the seat and I wondered whose pretty bare bottom had nuzzled into this spot today.

It was a nice little moment, but it drew too much on my own imagination, which I could use anywhere. I'd come here for *them*, for some word from the others. So after a few moments more I pulled my hand away and I backed out of the stall and entered the next one. Which had no words either, and I was getting worried, though there were a couple of smudges on this wall where things might have been erased.

In the third stall, however, I found words: Mary T. loves Danny G. and he loves her. I was more disappointed by this than by the silence. This was public stuff, no more personal than a girl wearing a letterman's jacket and it made me a little angry, as if they knew I was listening and they deliberately held back.

There was one more stall and I stepped in and at first glance it was just a bland repetition. Mary T. had been in both stalls and she loved Danny G. enough to say it twice: Mary T. loves Danny G. and he loves her. But then I noticed three words in a tiny, precise hand written just beneath the declaration: big damn deal. This wasn't the secret I was expecting. I guess what I somehow expected in this place was to hear the girls speaking of their bodies or drawing pictures, like the boys sometimes did, of their own secret parts, sure to be more accurate, or of our parts, full of girls' imaginings and yearnings.

Nevertheless, the three words of Tiny-Hand made me sit down right there and read and reread the message. Jealousy and loss were also things you could see in public, but this girl was suddenly present in that narrow private place with me. I could hear her desire for Danny G. and her hatred for Mary T. and suddenly I could also hear Mary T. and her self-doubt. She did not simply draw a little heart with the initials in it. She did not simply declare her love for the boy. She used a lot of words with her pen running dry every few seconds because it was at the wrong angle. She sat there and jiggled the ink down over and over so that after her own declaration she could emphasize "and he loves her." It was the emphasis of insecurity. She even wrote it as if it were in the voice of someone else, an objective observer, as if others could see what she was afraid only she could see. And Tiny-Hand missed this. She would've had a much more devastating rebuttal if she'd understood her rival, but she didn't. Big damn deal, she said, as if it wasn't a big damn deal, but you knew that it was a very big damn deal for Tiny-Hand.

I sat thinking about all of this for a time and I knew I could make both of them happy if only they could be made to understand who I was. And that's when I got my idea. Occasionally the boys' room would have a tempting note, like the one I'd seen that morning: Blossom McCoy loves to fuck. Everyone knew about Blossom, I guess. She had buck teeth and bad eyes that no one ever corrected so she squinted all the time, but she had the body of a fantasy truck-stop waitress and she wore very short skirts and we all figured we knew why her kneecaps were always dirty, and we all thought constantly about the rumor that she never wore underpants. Though every boy jockeyed for position lagging behind her going up the bleacher steps or the winding main staircase, nobody ever really confirmed that rumor, as far as I know, though many claimed they did.

But it was the little note about Blossom that connected to that moment and before I could even consider what I was doing, I had my pen in my hand. My only hesitation came as I lifted the pen to write and I realized that the handwriting was critical. It had to seem like a girl's. Tiny-Hand gave me all the inspiration I needed. She printed in block letters and I did this, adding a backward lean to the words so that Tiny-Hand wouldn't be implicated. I wrote: *Ira Holloway is a great lover*.

Maybe a week passed and I jumped at every ring of the phone, though I knew that only in my most overheated of just-before-falling-asleep fantasies was a girl going to call me up and say, "Listen, Ira, I've been hearing some good things about you. Let's meet after school today; my parents are away on a business trip." A walk-around-in-the-daylight fantasy was that at least Blossom McCoy would call, but I always figured that everybody was wrong about her, I figured there was more to Blossom than anyone realized, and so I never let that thought go too far.

What I mostly concentrated on was the search for the little sideways glances, the brief lifting of the eyebrows or widening of the eyes of the girls as I passed. And even looking for these things, even ready to imagine them based on the tiniest little hint of something, I couldn't see the slightest change in anybody. Well, once. The high point of that search occurred right after homeroom about a week later. I was nudging my way through the clot of students at the foot of the main staircase and a pretty girl I'd been noticing since the first day of school was standing near the water fountain, and even though there were students eddying around her, I could clearly see her face turn to me and then her eyes widened, just as I expected, but frankly they widened even more than I expected and then her face jerked to the side and she cried to somebody in the crowd, "You stepped on my damn foot."

It's a measure of my yearning as a sixteen-year-old that what should have been a little epiphany for me, what should have caused me to plunge into the crowd goose-pimply with shame instead made me stop and stare at the girl and wonder if this was Tiny-Hand. It was a rare girl in 1961 who would use the word "damn" so readily. Big damn deal. You stepped on my damn foot. Could it be her? She had long, straight hair which I have always particularly liked and heavy eyebrows which I also found that I liked, but if this was her, then it was Danny G. she loved and that made me move off down the hall realizing what I needed was a second endorsement.

So that night I slipped back into the school and into the stall and only at the last moment did I fear some scathing rebuttal to my earlier claim on this wall. I feared this just in time, before I let myself look, and I almost backed out of the stall and walked away from the whole project. But after a moment I decided the risk was worth it. I looked at the wall and the words were the same as I'd left them. No one had taken issue with me and I was lifted by this. I think I even rose up on my tiptoes for a moment with the joy that this idea about Ira Holloway was at least not so outrageous that somebody had to take issue. And surely Tiny-Hand would've done so, if it was. So I bent to the wall and beneath the message that Ira

Holloway was a great lover, I wrote in an impromptu imitation of a large, filigreed, girl's hand: *He sure is.*

Nothing changed. Not a word was spoken, not a glance or gesture was altered. And that should have been that. If it had, though, I wouldn't have spent this much time talking about a teenage stunt. But I went back a third time and I sat for a while and stared at the wall. I'm not sure what was in my mind. I guess at first there were the things you might expect: wondering if anyone even read these words, imagining the images of me in the minds of those who did. But I don't think that lasted long. For a time I just blanked out and stared. I wish I could recall the things that were in me when I took out my pen once more, but I can't. I probably couldn't have done that even moments later. All I know is that I had been thinking of girls just about all my recollectable life and I was inspired— like the inspiration of suddenly saying a thing that you don't quite recognize even though it's you saying it and it's just the right thing that makes a woman's eyes soften and her head angle slightly to the side and you realize that she has just fallen in love with you and you don't even know where the words that let this happen came from. I was inspired, like that perhaps, and I wrote this:

What's all this talk of Ira Holloway? I doubt if you really know him the way I do. I have been his secret girlfriend for a year. I saw him at the pavilion at the park swimming pool. I was floating on my back and my body was feeling real lazy. My breasts—which are very large, larger than the breasts of any of you who are claiming Ira for your own—my breasts had that loose sprawling feeling, you know how it is when you have large breasts and you lie on your back and you're real relaxed and they seem to flatten out but of course not really, they're like two cats fast asleep in a soft rug. And my nipples were hot like melted butter. And I was thinking about my body like this when I looked up and there was Ira Holloway looking down at me from that little second-floor pavilion and I have to say I liked the look on his face. You can have the soft snarls of your Elvis or your Fabian or your cheap imitations all around you in the halls of this school.

Now, writing all this was taking a long, long time but I wasn't really aware of that. It was like I was learning their secrets after all, writing in the voice of this girl. And so when the rest room door opened with a bang, I jerked up so hard I dropped my pen and it was all I could do to stop an audible gasp. At first I thought it was morning, that I'd been here all night and this was a busload of girls rushing in to find me here. But I heard a hard slipping scuffle and a man's voice cursing and I knew it was the janitor, which was bad enough. I quietly dropped the bolt on the lock and lifted my feet and pressed them against the door.

The janitor kept mumbling as he lurched about the room and it occurred to me that this man had access to this special place every night. I gagged with anger at that thought, in just the same way as I gagged whenever I learned that some really lovely girl I'd noticed was going steady with some really dumb guy. I wanted to leap out of the stall and pummel the janitor, but I just listened to him empty the trash and he was talking all the time, saying words too low for me to understand. It was clear that he wasn't doing a thorough job, that he'd maybe had more to drink tonight than usual, and that was my hope to get away with this.

Finally I heard the slobber of his mop and after a few moments out in the center of the floor, he opened the stall at the far end and his march down the row began and my knees went so weak that I could hardly keep my legs up against the door. He mopped and then flushed and swished the toilet bowl with the mop and moved on. He did this twice more and then he was standing in front of my stall. He tried the door and it did not yield and he said, "You little cunts."

I was breathing only from the lip up and my legs were beginning to quake. Surely the janitor had a trick for opening these doors from the outside, and there was a stillness now on the other side of the door that scared the hell out of me. No more cursing, no more mumbling, no motion now, just this silence, though I knew he was there. I waited and waited and my legs were shaking and I thought for sure he could hear it, I wondered why he would wait so long if he knew about me and if he didn't, why he was suddenly silent. Then the door moved just a little, like a great weight had been brought to bear against it, and I thought it was over.

But instead he said, "Oh this fucking head," and the weight lifted and groaned and then his mop came in under the door and waved around at me from the floor, knocking my pen away, and my only thought now was that he'd find the pen and take it and I wouldn't be able to finish. But the janitor had no more time for all this, and he jerked the mop out of the stall and I heard him stagger. He must have been bending over to mop under the locked door and this was a big mistake. He seemed to be struggling to stand up and he lurched out of the rest room and I heard the door close and I lowered my legs to the floor. It was a long few moments before I could stand, but I did and I went out and retrieved my pen and I returned and I wrote:

Ira was looking at me from the pavilion as I floated on the water and you'd think I was a bed with sheets that were dried in the yard in the sun and he was trying to just gently open me up and crawl in and rest inside me. He made me feel that way and that's just how I want to feel. My thighs were bare all the way up to that tight clutch of my swimsuit and I wished I could open up for Ira Holloway right there, just part my sheets and let him crawl in. So don't talk about Ira Holloway unless you can feel that about him. And I do. I really do.

I never met the girl of this voice, of course. Not in all the years that followed, not even among the women in my life whom I've loved with the abiding ardor of that sixteen-year-old still inside me. But every bit as important as the first woman you touch is the first woman you clearly imagine, and I feel the same way about her that she does about me. I really do.

So I called the number Fiona had given me and it was a Saturday morning and the city haze was burning off and it was going to be clear and she said she wanted to go to Coney Island. "Okay," I said. "I'd like that."

"I can't see your eyes now," she said, and I understood at once what she wanted.

"I'm smiling and my eyes have gone soft," I said.

"Good."

The mystery again: the things you say and do that inspire love in another; the things you see and hear in another that make you fall in love with her. They happen, they fling you from the thoughtless orbit of your life, and yet, subject to reflection, they can appear to be small things, not the gravity of a star but merely stellar dust. Still, you dash on in some drastic new direction because of them. This much I know: These words I am compelled to speak are not simply the story of Ira and Fiona; I have fallen in love many times and for what seems to be an infinite variety of reasons, and it is *all* of this that I must try to understand. But Fiona was different in some way, right from the first, and these are the little things from that day at the beach.

We sat on the fine sand and in the shadow of a pier and her skin was so white that I moved us twice as the shadows crept away and the sun fell upon her and I did this without explanation and the second time she touched the back of my hand and she whispered, "You're taking care of me, aren't you." I turned my hand to take hers but it was already gone and we were standing briefly in the sunlight and before us there were bare chests and legs moving and flapping towels and a great stretch of city gray ocean and I saw it all as if out of the very corner of my eye, blurred and indistinct, and I turned and watched her and this was clear: the short straight line of her nose, her mouth puckered slightly in thought. I already knew to expect the direction of her thought. Art was her work, I'd learned on the subway ride. She had degrees in art history and she was working in a gallery in SoHo. Now she watched the beach and said, "If I were a painter, I'd do a life's work right here. Like Monet and his lily pads. These bodies, shifting and arranging, and the light catching them and letting them go."

"Why don't you try it?" I asked.

"I'm too much a coward to be an artist," she said.

I waited for more but she fell silent and still I waited, and it's her voice, I realize now, that I remember so much from the beach. It was her voice I was beginning to fall in love with, even then. It seemed from the beginning to be a private voice, a whispered voice, ready to speak whatever was roiling inside her. And what was inside her came to seem familiar to me in an entirely unexpected way. We sat on a bench on the midway and there was popgun fire, the tinny clang of falling ducks, the ratchet of wheels of fortune spinning, the smell of cotton candy and of old piss on concrete, and she took up the thought again: "If you're an artist, you have to live completely in your body. You know? You have to tell your mind to fuck off."

She stopped me now and looked at me sharply, as if I'd spoken something that surprised her.

"What is it?" I said.

"I heard myself just then. Do you mind if I say 'Fuck'?"

"No," I said, and then corrected myself: "*Fuck* no."

"I wonder who I got it from, that word. Other people shape our voices, you know. And how we see."

"Like your artists."

"Yes," she said and then she gestured to take in all the midway, the people moving. "But the good ones let all this shape them directly. That's what I don't have the guts for. I'd keep letting my mind intervene, trying to keep it safe, trying to step out of my body."

The phrase stirred me—even that simple thing, the passing, general reference to her body. She was wearing midthigh shorts and her legs were stretched out and crossed at the ankles and the palm of my hand closest to her prickled with desire, just to reach out and fall softly somewhere upon her, anywhere, and rest there, but I kept my focus on Fiona's face and she looked at me and she smiled. "Your eyes again," she said. "I like what they do when I talk. They widen just a little bit and they're trying not even to blink, not to miss a moment of looking at me. I hope that doesn't sound conceited. It's not. Believe me. I can't even look at myself in a mirror. But I can see this in you and recognize it."

And she was right, of course. I simply nodded, not wanting to interrupt.

"And this I like," she said, touching the center of my chin with her forefinger. "I like a cleft there, even a dramatic one, a Cary Grant one. It was like Cary Grant's brain, that cleft. He had a right side that was him doing a tap dance, and then the left side when he was flashing those eyes that were so smart they could see right through you." She paused and her own eyes narrowed on me. "Does this bother you," she said, "my talking about another man like this? Admiring his chin?"

"No," I said. "It's fine."

"It could bother some people. I don't think I'd like for you to tell me about Veronica Lake, the way her hair fell over her eyes and that you loved when it did that."

"I won't say a word about it."

It was an odd moment, I suppose. But all I could see was what seemed to be her desire for me in this rather creative bit of jealousy, and I took that as a hopeful thing, a pleasurable thing, even. Besides, her fingertip returned instantly to my chin.

"But it isn't Cary Grant that I'm sitting here admiring," she said. "He was just an example. Your dimple is very different and I love it. Even more. It's very subtle there. It took me a while to notice it, really. Like some sweet little twist to your personality that suddenly came out. Like back on the boardwalk when you smiled and returned the nod of the guy wearing three sweaters rummaging in the trash. Did you realize you did that?"

"No."

"You did. He can't help being what he is, probably. And even if he could, it's none of our business. You made him feel like he wasn't some kind of pariah when you smiled and nodded back to him. Your dimple is like that. I saw it all of a sudden, in the sunlight on the beach the second time when you were trying to take care of me. Can I kiss that spot?"

We had not kissed at all yet. We had not even held hands. Her words stunned me into silence and I knew I could not muster a voice to even say yes. She seemed to know it, too. She did not wait but leaned to me and kissed me lightly in the center of my chin and she pulled back and I wanted to take her in my arms and return that kiss but I did not move because I had a strange calmness in me, as if we had just made love, as if we'd just connected in some momentarily complete way, and so I sat there and felt the faint coolness on the center of my chin, the touch of her lips evaporating, and the only clue I had to what was going on inside me was that I thought of Miss Chien's knuckle, the notch in the upper curve of Miss Trang's ear. Fiona saw my chin the same way.

Finally I did say, "It sounds as if you can live quite well in your body."

She grunted at that and turned away and I was afraid that I'd caused her pain and I began to thrash about in my head for words to take it back. But before I could say anything stupid, she said, "Sometimes I can. It comes and goes."

Now I simply sat beside her and pulsed with regret at saying anything at all, at not simply taking her in my arms in response to her kiss on my chin. She still kept her face turned slightly from me. Her eyes tracked back and forth, watching the passing crowd. Then her gaze settled for a time and her lids drooped a bit and I wondered if at that moment she was in her senses or in her mind, and I thought to speak to her about her eyelids, the curve of them, and then kiss her there. But before I could speak, she said, "They're brother and sister."

I followed her gaze to a coin-pitch booth in the center of the midway. There were four people gaggled there but I picked out the two she meant, right away. They were in their late teens and they were probably twins, both tall, taller than the other boy and girl with them, who apparently were their dates. My own attention moved from the brother and stuck on the sister. She had long black hair, familiar, at first glance, with my eye still predisposed by Vietnam, but she lifted her face and her hair fell away from her shoulders and down her back and her hair was thick and I knew my hands would wade slowly there, not plunge slickly through as with the Saigon women. And then she laughed and her throat was very long and Fiona said, "You can see that they're related even in the smoothness of their throats. It's nice in the boy. He's beautiful there, with the Adam's apple hidden."

I glanced at the boy and perhaps she was right but I went back to the girl and her face came down as the laugh died and I knew not to say anything about her beauty to Fiona. And I was surprised at myself: I should have been having a sharp little twinge at her admiration of the boy's throat, at the feeling I had that she wanted to kiss him there, but I did not. I was not jealous at this quick sensual current in her, even though I was keenly attuned to the potential of her jealousy. She'd warned me, after all, with Veronica Lake as a safe example, but I sensed this in her even without that, I sensed it in her even though she had opened herself up—willfully, it seemed— for what would be a most natural and unwittingly destructive comment on my part. But I don't think she was testing me. She was in her body at that moment, not thinking things out, and that made her vulnerable, and I kept quiet.

Then she said, "What's the mechanism, do you suppose?"

"What do you mean?"

"That keeps her from wanting him. A sister and her beautiful brother."

"I don't know. I'm an only child."

"I am too."

"I've never desired my mother. Never. It's even more common for a boy to want his beautiful mother, isn't it?" This came out unexpectedly. And I realized then that I was falling in love with Fiona. I was ready to speak any feeling to her. I looked away from the girl and there was no image of my mother before me, really. Maybe my head was doing what Fiona had been talking about—keeping things safe. "I don't know what that mechanism is," I said and then I turned back to Fiona and her face was bowed and her hands were clutched in her lap. "What's the matter?" I said.

"I like you already, Ira. Quite a lot. I hate to put any barriers between us. It's just that I have trouble with this parent thing. It's my own fault. I provoked it. I'm having trouble using my head around you."

"That's my trouble too," I said. "I spoke without thinking."

She lifted her face and she turned to me and her eyes were heavy with unshed tears and she said, "It's you here, Ira. Just you." She was silent then for a long while and she studied my face, carefully, as if we were about to part forever but she didn't want that, and I held very still and slowly her tears disappeared, evaporated like her kiss from my chin, and then she said, "I love this eyebrow about as much as the dimple." Her hand came out again and ruffled the place over my nose where my eyebrows joined.

Now I knew to take her in my arms and we clung to each

other as the coins skipped over the glasses and the popguns fired and the wheels of fortune turned.

I met Fiona for lunch at a restaurant in the West Village on the following Monday. I still didn't have a job and she had the afternoon free and we sat in wicker chairs at a wicker table on the sidewalk, a scalloped awning shading Fiona's skin from the high sun so I didn't have that nagging little worry about her that I'd had at the beach. And this restaurant must have been near a dance studio because for the third time now in ten minutes a different young woman passed that I saw instantly to be a ballet dancer, swan-neck thin, hair tight in a bun, moving with grace, yes, but with strength too and with feet splayed.

This third one I actually turned my head briefly for as she passed and Fiona followed my eyes and then came back sharply to me, a little echo of her lightly danced jealousy from Coney Island. I let myself have only one brief beat of pleasure at this—pleasure not at evoking her jealousy, for already I wanted to keep her feelings as safe as her skin, but at being the object of the jealousy of this lovely woman. I wish I could say how badly I may have acted in those early months. I know I was conscious of her sensitivity about my reflexive love of women, and I did all that I could not to let these fears rise in her, no matter how flattered I felt by them. I wanted very badly for Fiona to have peace. Perhaps she does now. I don't know. I wanted it for her then, from the first. I know this: When she looked sharply back to me after my eyes had moved to the dancer going by with her gym bag slung over her shoulder and the nakedness of her flowing from her throat down almost to the point of each shoulder, I focused instantly on Fiona's eyes and made mine as soft as I could. "You are so very beautiful," I said to her.

The sharpness went away from her at once, though it was with a dip of her head and a great lift and drop of her own shoulders, a genuine spasm of skepticism. "I hear that now and then," she said, "but I can't see it that way, I'm afraid."

"Then just look in my eyes," I said.

"Okay," she said, and she put her square chin on her fist and I was on the spot. I put my own chin on my fist and I about squeezed my eyes out of their sockets trying to be soft and loving. I kept waiting for her to laugh at my efforts but this went on and on and her gaze did not waver on me and her mouth was flat and still and then it occurred to me that she really was trying to see herself as beautiful in my eyes and even as I thought this I stopped trying to force my look and she knew it. Her head cocked ever so slightly without leaving her fist and I was lost, I thought, I kept looking at her but I could only think how wonderful she was to be reading me so closely and how stupid I must have been looking. And then she said, "Now. Now I see it, Ira."

"Good," I said, though my voice was much tinier than I expected it to be.

Fiona sighed and it sounded almost like contentment and she took down her hand from her face and I began to listen now for her inner voice. I was listening already and there was a faint whisper of it. No words yet. But something. "I think they're ballerinas," she said.

"I do too," I said.

"They are always the same," she said. "These girls are from Degas."

"Their feet," I said.

"Yes," she said. "Ducks."

"Ducks," I said, very seriously trying to agree.

"That's why I'm not an artist," she said abruptly, but with a faint smile. "I'd make them ducks because I find them beautiful and can't stand the sight of them for it. Degas found them beautiful and painted their feet like the cosmic things they are."

I had no reply to this, of course. I put my chin back on my fist, and after she watched still another ballerina go by, she did too, and I think we stayed like that until our food came.

And then, still early in the afternoon, we ended up at her apartment on the Lower East Side with the dopers and the bottle gangs and the building next door to hers falling into rubble but also with women in aprons leaning out of windows and people going past and stopping and talking and they could be warm, could show something that seemed like real affection for each other even shouting down to the street from four stories up while their children played on the stoops, and men in cutoff T-shirts weren't afraid to pick up their kids and kiss them. This is what Fiona loved about the place and we walked up five floors to her apartment and the roaches scattered and the sunlight splashed in from a skylight and the tub was in the kitchen and I noticed it right away and I wanted to be sure and bathe with her there before all the sunlight was gone— that is, if things went as they seemed they were about to go. I had to stuff my hands in my pockets to stop them from shaking. Not from fear, you understand. My only fear was not knowing everything about this woman who was standing in the sunlight and lifting her face to it.

She said, "Do you think Van Gogh really saw the sky and the sunlight like that? Like something thick and agitated, like a man trying to make love to you and you don't want it?"

She lowered her face and looked at me and her hair was a tissue of soft flame and it took me a moment to hear what she had said, though when I did, I wasn't sure I'd heard right. The part about a man trying to make love with her and her not wanting it suddenly sounded full of implication about her attitudes on the coming afternoon. She must have read something in my face, because her hands lifted and flapped at me in guilty record straightening. But it was a different mis-impression that worried her. She said, "Please understand that I'm not suggesting anything about Van Gogh's sexuality. The metaphor was mine."

"I gathered that," I said and my voice surely betrayed a concern for something other than Vincent Van Gogh's post-humous sexual reputation.

I think she picked up on that, though maybe this was her next thought anyway. She lifted her face once more to the sunlight and said, "I don't see it the way he did. I love his art and I respond to it very strongly, but that still isn't enough to change the way I see things."

I said, "If all the artists you loved changed you, they'd hack you up in little pieces and you'd never get back together. That, or you'd end up loving only one artist forever."

She frowned at the sky. "Nasty choice."

I took a step toward her but I was afraid to touch her yet. Not while she stood in that shaft of sunlight. "Look. I don't even know what the hell I just said. I just want to give you sweet choices."

This made her smile, made her turn to me and step from the sunlight. She drew very close and on her breath I could smell the strawberries we'd eaten from a paper carton on the way here, the faint stickiness of them still on her fingertips as she took my hands. "Sweet choice number one," she said. "Do we walk to the bed hand in hand or do you carry me?"

And this was our little motif for the first time we made love. Sweet choices. Do you undress me or do I undress you? Do you go down on me first or do I or do we do that at the same time? Do I start on top or do you or do we lie on our sides? It was charming at the time, I guess. But I sensed that some-thing was wrong: I was involved in the little game and I was missing too much, missing the things I loved to linger with and concentrate fully on. The first sight of all the special places, the first touch of them, the first dew rush of wetness. None of this remains. Not from the first time. The sweet choices did their work: there was appreciation but no one was changed.

And to be honest, I get a little queasy feeling, thinking back now on all the cute talk that so often went along with the wooing. I shiver at it. Really. I've had plenty of male friends who love all that. They love to think about the lines they use and they trade them off and they run them over in their minds. I was telling Fiona the truth when I said I didn't know what the hell I'd said. Sweet choices. What kind of bullshit is that? That was just something that got in the way, another layer of clothes that you put on just before you want to be naked and you can't ever quite wriggle back out of them, the buttons catch, the zippers stick, and you end up never really touching.

So when Fiona and I had finished and she had curled beside me to doze, I tried to clear my head. And it was pretty good after that. There was laughter down in the street and salsa music coming through the walls and a child crying somewhere and I turned my face to the foxed window shade, half-raised, the braided pull loop fluttering a little, and a pigeon dashed by soundlessly and across the way I could see an open window and a TV screen flickering in a dim room. All of this made me comfortable where I was, surrounded by a kind of scruffy thing-ness that I'd often felt in Saigon, too, just the year before. But I resisted any drift back to the Orient. I was determined to place myself with this new woman and I looked at her and she was on her side, the sheet lying across her hip, and only the upper curls of her pubic hair were visible. That was all right for now. Since most of the mystery of that had been preserved by my earlier distraction, I'd let it linger. Her arm was twisted up in sleep across her chest and hid her nipples and that was all right for now, too. The soft afternoon light from the window framed her navel and I would start there, happy to, for I love a woman's navel, made more special because it's so rarely seen, and Fiona's was a taut little tuck, curved lightly to make a crescent, and it stirred me now, Fiona's startling white Irish skin with her faint smile of a navel and a navel is an intimate thing, after all, the mouth of a woman's life in her own mother's womb, and all navels are different—their size, their puckers, their turnings, their dark depths, the shading of the skin—and so this was Fiona here, a sweet little wry smile of a navel and like all navels, it suggested, in sweet miniature, a pussy.

And when I say this now—pussy—I name the place with a foolish little word, a reductive, hissy little word, but there are no others that are better. Vagina is a cold eye, legs in stirrups and rubber gloves. Cunt is angry. Cunt sees no beauty there and is afraid. Pussy at least can be gentle, can be soft-edged, and that's how I say it, knowing that the word is absurdly inadequate, knowing that it will take every word I will speak in this story of mine to be able even to draw near this place and begin to understand why I love it so much.

And so from this place that has no name Fiona's smell hung lightly in the air and I flared my nostrils to it, drew it in, and her navel blew a brief kiss to me as she breathed deep, and then she let the breath out softly. I looked at her face and her eyes were moving beneath the lids and I hoped I was the one in her dream. But—to my surprise—I felt it wasn't necessary, really. I was close to her in a way that I couldn't quite bring into focus and it was a way that made me sigh a bit—even with the possibility that there were other men moving in her dreams—sigh just as she had sighed at the wicker table in the West Village. And I crept across the bed and brought my face very near her navel and in the light from the window I could see the lick of pale fuzz rising from it. She once lived in her mother's sea through this spot and my hand came forward and I put my thumb and forefinger in her very softly, I opened her up, and her navel swirled down into tighter depths as if I could go farther still, much farther, but I bent to her now and kissed her there, touched those deep turns of her flesh with my tongue. I closed my eyes and on the tip of my tongue I felt this deepest pinch of her and I thought I could imagine her voice, the voice that is never spoken. I thought I could open eyes in my own head as if they were her eyes and I thought I could hear her voice:

I know I am dreaming but I know that it is my true life: I sit, knee-weary, in a gallery at the Met with a pointillist haystack floating before me and I lower my eyes and slip off my shoes and a shadow passes over my face and I see his hand, young-skinned but corded with veins of a flat Dufy blue, and I look up and I see only a brief flash of his dark eyes and he smiles a quick smile from the corner of his mouth and he is gone and I will never see him again and I do not move for a long while, I cannot move from a deep sense of him, and a man I loved for only an afternoon lies beside me on a beach in the south of France and he sleeps and dreams beside me and I follow the whorls of his ear with my eyes and I want to put my finger there and follow them but I do not want to wake him and so I touch his ear only with my eyes, memorizing it, and he sleeps on but I do not. Instead, my dream begins to end in an odd way. This new man, this Ira Holloway, is above me in my dream. We are making love and I arch my back to him and he is inside me, filling me up, but he is also floating. He is lighter than air and floating over me and I look up into his eyes and they are blue, like holes through him and I can see the sky, and there is a stirring in the center of me and I awake and I see a bird rush past the window and I know I am awake. But there is still this feeling in the center and I look down and he is kissing my navel, filling it up with his tongue, and I look down at the top of his head and his hair is what the artists call bone black and there is a part through it absolutely straight, baring the whiteness of his scalp. I like this straight part, this Ira Holloway of clear direction and precision, and I make my hand straight and I lay the side of it in his part, fill it up.

And this she did. I felt her hand on my head and I realized

that the delicate nakedness there in the parting of my hair was suddenly covered up. I filled her navel with my tongue and rested against her and she kept her hand against my part for a long moment before finally stroking my hair flat and then changing her mind and tousling it. I lifted my face to look at her and her mouth was drawn flat, though her eyes seemed soft, looking at me with what I hoped was love.

But the voice I'd heard in my head was wrong. Not about the men. All the men Fiona had ever loved—and I had no idea at the time how many that might be, though I sensed there were many—did indeed reside inside her. But I thought that gave her joy. I was happy for that. Happy. And I was comfortable then about the women who lived always in me. I was even suddenly cured of a niggling, retrospective jealousy that often scrabbled its way through me with a woman, particularly at the beginning of things, before we had our own memories. But I was wrong. There was no joy for Fiona in her memories. And even as I put these words together now I can see her on that afternoon when she placed her hand in the part of my hair and I looked at the tight pinch of her mouth. Now I can hear her true voice: *I woke and he had his tongue in my navel and that was something new, I think, something that should have made him special somehow but it never worked the way I expected it to. The bed was suddenly crowded. Over Ira Holloway's shoulder was a redheaded man—some guy I'd met at a bar—and he was coming up for air and he put his chin on my cunt and he was suddenly wearing my pubic hair for a beard and it struck me that the color was just the same as the hair on his head and for a brief moment I was convinced that he liked me, only for a moment, you understand, because there was this impossible proposition at work: that he might know more about me than I do myself and he can come up with his face dripping and say that what Fiona Price thinks she knows about herself, knows down even to the roots of her pubic hair, is all a big mistake; in fact she's worth drawing another breath on the planet earth. But in an hour or two hours, whenever he's gone, I lie back on the bed and my eyes fill with censer smoke, a man's hand swinging a chain and even the hand disappears in the smoke, and every pore in my body pinches shut and I feel that whole process going on, a million little spots all over me, each making a judgment, shutting down, mea culpa, and I strike my breast, and if I am lucky the hand in the smoke does not belong to my father, does not come gently toward me now.*

This was her true voice. I came to know that her father was always there in her true voice. This was her voice except perhaps for the naming of the sweetest part of her body. Maybe that was her voice also, for her self-loathing was very strong, and the word I hear, cunt, carries that. But maybe not. If the words for a place so softly, so complexly portaled and swirled, a place so prone to weep in joy, seem ridiculously inadequate to me, then what must they seem to a woman? For a woman to have a place at the center of her that she cannot really see— not like my part, which yields its whole shape to the slightest glance—for her to have a place that is like the mystery of personality, difficult even for itself to apprehend, for a woman to have such a place in her body that gathers a man into it from his deepest yearning, a place that also cries forth a new child into the world, for her to have such a place full of the mystery of love and desire and the creation of life, I am sure she has no name for it in her truest voice. Just as there are no names for the feelings in myself that I am trying in all of this to understand. I speak now, speak in the ways I do, because I am ravished with love for this center of a woman's body that has no name, that can't be turned into a thought, that will not yield in any way but through my senses.

And so, because I give words to whispers, to sounds like the faint hiss from the edge of the universe, there are these little bits of broken translation when there are no names. Still, I sense that this too is Fiona's true voice: *I stood once on a balcony on a tenth-floor apartment in the south of France. It was dusk and I was naked and there were lights in the harbor and a man was sitting in the room through the sliding doors behind me. I was wet still and sticky on the thighs and I heard a voice behind me but it was speaking the news, the man had turned on the television, but I wouldn't let myself think about the choices he was making now, with me naked here, leaning against the ironwork balcony, visible to the street, and so I turned off the French in my head. Suddenly a man's face was before me, his eyes looking in my eyes and then sliding down to my breasts, quickly, my cunt, my legs, and he was gone. I heard the sound of him hitting in the street below—even the quick exhaling of his breath, like he'd just come—and I knew he must have jumped from a balcony a floor or two above me. But all I could wonder was if he liked me, if he liked my naked body that flashed before his eyes. And I knew he didn't.*

Sex and the dead are the only things that can interest a serious mind. I think that's William Butler Yeats. Fiona quoted it to me in the early days. Not in connection with the south of France. She spoke of that much later, and then it was with only a few words about being with a man there—a gallery owner, I think it was—and nothing about her being naked on the balcony or thinking at that moment about how much she despised herself, though almost from the first I knew she thought about that all the time. In spite of some early errors—critical ones, I suppose—her voice, her secret voice—the puckers and the tucks and the turnings and the skin shadings of it, the secret pussiness of it—eventually became known to me. Known to me and to no other, not even, much of the time, to Fiona herself.

But when she quoted Yeats, I felt her warmth near me and these things—sex and death—had passionately joined in my life less than a year earlier, and in spite of my being smart about Fiona's jealousy a few times already, this time, without thinking, I told her about night bunker guard at a base camp called Homestead, where I was stationed in my first few months in Vietnam, before I was transferred to Saigon. We all pulled that duty. At dusk we'd climb a shaky wooden ladder up about fifteen feet into a square, timber, tower room. The wood was bare and held a mustiness that was one of the first things about Vietnam that seemed familiar to me, that connected directly to something that already was part of me, a musty woodshed in a ragged yard, a girl with a gap in her teeth and a star map of freckles on her face, my distant cousin, and she kissed me hard on the lips in the fly buzz and the musty smell of the shed, my first real kiss, I think.

In the tower we watched the hundreds of yards of our perimeter, gullied and wrapped in concertina, and beyond it was Highway One, leading to Saigon. There was a tall wooden bench at the highway side of the tower and we'd sit there beside our M60, the two-hundred-round clip snaking away from it, and there was a turning of a stream beside us; it made a tight arc and flowed beneath a little bridge at the highway and on into Bien Hoa, the town nearby. You could see two suns, one growing fat just over the horizon and one in the stream, below the bridge, and then everything went black and we'd wait out the night.

Like everybody else I was scared shitless for the first few weeks. When the night came, often you couldn't see a thing except the stars and a few spots of lamplight in the town and once in a while there were dogs barking far away, a hollow sound, like they'd all been thrown down a well and were frantic to get out. A couple of times a night somebody from a bunker down the way would get nervous and pop a flare, but mostly it was darkness and the clamping in your chest because everybody talked about how all these bunkers and the marsh behind us and the first two streets of hootches beyond that, including mine, had all been overrun by the VC in the big Tet of '68.

We'd whisper in the tower and pop a flare every so often just to look around out there, afraid of what we'd see but even more afraid of not seeing it, and we'd shake each other if we dozed and we'd keep glancing back to the ladder up into this place, waiting for the Cong to suddenly appear there, though it would be just a couple of grenades thumping and rolling under our feet, if you wanted to be real about this thing. We'd hardly have time to sort that noise out from a dropped coffee cup before it'd all be over.

But the thing about Vietnam wasn't how scared everybody was. It was how routine it became. How you got so bored most of the time you figured you'd beaten it for good, you'd never get scared again. That could always change real fast, but usually it didn't. And the nasty Tet was more than a year ago and things were pretty calm here in our camp's little corner of Vietnam. So I guess that's how Betty and Jane started coming to our tower in the middle of the night.

I don't know how it got started, but one night the gangly motor-pool sergeant they called Flamingo cried up to us in a stage whisper from the darkness and said he had a surprise. Understandably we all spoke very little, so I never learned their Vietnamese names, never even got a good look at them except for a brief glimpse at the face of one of them. Flamingo whispered how much they charged and we paid it gladly and in the dark one of them sat me down in a back corner of the tower and she unzipped my pants and drew me out and took me into her mouth and I could hear the dogs barking down in that well and I didn't let myself hear the soft sounds in the far corner of the tower. I listened to the dogs and the chirping of the lizards and the sweet little grunting sounds of this woman who held me in her mouth.

I pulled the tower every fourth night and for three or four of those times in a row, Betty and Jane—BJ, Flamingo laughed at mess one morning as if I hadn't already figured that out— Betty and Jane appeared in the dark and sucked us dry. We all knew how crazy this was. We all knew that Betty and Jane and whoever they might have been working for could have had our lives any night, our lives and the lives of half the sleeping camp, probably. But the two women would flash a penlight at the bridge at 0200 hours every night and Flamingo would flash a penlight back at them and they would wade in and slip through the concertina wire in some place that I don't think even Flamingo knew about, exactly, and there they would be, their feet wet and their mouths hungry.

The last time Jane gave me a blow job, I yearned to see her face. It was just the two of us. Flamingo was pimping Betty in a different bunker and the other guy in my tower took a walk. The wonderful thing about a woman sucking you is her face: all its particularity, made so familiar by constant exposure, suddenly is part of the secretness of sex, and my hands were on Jane's hair, at first gently tracing the center part, touching her scalp with my fingertip, and then as I grew tighter, lifting her hair, letting it flow between my fingers, but this night I wanted to see her face upon me and my hand acted almost on its own, letting her hair fall and reaching out, stretching far to my left and I found the flare gun.

I leaned back and angled my arm out of the tower and I shot the flare and there was the rising hiss and the pop and the world bloomed orange outside. The darkness remained inside for a few moments, but the flare was parachuting slowly down and the shadows around me began to move, the blackness suddenly had a broad, sharp edge and it moved down the far wall and across the floor and then I saw myself stretched hard into this face and the top of Jane's head made my chest collapse with tenderness, her long black hair fell from the part and I bent and kissed her there and before the shadows could wipe back across us, she lifted her face slightly without taking me from her mouth, her eyes rose to mine and I was very tight now, full and focused on the tip of me, and she sensed it and her eyes closed softly and then opened, and as if in rapture her eyes rolled back, rapture I thought, rapture, and two days later she was dead. Flamingo came down with the GI shits and he wasn't out there on the stream and there were a couple of guys new in country in our bunker and they popped a flare and saw a couple of intruders wading up the stream and the M60 cut them to pieces. Jane rolled her eyes back in my dreams for weeks. I was hard and I was in her mouth and I was part of her but she was dying, gasping for air, and her eyes rolled back in pain and she was dead.

Why would I tell Fiona this story? Even if the impulse came in a direct way from my feeling of closeness to her, my love for her, even if my hands quaked and my voice grew thick as I spoke, I should have known better. Last week I was in a grocery store and the checkout counter had one of those new cash registers with a synthesized woman's voice that speaks the price of the item as the clerk scans the product code. The voice was, of course, flat, unexpressive, though it was clearly a woman to me and I watched the numbers coming up as she spoke them. "Two twenty-seven," she said for a TV dinner and "Two twenty-seven" for the second one and "Ninety-nine" for a jar of mayonnaise. You know how it is that when you talk on the telephone to someone you've never laid eyes on, you automatically see a face. This one, from the voice talking through the cash register, was a thin face with a pointed chin; her wheat bread brown hair was pulled back sharply in a bun, though she was still young. The clerk who was scanning the groceries was a pasty-faced high school boy with a bad overbite and I wondered if he saw this face, too, if he was haunted by this bland face in his dreams, after listening to the voice all day long.

But he had now reached my twelve gourmet strawberry yogurts and the price was sixty-nine cents and the woman's voice began to call out, "Sixty-nine, sixty-nine, sixty-nine." I turned to her and her voice no longer sounded flat. It was full of longing; it was insistent, driven by desire, and she went down on her knees before me and she undid the knot of her hair and let it fall and she took my hands and tugged at me. "Sixty-nine," she pleaded. "Sixty-nine."

I gripped the check-writing stand and tried to break the spell of this sexual iconography. Sixty-nine, the perfect little yin-yang of a position, and this voice was calling me to lie beside it, face to loin, face to loin. Surely the whole store was alert now with all the grimacing old-lady faces and the leering men with seed caps turning my way. But when I looked around, no one was paying attention. Even the clerk was bent single-mindedly to the scanner in the countertop. It was just me and the woman in the machine. "Sixty-nine," she cried. "Sixty-nine." And I broke into a sweat of desire for this woman who was worse than dead.

Fiona reacted strongly on that very early day to the story of Betty and Jane, and I don't blame her. Even at the time, instantly, I understood that this was a very stupid thing to tell a woman. She thought there was something seriously wrong with me. Maybe it wasn't a thought exactly. She threw a chair at me. A big wooden chair, like something an immigrant had made to go with his wooden bathtub in the kitchen and then it got passed on down with the apartment for decades. Fiona's strength surprised me, but she was very upset and I skipped out of the way pretty easily because she couldn't throw it very far, no matter how much strength her fury gave her.

"What?" I cried. "What is it?" Though I knew what and I was really trying to think of some way to take it all back.

She could only sputter and I was standing in the middle of her living room floor at this point and she was in the doorway to the kitchen, looking around for something else to throw. She turned to the refrigerator next to her and I thought for a moment she was going to give it a try. But instead she snatched a happy-face magnet from the door and threw it, way off the mark.

"Fiona, what is it?"

Her hands were flexing furiously and she was gyring there just inside the kitchen doorway. At least she didn't seem able to move very well, she wasn't heading for the drawers to get knives or whatever. I guess by now I could figure out basically what was wrong, though we'd known each other for only a few days. She threw a hand towel and so I moved closer to her. I wanted to tell her that I was a fool but the only words that came out were ones I didn't mean, justifying things: "You were the one who quoted Yeats," I said.

"Yeats gets me the tale of your favorite blow job?" she cried, and for her to go so fast from sputtering and gyring to this sharp little indictment made me want to take her in my arms, made that neat little scimitar of a navel seem wonderfully expressive of her.

"Not my favorite. Surely that's clear," I said and I flinched at how out of control my own words were.

"Oh great." She flapped her arms. "I've got your favorite still waiting for me."

There was the sudden calmness of irony in her voice and I drew near and finally I could say something I meant. "I was a dumb shit to tell you that story."

"Yes. Yes that's true."

"But this was a thing I'd never spoken before to anyone. Can I be wildly insensitive to you and deeply respect you with the very same words?"

She lifted her face at this and considered it. "Yes," she said. "Perhaps so."

I thought that was a moment of real understanding between us. But it would be months before she herself mentioned the guy jumping from the balcony, and even then it would be just a few bare facts, just that such a thing happened to her once.

I learned the details from this voice of hers that's inside me, a voice that says much more because of all the things about her that I've learned face to loin, flesh to flesh, lips to ear, and because of all the whispers in half-light and shrieks in a kitchen door and chairs flung and because of a child—a son, my son— and because of all the years that were to come. I know that her voice inside me is true.

But I was wrong to bring up Betty and Jane. Yeats was just small talk. I was wrong and I knew it and this encouraged me to understand Fiona's jealousy in a certain way, and that lasted until it was way too late. Something earlier that night should have been a warning, but I ignored it. Her mouth clamped tight at the table from the first moment the waitress appeared, a dusky-skinned Oriental woman, Thai probably, with a pony-tail. I smiled up at her and thanked her for the menus and there was nothing in the smile at all, I was still very much focused on Fiona, my knee was touching hers under the table and our bodies were so new to each other that even this touch-ing was breathtaking. I just smiled a thanks-for-the-menu smile and the waitress was gone but Fiona already was furious. I ignored it. I didn't learn what she thought until after the chairs had flown later in the evening and by then I was blaming myself for Betty and Jane and I didn't stop to think that the thank-you for the menus had set her off almost as badly.

Only once during the meal did I do anything that could rightly give her a twinge of jealousy, and there was no way she could possibly have known about it. Indeed, she had dragged herself away from her earlier pain and was talking compulsively about poetry and Ireland and all of that and she never missed a beat even as the waitress left the fresh bottle of chilled wine on the table. The young woman had disappeared already, but on the side of the bottle I could see a corona of foggy conden-sation around the place where her fingers had touched the bottle, and the quick faintness of desire came over me at this vision of her fingertips. I placed my own fingertips over hers and Fiona's words flowed inexorably on, leading us to Yeats and then to a deep, deep silence that lasted through the cab ride and up the five floors and into her apartment and the first big fight.

Talking like this, I know sometimes I sound as if it's just Fiona I'm trying to understand. She's very important, of course, but in some sense that waitress is just as important. She and a great metropolis of women are inside me and they teem into me still, they never stop, the tiniest intimacies about them, their fingertips fading on a cold bottle, make them part of me.

A couple of years ago I received a booklet in the mail from a guy in my high school graduating class who'd organized a fifteenth reunion. I was in Europe when it took place and so he sent me this booklet they'd put together. It was full of little profiles of all the people who graduated with me, and I found that Blossom McCoy was dead.

I never touched Blossom, in spite of her reputation and the indiscriminate bellow of my desire in high school. Even if what the rest room walls said of her was true, she seemed unapproachable. And I have to admit that for most of the time I knew her, the homeliness of her face put me off, no matter how terrific her body was.

Then one day I was on a hall pass doing an errand for a teacher. I had to deliver a note to a student in the boys' gym and I knew what a special chance this was. To get to the gym I could reasonably go down the canopied outside walkway that passed the entrance to the girls' locker room. There was a frosted glass door that led to an inner hallway and then another door straight into the lockers. On warm spring days like this one, the outer door was often propped open and then, it was rumored, if you were free to walk by during this last ten minutes of a class period and if someone were to open that inner door at just the right moment, you could maybe catch a glimpse of a naked girl straight from the shower. A couple of guys claimed to have done this: one a slide-rule type on a hall pass who said he saw the head cheerleader full-front-naked—a claim I did not believe—and the other a guy with a ducktail hairdo who was cutting class to sneak a smoke and who claimed to have seen only the rather large bare backside of a sweet-laugh fat girl who no one cared a damn about sexually. That one I believed. And I figured if one day it's the fat girl, the next it might be someone even more exciting.

So I hit the walkway and I could already see the outer door propped open and my groin clenched right away. I walked along and tried to look nonchalant. I even whipped out the hall pass and pretended to check something on it, a silly little ruse to wave this flag of my legitimacy. But no one was watching anyway. I slowed way down, and as I drew even with the door, I dropped to one knee and began to fiddle with my shoelace. Then I slyly lifted my eyes. The inner door was closed. It was a heavy metal door with no glass, not even frosted, and it was shut tight. But through a gaping transom I could hear the sound of showers and girls' voices and I wobbled on my one-knee crouch and it was all I could do not to fall over.

I delayed as long as I could, but I finally had to get up and deliver my note. I knew, though, that I would have another chance on the way back, and as I approached the entrance from the other direction, I was ready to work on my other shoe. But this time the inner door was standing wide open and I reared back and gasped. A girl was standing there, her back to me, and her hair was frizzed and wild but put up in a temporary ponytail and all the rest of her was breathtakingly naked. I followed the indent of her spine down between the tuck of her waist to the flare of her hips and from where I stood I could not see the wetness from the shower but I knew it was still there, still beaded on her back and in the straight cleft of her sweet bottom and in the faint indents of her sacral dimples.

All this I took in instantly and the gasp came uncontrolled and to my horror, the girl heard me and she was turning.

I expected her to scream and then I would be caught there flat-footed, both my shoes clearly tied and no excuse at all for this forbidden privilege. But it was Blossom and it was I who thought to cover up, to whip out my hall pass and cover myself with it so she would somehow not see me. Blossom herself made no move to hide. She squared around and faced me and I gasped again, more softly, at the vision of her nipples the color of my tongue and the thick arrow of her pubic hair pointing to one of the two places—the other being the soles of her feet—that I had not seen in the past few seconds.

She did not make a move. She stood there squinting at me and her face suddenly didn't look so bad at all. Her mouth was open a bit and though perhaps it was really for the sake of her protruding teeth, it seemed to me like the drawing of an excited breath. And I even felt a sudden tenderness for her squint, which seemed now like a squint into the sun by a strong woman, a pioneer woman maybe, like if the movies had had guts enough to give John Wayne his equal to fall in love with. Seeing Blossom naked made her face beautiful to me and we stood there watching each other for a long moment before I figured I'd pushed my luck far enough. I sort of smiled at her and she made the faintest nod of her head and I moved away.

I was sixteen when I saw Blossom naked. It was in the late spring of my sophomore year and I still had never been inside a girl. Blossom was in none of my classes and in the few weeks following, I saw her only a couple of times, passing in a clogged hallway between classes. She always noticed me, it seemed, but with that same faint nod, nothing more. Wabash was a steel-mill town of about forty thousand people and it lay in the river bottoms just across the Mississippi from St. Louis. It was 1961 and we still didn't have an air conditioner and I would lie sweating in the dark with the window open and the sky orange from the hot strip plant and a faint smell of naphtha in the air and I would conjure up that blessed few moments of Blossom standing naked before me, willing to show me her body. I could touch myself then and on those nights I felt closer to Blossom McCoy than any girl I'd ever known, closer maybe in a certain way than to any person I'd ever known, even putting sex aside, though that was the way I was reaching her. I figured I saw her face the way no one else saw it, the beautiful face of this strong woman.

But still I did not act. Of course part of my dreaming in the nights of that spring included a true joining with Blossom. And on a hundred nights in a dozen cities scattered over the nineteen years since then I've cursed softly into the dark in regret at not having approached Blossom, taken her away somewhere—to the levee or to the bluffs or maybe even back to her own trailer—and made love to her. I wanted to kiss her eyes, run my tongue across her teeth, rest in the softness that I knew was inside her and that I never even had a chance to look at.

Blossom did not give me my first orgasm inside a woman but she did bring about my first postpubescent fistfight. Shortly after I'd seen her naked, some guys were talking about her in the lunchroom and one of them said that he'd sure love to fuck that cunt, he'd just throw a paper bag over her head, and I called him a piss-ant asshole and he was also dead in the reunion booklet I got in the mail, dead it said from a motorcycle accident, though it said nothing of how Blossom had died. But this guy jumped up and threw a punch that glanced off my ear and I jumped up and full of love for Blossom McCoy I hit the kid in the nose with a straight right. He went down and in clutching at the table as he fell he brought his tray of food down on him. This was my first fistfight and also my last and I felt okay about it. I knew even at the time that there was some principle involved, something I felt very deeply about but didn't really understand.

Later in the week I had the family car for a couple of hours and instead of heading for a friend's house like I'd promised, I drove south, past the high school and into the numbered streets with their tar-paper shotgun houses and then the vast skyline of pipes and stacks and furnaces at Wabash Steel's blast-furnace plant. The smell of naphtha filled me up and at first it was a smell of night and dreams of sex, the link to my open window and my bed, but the smell grew stronger and stronger until it scared the shit out of me, taking away the control I had over my own fantasies, making me dizzy with the possibility of something real.

The street brought me up to the cyclone fence at the plant and I leaned forward and looked up the towering bleeder valve with its gelatinous flame, almost invisible in the sunlight but undulating there, I knew. I turned onto the Collinsville Road and went out past the horseradish fields and over the Illinois Central tracks and after a little run of farm stands and a bait shop and a tavern, the water oaks thickened into a wood and then they thinned again and scattered beneath them were trailers and I was tempted to accelerate away. But I didn't. I slowed and turned in by the hand-painted sign: OAK VIEW TRAILER PARK, electricity available.

There were two parallel dirt roads before me and I chose the one on the left and I crept along it, white-knuckling the wheel and sweating badly and sorting out the place going by— the ragged laundry flapping on lines, the babies without pants playing in the yards, the turn of a long-jawed woman's face to watch me, the leap of a cat from the fender of a beat-up late forties Plymouth up on cinder blocks—and I came up to the end of the first road where two strands of wire fence were strung at the edge of a wide grassy field. Across the field I could see the snaky line of the Illinois Central tracks heading for the distant bluffs.

I turned into the second dirt road and about fifty yards down I saw two women working in the yard before a little house trailer painted a most extraordinary color, lavender, fresh still, unblistered, unstained, and I knew from the color that there was no man in this trailer, it was just Blossom and her mother, and the two of them were in the yard, on their knees tending the flowers in a brick-edged apron going round the trailer.

I slowed and I realized that my penis was lifting and Blossom was wearing jeans that were cut away to the swell of her bottom and now there was only one place I had not seen, for her feet were bare and the soles were turned up to me and as I approached her trailer, Blossom turned her head and saw me and she put her trowel down and she rose, wiping her hands on her jeans. I wanted to stop, to rush from the car and embrace her, but her mother also turned her head. She had very thick glasses and her face came forward to see who I was and I looked at Blossom and she smiled that faint smile once more.

There were many little things, I suppose, that made me drive on without stopping. The mother straining her bad eyes to see me. The fear of Blossom saying no after all, since every straining penis fears rejection more than anything, I suppose, and never more so than when no one has yet said yes to it. And the lavender of the trailer made me feel that this was no place for me, that I was right about Blossom McCoy and her trailer was indeed the opposite of the great hole of free fucks that the boys at school all assumed. This was a soft place, a woman's place, and I did not belong no matter how sweet Blossom's faint smile was. And I also knew that I could not step out of the car without the world instantly seeing how wildly erect my penis was. The mother's magnifier eyes would drop to my pants and she would burst out laughing at my desire and no matter how much Blossom would try to put me at ease, I would have to flee anyway. So I just waved at her. A goddamn stupid little wiggle of the fingers was all of myself that I gave to Blossom McCoy and I drove off with the perfect knowledge that it was my last chance with her and I would regret this forever.

So the thing that I did that was maybe a little bit crazy was when I read in the reunion booklet that Blossom McCoy was dead, I sat down in the guest bedroom at the back of our house for a long time and I didn't turn on the light. I sat in the gathering darkness, and I expected the thing that drove me there to be a profound something but almost immediately I was distracted by that faint buzz a completely quiet room makes and I wondered what caused that and then my heel began to itch and I slipped off my shoe and I scratched that spot like crazy for a long time, completely caught up in that wormy little sensation. The crazy part of it is that I had a business trip to Chicago the next week and I contrived some reason to make a side trip to St. Louis and night was coming on when I got there and I rented a car and drove over to Wabash and down to the south side of town and out past the blast-furnace plant roiling in the dark, washed by steam and blazing with light, and the bleeder-valve flame was immense and tonguing the night sky. I hadn't smelled naphtha for quite a few years but I had come to this place for one reason only and I didn't let myself go to any memory but one. I rushed on past the mill and past the great broken black shapes of the slag heap and away from the town, out into the horseradish fields and over the train tracks and it wasn't until about now that I stopped to wonder what the hell it was that I was doing. Blossom was dead. But I could hear her voice.

The first guy I ever had feelings for, you know, sexy feelings, was Wally Moon. I was nine years old and he was a rookie right fielder for the St. Louis Cardinals and my momma took me over to the game in Sportsman's Park. He was from Arkansas, which is where my momma once said my daddy is from, but that didn't have anything to do˜ with my feeling. It was Wally Moon's eyebrows. They were thick and black and they didn't stop there over his nose, they went clear across. Looking at him loping through right field and seeing that face of his made me feel like I did when I was all wet right after a bath and I touched the dial on that old radio Momma kept on the back of the toilet. All the little hairs on my arm stood up and I figured I better let go quick or this shaking inside would take me away. It was something like that when I looked at Wally Moon and his one big old shaggy eyebrow going all the way across his face.

And that was what this boy had who stopped and looked at me through the locker room door. He was skinny and dark and he had eyebrows just like Wally Moon. I knew that door was open all right. My momma calls me shameless and I come in for a lot of rough talk all my life, but this is what it was for. I was the first one out of the shower and I was alone down there at that end of the locker room and I opened the door myself, pushing it far enough that it stayed open and then I turned my back to it and I started to dry myself real slow.

This isn't shameless. It's full of shame. Not that I mean I should be ashamed for doing it. I'm talking about the shame of my face and the shame of the way I talk and the shame of whatever else it is that makes men look at me like they do when they look at my face, like this is something ridiculous and it makes them angry, even when they let their eyes go down to my tits and my legs and then my crotch, it's like they're tearing around some corner real fast because their faces stretch hard in some new direction and I guess that means they like what they see down there, but it never does me the good you'd think it would. 'Cause I've already bought that first look and the words I know they say behind my back and what I dream of is somebody looking at my body and then looking me in the eyes and not seeming like they want to hurt me.

That's what this boy done who was standing outside the locker room door. That's what I leave that door open for sometimes, looking for just this boy, though I figured the chances of him ever actually walking by one day was pretty close to zero. But things can happen and this time I knew somebody was behind me because my ass prickled. I was still wet and it was like some cold breeze come through, but it wasn't no *breeze, it was this boy's eyes. So I turn around real slow and there he is with his dark pompadour and his Wally Moon eyebrows and these eyes that you'd expect to be dark too but they're not, they're blue of all things. And what's in those eyes is no anger at all. Nothing like that. And I know I'm in love already because it feels like all my pussy hairs have jumped up, just like they was fans at Sportsman's Park and Wally has hit one of his twelve home runs his rookie year. And the best of all is that I can see how this boy is looking at me different.*

And so it's no surprise that a few days later I'm working with Momma in our little garden and a car comes grinding by and I look around and it's him. This makes me real happy and I stand up and I wipe off my hands because when he stops I plan to touch his elbow propped up there in his door window, just a little touch to let him know he's the one I've been waiting for and he'll look me in the face and there'll not be any anger there at all, nothing but love. And I even know what I'll say. I plan to tell him how he looks like Wally Moon and I figure if he likes my goddamn face he won't mind me being a baseball fan all on my own.

But I let her down. All I could do was wiggle my goddamn fingers and after that I stayed away from her. We never had any classes together and since there was only one high school in Wabash it was crowded and I could just hug the walls and stay away from her and this is what I did. Because the shame was mine now, all mine, and I didn't know how to make it right. And so I let us both down because there was something really important that I never learned, something only Blossom McCoy could whisper to me, and as crazy as it seems, that's why I'd rented a car more than fifteen years later and I was heading east on Collinsville Road and I was suddenly nervous about the bright splash of lights up ahead, something new, and a billboard said that it was half a mile to Wabash Speedway, Stock Car Racing and Demolition Derby.

I pounded the steering wheel at this, for though I knew how

quixotic this whole thing was from the start, I sure as hell didn't want a goddamn demo derby track to sit in the place of Blossom's trailer park. But the track was still half a mile off and I was already passing the little clumping of water oaks, the oak view of Oak View Trailer Park, and I thought of Wabash, Illinois, to give me hope. The place had long been a Rust Belt town with only one of its two steel mills operating but it also had a reputation for being a find-your-own haven for Southerners having hard times but thinking they could maybe go north and make something of themselves in a place like St. Louis. So I figured there was probably nothing more permanent in Wabash than a trailer park. And in the park there were those who came and went real fast, but there was always a hard core of residents who took the place as their rooted home and the wheels under their houses simply as souvenirs of their youth.

And it was still there, the Oak View Trailer Park, and when I turned in, from what I could see, it was much the same as it had been, except the two parallel streets were macadamized. There was even some laundry on a line, limp in the darkness, and backlit in a trailer door was a baby without pants and in another doorway was a woman with a long jaw watching me pass. It was all the same, as if this were the same laundry and the same child and the same woman who had watched me roll through here long ago.

I followed the same path I had the first time, down to the end of the left-hand street and then a turn at the field and another into the next street. I remembered clearly how far down I'd seen Blossom and her mother, but when I got there, the trailer was different, much bigger, taking the space of Blossom's little trailer and the one next door as well, and I could see a wiry man, maybe forty, gesturing angrily in a window to somebody out of sight.

I hurried on now, embarrassed at last by this crazy little quest. But I knew I'd simply obeyed an impulse like the one that had sent me into the gathering dark in our back bedroom to sit and try to think about Blossom when I'd read that she was dead. I'd come to this place where she and I had once been together and I hoped to learn something from her, if not the secret of her sexuality then the secret she knew now, right now, the biggest secret of all. As I drove on down the street, I tried to see Blossom's face from the day when she rose up, wiping her hands, and smiled faintly at my ardor. Was there something in her face that foreshadowed an early death? That's what I wanted to know. In her face with its squinting eyes and bad teeth that I'd come to see in some really special way, was there something that could explain what would happen far too soon? If I could see beauty in her face that no one else saw, maybe I could see destiny, too, and then maybe I could look at my own face or the face of someone I love for those same signs.

I neared the end of the street and all my attention had turned inward, but a sound started up in the distance that made me look around. A great cycling whine began, like a forest full of monstrous cicadas. These were the engines of stock cars, I realized, a race had begun at the speedway, but in turning my head I now found, on what was probably considered the prime corner lot, a little trailer with a skirt of bricks. I couldn't make out the color in the dark, and it didn't have to be lavender this many years later for me to sense at once that this place belonged to Blossom's mother, like other old women in Wabash still living in the only home they had ever owned. But at least the wheels had turned again, if only to move into a better spot in Oak View.

I stopped the car and there was a light on in the trailer. I hesitated now, feeling foolish at each separate stage of this thing. But I'd come this far and I made myself step out of the car and into the night that smelled of the mill and roared with distant stock cars and I moved to the front door and knocked.

The face was unmistakable, the eyes bulging behind the

thick lenses of her glasses, even the pucker of a mouth full of unruly teeth; this was Blossom's mother and she said, "Who are you? What do you want?"

"Mrs. McCoy?"

"My name ain't McCoy," she said and she was ready to pull back into her little house and close the door.

"Did it used to be McCoy?"

"In a manner of speaking."

"I went to school with your daughter Blossom."

"Don't have a daughter named Blossom." She said this without missing a beat and the words were flat, uninflected. Was this a way of her saying that Blossom was dead? Was this the residue of a years-old split from her shameless daughter? Or was it semantics? Oddly, this last thought was the one that I sensed was the truth. This was a woman reared in some tight-doored hill-folk family and the substance of what I was saying, the images of her daughter, hadn't even entered her mind. This was word play and it was a reflex to keep her distance from a stranger.

I said, very courteously, "I knew a girl named Blossom McCoy who lived with you in this trailer park in 1961 or so."

"My daughter was named Vera."

"Vera?"

"There's nobody to call her that fool name anymore."

"The fool name being Blossom?"

The old woman cocked her head at me, thawing a bit, I sensed, as I played her little game with her. She nodded. "That's the fool name I'm talking about. I sure don't mean Vera, which is a pretty name if you ask me, one that I thought about a long time."

"I went to school with Vera."

"Were you one who helped make her a bad girl?"

"No, ma'am."

"You know what I mean?"

"Yes, ma'am," I said and there was a sudden release of the

engines in the distance, a drastic cycling down of them all, maybe in response to a red flag, some accident over there, but the air suddenly seemed to ring with silence, even though the cars continued to mutter. I don't know if it was a coincidence or if the woman lived in a nightly emotional cycle controlled by the speedway, but Blossom's mother seemed suddenly to relax, even though she voiced a suspicion.

"You sure?" she said, but softly.

"Sure that I know what you mean?"

"Sure that you didn't make her a bad girl."

"Yes, I'm sure. But can I say something without making you think I was ever her . . . boyfriend? I don't think she was a bad girl."

"It don't make no difference now," she said. At last she appeared to think about the death that brought me to her doorstep. She took off those thick glasses and wiped her eyes hard, with her wrist, though I didn't see any tears. Then she put her glasses back on and faced me once more with suspicion. "What do you want with me?"

"Maybe just to talk a little bit."

"What about?"

"About . . . Vera."

"Vera was a little girl. Just five or six years old. That's all I remember. You don't want to know about *her*, do you?"

"Then how about the woman called Blossom?"

"Don't remember her."

The cars had started up again and I started to whine inside just like them. It was the stock cars that made this woman a little bit mad, I decided, and I knew if I stayed around much longer I would go mad, too. I nodded at her and turned to go. Her door was closing fast, but at least I had sense enough to call out one last thing. "Ma'am," I said and she left me a six-inch crack in the door. "How did she die?"

"She fell out of a plane."

"What?"

"She loved some no-account crop duster and she fell out of his plane. Doing what, I don't even like to imagine."

She slammed the door in my face, and I stood there for a long moment wondering if this was true. But when I moved off, heading for my car, I heard Blossom's voice: *I was right behind him in an open cockpit and he wore a leather cap. A man in a leather cap flying a plane saw something about me worth his putting that thing he loves so much inside me. A man in a leather cap who does what he does and he's done and then he rolls off and turns his back like he's suddenly really pissed off at me, like now he can't stand to look at me, which you have to realize is something I understand only too well.*

But fuck him. There've been plenty of others in seed caps and in ball caps, in fedoras and in golf visors, and bareheaded too with all kinds of hair and that's where I keep my eyes most of the time when it's going on, somewhere up there along the hairline and I say to myself, "See? See? It's okay. It's okay." And if they roll away, if they all roll away after they're done, then fuck them. A few minutes ago they knew what I am. And right now, somewhere in Wabash or in St. Louis or somewhere around these parts, there's a guy who's ready for me, who can see real clear what I am for ten minutes or so. He's ready.

It's just that they're all idiots and they have no memories, they can't none of them remember something for even that eleventh minute, so I just unbuckle the belt that's holding me in the plane, and this guy in the leather cap looks back over his shoulder and he gives me a thumbs-up and the wind is beating at me and I haven't looked down even once yet. But then I'm suddenly pressed back and looking straight up and he's climbing. When he does the first loop, I'm surprised to find a real clear force, like some man's rough hand, pushing me into the seat. Then we're flying level and the guy in the leather cap does a barrel roll and again there's this pressure and I'm still sitting there and so I say aloud, "Get your fucking hands off me, creep" and I know it's God I'm talking to and he's just another guy pawing at me, if you want to know how I really feel. Then the pilot looks over his shoulder and does this thumb thing again like this is going to be really something, and it is. He does half a roll and starts to fly upside down and I'm outta there.

The next part is okay. It's like I've just opened the door to the girls' locker room and I'm standing there naked to see who shows up, that's why I undid the belt: I'm falling and I open my legs and I spread my arms and suddenly somebody's got his eyes on me and there's no looking away, his eyes are looking into my face and there's no anger at all. He likes what he sees and he's ready to take me in his arms even if I called him a creep.

In Vietnamese language school, we sat in a lab for two hours every day. We wore headsets and hunkered into cubicles and we talked to Vietnamese speakers on tape, responding to their questions, telling them it is a beautiful morning, thank you very much, I am weary and wish to sleep, can you turn out the light? And we took tests from these tapes, as well, and it was always the same woman's voice. We had native teachers in our language school and finally I got up the nerve to ask someone, but the woman whose voice was on the tape was not one of ours. Nobody knew who she was. We were in school in Arlington, Virginia, and everybody thought she was probably out in California, in the bigger Army language school in Monterey. Somebody else said that the tapes were made in Saigon, she's over there. I don't know. It finally just made me restless trying to figure out her other life, so I stopped thinking about where she might be and I concentrated on what I had of her.

The test was very formal. She kept her voice steady and uninflected beyond the natural rise and fall of the Vietnamese tones. It was a slightly nasal voice, pitched only a little above what might register on your ear as a child's voice. But every now and then, in between a section on the test, moving from vocabulary questions to the dialogues, say, you could hear a faint tinkling sound on the tape, like a little bell, and it took me a couple of minutes to figure it out, but she must have had on a piece of jewelry, a bracelet probably, that's how I finally heard it and it seemed exactly right—a bracelet—and it thrilled me. She'd finish one set of questions and before the next she'd shift the microphone from one hand to the other and the bracelet would make a faint ringing sound. I felt weak with tenderness for her, for this bracelet that she loved, that she clasped around her thin wrist every morning to come and sit before her tape machine and speak these questions—directly to me, I imagined, knowing that she could never hear my answers. Could you post this letter for me, please, she would ask, and I would answer in Vietnamese, Yes, yes, I will post it for you but I will also write to you, I will send you letters and tell you how much I love you. And at this my teacher, a sinew-and-bone, been-through-too-much-already matron of a Vietnamese woman who was listening to my answers, would interrupt and tell me to stick to the text of the lesson. But the sound of that bracelet would loosen my Vietnamese words, let me speak with ardor in this musical tongue, and it made me listen even more closely and sometimes I could hear my lady of the bracelet breathe. I could hear a soft slip of air just before she'd speak a sentence and I could feel her chest fill, her breasts lift just a little bit, and I loved her.

And she would ask, Where are you going? And you could hear the murmuring in English from the other cubicles: The fucking Nam. I would answer her in Vietnamese, but I would say, I don't know, I don't exactly know where I'm going, but I know it will lead eventually to you. And I can hear her right now, hear her question: Where are you going? I wish—devoutly—as I try to put all of this together, that I could already see a direction, that things were taking shape like a proper life story and I could make it clear where I am going, but it's in the very nature of what I seek that I seem to wander, to digress. There's no other way. If the sex you trembled after was something clear and whole, and you knew what it was, and you went to a woman and she took you inside her and she fit perfectly and completely and you fit her, just like you both figured, then there would never be another broken promise and I could say it all really simply right now. But as much as I yearn and love, as intensely as I listen for the whispers, the answer of each woman does not prevent me from yearning again. And it's the yearning I have to understand, that and how all the women I've ever loved still exist somehow inside me. And the ways you usually try to understand things like this—by thinking about them, by breaking them down and fitting them logically together, by carefully fixing yourself in this linear, practical life we cannot avoid leading—these ways feel as if, in fact, they would carry me farther away from the understanding I seek. I cannot say any of this unless I say it in the way the whispering and the yearning and the remembering all come upon me, and that is unbidden, unconstructed, uninterested in psychological origins, unbeholden to the time and the space we are used to dwelling in. The very shape of all these words must be the shape of the yearning itself if I am ever to understand.

For the moment I only have to wonder why Blossom's voice could be so strong in me if I did not make love to her, if it turned out there was that one place on her body that I never did see, much less taste or enter into. Because sometimes I know that touching and kissing and entering that part of a woman is so I can find my way to her voice, her secret voice, so I can hear it in my own head. But then sometimes it all seems the same: the women I knew every tuck and wrinkle of and the lady of the bracelet; the woman I married and the woman I glanced at through a subway window maybe five years ago and we were rushing along in different trains on parallel tracks and staring at each other through the scrim of fading spray paint and we didn't let our faces change at all, not at all, not in New York City coming up to the end of the twentieth century, but we didn't look away from each other either, and that meant something, we looked at each other, passionate in our inertness, and she had corkscrew curls and a thin nose, faintly crooked, and the trains ran together for only a few moments and then she was gone.

But, of course, as abiding as that face is, I can't quite hear her voice. Perhaps all I would have needed was to run my tongue down the line of her nose to begin to hear her, but in my mind the faint turning of her nose has always been echoed there between her legs, the lips of her loins bent just the same way, and if I knew that for sure, then the woman would tell me everything. And as for Blossom, since that one place died and dissolved away without my ever touching it, perhaps her voice is really Fiona's, for the two shared a certain kind of pain.

And oddly enough, there was even a night when Fiona spoke of being caught naked in a girls' locker room, though hypothetically. This was pretty far along, in maybe our sixth month, and we actually had some friends, some couples, and three pairs of us were eating dinner in the apartment of one of them. Our hostess brought it up, the wife of one of the guys from the little public-relations agency where I worked at the time. She was very pretty, and the whole internal ritual you go through to mute your reaction to a woman who's married to somebody else, somebody you know and even like—that's a whole other subject. But she was still clearly very pretty and she had collarbone-length blond hair and she fondled a long lock of it as she talked, she caressed her own face with it, and when somebody else was talking she even stuck it under her nose and pushed up her lip and wore the lock of hair like a mustache. In short, she made things really difficult for me, but I knew Fiona by now and how she reacted, so I almost never looked at the blonde directly. I'd just steal some side glances once in a while, at the moments when she was speaking and it was perfectly natural for me to be looking, and I'd let it go at that.

Her name was Sam and she brought the subject up. What would you do, she asked the other two women, if you got caught coming out of a shower and there was a strange man just about to walk in and you couldn't stop him and all you had was a washrag? What part would you choose to cover with the rag? The third woman at the table, the redheaded wife of the handball partner of the guy from the agency, spoke up real fast, but it was odd because she was leaping in only to mince words. "Oh, you know," she said. "*That* part, of course."

Sam laughed and said, "No, what part?"

The other two men and I looked at one another and I don't know why, but we all just decided wordlessly to bite our tongues. We weren't talking.

The redhead laughed too and said, "Christ. *You* know. Harry likes me to say that word for him at . . . um . . . critical moments and I don't want to embarrass him."

We all laughed at this, even Harry Handball. Then Sam said, "Maybe so. Maybe that's the thing to do. Then you've got your other arm to put across your titties." Sam leaned on the word "titties" and I think she even glanced at Harry, who picked up on it right away.

"Oh brother, now you've done it," he cried rolling his eyes and dropping his napkin into his lap like he was covering something up, and we laughed again, but I looked over to Fiona and she wasn't laughing. She probably hadn't laughed before, either.

For the first time I had a nibble of fear about Fiona. Not that I could yet imagine her demons coming at her over anything other than sexual jealousy. But when I glanced at her it seemed to be that very thing, as if somehow it was jealousy that she'd sucked out of all this and she was going to make a scene. If she had, maybe I never would have married her. I would have known something was really wrong. But she surprised me, and in my relief, I radically misjudged her. As soon as the laughter had died, she said, deadpan, "I'd cover my face."

Nobody laughed, but you knew they approved. They all sort of went "Ah" and Sam clapped slowly with an exaggerated nod of her head, that loose lock of her hair falling away from her upper lip, the mustache disguise abandoned now before this truth. And I heard it as that, a truth about bodies, and I felt very close to Fiona at that moment. She even turned her face to me and she was thinking, I knew, about how she always wanted to look me in the eyes when she came and that was exactly my impulse too, though I would eventually figure out that it was for a different reason.

But she was right, you have to know the public thing to make the private thing real, and I told her so on the way back to my place after the dinner. Out in the chill of the autumn night, looking up West End Avenue for a cab, our mouths still a little stiff from our farewell smiles, I said, "You were right about faces. All the stuff that's hidden has no meaning if you don't know what the face is."

And Fiona said, "Did you have fun seeing her naked in your head when she was doing that insufferable little act about not naming her cunt?"

For something that seemed to come out of nowhere, I knew real fast what she was talking about, though I feigned ignorance. "What?" I said like she had just spoken in some other language. Even Fiona's striking powers of observation could not have read my thoughts from anything I'd shown on my face, surely not, not when everyone had been justified in watching the redhead as she thrashed around. I'd just watched and smiled like everyone else at the table. But still, Fiona knew. She knew that as soon as the redhead started talking about where to put the washrag, I had her there in a locker room in my head. Hell, I had her in Blossom's locker room and she had just

· *61* ·

stepped full-front into the open doorway and I was tying my shoe and there she was and her hair wasn't Fiona's pale, fading-into-something-you-might-even-call-blond kind of red but a Klaxon, this-is-why-they-call-it-a-red-light-district kind of red and her pussy hair was exactly the same color.

A cab pulled up in front of us and we got in before I had to say any more. It was a Spanish cab with the dashboard pasted with family poses and the rearview mirror wearing a fuzzy bedroom slipper and dangling a Christ on the cross. I gave the driver the address of my little apartment on Seventy-second Street—we never went down to the East Village when we were out late. But when we peeled away from the curb and Christ started twirling in the front window, I felt certain— even then—that it was this crucifix Fiona was staring at and she said, "I'm not so sure."

This could've meant a lot of things. I said, "Not sure of what?"

"This might be a big one."

"This what?"

"The argument we're about to have."

"If you can sit there and calmly talk about how big this is going to get, then how can it get out of control?"

"One thing's going to lead to another. I'm not so sure we should be going to your place."

I looked out the window, just watched the building facades go by, solid there in the scattered light of the street, and I wanted to get myself really pissed off and do the simple thing, drop her off on Avenue C and beat it back uptown and spend this night alone. But Fiona was full of more mysteries than I knew how to handle and she was liquid beside me, sloshing around in her clothes, and I wanted more than anything to plunge my hands into her, hold my breath and push my face in and open my eyes. I turned to her and she was still watching the crucifix and I said, "Let's just not start it."

"It's already started," she said in nearly a whisper, still perfectly calm, and I have to admit it was a little scary. But Christ Almighty her profile in the flickering of street lights was beautiful, the wide mouth set hard and her sharp thin nose just starting to think about flaring and the broad quietude of her forehead, binding in those images that were tormenting her, and I put my hand over hers and she ripped it away and hissed my name in reproach and when I retreated, she sat still again.

"Do we have to do this?" I asked softly.

"Yes," she said. Then, as if she thought she owed me an explanation, she looked my way and leaned to me slightly. She said, "I love you, Ira. I want you to be the only man against my body and in my head and in my heart. I don't want to sleep with ghosts, I don't want to touch some part of you and think of some part of someone else. Are you following me?"

"Yes," I said and I thought I was. I loved her for this declaration. I still thought the touches of other men had been very sweet for her—I'd think that for several months to come—and she just wanted me to be the sweetest one. I was happy to help her in this. There was a residue of my own retrospective jealousy that would be put fast asleep by this very thing. And I got the idea to find sexual things that we'd never done with anyone before. I thought of some hint Fiona had seemed to drop not long ago, a sigh and a word or two that I couldn't quite remember, "that's new" or something like it, so now I asked, "Is it really so that no other man ever came on your nipple?"

She looked at me with what seemed sadness in her eyes. I realize now how hard it was for her to be forced to think this through and then not to lie to me, as I later learned she had done before on matters of her past. But she said, "Which nipple?"

Fiona was a smart woman, and as soon as I realized—and this was almost instantly—that she wasn't making a joke, I think I gaped a bit at the answer, and she said, "Remember what you're feeling right now. It will help you understand why we will fight for the next few hours."

She thought I was jealous. And at that moment she was right. Maybe that bit of me roused briefly and mumbled in its sleep. Though the feeling was complicated, for at the same time there was the soft murmur of understanding between us. I believed that she was shaped inside the same way I was, and that was unquestionably a comfort to me. But trying to remember which nipple I'd come on, I understood by implication that one of them had already been taken, that some other man had come there. It was all right for me if *she* remembered her passion for him, but *I* didn't want to and I could suddenly see Fiona sigh and smear this man with her fingertips around and around the nipple, going higher and higher up her chest until she touched her fingertips to her lips, just as she had done with me, and the thought of that made my forehead break into a brief sweat of jealousy.

And it was just this kind of jealousy that Fiona had come to. And she explained that pretty clearly to me, pretty rationally in the cab ride. She said, "Knowing what was in your mind tonight about the redhead has just started the whole thing, you see. It makes me think of that mind of yours and the images it holds."

"Like yours," I said.

"Of course like mine. I'd never dream up this kind of problem for myself if I didn't know firsthand what it was."

"I'm glad to hear that."

"Pay attention," she said. "This isn't going to stay friendly very long." And I could tell she was right, for she was twisting her hands in her lap, linking the fingers and wrenching her hands in opposite directions, first one and then the other.

But she held off for a while longer, though I knew it was only because of a great struggle to do so. She pressed her lips into a thin hard line and she said nothing at all, not a word, for the next words would have to be the beginning. She waited until we arrived at Seventy-second Street and we got out of the cab and I paid the cabdriver and I turned and she was already past the doorman and I followed and she even waited until we were up the elevator and along the blood clot red carpet, her leading the way, her standing with her eyes closed as if very tired before my door, and she waited until we were through the door and inside the dark room and I went ahead of her now, knowing how she liked the view, so I went straight to the window and drew open the shades and I wanted her to look at the dark stacking of rooftops like foothills leading to the bright rise of the United Nations building. I actually thought the view that we'd held each other before might soothe her, dumb shit that I was.

But her hand was on my shoulder, turning me with a hard, grasping rub like she was trying to wipe something off her palm that was dark and sticky and repulsive and wouldn't wash clean. "You're always thinking of them, aren't you," she cried.

"Why do we have to do this?" I cried in return, consciously matching her intensity.

She shoved the shoulder that she'd grabbed. "You're always thinking of them. Tell me the truth."

I pressed back against the window and I wanted very much to tell her the truth. Of course I did. Lies are like the cute talk of wooing. Lies are more clothes with stuck zippers and what I want is to be naked with a woman, utterly naked. I even believed that she would understand the truth, in some calmer moment. But for now Fiona was clearly in the grip of a sharply gathering pain and I knew what it was about.

She shoved me again. "There's nothing complicated here. And don't try to hide behind semantics. You know what I mean by 'always.' Yes or no. Do you think of them?"

But what exactly was the truth to tell her? The women I've loved—in all the great and small ways—are always there. That should be clear even in what I've said so far. This story is about *all* of them. So the answer was yes. But I never thought of anybody other than Fiona when I was looking at her or touching her or smelling her or tasting her or listening to her breathing or her murmuring in her sleep or her talking about an artist's work in a headlong voice. At those times it was only Fiona. As it was with every other woman whose spoor I followed through my senses. When a woman is present in me, then there is only that woman, even if she enters me merely through the tinkling of an invisible bracelet in the pause of a faceless voice. There is only that one woman in all the world, and so the answer to Fiona's question was also no. Either way, yes or no, there would be a distortion, a lie, and I hated this but I knew enough not to try to make these distinctions to her because she would take that as bullshit, as a way not to say the true answer which she would understand to be yes. And so I chose the distortion that would hurt her the least. I said, "No, Fiona. I never think of them."

"I know you're lying."

"I'm not lying."

"How many have there been?"

"What. How many what."

"Women you've fucked—I'm sorry I use that word but it's how I feel at the moment and I can't help it—how many women are there in your goddamn blood, is what I want to know, how many women that come to you in your head, and their hands are on you again and their bodies are against you. You know what I'm talking about." She brought her face really close to mine now but she didn't stand still and focus on anything, she was bobbing and weaving like a boxer and there was no punch ever thrown that she couldn't slip and all the movement was making me a little dizzy and I was already pressed back against the window and her face veered so close to me for a moment that I could smell the shrimp from dinner on her breath and I caught a spray of her spit on my lips and her fists came up before her but I knew somehow not even to flinch and they suddenly pressed hard against her temples and she wasn't getting off this question. "How many?" she cried.

She fell back a little and I slid away and crossed the room and I was trying to make a quick count, if that's what she wanted now. And she brayed behind me and I felt her rush more than heard it and she pounded once on my shoulder blades. "You're fucking counting, aren't you?"

I turned just in time to catch her striking hands at the wrists and I hoped that stopping the motion would make the impulse go away but it did not and she strained so hard to strike again that I felt her wrist bones wrench and I let go fast, not able to tell if the pain she must have felt was simply from her struggle or from my own intent, my own angry hands. I flinched backward but she just crossed her wrists below her breasts and I said, "Isn't that what you were demanding? A count?"

"You say two. You say three. You say that's all there ever was and you say it's like even those never happened. You say I'm the only one."

"Why don't I just say I was a virgin till I met you."

"I wouldn't believe it, goddamn it."

"You'd believe two or three?"

"Not now," she said and she crumpled before me, sank to her knees and wept, her head bowed. "Not now. I can't tell you what to say. You're so incredibly stupid. It doesn't do any good if I tell you what to say."

I thought for a moment this crumpling would be the end of the fight. I sank to my knees to be with her on the floor but she lifted her face suddenly and looked at me with wide eyes, no tears, not a sound, just her eyes getting wider and wider like she couldn't believe what she was looking at, it was so outrageous, my being there on the floor with her. We had only begun.

And I can hear her voice. Clearer now than it could ever have been at the time, though I yearned to hear it even then.

The voice in her head: *How much more would this man put me through how much more of this swelling of every drop of blood in me my blood pushing outward like some terrible weight has been dropped in the middle of the sea of my blood and has sunk out of sight quickly but its mass is pressing all my blood outward and heating it up, this sea boils hot inside me. I have the pain of swelling and burning but my skin not yielding at all, not even turning red from the heat. I look at my hands and they seem pale and very small. I have small hands. I put them on my face, fist them and dig at my temples but they aren't strong enough to reach the pictures there, another woman's hand folding around the cock of this man I am falling in love with, it's no longer just him and me but there are others in the room and the great weight that fell into me rises and there is smoke in the room and I wake and it's like at Mass when I sit in the front pew and the smoke of incense rolls over me and I see nothing for a moment but am filled with a smell so sweet it burns my throat, and hands come through the smoke and a voice, My baby, it's Daddy, we have to go, and his hands are on me and it's not church but my room and I am heavy with sleep but there is smoke everywhere and it's as if I had to name it to feel it for when I know it's smoke I feel it then in my lungs and I begin to cough and my father's hands are on me to carry me away from here, though I can walk I can run faster than any girl in my school but I let my father put his hands on me, one in the center of my back and the other on the back of my legs, just above my knees and he lifts me and when he holds me against him his hand slides up the back of my legs, my thighs, and I can feel it very clearly, his hand is inside my nightgown and we are running through the smoke and I know that my house is on fire and we are on the steps going down to the first floor and he holds me against him, I feel the rough tweed of his suit against my face, my arms, and now I can hear him coughing and the cough is so deep that it makes me picture his lungs, deep wells inside him breaking apart with this sound, crumbling, I must be coughing too but all I can hear is my father's cough and I think for a moment that he will surely die but his hand is alive, it slides easily up me now to keep me from falling and his broad palm nests the cheeks of my bottom I can feel his hand damp there and we are going down the steps and all this time I can feel the curve of the staircase. Then I feel the touch: his palm turning a little and the crotch of his thumb nuzzling down there between my cheeks and his thumb going out then and covering a place that I do not know feels prickly with exposure until he covers it and the tip of his thumb gently presses open my secret lips and does not move again, just covers me there and all I know to do is hold on tighter to my father because my house is on fire and he is carrying me away.*

How is it that I came to know about her father? Most of it flows from her inner voice that I heard in our intimacy, the woman voice whispering to me. But there were two clear moments from later on. One was on another trip to Coney Island. Early one Saturday evening Fiona was chatty with nostalgia about our first date and we got on the subway and we held hands as we flew over the rooftops of Brooklyn and it was dark when we arrived. We turned away from the main midway and floated toward the great white wooden web of the Cyclone, Coney's roller coaster, the lifts and falls of it strung with running yellow lights, and we turned down the street beside it, which was filled with the squeal of coaster-car brakes and the whooping of riders sliding into the station beyond the fence, and the air smelled of the sea and musty wood and Nathan's hot dogs and the scorch of brake shoes and Fiona and I entwined our fingers and we swung our arms as we walked and I said, Would you like to ride? and she said, No way, and I started to try to persuade her but she said, Really, and I said no more. Then we stopped and talked briefly about where to go first and when we decided not to get a hot dog but head to the beach, the riders were filing out of the Cyclone and Fiona and I turned just as a man and a little girl, not much higher than his waist, came wobbling out and he was holding her hand and he had a fringe of sandy hair sticking out of a dark cloth Mao cap and he was wearing black horn-rimmed glasses and so was the little girl and she lifted her face to him—she angled her head sharply back and looked into her father's face—and she was laughing and she reached up to her father and he took her in his arms and she hooked her legs around him and put her head on his shoulder and I looked to Fiona and she was watching them, of course—she seemed never to miss anyone who passed—and I expected her to be smiling but she wasn't, she grabbed my hand and dragged me off in the direction of the beach.

When we were clearly out of the hearing of the father and his daughter and Fiona was still walking with a sense of urgency, I said, "What's wrong?"

"Nothing," she said, a firm thump of sound.

But I pressed her. "What. Tell me."

"He shouldn't take a little girl on that thing," she said.

"That doesn't sound like what you really want to say."

"It is."

"You don't think a little girl should be kept out of fast things or rough things. I know you well enough already to know that."

She dropped my hand and stopped so abruptly that I took two steps before I could respond. I turned to her. She was standing very still with her hands at her sides. "Come back here, Ira," she said and her voice was surprisingly soft. I moved to her and she immediately asked me, "Are you going to be a good father?"

"Yes."

"I'd worry about a daughter."

"That I'd take her on a roller coaster?"

"No." She looked hard into my eyes with this and then she turned her face sharply away. "I'm sorry," she said. "I love you. It's not you." She was trembling now and she began to weep softly. I could think of only one thing to conclude from this. There had been something very bad with her own father.

I wanted to touch her but I was afraid to. There were memories of holding, I knew. I waited for her but she kept her face turned away and she did not move and she wept softly and it seemed to me then that she was waiting for something from me. "Talk to me about it," I whispered.

"No," she said, just as quietly.

"I love you," I said.

Now she looked back to me, her tears twinkling with the yellow lights of the coaster, and she said, "It should be clear to you that somebody touched me."

"Yes."

"You can understand that I don't want to talk about it."

"Yes."

"Then just hold me now. I want you to take me into your arms and look me in the face."

"I will," I said and I did. We pressed close and she kept her face lifted to me, her head was angled rather sharply back and we held each other's gaze and to my surprise it was very difficult for me to hold still, I wanted to break this off, because I could not keep the face of the little girl with horn-rimmed glasses from my mind, her face lifted to a man who could make her whole or shatter her to pieces.

And on the night after the dinner party, the argument went on for a long time. She came at me, physically, not hard, not with any real intent to strike out but putting her anger into movement only, but I did not let her feel that I wanted a confrontation, I kept moving and so did she and she seemed to have no judgment about where our two bodies were, I'd slow down and she'd bump into me and if I tried to hold her then, she'd fight me off like I was trying to attack her and I'd move away and she'd start following me again. And all the while she was demanding details about the women I'd had sex with of any kind and she'd veer into the subject of some glance she thought I'd given a woman in the street or in a restaurant or in a gallery, and this from weeks ago, months ago, and she hadn't even made an issue of it at the time. And this went on and on in a manic choreography, I'd circle and circle the room and she'd follow until finally she broke away and then she'd grab something off the desktop or the chest of drawers and almost throw it but put it down instead and move off and I'd follow her thinking she was beginning to control herself but follow only until she realized what I was doing and then she'd turn on me and I'd back away and the circle would start again, me moving and her pursuing until eventually she would veer off and grab one of the objects she'd picked up earlier and throw it across the room, but never at me, as if this was merely some unfinished business that had been worrying at her and she finally just took care of it.

This would bring us to a temporary stop and at moments like these another theme would begin. I can see her clearly even now, even though she stood only in the dim light from the city—we fought this night after the dinner party almost entirely in the dark, only one pale bulb burning by the front door and that merely darkening the shadows around her as she slipped away from the desk, the clang of the letter opener hitting the far wall still hanging in the air, and she went only a few feet, almost aimlessly, and she stretched out her hand and leaned against the wall and she said, "Listen to me. Why are you still interested in me, Ira? I must look terrible when I'm like this."

Even before I could make my legs move, even as the yearning to touch her rushed back into me, she stopped me. "Not yet, Ira. It's too soon. I'm such a worthless bitch that if you do what you're thinking of doing I'll probably try to scratch your eyes out." And this she said with such sadness in her voice, such calm self-awareness that I wanted all the more to touch her but I took her advice and let that desire wait and grow. Meanwhile, I could see only highlights on her face, scraps of light fallen there on the line of her cheekbone, her temple, and I could not even see her lips gently part to sigh, as she did now, she sighed and then she began the rage again. And I never stopped loving her at all. That sigh in the midst of it, this was a wonderful thing to me. The quick mind that moved even beneath her rage was very beautiful.

And in her sigh I thought I could hear the end of the fight approaching. We circled the room a few more times but the edge of her voice had finally worn smooth and though the words she spoke were basically the same, the anger was almost gone. She was demanding for the second time to go through the things we did together sexually that she could be assured had no memories for me. The first time, I'd known to avoid answering the question. I knew that her focus would go at once to the activities and body parts I was leaving off the list and it would only make things worse. And frankly, I'd gotten distracted by a big, ill-tempered mutt of a feeling of my own, the same one that shook itself awake briefly in the cab. So instead of answering her question, I said, "This is why you said to remember what I felt. In the taxi. When I asked about coming on your nipple."

"That's right. It's time for that. Tell me."

"What about a list for me? Are you going to do the same for me?"

She flailed her arms and growled. "I don't care about that."

But I did care about it now, all of a sudden. Maybe there was an old reflex of competition about it. You *win* the girl, hasn't that always been the way you learned it? But when she gets won time and time again, when we all finally live in an age that says do what you want with every crevice of your body if it pleases you, equally, man and woman, then a man can still maybe feel this little whimper of a challenge from the men who have visited the secrets of this woman's body already, and a man might ask very gently—fearing the wrong answer and knowing how the question itself pisses most women off, but he asks anyway, very gently—was I the best ever for you? was mine *big*, compared to the others? since I can't win your past or even, to be honest, any certain future, since I can't carry you off to a place where there is no memory, can you at least tell me I was all-alone-nobody-ever-like-me special in some way, no matter how small?

So I risked setting her off again and I pressed the point just a little bit. I said, "Wouldn't it be even better if we can find the things that *neither* of us has done?"

"All right," she said. "Maybe so. All right. Just don't try to make me think about the things I *have* done."

"Fine. That's fine," I said and she was even standing by the window now and she glanced over her shoulder toward the UN building. I watched her for a moment, very happy at what clearly seemed to me to be a sign that she was going to be all right.

"Get on with it," she whispered without looking at me. I could see her eyes in the spill of light from outside and she closed them, as if she'd had a bite of pain.

"Your toes," I said and this was a lie, of course, I was pressed for a body part right away and I didn't have time to think, so it was natural that I would start with a lie. A woman's toes, in the climates where I grew up, were hidden for most of the year and they built up their erotic secretness and then, when the weather grew warm, they emerged in all their quirky uniqueness and they were rows of sweet little faces, each a special, separate quality in the woman, and I made it a point to kiss the toes of any woman I touched, and Fiona turned to me, her face going dark in the shadows but I knew it was full of disbelief.

"You've never kissed another woman's toes?" she demanded.

"Kissed, yes. But no more."

"Sucked?"

"All right. Sucked. Yes. But I . . . never came on a woman's toes. Or from the touch of them."

She lifted her chin in thought as if to decide if this would do. I tried to help. "You think your feet are pretty, don't you? You paint your nails, pumice off the rough spots. I've seen you."

"Yes."

"And so they are. And I know you're sensitive there."

"Yes."

"So you can touch me with them. It's all ours. Honest."

"Maybe."

"Can we put it on the list?"

She came away from the window at this. I was afraid at first that I'd sounded flippant to her. But she stopped there before me, just out of reach and she said, "Okay. Yes. I'd like that."

"And your instep," I said. "Sometimes when I come inside you I will draw your foot up and you can curl your toes and I will kiss the sweet little ripple of flesh there in your instep."

"That one came too easy. You've done that with someone, haven't you. Are you starting to lie to me?"

"No," I said and I meant it, this was something I really hadn't done, though saying it made it seem as if I should have, as if it was unusual that I hadn't. But I wasn't lying about this and my innocence must have shimmered out of that denial, because Fiona came closer still and she nodded.

"My armpit," she said. "I'm very sensitive . . ."

"You'll draw your arm forward," I said, "and make a great hollow for me there."

She came very close now and I could hear her breathing, she was beginning to pant faintly, but I held back my hands for a moment more. "The crook of your arm," I said. "Where they draw blood."

"It's very sensitive."

I took her arm and drew it to my mouth and I kissed her

in the bend of it, I nipped at the place where a doctor's needle would probe her and I bent her arm further and followed the crease with my tongue. "These things are all new for you, as well?" I asked.

"Yes," she said.

"And they'll make even the old stuff seem new."

Fiona answered this by clutching me hard against her, her hands swarming around my back, up to my head, down to my butt, and she hooked one leg around me and said, "I love you, Ira. You understand. I know you do."

I lifted her now and we did not waste time by moving to the bedroom. She hooked her other leg around me and I carried her to the couch, our mouths bellowing soundlessly against each other, and I bent to lay her down, tangled in the vines of her arms and legs, and as soon as she touched the couch she hissed, "Oh shit."

My first thought—not a thought, really, more a hacksaw swipe across the back of my neck—was that I'd done something wrong again. But when her hands fell away from me, they did not reattach themselves to my throat, where some little cowardly part of me expected them to. Instead, they lurched against her own face. "My period started this morning."

I did not hesitate. "Then this will be ours alone," I said, and her astonished hands flew up and intertwined at the back of my neck.

"Ira," she whispered. "You're going to make me sane."

She pulled my face down and she kissed me hard and then she slipped from beneath me and said she'd be right back. I began to undress in the dim light and my hands quaked faintly, partly in desire, partly in a sensation I'd already come to know and would know much more intimately in the years to come: the prickle of silence in the room where only a few moments ago we'd circled and shouted and scrabbled against each other over these things roiling in Fiona. I could not hold my hands steady and then she was beside me, luminous in the dim light, so naked that my hands stopped and my breath as well and she stripped me quickly and we went straight to the thing that was new for us both, I slipped inside her, and she was so soft I worried that if I moved I would rip all this out of her but I moved and the wetness of her was thick with things never spoken never thought and her face was laid against my throat and very still there and we both concentrated on this movement, this swimming in the viscous river of her, and we did not speak until she was trembling and close and she pulled her face back and cursed the dark and reached back to the end of the couch and my eyes flashed and then cleared and she was in the light and staring into my eyes and pushing me a little away to see better and I shifted my knees and drew my body upright and I lifted her legs and laid them against my shoulders and the couch cushions moved beneath us and she was panting and calling for my eyes and I looked at her and I was conscious of her feet pulsing at each side of my face and I should have let well enough alone but I turned to her instep to kiss it as I'd promised and with her ankle she tried to push my face back to see my eyes and the cushions moved again and did not stop and we fell from the couch, tumbling onto our sides and I slipped out of her, feeling the cold grasp of air on me there and I rolled onto my back and she came up over me and I looked down to ease myself back in and my penis was red and her thighs were red and my thighs were red and I was inside Fiona again and a month later we were married.

When the lights went out in our little Paris hotel, Fiona and I had already begun to kiss deeply, had cast ourselves across the bed, weary after walking the quais but ready to make love, and then the lamp on the nightstand fluttered and went dark and some of the faint light coming in the window blinked out, too, the bedside lamps in all the other little mansard-roofed French hotels around us losing their juice as well, I imagined, and that was okay with me. I shared Fiona's preference for light, I loved the look of her too much to miss it when we made love, but this seemed like a nice little moment to me. If once in a while you couldn't see, then your focus on the touch and the smell and the taste and the sound of each other was even more intense. But Fiona's mouth went hard and she jerked her head away and pressed me back from her.

"What's happened?" she said.

"I don't know," I said. "The power's out."

I tried to pull her close to me again, but she put her hands on my chest and said, "No."

We had been forced by our jobs to put this honeymoon off for about six months. So by now I'd known Fiona for a little over a year and it wasn't until that hand spread open in the center of my chest that I realized we had never made love in the dark.

I brought my face close to hers and whispered, "Fiona, it's okay. All the couples in all the rooms around us are sighing and stripping each other and letting the starlight do."

She touched my chest again, softly, and dragged her fingers down it. "Such bullshit, Ira," she said, but gently. "Sweet. But bullshit. How do you make it up so quick?"

I opened my mouth to say some more and she touched my face with her hand, groping her way down till she pressed my mouth with her fingertips. "It's you, isn't it," she said.

I thought—wrongly—that she meant it was like me to speak bullshit. I had never mentioned my discomfort about all the "sweet choices" stuff when we'd first made love, and the sighing and stripping and starlight was the same as that—she was right—and I took all this now as just another moment of her inspiration, when she could see deep into me, and I was grateful for that. So I confessed instantly. "Yes. It's me."

Then she said, "Forgive me, for I have sinned." Her hand left my face and she shifted away just slightly, and I realize now, lying again with her in the bed on that night, that I felt a movement of air as she crossed herself. Of course, I knew then that Fiona had grown up a Catholic, but we had never spoken more than a few dozen words about it, and those simply to note the fact and go on, and so I listened in ignorance. She spoke to me in the dark and it was not in my head, this was her own spoken voice, from outside of me, entering me. She said, "It has been a lifetime since my last confession. I have sinned in the flesh. A man has come to me in the dark and it was a dangerous time, there was a fire, and it was dangerous and that was how it began that he touched me. A man came to me and he was a man who should not touch me, he was the one man who should not touch me but he did and I let him do that and my body was ignorant, the places on my body are ignorant and they have sinned, they have taken his touch and they have trembled and even have grown wet, even for him, and I have sinned and if only I had grown wet before him and I was wet enough to put out the fire at once but the fire came first and I was lost."

She stopped speaking and I understood everything from this and she was inside me and I trembled and I did not know what to say. If only I had understood the rituals then as I did later I might have said the right things instantly, without prompting, I could have spoken the words of absolution and maybe she would have had the peace that they talk about in their churches, the peace of God that passeth all understanding, but she had instead the pain of God that passeth all understanding and I sensed her waiting and then she said, "Am I forgiven?" and I said, "Yes," and I began to move to her and she said, "No. Please. Not in the dark, Ira. Wait for the lights." And I eased gingerly back down and Fiona and I did not move for a long while and I thought I heard a faint, sweet moaning from some window outside and Fiona and I lay side by side and then at last the lights came on and I turned to her. She did not look at me. She was laid out on her back and the sheet was pulled up nearly to her chin and only her naked arms were exposed and they were crossed on her chest and her eyes were closed and she said, "I am going to say this very calmly but please understand that this is perhaps the most important thing that I've ever said to you. You must never mention this to me again, what I've said. You are under the seal. Do you promise me?"

I wanted desperately to help her stop the pain. But I had no way, no right, to doubt that she knew what was best for her in this. "I promise," I whispered and I would keep my promise in the years to come, though it was very difficult, very difficult except for the fact that I could not imagine what to say anyway.

Her eyes opened and she turned her face to me and her eyes fixed me with a gentle fury and I could feel her concentrating on the sight of me and I understood the lights now, of course, I understood what she'd meant when she touched my face and said it was me. She had to make love with the lights to know that it was not her father, and then she said, "Hold me, Ira."

The next day she took us to the Catacombs. We woke to a thin little butter-based gruel of sunlight and she was in my arms and her eyes were still puffy from crying and I asked her what in all of Paris she wanted to do today and she said, "Something Grand Guignol."

"I love you," I said.

She turned her face to me, looked me carefully in the eyes. "How do you make it up so quick?" she said and there was a sharp edge to her voice.

"I don't. Not about that. Ever." I said this instantly and she strained to see in my eyes if I was lying. I wasn't lying, and she clearly didn't doubt me, but her scrutiny persisted and we kept our eyes connected for a long time and it was equally clear that she wasn't quite believing me, either. I think it was at that moment I understood something more about her needing the lights on when we made love. And it didn't involve just me. It had to do with all the men she'd ever gone to bed with. I'd been right in sensing that they all lived on in her and that the whispering and the yearning and the remembering could come upon her unbidden. But I'd been wrong in thinking that gave her joy. She had always struggled to keep each of her lovers fixed before her in the light. She needed them to drive her father out but they always threatened to draw him back to her.

She looked long and hard into my eyes that morning in Paris; she rose up on her elbow beside me and the sheets were rumpled like a stormy sea all about her and the light from the window made her skin seem as white as the white of her eyes and we looked and looked and I think even at that moment I heard her voice. Even when I knew what to do next and even as I did it, I think that somewhere inside me I was hearing her voice: *I watched these blue eyes, his blue eyes, and I never have quite gotten over them floating there beneath that thick black brow and it makes his eyes very hard to read, especially when we aren't touching, especially when he's not inside me, especially when I need the most desperately to read him so I can think it's okay to draw this next breath into me and maybe even the one after that, so I can think that my being alive is not an offense to somebody powerful. Who can that somebody be? I wonder sometimes, but the fact is inescapable that the somebody exists, that there really is some sentience behind all the things we can see and that sentience is sitting there some-times thinking, There's been some big mistake, what the fuck is this woman doing here? and sometimes thinking, Okay, okay, let her be, if that rascal on top of her is so enchanted that he can forget his own foolish self for a while and realize there's somebody else around besides him and the proof of it is that he's looking in her eyes at a time like that and even liking what he sees, then maybe there's some use to her, let her go, let her draw this next breath. But it's always a struggle. Look at me, I say. Not to Ira. I don't have to say it to Ira. He's always ready to look in my eyes and that's the strange thing because*

I have trouble with those blue eyes, they just burn beneath his dark brow like an alcohol flame, I can't see the nuance, though it's better when he's coming, one eyelid droops ever so slightly and the other opens ever so slightly wider, that's what happens, and then his head rolls a little to the side but his eyes keep fixed on me like they can't let go and that's real nice, that's when Ira is telling me it's okay to walk across the floor and open the shades and throw a silk robe around my shoulders and make a salad maybe and read the newspaper and run a comb through my hair, it's okay to do these things, they don't have to seem ridiculous just because these are the daily things of people who fit and it's okay for me to feed myself and wash myself and lie down when I'm tired, I don't have to look in a mirror and see the tangle in my hair and feel like my arms are too heavy to lift and hear the crackles of the filament of the light above me and hear the canned laugh track through the wall and look again at my tangled hair and think it's just right, really, it's just the way I am. Ira's eyes tell me that it's not the way I am. And with Ira it's not a struggle for me. I don't have to say, Look at me, and I get only one fucking little glance and there's a glaze as thick as cataracts on the eyes of whoever the asshole is this time and then it's just the bottom of his chin again, with fucking stubble there, he can't even make the effort to shave properly for me, and I say, Look at me now goddamn you, and he does and all his eyes can show is a little puzzlement and I know it's going to be a bad one, though there were some good ones too, some with deep V brows, like a knife of pleasure plunging between the eyes that nearly shut from the okay of it but wouldn't shut quite all the way because they had to keep looking at me, and some others with the skin of their faces stretching so tight from the rush of what they felt in me that I let myself look past their eyes for a moment to see their ears move straight back in this reflex and then I would return to the eyes and they were fluttering, like silly schoolgirl eyes. Okay Fiona, they'd say to me. Okay.

This was the voice speaking in me very low, not quite audible, even on that morning when I knew enough to prove that I loved her by immediately taking her in my arms and entering her quickly in this pallid sunlight. She clung and cried out and fixed my eyes with hers and when we came nearly at the same moment, I did not have to prove anything more, I felt what I felt and it was what she wanted me to feel because I did love her and my eyes must have told her this was true because her own eyes grew soft even as she clawed my back and kicked my hams and even as she roared and shrieked so that they must have heard her clearly five floors down in the lobby but while all this happened, her eyes grew soft looking at my eyes, her lids closed slowly and opened again and her eyes did not move, though not from concentration now but from peace, even as her body and her voice wailed on in the rush of sex, and I knew that for this day at least she was okay.

Still, she wanted Grand Guignol, the Catacombs, so we took a cab and the driver cut across the Ile de la Cité, right in front of the Cathedral of Notre Dame, and this was our first view of it, up close. We both gawked as those great towers went by with their flat heads, striking me as not quite so sure of themselves, hesitating to point to the heaven that their priests had always sold to the people. I sat back around in the seat and I thought of her old Catholicism—not really tying it, even, to the words in the dark last night—to explain why she did not draw away from the window now but pressed her face to it and then turned around to look out the back and then quickly rolled the window down and stuck her head out and kept staring at the receding building as if it were a lover's eyes.

"We can go there later," I said.

She pulled back into the car and didn't say anything. Now I decided she'd been cursing the place under her breath as she watched. "Or we can stay far away," I said.

She looked at me and said in a voice more weary than angry, "Stop trying to figure me out."

"Sorry," I said, and she squeezed my hand gently.

I was glad for the reminder, really. At the Catacombs she took me by the hand and led me quickly through the outer passageways and then into a great stone antechamber—this depository of the bones of perhaps 5 million dead was made in the eighteenth century from a rock quarry—and then without pause she drew me on through a doorway beneath a stone lintel carved with the words ARRÊTE! C'EST ICI L'EMPIRE DE LA MORT. The Empire of the Dead.

Now we were walking in winding tunnels, cool, rough-hewn sweating stone, cobbled beneath our feet, arching low overhead, Paris above barely held up by pillars along the way, faintly leaning piles of massive, hand-chunked stone. And left and right were the long galleries of bones, the walls of the place invisible behind the endlessly stacked bones, arranged with a neatness that suggested some force other than human, an old notion of Nature or of God that gave order even to all of this, the bones layered there like the implacable record of eons passing, a long thin stratum of skulls, then a dozen of the nub ends of thigh and leg and arm, then another of skulls, a dozen more of the body bones, and on and on, mounting into the darkness of the ceiling, and all these faces from each era of the skull watching us pass, wide-eyed, their heads jaundiced, leathery, crossed by sutures as if inscribed by a delicate hand, the marks of an ancient tribe, and Fiona lead me more slowly now, her hand still on mine, and she was erect with shallow breathing, not from fear, I sensed, but deep attentiveness, moving and taking in all that passed on both sides, a way that she often took me through an exhibit of art that she recognized and loved, wanting to get a moving overview first before going back and lingering before the pieces she admired the most.

But she said nothing and I said nothing and our feet rasped and echoed as we followed the turns of the tunnel, passing through the scattered splashes of bare bulb light, our skin yellowing like the skulls and then going black and then yellowing again, and Fiona slowed a step suddenly and let me get near her, but she still held my hand, grasping it hard, and we moved on, pressed against each other, our clasped hands held low, against her thigh, and I was very conscious now of Fiona's body, fully fleshed, the bones invisible, and I stopped her and kissed her, knowing that all that kept her upright before me, that let her lift her arms and hold me against her, was invisible to me and always would be invisible to me and when our lips met and I closed my eyes, I was still thinking of these bones that shaped her every movement and this was where her untouchable pain was, I felt, in her bones, and I was animated with a despair that she took to be passion and her tongue lunged at mine and I tried to throw off this feeling, tried to concentrate on this tongue of hers that surely spoke of the deep dumbness of her bones, the deep irrelevance of them, surely this tongue was more important and yet I suddenly saw Karen Granger's toes in the green glow of the X-ray machine in my uncle's shop and I wondered how many men Karen Granger had kissed by now, I wondered how her tongue felt, I wondered if anyone had ever kissed her toes and I felt a deep scrabbling of desire in me, wanting to kiss those toes that I knew better than anyone's, and the impossibility of that kiss made me open to this tunnel I stood in, even as my kiss with Fiona grew more insistent, and a row of dark eyes watched us and I wondered which of them were women.

A skull directly before me seemed smoother than the others, thinner across the cheeks, and I felt certain it was a young woman, dead from pneumonia at age eighteen, dead without touching a man, this skull the secret beneath the delicate hollow of her cheeks, and I yearned to know which thigh among all the thighs stacked below and above this private face was hers. And her face seemed wistful to me then, as she watched this long kiss that had never been hers, and I closed my eyes with the face of a Vietnamese woman before me now, a bargirl, the first Vietnamese woman I ever touched, my first night in the little side-street bars in Bien Hoa, and her name was Xau, which meant "ugly," though she was not ugly at all and I did not learn this real name of hers until later in the night—she was called Kim in the bar—and we went along the street to her tiny second-floor apartment and I learned her name when I was lying, spent, within her, not wanting to draw out, happy to grow slack there. When she realized I wanted to remain inside her even after coming, she pulled her face back and her dark, dark eyes looked at my face as if she couldn't believe I was real and she kissed me a quick, noisy little kiss that seemed sexless but was not, was in fact her first truly felt kiss of the night, I realized. Then she told me her true name and how she was the daughter of very poor rice farmers and how her village had the custom of naming their first children degrading names so the spirits would be fooled and not come in the night and carry off the babies' souls. She was named Ugly so that she could live. She laughed at this and she moved slightly and I began to slip out of her but she realized at once and she stopped and quickly put her hand down there and tucked me back inside, shifting a little and keeping me there, and she said that she made love for the first time when she was fifteen and she was cast out of her family because of it and she said she let her virginity be taken out of marriage and so early because another belief of the village was that if a girl died a virgin, her head was very valuable and often was stolen. The head of a virgin could be turned into a powerful talisman and whoever had that talisman could never be killed by his enemies. Xau made sure she lost her virginity as soon as possible because for years she had been dreaming of dying young and having her head stolen and the loss of her head frightened her more than death and more than the rejection of her family and even more than a man's cock. When she said the Vietnamese word for cock she giggled at this and she kissed me again, this time quietly and with her tongue shyly presenting itself and she sighed an undulant sigh when she felt me growing hard inside her once more.

Fiona and I were moving again through the tunnel, our arms about each other and I realized with a brief regret that I'd forgotten to take a last look at the young woman who had watched our passion. But I felt uneasy about that whole, slightly crazed little wandering of my mind and I tried to concentrate on my wife, my wife who had brought us to the Empire of the Dead, and we were strolling now as if down a woodland path, her head tucked against my shoulder, my face burrowed into her hair and we splashed through the puddles of light and the air was damp from the sweating of stone and a sound began to come from before us and Fiona's head rose from my shoulder.

She took me by the hand again and she led me more purposefully.

"What is it?" I said.

"I don't know," she said.

There were many voices, chanting, and at each turn of the tunnel, they became clearer. They would chant and then a single voice would rise alone and then all the voices would sound again.

"It's Latin," Fiona said. Then she squeezed my hand in recognition and said, "The Latin Mass." She pulled at me, dragged me as fast as she could, and the voices became very clear. I caught, at the beginning of a passage from the many voices, "Ad Deum . . . ", to God. And when the single voice, a man, spoke once more, Fiona spoke with him, softly, next to me, and she slowed us down as the voices were very near now.

"Adjutorium nostrum in nomine Domini," Fiona said.

"What is that?" I whispered, but she shushed me and we turned a last corner and in a gallery off the tunnel several dozen people, mostly women, their heads covered in lace, knelt on the stones before a small table draped with silk and a priest with his back turned, and beyond him, of course, was a vast choir of bones.

Fiona stopped us in the shadows of the tunnel and she drew me near, the gesture seeming not so much an embrace as a way to keep me still. The congregation began to speak. "Confiteor Deo . . ." and I stopped straining for the words but I knew they were confessing their sins and I knew, too, though I was not Catholic, that the Mass in Latin had ceased several years ago and it struck me that these were ghosts here before me. The bones of the faithful had reassembled themselves from the wall and were having their Mass and would soon return, and as I thought this, they all struck their breasts with their right hands, and as they did, Fiona let go of me and struck her own breast. "Mea culpa," she said with them. And they struck and spoke again. "Mea culpa." And again. "Mea maxima culpa."

And then the priest went on and Fiona and I stood there like that for a long time, listening to the words, and when the priest turned to begin giving out the bread and wine, she let go of me and I looked at her, expecting that she would go forward to receive these things, but her eyes were full of tears and she looked briefly at me, an angry look in spite of the tears, and I feared that she understood I was in love with the young woman in the tunnel, but the look began to change even before I could clench in dismay at the possibility of another argument. Mine was a shallow thought anyway. It was her memories not mine that made her look turn now from anger into something else, softer but more despairing: *I can't blame you for not making me whole, Ira. I'm the evil one.* Then she fled into the darkness of the tunnel.

I didn't catch up with her until she was above the ground, out on the street and already hailing a taxi. I believed the voice—Fiona's voice—that I'd heard inside me back in the tunnel and I loved her and desperately wanted to exorcise that guilt in her. But at moments like this it seemed as irreducible as her bones and her back was to me and already a taxi was pulling up to a stop and it seemed as if she wanted to get away by herself. So I did not speak and I did not move. I slumped against a wall and watched the pale red of her hair splashing down her back and it made my flirtation with bone seem foolish. This soft flare of color, this delicate animation, was surely the only thing worth loving. I wanted to rush forward and embrace her, but I didn't want to provoke her, either. If she wished to be left alone, I knew to let her do that.

But she leaned into the taxi and spoke to the driver and then turned and found me. "Come on," she said.

I rushed forward and followed her into the back of the taxi and we were off. She must have given the driver our destination when she leaned into the cab because he drove as if he knew where she wished to go.

I wanted to say something now, tell her that all the ritual downstairs signified nothing, particularly not her own guilt. But I knew she wanted no words. I glanced at her and I made no sign as if I were about to speak and it was clear she noticed that, because though her eyes were still brimming with tears, she gave me a faint, at-least-I-can-depend-on-you smile. This made me inordinately happy. I looked out the window and my own eyes filled from that strange combination of anger and fear and gratitude and love that Fiona could inspire in me.

Then she leaned to me and whispered, "We are going to Notre Dame so that I can confess to a priest."

I turned to her and she was startled by the tears in my eyes. She smiled and took my face in her hands and drew me to her and her lips came for my eyes and I closed them. She kissed my left eye and said, "If I am to survive, my darling . . ." Then she paused and I did not look—I sensed her lips moving like a priest's hand from one tongue to the next—and she kissed my right eye and said, ". . . we must return to God." I opened my eyes now and hers were filled with new tears. She seemed suddenly very happy. What was I to say? And two months later she took it as a final, absolute sign of the rightness of this resolution that on one of those nights in Paris, in the light from our nightstand, she had become pregnant.

M y mother is dead. She was already dead when my son was born and that was a great regret for her when she turned her eyes to me in her bed and died, a regret she had been talking about almost exclusively for hours before her life ended, the regret that she would never see her grandchild. She was dead already, long dead, when I first met Fiona, but there would have been no regrets for my mother over that. She would not have liked Fiona. She would not have liked any of the women in my life. She died when I was eighteen and she did not have to worry about me going to war and she did not have to wrestle with the profound mystery of my attraction to women. I know that would have been a mystery to her because there are a dozen memories of my mother, beginning very early on, where she is smudgy with the scent of lavender and a woman is passing by on the sidewalk or down an aisle in a store or along the shore of a beach and the woman is dressed in shorts or a swimsuit and her thighs are naked and maybe the lower curve of her butt is visible and I notice all that, even when I am very young, even before I am ready to take Karen Granger to the X-ray machine. And my mother bends to whoever is near— her own mother or her sister or my father or sometimes, if we are alone, she simply bends to me, smelling like a garden trellis—and she says in a stage whisper, "How ugly." She says, "It's disgusting when a woman shows her body like that."

And nobody ever contradicted her. My grandmother nodded and agreed. Her sister repeated the refrain, *ugly*. Even my father grunted in assent. I never knew what to say to her. She even did this thing in the hospital a few days before we took her home to die. Both her breasts were in a bag somewhere in a dumpster in the back of the hospital and it occurred to me that she was taking some consolation from all of this, that at least she didn't have to worry anymore about somebody seeing her breasts. This thought came to me while I sat beside her bed and she clutched my hand and said she loved me— and she did, she never left any doubt about that—and it felt like my face could light the room, it was so hot with shame at the thought I'd just had about her.

Then it simply seemed that I was right, for a nurse came in to take her temperature and bent over the bed. The nurse was very pretty. I would fantasize that same night before falling asleep about having appendicitis and this nurse would come in with a bowl of water and a straight razor and she would lift my hospital gown and shave my pubic hair and from out of the lather my penis would rise and she would exclaim in delight and she would go to the door and close and lock it and she would open the blouse of her uniform, which was already open two buttons down so I could see her cleavage, and this is where my dream abruptly ended, for I could hear my mother's loud whisper from that afternoon. Her eyes were narrowed at that cleavage all the time the thermometer was clenched in her teeth and then, even before the nurse was all the way out the door, she said to my father and me, "How ugly."

And nobody ever spoke up to her on this subject. Nobody ever told her she was full of shit. Her feelings were easily hurt. She would weep quickly and softly when I disagreed with her even about some little thing and if my father was in some far part of the house he could hear this nearly soundless weeping and he would be at my side instantly, clutching my shoulder and guiding me out of the room with a dark, deep oath. I could not hurt this woman's feelings, he said, and by the time he had deposited me in my room, my shoulder was burning and the imprint of his grip would linger for an hour. So certainly my father was not prepared to defend the beauty of the bodies of women.

Indeed, I came to think that he actually deferred to her

judgment on the matter. He often did on other things. He worked at the steel mill in Wabash and somebody had convinced him—I'm not sure who; I've never asked—that the mill was the best place for him. But he knew my mother was smart and I was present one night when he watched my mother drop the newspaper beside her chair, a slow crumpling and releasing of it, like what she had just read was very sad. "What is it?" my father asked.

"There's so much going on and I know so little," she said.

"You have to go to school," he said. "It's where you belong."

She said yes right away, but she said it to me. She turned her face to me and smiled and said yes, like I was the one who had inspired it. They obviously had been discussing this for some time and I was part of the reason somehow. It was never explained to me and I never asked. So three days a week for the next four years she went over the river on the streetcar to St. Louis University, and I expected to hear a lot about it, all the things she was learning that she could pass on to me, but after the first few weeks there was very little. It was like a job she went to and never talked about. I don't think she approved of what she was learning. But she would not quit. And she never seemed to get any new ideas. Most Sunday mornings she would talk at some point about how the Church was really in your heart. Occasionally over the evening newspaper she would mutter darkly about the Democrats, saving her sharpest scorn for Adlai Stevenson who she suspected of being what she called "a tomcat in an eggshell." And she still was dismayed at the bodies of the women in the streets.

I realize how little I know. I wish I could hear her real voice. I wonder if my father ever did, if anyone ever did. For some few months forever severed from my conscious memory, I sucked at her breast. My mother had a nipple that I never saw again but for a time I put my mouth to it and sucked there and all the sweet lovers I've bent to ever since would whisper their secret voices to me when I plucked their nipples erect with my lips, but my infant's mouth never let me hear a thing. Or maybe I did hear and like all the images of all the moments of those first two or three years, the voice is simply beyond recall.

It doesn't make any difference. All of that came to an early end. But she did live long enough to wind up with my father in the principal's office at the high school and there was a big mystery about why they were being called in along with me, though I certainly had my own suspicions. She figured it was some special honor. Our principal, Mr. Sims, was a little man round enough that his arms never quite lay flat against his sides, and he was always using his handkerchief to mop his forehead and then high up into his receding hairline, as if keeping it dry up there was some kind of hair-restorative therapy. He met my mother and father and me at the door of his office and he put my parents together in a pair of chairs to the left of his desk and me in a wooden chair in the middle facing him.

He apologized profusely to my parents but this was a very serious discussion and it was his experience that if the parents were present, the truth always came out a little quicker. My parents looked at each other and then at me and I was already prepared for what I now knew would soon follow. It helped me to stay blank and cool by focusing on my intense curiosity: how would Mr. Sims say all this?

He lifted his chin and mopped his head and said, "All right, Ira, a certain something has appeared in a certain place and I want you to tell me what happened."

Now it was a struggle for me to keep my face straight. He was trying not only to completely dodge having to state the offense himself but he figured he could get me to do it for him. I wanted to laugh or sneer but I channeled all my facial energy into a puzzled frown. "What do you mean, Mr. Sims?"

He rolled his head in the direction of my parents, but they, of course, were as puzzled as I pretended to be. He mopped his head again and returned to me. "Oh come come, Ira. You surely don't expect me to believe that this sort of thing was written about you."

"What was that, Mr. Sims?" I asked.

He creaked forward in his chair. "Don't play games with me, Ira Holloway."

And now my mother intervened. "Mr. Sims," she said so sharply it made him flinch. "My husband is working the night shift this week and he should be in bed. I should be home doing my housework. You drag us both into your office without making it clear what for, and you tell us you're after some truth that is obviously still undetermined or we wouldn't be here, and now you're acting as if you already know the truth but you won't reveal it. Now you either speak up, Mr. Sims, and prove what it is you're saying, or we're leaving, all three of us."

I felt an odd thing. This was the same part of my mother speaking that made audible the whispers about what she perceived as immodestly dressed women. Here, on my behalf, facing down whatever damn fool she saw as a threat to someone she loved, she made me feel a brief twinge of regret that I'd given her an unjust cause to fight for. I glanced at her and saw my own blue eyes replicated there and I could see my father looking into those eyes as she stepped down off the trolley on Grand Boulevard in St. Louis and he couldn't believe how beautiful those eyes were, he had to love this woman no matter what. Then the feeling shifted in me. She was going to clear me and all the while it was true, I'd been sitting in the girls' room, writing about their bodies and mine and there was nothing ugly in it, I was thrilled to sit where they put those bare bottoms. I struggled again to keep my face still. This was a grin-worthy irony, it seemed to me. Let her fight for this cause.

I looked back to Mr. Sims and waited for the handkerchief to rise but it did not. He put his hands palm down on the desk and he tried to fix me with a steady gaze. He said, "Over the past week or so certain . . . writing has appeared on the walls of the rest room . . . the girls' rest room, that is."

That's all my mother needed to hear. Sims didn't get out another full sentence for the rest of the meeting. When he finally communicated the suspicion that I had actually written the words myself, she leapt up and I thought for a moment she would fist his shirt at the throat and lift him from his chair. But she just leaned over his desk and challenged him to match the handwriting with a sample of mine. She was ready to drag him down to the rest room right then and there. Sims said that the graffiti had already been removed from the wall and he lifted his handkerchief, and when my mother turned her eyes to his rising hand, he stuffed the handkerchief into his pocket and left it there, afraid, I'm sure, that she was about to make him eat the thing. The meeting was at an end.

That night when I got home, she came to me at the door and put her arms around me and laid her head on my chest and she said, "I'm so glad you're my son." I did not lift my own arms to return the embrace but I don't think she noticed.

Nor did she notice how I kept my right hand hidden when she met me at the door one night that following summer, late from what she knew was a date, and she certainly had a niggling little fear that something would sometime happen, but I hugged her with my left arm only, spinning her around and telling her she was prettier than my date, and if that was—I now realize— objectively true, it certainly felt like a lie at the time. People always spoke of how pretty my mother was, but I almost never saw it. That night it was just a good distraction and I kept my right hand down low, out of sight, though there was nothing unusual to see, really, it was the gentle crusting that was coming upon it and the smell of it that would give me away and I told my mother that I was really tired I was going to sleep, and still blushing from the compliment, she let me go.

In my room I closed and locked the door and threw myself on the bed beside the open window. I was sweating—the nights were always hot in the Mississippi River bottoms—and I waited for a while with my arms extended at my side, waited for my heart to calm and the house to grow quiet, and then I turned my face to the window, looked off to the west, where the hot strip at the mill was always going, all night, turning the sky red. And a train whistle blew, faintly, in that summer-night distance, and usually when I heard this sound in my room it spoke of a future that would take me away but was still deferrable, and that was all right, the room was comfortable and private and held me close and to know that the women in the two nudist magazines behind the loose ceiling board in my closet were sleeping now, naked in their tents in their forest camp, that was enough for me when I heard a night train from my bed with the door to my room locked.

But on this night I'd lain with a girl named Amanda on the great grassy bed at the top of Sun Mound, the pre-Columbian Indian burial ground a few miles north of the blast-furnace plant on Collinsville Road. North, too, of the trailer court where Blossom lived, and I drove past there with Amanda and I wished that Blossom knew where I was going and what I would do so that she wouldn't think I was totally backward sexually. But I erased that thought right away. I hoped she never heard anything, ever, about me and any other girls because then she might think that the fault was hers, that I drove on past her that day when I was sixteen because I didn't like her face or because I shared the feelings the other boys had about her.

I turned to Amanda and she was talking about Mr. Sims, how he stood by the water cooler between classes and asked every girl who drank there how things were, and I focused on Amanda's profile, her faintly aquiline nose, and I put Blossom out of my mind, and Amanda's skin was dusky and she looked like the image I had of the Indians who built the great Sun Mound and disappeared six hundred years ago, and Amanda and I climbed the path to the top of the mound and we lay down and watched the stars and she came near and a train cried in the distance and out here, the sound also spoke of the future but it made me impatient for it, made me stir and hold Amanda close now.

I instinctively found that comfortable place for my arm, stretching beneath the curve of her neck, drawing her cheek to my shoulder and curling around to let my wrist fall across one breast and my hand rest lightly on the other one. This took my breath away, both the soft pile of her and the perfect fitting of these body parts, a perfection that I credited myself with, like I'd just invented the wheel. We watched the wild scattering of stars and she said she'd visited this place with her class. Did I know, she asked, that a few years ago they'd found an ancient king buried in one of the smaller mounds just south of this one? He was laid out on a cape of polished shell beads and in a pit beside him they found the skeletons of fifty-three women between the ages of fifteen and twenty-five, his wives and lovers, who had each been ritually strangled to accompany their lover to the afterlife.

No, I said, I didn't know that, but my voice was barely audible. I was stricken by a violation of some instinct in me, something I can only call protectiveness. Like when you hear about the death of an animal or a child. And by this I certainly do not mean that all those women seemed like animals or children to me. Quite the contrary. Even with a great and awful panorama opening in my head of the naked skeletons of all these young women, I knew that each of them was a terrible and wonderful mystery to me, fifty-three women, like a great gym class in their locker room and the water was running and I was peeking in the window and dazzled beyond all imagination. But at the news Amanda had given me, the first thing I felt was a restlessly violated sense of protectiveness for that soft and summoning part of each of them. Never yet having touched a woman's pussy or even seen one in the flesh, I nevertheless felt it was something so vulnerable and so gentle and so sleepily helpless that I yearned desperately not only to touch and kiss and enter it but also to cover it and cradle it and shelter it.

"I can't let that happen to you," I whispered to Amanda.

She laughed softly and turned to her side and her hand touched my chest and we kissed and I realized that there was a faint tenseness in her body only by feeling it fall away when we kissed and I turned a little onto my side as well and my free hand, my right hand, rose and came to rest on her hip and her lips pressed harder against mine. For a moment, my hand was held there on her hip by a sudden strong awareness of her hipbone beneath my palm. But this time there was something more secret even than bones to touch and I drew up her dress and I moved down the tight little line of elastic on her panties and then beneath it and her pubic hair was spongy and a little damp and I spread my fingers there to take it all in and I waited for her own hand to come and make me stop, but it did not. She kissed me harder still and though I wanted to linger there in this lovely hair that was smudged out of the photos in the nudist magazines, I did not want her to change her mind. So my hand crept on, and the first thing I did was to cup her there, to cover her whole pussy with my hand and her secret lips kissed my palm and I held her tight and nothing would hurt this part of her, I would see to that. The kiss of these lips grew very wet and I put my fingers in her and nothing was as soft as that: this place in all the women I've ever loved has never ceased to startle me with its softness but that first shock of it, with Amanda, on the top of the Indian mound, made me gasp.

"What is it?" she asked.

"Nothing," I said. "It's just that I can feel how beautiful you are."

And in my room that night, my face to the window, I finally let myself raise my right hand, which I had carefully not wiped, which I had even kept off the steering wheel on the drive home. Amanda was sweetly responsive to my touch, panting softly and then crumpling at the last, but she never thought to touch me and I was so thrilled for the great good fortune of my right hand that it never even occurred to me to suggest it. So on my bed I raised my right hand and laid it against my face and I drew her in, the rich smell of her that reminded me at the time of both the earth and the steel mill, the newly turned black earth of the cornfields that you rolled your window down for when you drove by in the spring and the great steaming banners of smoke from the night fires of the blast furnace. And I touched myself then, for the first time with some real link to a real person and it was not what I wanted, it was lonely at last, but the smell of her on my hand was something that I felt gentler and gentler and gentler about and gentler still until I rushed into that smell of her and I knew this girl and she said to me, *I wish now I had touched you, but your hands were the first and they seemed complete inside me, I didn't have to move to be loved, I didn't have to do anything but lie against you, and if I believed, really believed, that we had bodies of the spirit and there was eternity before us all and I loved a great man very much, I would perhaps have knelt down to the ritual cord about my neck and there was no more that I would've had to do. I would've been filled only with love.*

It may be very easy to misunderstand me: Fiona seems now to be central in what I'm trying to say, and, of course, in some ways she is. But Amanda is also important even though she moved away at the end of the summer and we never did get as far as making love. On the fourth and last time we lay in the grass somewhere in the summer heat, as my right hand nuzzled into her, her own hand did at last move inside my pants and down to my penis and she curled her fingers around me, but that was all she did, she just held on, and then she was gone. And yet, I feel that she too is at the center of what I'm trying to understand, and so are all the rest of the women I've mentioned and many more, they're all in the center of me and they don't come back as a way for me to avert my eyes from Fiona and all that happened between us, but rather as a natural part of something much bigger. Not just a part of it but a palpable sign of it. Which is what they call a sacrament.

I sound strange even to myself sometimes. Maybe it has something to do with Fiona dragging me into the Catholic Church as soon as we got back from Paris. We had already moved into a two-bedroom apartment in the West Village and it was the first Saturday that we were back. She hadn't said much more after her confession at Notre Dame but there was an odd little brooding going on in her. We had no more fights about jealousy and we had some lovely, quiet sex and later, one moment stood out in my recollection, months later, as I tried to examine those few days after something took a turn in her in the Catacombs. It was our last night in Paris and we were naked and touching and kissing and trying first one favorite part then another. Her insteps and the crook of her arm were slick and happy, as were other places we'd settled on as special for us, like behind our ears and the backs of our knees and our tailbones, and she seemed calm and I was feeling a breeze from the window on my sweaty back and smelling rain that was coming our way and she turned me over and clambered down me to take me in her mouth. She mumbled the head of my penis around in her mouth for a few moments and then she stopped and she took me out but without touching me. She even clasped her hands at her back and she stared at that yearning tip of me for a moment and then she opened her mouth again and I could see her tongue come forward a little bit and curl at the tip and she took me onto her tongue and sucked me deep inside her, her shoulders hunching, her hands still clasped.

I didn't make any connection with this moment and my first Catholic communion for a long time, and maybe there was no connection at all in Fiona's mind. Her voice is silent in me on this point. But on that first Saturday back in New York, we made love and then wrapped ourselves in light robes and we stepped onto the front fire escape, just outside our living room, and we strained out to see the sky going red as night came on. And Fiona said, "We have to go to church tomorrow. I feel something is happening in me."

"Church?"

"You're not going back on our plans in Paris, are you?"

"I don't remember a plan," I said, being particularly stupid. The plan had been detailed and complete in her head and all I had needed to know was that simple notion of getting back to God.

She faced me on the fire escape and I could see the exasperation in her face and she could always surprise me because instead of saying anything, she just slipped off the robe and threw it over the railing. She was naked in the dying light and though we were five floors up and there was a warehouse across the street, she seemed naked to the whole of New York, to all of the world. "I have no defenses," she said.

So the next morning we went to a little Catholic church behind an iron fence in the West Village: *Ira touches my hand briefly, just a fumbling little squeeze as we step through the gate, and I take it to mean that this is the right thing to do and it is, clearly it is. Ira is a good man. He thinks he loves me, and maybe what's inside this place that we approach in a Sunday-morning mist rank with bus fumes and doorway piss will make that real at last. I don't know. But the piss smell that seems to fall with the rain grows stronger as we move under the arch of the portico and it is here that I want to begin to feel the first stirrings of change, it is now, right now, stepping into the shelter of this doorway, that I want to have that first intimation that no matter how many years of reparation it will take, I will be made clean this way, and even as I want this so badly, I smell the piss spoor of the homeless and it makes me angry. They can't help being what they are—which of us can?—and I make sure I always act from this attitude, I often* buy them food on the street, this is something I've done often, but with a single thought I wipe away all that I've gained for my soul from any good works. My head snaps to the dank corner where they slept and pissed and if they were there right now I would stand before them and tell them to get the hell out of here, this is one building where they can't just whip it out and piss, and knowing I would do that makes me stop short and Ira turns to me and his hand comes out and I bat it away and this smell touches me with something else: a doorway into a building uptown, thirties Moderne with no straight edges, everything curved and grooved and metallic and this smell is there, very strong, I never see the men but every week when I go through this door I know they've been here the night before, and up on the twentieth floor is the man who taught me everything about psychiatry, he waits for me and only when I enter his office does the piss smell fade with the smell of leather and book paper and on this man's hands the smell of soap—he has a little toilet off his office and I sometimes catch him washing his hands as I come in, washing the previous patient off his hands and after our forty-five minutes are over, as soon as his door is closed, I sometimes linger and I can hear him rise and go into the toilet and wash his hands, though he has touched nothing while I was there, only the desktop and a notepad and his own lapels. I have made him dirty.

And from when I am sweet sixteen until I am twenty-three, this is what he gives me: he lets me talk and he never interrupts me and he never asks about anything but what I dream and I can never remember so I make dreams up for him and he writes a prescription and every morning for those seven years I stand before my bathroom mirror and I extend my tongue and what feels light in the palm of my hands feels very heavy on my tongue, it is hard and very heavy and I can't imagine it dissolving inside me but it goes down and then my blood pounds and I am going so fast that I can outrun any feeling I want for a while, I can run very fast, even faster than when I was a little girl in school and was faster than anyone. And then at night I stand jittering and exhausted before the same mirror and I extend my tongue for him again and this time the pill is so light in my hand that I have to look at it again and again to see that it's actually there and I have to be very careful that it doesn't jump off my palm and down the drain and when it's inside me, my blood goes thick and slow like I've been slashed open across some fatty part of me and the blood is just oozing out on the floor and puddling there and I sleep.

So this is why I curse the homeless in my mind on the portico of the Catholic church, for making dirty this place that I hope will make me clean and maybe I'm just as bad as the man on the twentieth floor, it's like I'm wanting to wash my hands though I haven't touched a thing, but of course it's different because his hands are already clean and mine are dirty and I know it's not from the piss in the shadows. But Ira is giving me that oh-shit-what's-happening-now look and that beautiful long eyebrow of his is wrinkling up like it's a big black worm on the sidewalk after a rain and the sun is out and desiccating its body and now it's Ira making me angry, not having faith in what we're about to do, not realizing that this is a long-term thing, a commitment, something that we can't expect to work overnight, but this just shows what a hypocrite I am on top of everything else because it's my own lack of faith, stopping here and getting angry at the guy who slept in this doorway last night, that's worrying Ira now.

I move to him and take his hand and I say, "It's okay." He seems very grateful at this, and we walk through the door and I am very happy for a moment. In the narthex I stop again and look through the doors into the nave and it is very small, really, holding only a few dozen aisles and rising into a low, timbered ceiling and it is nothing like the great hold-the-whole-neighborhood Catholic churches I grew up in and this is such *a relief that my eyes fill with tears and I slip my arm around Ira and give him a hug so he knows I'm all right, these are good tears.*

And it's strange, really, to hear English words in the Mass, and this makes it different from before, too, and the priest is facing us when he lifts the host turned now into Christ's body and the chalice of wine turned now into Christ's blood and I don't tell Ira that he isn't supposed to go forward and take the body and the blood without being officially a Catholic because I don't want to give him a reason to reject these things and this is something I don't agree with anyway and I want Ira beside me, I realize, and this is working out better than I ever imagined.

So when the time comes, I nudge Ira and lift my chin toward the front and he looks and understands what I want us to do and to his credit he hesitates only for the briefest moment, not quite long enough to set me off, and then he is getting up and even the little hesitation seems sweet to me—if he'd gotten up instantly, I would have known how easy it was for him to tell lies with his actions just to try to patronize me—but I also know that if he had hesitated for even a few more seconds I would have had trouble keeping it together. But we get up and we join the line in the aisle and I close my eyes and I pray very hard: Come into my heart, Jesus. I am open to you, please come inside me and make me clean. And I am kneeling on the altar steps and Ira is beside me, on my left, and on my right is some old woman and beyond her a row of others and we are all here to be made clean, we are all dirty together, and I can hear the priest's voice murmuring, coming closer: "The body of Christ . . . The body of Christ . . ."

I am supposed to keep my eyes cast down, but I glance along the row for just one moment to the golden ciborium in the priest's hand and he takes out a wafer and he says "The body of Christ" and I cannot see the wafer very well, it is small and it has disappeared right away but the hand is large and very smooth and I look at the priest and though I have been watching him for some time, now that he is drawing near to extend this hand with something that feels like a chance for me, I can see that he is young—younger than me—and he has a faintly fleshy face but nice, really, its hint of future jowls redeemed by a thin, straight nose and a wide mouth that moves very sweetly with each offer of this body.

But I catch myself beginning to stare and my eyes drop once more to the priest's hand rising from the ciborium and now the host is visible to me, white as my skin, and I square around and lower my eyes and soon the priest is before me and he smells of Old Spice, I lift my face and look at my nose bulbous in the gold mirror of the ciborium and I am ugly there and I am sure the priest can see how ugly I am but still he says "The body of Christ" and I whisper "Amen" and I open my mouth and I bring my tongue forward: softly, softly, the air is cool on my tongue and I feel naked and I curl the tip of my tongue very slightly and his hand comes forward and the host touches me, and it is very light on my tongue and I can feel my blood speed up, pounding in my head so hard I am afraid I will faint, but I close my eyes and concentrate on the body of Christ in my mouth and it is as light as a soul and I close my mouth and hold Him inside me.

And Fiona was happy in that moment. I could feel her quaking with happiness and the priest was then before me and I took the wafer into my mouth and I did something that Fiona later told me was wrong to do. She told me with elaborate patience, but I could sense another kind of quaking behind her words. She was angry. I almost spoiled things for her. But even she realized I couldn't have known. I chewed. I ground the body of Christ between my teeth and when she later told me about it, I understood at once how people who believe in all that could be offended. I would soon become very adept at imagining the point of view of those who are institutionally religious. But at that first communion, I chewed the bland little wafer all up and fortunately the sound of it didn't go very far. But part of what made me chew was my watching Fiona's tongue. I was jealous. I chewed hard and I shot one look of resentment at this soon-to-be-pudgy young face passing by, though I knew priests were celibate and maybe this guy didn't even realize his privilege.

But I was jealous not just about Fiona—she was only a very small increment of it. When I rose and left the altar and I moved past the pews full of worshipers who had already taken communion, I saw half a dozen women who could stir me, a dozen, more, and the tongues of all these women had slipped forward from their mouths, yearning toward the priest's hand, and the tongue was powerful for me in its hiddenness, the little glimpses during speech only making its mystery greater. It was this, which the priest had, that I wanted for myself: the slow, full exposure of a woman's tongue, hollowed and soft, the faint bumpiness of it ready to taste. And they came to this priest one after another, all these lovely women, and they gave him this vision of themselves, this secret, and they let his hand come to them, come very very near the yearning tips of their tongues, and with no wafer left in my mouth as I followed Fiona back to our pew, I ground my teeth now in jealousy.

After Mass, the mist outside the church had turned to rain, but Fiona was happy. "It's okay," she said as I hung back in the shelter of the portico and she dragged me into the rain. We walked back to our apartment and no matter how often I tried to pick up the pace, she slowed us down, as if she was determined to get soaked to the skin. I should have been smarter, I suppose, about what was happening, but maybe that would have just made things harder for me. There's not much I could have done differently. I loved Fiona, after all.

"It was wonderful," she said even before we'd gotten out of the iron gate.

I nodded, more concerned about the rain at that moment. And only now does it strike me as a little odd that the rain should have bothered me that much. The morning was warm and I'd been soaked by rain many times and it was never a problem. But if in fact Fiona wanted to immerse herself and come out a different person—some sort of baptism was in her head—I guess I must have been unconsciously responding to the same thing and I was resisting any change, and that's a little spooky to me now, I guess, my instinctively buying into the symbolism enough to feel I had to reject it.

"You made one big mistake," she said, "but it wasn't your fault, really."

I looked at her to see how the next few hours would go and she made herself smile. "Don't worry," she said. "It's really okay. You'll learn."

This made me turn my collar up against the rain and walk a little faster, but she did not move to catch up and I wonder what would have happened if I'd forced the whole issue right then. But I loved Fiona. She was smart and she could be very gentle and she was fighting with real courage, it seemed to me, against demons that I could only vaguely imagine. And for myself, some part of me was already saying, Okay we're going to be soaked to the skin and we'll be home at last and we'll start some coffee brewing and we'll strip the wet clothes off and dry each other with fresh towels and then we'll make love, looking for the places where the dampness has lingered, and we'll smell coffee when we come and we'll cling then before we rise to eat and drink and we'll listen to the rain going on and on. And this is exactly what we did, and on that Sunday morning, lying with Fiona against me, our thighs wet with each other, the taste of her tongue on my own, I turned my face to the blur of rain at the window and I wondered if maybe it was really this that people called grace.

Two things astonished me about the women of Vietnam—all the many women I made love to, most of them bargirls, some briefly, one night only but full of their family photos and soft sighs; some for a longer time, after the second night a schoolgirl jealousy setting in and talk of forever; and one woman, no bargirl at all, for what might have been much longer, if not really forever then at least for years—and these are the two astonishing things: though the pussies of these women made my face as wet as the afternoon rains, they had almost no scent at all, not one of them; and every one of the women was religious. Every one had an ancestor shrine—most within sight of the bed where we made love—and this bit of Confucianism was almost always in addition to some other religion. Even the two Vietnamese Catholics I made love to prayed at their little altars to a dead father or grandfather, though perhaps this was easier for them to reconcile than other Christians, the Catholics always ready to pray for the souls of the dead. Confucius said that the spirits of the dead could dissolve into nothingness if the living did not work at keeping them alive through prayer and veneration. And this they all believed.

Even Miss Xau, whose family had taught her to fear her head being stolen if she died a virgin and then cast her out for doing something about it, had her shrine. The second time I visited her, I found her at her prayers, the incense smoke rising from her hands and her father's picture before her, framed on the altar between two vases of flowers. She had come to hate this man, I already knew, and he had died only the year before and so he was particularly confused in the spirit world, and I slipped softly into the room and sat on the floor and I could see her face and there were tears in her eyes and a furrow of worry in her brow as she prayed. The incense burned low, lashing up from her very fingertips before she set the stalks aside and finally turned her face to me. Later, after she had held my penis in both her hands and stroked and caressed me and then rose up and straddled me and settled down on me and her hands were free, I brought them to my face and they smelled strongly of jasmine, the incense, and I imagined that my penis smelled of jasmine now, too, and still later, when she was on her back and coming, she turned her eyes briefly toward the altar. I wondered if she did this in spite or in sorrow, but I never asked.

And I made love to a Taoist who stripped herself before me only at the precise hour her astrologer prescribed and who sensed the room full of spirits and fairies and I made love to a Cao Daist whose religion began with a crow tracing a message in the sands of Phu Quoc Island and revered Victor Hugo as a primary saint and I even made love to a woman from the Mekong Delta whose family followed the Palm Tree Prophet, a man who spent every evening in holy contemplation in the top of a palm tree and who once broke into a Saigon meeting between Henry Cabot Lodge and Robert McNamara to show them a cat that suckled mice, though the Americans apparently missed the spiritual message. This woman still went with her family on a pilgrimage to the prophet every spring, her parents never speaking a word to her on the whole trip as punishment for her way of life in the Saigon bars. The two Catholics I made love to wore Miraculous Medals around their necks and one of them had a plaster statue of Mary on her ancestor shrine. The other wasn't a bargirl but a woman I met at a reception at city hall. I made love to her, at her suggestion, in my own room at the Metropole, an old French hotel that had been taken over by the Army. Whereas the bargirls spoke always of love and almost never of money, this woman clearly didn't like the Spartan furnishing of my place and sharply asked "Where are your things?" when she first came in, and after I made love to her with a ghastly sense of her attention being elsewhere, she began to tell me what a nice man I was and how much she needed to go to America and she told me all the things she would have in her American house someday, naming the brands—Kelvinator, Whirlpool, Zenith, Hoover—and after she was gone I went out into the streets and it was dark and I walked the alleys, and the doorways and tiny back rooms were full of people crouching and talking and playing cards and someone was cooking soup pungent with fish sauce and someone was twanging a Vietnamese guitar and the faces turned up to me from the puddles of kerosene lamplight and always smiled and when I would speak a word of Vietnamese the faces would crack open in pleasure and I finally accepted one of the invitations and crouched flat-footed with a farming family from Hue, eight of them living in two small rooms and their eldest daughter, perhaps twenty years old, was very beautiful and she was beside her mother and she looked at me with her head slightly bowed and the father made me eat the only piece of chicken from their soup and his eldest daughter put her hand over her mouth to smile at my Vietnamese while all the rest of them cried out at my skill and I knew that I would never be able to touch her, though I longed to, not because the family wouldn't encourage it, for they would, not because she didn't want to, for after a while her face lifted slightly and her eyes softly fixed me and told me she did, but because what they all truly wanted was a son-in-law, even an American son-in-law—perhaps especially an American son-in-law—and they all wanted true love forever in a distant place that seemed to them like paradise. I opened myself to her eyes and let her sear me there in our tight little circle of nine people, her youngest brother hanging on my shoulder, her mother keeping my bowl full, all of them crying out in pleasure at my slightest turn of phrase, and I loved her very much for that two hours, though our skin never touched. And she was a Buddhist. The family had the iron Buddhist swastika from their field propped in the corner of their front room. The father spoke of the great pagoda in Hue on the bank of the Perfume River and I could imagine his eldest daughter walking with the family, lagging behind in her purple ao dai and with her conical palm-leaf hat pulled down to half hide her face.

Most of the women I made love to in Vietnam were Buddhists. Though they all made it clear that they were actively religious—each in her own way, by a passing but sincere reference to the persistence of the spirit, by a pause to pray, something—it was rare that the passionate connection of our bodies caused them the slightest hesitation. I didn't like to think of my ardor as eddying about within the great current of the Middle Way, but somehow that also appealed to me, in the same way that I relished knowing the language and picking up on details of the secular culture. And the most ardent of the Buddhists, as it turned out, was Miss Tran Thi Hoa. I met her in my second month in country. Before I was transferred into Saigon I was jobbed out at Homestead to various sorts of units. But much of the interpreting I did was for a military-intelligence captain named Hank. When I was with him we wore civilian clothes—PX chinos and PX button-down shirts and PX Hush Puppies—and I don't know who we were supposed to fool. But I was on call for him any time of the day or night and it was very nice to get out of the fatigues and jump into his jeep and bury my eyes in the landscape for a few hours and then talk to people who weren't inevitably military. One of my lingering early memories of Vietnam—from my first week—is of that jeep careening through the night along the narrow country roads from the camp out to Bien Hoa Air Base and though I imagined the darkness full of the Viet Cong silently raising their rifles at my shape passing, I was too thrilled to be truly frightened, thrilled with the surprising chill of the air and the children running along the road with sheaves of burning grass and the Vietnamese people—I had seen so few of them yet—moving in the dim lights of their little houses of scrap wood and corrugated tin. And every one of these houses stirred me, the darkness thick and unremitting and then the sudden shape, a square of kerosene light and a figure bending to a table or another house with no one in its window but shadows or another with fluorescent light and the shaking of long black hair or another with an inner doorway hung with strands of beads. And for each it was the same: I sensed a woman there, a new woman, full of mysteries that were ravishingly compounded by the invisible rice paddies with their pocked stone tombs and the night sky filled with clouds wispy as a mandarin's beard; each house prompted the sweet yearning for a woman, a woman just out of sight, waiting behind a beaded curtain or on a pallet in the spill of kerosene light.

It has always been like that and it remains so. I am thirty-five years old and it remains so. Three weeks ago I was in the state of Louisiana on business. I rented a car and drove west from Baton Rouge and then north on a two-lane and it was twilight and the scattered houses set far back from the highway with their porch swings and pickup trucks were beginning to light up and I was very conscious of them: the windows across the deep lawns stirred me just like in Vietnam, whispering of women inside. A pickup with spoilers and a gun rack had passed me on the interstate an hour earlier and the driver was a young woman with teased blond hair and she eased past me very slowly, though she did not look my way. She had a delicate profile with a long nose, very pretty, and she looked ludicrously fragile in the cavernous cab of the truck and I wondered where she was now, as the bright windows drifted past me on the two-lane. She was behind a window like these somewhere and she was sitting on the edge of her bed with her boots off and wiggling her toes and thinking about a shower and the guy who bought the truck was out of her life now and because the son of a bitch had skipped off to Texas and left her with the payments it was all she had to get around in, though she could handle it better than he ever could anyway and the gun rack was empty now and she would figure out how to take it off the back window one of these days. She rose from her bed and began to unbutton her blouse, her fine, thin mouth set hard against the cowboy, and she was thinking how she needed a man of a completely different sort. And this was what filled my eyes and made me hard driving alone on that Louisiana blacktop just three weeks ago and the light was just about all gone and the highway was very dark, trees roiling past on both sides of the road and then suddenly the woods cracked open and in a blare of orange light there was a tangle of pipes and tanks and a flare stack—a little oil refinery—and then it was gone and all I could think of was a woman waiting there, a woman in work clothes and she had a square jaw and she was sweating and alone in the place and I stood before her and she pulled off her hard hat and her hair tumbled down and it was black as number-six crude, even in the orange light, and she pulled her wrist across her forehead and smiled a crooked smile at me and I moved forward and she was as tall as me, exactly as tall, we looked straight into each other's eyes and then we held each other close and she was rich with sweat and I kissed it from her brow and from her throat and the hard hat fell at our feet.

So the way I first met Tran Thi Hoa was this. The captain named Hank came to my hootch where I was spending the last fifteen minutes of my lunch break listening to the sweet bite of Karen Carpenter's voice and thinking how sexy it was for her to be a drummer and he said there was a man he had to talk to. We drove east for a while on Highway One and the rice fields suddenly ran up to a vast expanse of tall, top-thick trees. My first sight of them, at our angle of approach, made them look bunched up and wild. But then we slipped into their shadow and they all fell into long, precisely aligned rows, immaculately cut with dark slashes in their white trunks.

They were rubber trees and Hank now shouted over the wind in the open jeep that this was the place. The trees broke and on one side of the highway was a stucco building of bright yellow with a brown slate roof—an office building, I gathered—and beyond it was a clustering of the workers' houses all in the same yellow stucco and brown shingles. Then the little houses rearranged themselves like the plantation into neat rows and we turned off the highway to the other side and we passed a tennis court ringed by mahogany trees and the villa was ahead. It was the same as all the other buildings, stucco and slate, but it was built high on concrete stilts and had a veranda running around it, the wood columns all painted bright red and these were the colors of South Vietnam's flag—yellow and red—and I figured all the shingled roofs on the plantation were once red as well.

We climbed the stairs to the veranda and Tran Van Loi met us with a bow and sat us down there on wicker chairs. The man spoke pretty good English and he and Hank already knew each other, so I just listened for a while to the two of them talk: Loi was clearly a Buddhist, speaking of the monks he supported in a nearby village and still referring bitterly to the ruin that a Catholic president (he would not even speak Diem's name) almost brought to his country; and Loi hated the arrangement he had to live with here—he was still the owner of his own plantation during the day, but the Viet Cong owned the place at night, allowing everyone to stay undisturbed inside their stucco houses but moving at will through the trees.

All of this seemed mildly interesting but there was jasmine trellised along the veranda and its smell distracted me, made my gaze wander from the porch to the ring of mahogany trees and the empty tennis court, and the smell of real jasmine had the rich prickle of authenticity so I thought of Xau and her incense only very briefly and instead I felt open to the future, to all the women who were far away from this empty landscape before me, who were moving through their lives unaware that in a year, five years, ten, twenty, they would lie down with me and we would whisper all that we knew to each other. Then there was a swirl of dust off the highway and a Citroën 15CV saloon—onyx black and easily thirty years old—headed this way. It was a beautiful car, the sneer curls of its front fenders framing its gently back-leaning silver grille. I expected a Frenchman in a rumpled suit and slouch hat to step from it, or if a Vietnamese, then an elderly man in mandarin dress.

But the car raced to a stop in front of the house and Loi

rose and we did too as a woman emerged. She was very tall for a Vietnamese woman and I'm sure this made the men in her circles very nervous and I could see past the first impression very quickly, even as Loi apologized for her. She was wearing loose pantaloons as black as the Citroën and a severe blouse of drab green and her hair was rolled up tight at the back of her head. Loi said, "My daughter is very modern. She takes an interest in everything and when she goes to the plant, she dresses like they do." "They," I understood, were the peasants, the process workers.

But she draped an arm over the open door of the car now and undid the bun at the back of her head and shook her hair down in a sleek, straight, black fall and I could see that she was very beautiful. She shook her hair until it was perfect, reaching nearly to her waist, and she turned her eyes on the three of us standing on the veranda and her face was long but her eyes were deep, shaped only by the Orient, knowing every mahogany tree, every water buffalo, every rack in the hot sky, and she smiled at us and waved.

Loi said, "Come up and meet our friends," and my breath snagged in me as she closed the car door and strode across the gravel and up the steps and the pantaloons were silk, I realized, and they rippled softly about her crotch and she was before me and Loi introduced the captain first, but I thought that Hoa did not look at him very long, her eyes already tugging away to meet mine, and then Loi was saying my name and I took over, greeting Hoa with great and even verbose courtesy in Vietnamese, letting her hear how well I knew her language.

"Well, what in the world is this?" she said in English.

"An American who has fallen in love with Vietnam in only two months," I said, and I persisted in speaking Vietnamese. She turned her face very slightly to one side and smiled at me like that, a gesture that seemed very complicated to me, at once coy but ironically so, a little patronizing but also vulnerable in its willingness to be charmed. This is how headlong I felt about Hoa, that I should already be so desperately analyzing the smallest gesture.

"Do you always fall in love so quickly?" she asked in Vietnamese, and only twice did she ever speak English to me again, and then only very very briefly.

"It was worse than two months, really," I said. "I fell in love at first sight."

Hoa looked at me from that slightly turned place for a moment, listening to the wooing in my subtext and then she dealt with her father. "Isn't it remarkable to find an American who loves our country?" she asked him.

Mr. Loi muttered some polite assent, clearly not charmed by our banter, and Hank, with all the Vietnamese words rushing around him, said, "Hey, what's going on?"

Hoa dealt with him too: "It is nothing, Captain. Your Ira Holloway is very good in small talk with Vietnamese."

After that, the captain and the father moved quickly to business and Hoa gave me a last nod and she walked away down the veranda and I thought about her most of the time while Hank and I were across the highway and beyond the workers' settlement at the processing plant—a vast shed with no walls and a high roof and full of rows of silver tubs and a maze of troughs and wringers and stacks of bamboo poles to hold the latex on the drying racks. We talked with a black-toothed old man who had been watching most of the night every night at his window on the edge of the workers' settlement. He was the only man with guts, Hank told him, and we went over the contents of a little notebook he'd kept of what he saw: how many Viet Cong were out there each night in the trees, which directions they moved in, what he made of the lights every night down at the water tower at the tree line a quarter of a mile away. None of the workers went down there anymore, not even in the daytime. And I was glad that I spoke Vietnamese well enough that the right words would come out while my mind was somewhere else, and I thought of the tiny collection of words and gestures I had of Hoa as if they were the tinkling of the woman's bracelet on the tape at language school, ridiculously little things, but they were working on me in some mysterious way.

We tooled out onto the highway heading back to Homestead, and I craned my neck to look at the passing villa, hoping to catch sight of her, and sharper than the old man's eyes seeing death moving in the night all around him, I spotted Hoa just before the villa disappeared behind us. She was a tiny figure from here, moving away from the house, but I could see two things: her hair was still down and she had a strong, sharp gait. I realize now that I had never heard a Vietnamese woman whistle and maybe the culture just totally prevented it—as a matter of fact, I don't remember ever hearing *any* Vietnamese, woman or man, whistling—but the impression I have, thinking back to her more than a decade later, is that Hoa was the kind of woman who would whistle.

I have always loved a woman who whistles, particularly to herself. There aren't many. I met Rebecca Mueller like that. I worked for a week with a client in their European office in Zurich. The offices were in an old Tudor building on a cobbled street that climbed a hill up from the Limmat River. The president had an office with a bay window on the top floor and on my first morning with him I took a break and moved down the hall in search of the men's room and it was very quiet, the heavy wood floor creaking beneath my feet, and then from one of the offices I heard whistling. I stopped by the door and it was the "Ode to Joy" from Beethoven's Ninth Symphony and for something joyful, the tune had so often sounded ponderous to me, beautiful but somehow a little too determined, but this sweetly reedy whistle told me it was a woman and she had transformed the tune, it seemed to me, made it joyful at last. I listened for a while and then I peeked around the corner of the door and a young woman was stuffing envelopes at a desk and she had hair the same color as the wall of August Swiss sunlight behind her. Though not a tall woman she was large-boned and carried a striking *thereness*, though not really a corpulent woman she seemed somehow stuffed tight in her body, and there was not the tiniest tentativeness in any movement she made, no matter how small. Her lips were rounded in the whistle and were bright poppy red and her eyes rose from the envelope in her hand—they were lovely large eyes and their delft blueness was clear even across the room—and when she saw me she lifted her eyebrows and winked and the Beethoven did not falter for even one note. I smiled and nodded, a bit overwhelmed, and I drew back and went on down the hall to the men's room and it is always strange to see a lovely woman in a public place and then seconds later to be holding your naked penis; though you are in the dank sterility of a public rest room, the near correspondence of the two things will not let go of some little twinge of something. So I pissed in the tiny WC at the end of the hall and listened to the whistling blonde and on the way to the president's office I passed the whistle and for a few moments she even broke out into a soft little run of words: "Freude trinken alle Wesen/An den Brusten der Natur." Without thinking, I looked into the office once more and said, "Can you translate for me?"

The whistling stopped and her mouth stretched out into a smile and she said, "What would you like me to translate?" Her words were very precise but without any trace of accent.

I said, "The words you just sang."

She rolled her eyes. "Am I singing again? I thought I was cured."

"You're not. I caught you red-lipped."

She laughed, a sharp, commanding laugh, and then closed her eyes and mouthed a few words, obviously trying to recall the phrase that she sang. Then she opened her eyes abruptly. "Was it, 'Freude trinken alle Wesen . . .'? That part?"

"I think so."

"It means that joy is drunk by every one of God's creatures from Nature's—this is a rough translation, you understand . . . you drink joy from Nature's big breasts." Her hesitation was not in the least coy but rather a kind of play, I could see, her eyes never letting go of their fix on me.

I am thankful that I resisted all the coy answers to this myself. I just concentrated a little harder on her eyes and said, "Thanks."

"You're welcome."

"I'm Ira Holloway."

"I'm Rebecca Mueller."

I tapped my right temple and plumed my fingers in farewell. She repeated the gesture exactly and I backed out of the doorway and her whistling resumed at once.

There was a good deal of table space in the room where Rebecca worked and I found a reason to spend most of the next day in there, spreading out the company's documents but concentrating mostly on her. She and I talked about Zurich and about New York and briefly about her childhood (I learned that Rebecca's mother was American and her father was Swiss German and that she was not quite yet thirty and uneasy about turning it) and even a little about Vietnam (she was particularly interested in the half-American, half-Vietnamese orphans they called "children of dust"). But as we spoke and worked and spoke again, the thing I grew most conscious of was her lips. They did not whistle, with me there. I watched them, though, and they were very full and they began the morning painted that bright poppy red, but Rebecca and I spoke and worked and with each thoughtful moue and pucker of her lips the paint grew fainter, and not once did she go off to refresh her lipstick but she let it go, and the paint grew fainter still and it was as if her lips were slowly undressing for me and their own true color—their pale, labial pink—began to show through, and then at last her lips were naked. It would be a long while, though, before I would kiss them. A long while, even, before

I would think of that morning with Rebecca and remember her say, speaking of her wrangling parents, "It's not easy being one of the 'children of chocolate.' "

And they lead one to another inside me. Rebecca's lips, naked at last, and Hoa's long legs striding out beyond the rubber trees and Fiona's breasts, wet from the rain and with the smell of coffee in the air and a boy child barely the size of a raindrop growing deep inside her, and it is Rebecca I return to: the first time I saw her after that Zurich trip—I did not kiss her in Zurich—she was playing tennis on a court at the Long Island estate of the owner of that Swiss company and she was not there because she was the lover of the man, that was clear enough, he had a whippet of a young woman on his arm all through the weekend and Rebecca was a different sort of woman altogether and I watched her play tennis with some marketing manager and she hadn't seen me yet and her legs were strong and just a little bit thick at the ankles where her socks had tassels and, perhaps with the "Ode to Joy" fluting in my head, her ankles seemed wonderful, really, thick clouds, thick dew, this flesh was kissed by flying tassels and I wanted to kiss them, as well, and as she bounced and moved and baseball-batted her forehand I could hear the faint little thump of her exhalation just before the thump of the ball and when I say that, I move from Rebecca to a vision now of a new woman on the professional tennis tour, which I love to follow, she was very young but clearly a woman in her sharp features and cloud of dark curls and her strong forearm and the announcer at Forest Hills said she was Maria Santini and she was from Argentina and she was a high seed and I saw her play this spring and she made a wonderful sound when she hit the ball, I let myself close my eyes to the fine, muscled flow of her racket arm and just listen to her cry at each volley, a strong, sharp cry now and now and now, as if she were in the midst of wonderful sex, and then she had a foot problem, blisters, and with her lovely cries still in my head she sat at midcourt and took off her shoe and her sock and I was nearby, behind her and a little off to the side and I could see her lovely bare foot and she was hurting there, my Maria of the Pampas, and I wanted to kneel to her and kiss these bare toes I could actually see now before me, wanted to kiss them and caress them until they hurt no more, until she placed that strong right hand on my head, gently, and cried out just as if she'd hit a passing shot down the line.

Rebecca and Hoa. They are so very different, but linked somehow. Rebecca and Hoa and Maria Santini. Rebecca and Hoa and Maria Santini and Olga Korbut from the Olympics a few years ago and of course I loved Nadia Comaneci, as well, but she registered as very much her age, a child still, in spite of her pirouettes and step-outs and cartwheels on the impossible thinness of the beam and there were moments in the peak of a leap, with her long legs rising high and straight and taut above her, when her body made a quick signature of the woman she would become, but Olga soared too and the pinch-your-cheek girl of Munich had become in Montreal a rough-hewn woman, the ragged twin ponytails still there, the sweet crumpling of her face in her smile, but she was a woman now, and she flailed on the bars, I turned away as she faltered and would not fly, but then she was on the beam and she leapt and she was in every movement strong and sure and she landed and raised her arms and she smiled that large smile full of uneven Russian teeth and there was a shadow in the hollow of her throat that I longed to kiss. Rebecca and Hoa and Maria and Olga. Rebecca and Hoa and Maria and Olga and Fiona. Rebecca and Hoa and Maria and Olga and Fiona and Xau and Blossom and Amanda and a woman in a passing pickup truck and a woman in a passing subway and Betty and Jane and Karen and Hue and Tiny-Hand and now that I've somehow talked my way into this momentary jumbling of them all together, there are so many others who are ready to come forward, but what it really feels like is when you're watching a movie and the camera floats out the window of a house and then rises up in the air and you see the house next door and then also the one across the street and then also all along the block and the camera keeps going higher and higher and you see all the blocks around and then the whole town and then the countryside all around and it's this one large place, all connected, everyone's living together. It's like that. All of the women who have stirred me in all their special and surprising ways: they are all connected, they are a vast landscape and it's only there that I can truly reckon time and space and it has nothing to do with this other time and space, the one that most people think of as *now*, and maybe this is one reason why I've got to say all of this, because for me, time is Hoa's hair followed by Rebecca's lips followed by Rebecca's ankles followed by Maria's toes followed by the hollow of Olga's throat and I have no choice about any of that, really, no more than I have a choice about whether or not seven o'clock will come tomorrow morning in that other place and my alarm clock will go off and I will put on a tie. And though I can't change the flow of my time, for that very reason I must believe that it is carrying me *somewhere*, that it will finally make some kind of sense. And I believe that this realm of my own has boundaries, has a shape, has a governance, a governance all its own.

And I did make love to Tran Thi Hoa. I contrived two more visits on my own to the rubber plantation and I saw her both times. Once, we were passing in the driveway, me in the jeep and she in her Citroën, and I was white-knuckling the steering wheel in disappointment because as the car came toward me I could see that she was driving and I turned my face to her and she turned her face to me and I can't imagine that we saw anything in each other's face, it all happened too fast and there was no way to really show anything, but we both knew to stop abruptly. I saw her in my rearview mirror, the plume of dust from her skidding front wheels, and my own foot was already on the pedal and simultaneous braking may not make any of the sex manuals but it was a thrilling little moment for me, as was the long, quiet moment afterward, the dust settling and both our engines idling, as was the slow whining reversal of our cars until we eased next to each other and turned our faces and smiled.

"Are you still in love?" she asked.

"Yes."

"Your feelings are too strong," she said. I knew enough about Buddhism already to hear something behind these words. For the Buddhist, strong feelings lead to suffering. But Hoa sounded ironic, applying them to me in this way. And that irony seemed to fit in with her clearly devout father's discomfort with his daughter, apologizing for how she dressed, how she related to the workers. I concluded that she was a maverick in religion, too.

I said, "Did you slam on your brakes to tell me that?"

She fixed me with her sharp-cut Asian eyes and studied me for a moment and then she smiled faintly and said, "Only the very holy among us are free of desire."

Now she had me. I hung in an exact balance between two impressions: a woman who was deeply engaged by her religion and was defining the barrier between us, and a woman who wanted me just as I wanted her and was inviting me to touch her. I tried to read something in her face but I became suddenly conscious of my own eyes, I could not hear Hoa's inner voice yet, but I could see my own face through her, the bulging, naked liddedness of them. I felt as if Hoa knew my every thought and I had not the slightest idea of hers. We sat there and my jeep was pinging and coughing and her Citroën was humming softly—I could hear it even beneath the racket I was making—and I was one ignorant young man, I knew that much, and at last I spoke the only thing that I truly knew at that moment. "You are very beautiful," I said.

She lifted her chin at this, as if she was about to shake her hair down to her waist, and I thought for a moment that I'd said the right thing, that the tight little bun of her feelings about me would tumble down into sight now. But she simply said, "Don't put me on a paper airplane," a common Vietnamese saying used to deflect a compliment.

I knew myself. If I didn't press on, I would make myself crazy running this conversation over and over and understanding less and less each time until I could figure out a way to see Hoa again. But she was still sitting there before me, at that very moment, and so I had the presence of mind to say, "My strongest desire right now is to know what the hell we're really saying to each other."

"You think that I am a beautiful woman."

"That much I know."

"And like you, my feelings are too strong."

"What kind of feelings?"

"It is a very odd thing," she said, "listening to you. You sound so much like a Vietnamese in the way you speak our language, but your words are so blunt. This is not the way of the Vietnam you love."

I lifted my chin now. "You drive your car very fast, Miss Hoa."

"Yes."

"You dress like the workers and you shake your hair down before strange men and you look me straight in the eye when you speak."

She smiled at this. "And so you expect me to be blunt as well?"

"At least to accept it in me."

"I accept it, Mr. Holloway." She pronounced my name with absolute precision and her car's motor revved and she was gone.

Which was ambiguous enough. So I did in fact make myself crazy running her words over and over in my head, and it went on until the captain sent me back to the plantation the next week to talk to the black-toothed old man with the notebook.

It was midafternoon and the Citroën was sitting before the house when I arrived. I went up onto the verandah and Mr. Loi came out to greet me. He sat me down very cordially but he did not make small talk with me. He ranted for a while about the Viet Cong owning the night and when he learned that I wanted to get an update from the old man, he apologized that he was expecting an important phone call and he'd have to get one of his foremen to take me over.

I'd been having a little trouble staying focused on Loi. Twice I'd associated Hoa with the car, and I sensed her nearby, though all I could see through the open front door was a dim corner of hallway, and through the window near me, a paddle fan moving slowly and a teakwood cabinet full of tusk carvings. A wind chime jangled lightly at the end of the porch and Loi was on his feet now, presumably to go find me a foreman. I rose and for a moment I was on the verge of actually asking Loi where Hoa was, but suddenly she was in the doorway and she seemed not even to look at me. She was dressed just the way I'd first seen her, in her peasant work shirt and black silk pantaloons, though her hair was down, and she leaned against the door frame and said to her father, "I can take Mr. Holloway across the road."

Loi turned to his daughter with a start. "I didn't know you were there."

"I was."

"I can find Mr. Cung."

"Cung's a busy man. I'll take Mr. Holloway."

The father looked at me and shrugged, as if he were trying to apologize for his daughter's bluntness. Hoa slipped past me and I had not yet caught even a sideways glance in my direction. This perhaps more than anything else quickened me, made me have a real hope that I would someday touch her. She went straight to my jeep and got in and waited for me. I slipped behind the wheel and I said, low, "I thought you'd want to drive me in your car."

"This is easier on my father. I still slightly resemble a woman to him."

I started the engine and we drove across Highway One and into the workers' settlement and I stopped in front of the old man's little house. Hoa said, "I'll be here when you're through," and I went in and asked my questions, but when I came back outside, Hoa was gone. The jeep sat ticking in the afternoon sun and beyond it was a scrubby field and a hundred yards away was the line of trees sweeping left to the highway and far to the right, past the distant water tower and on toward the blur of forest half a mile or more away. Maybe a mile. I had no sense of distance suddenly, just a sense of things being stretched far and there was no one in sight and then Hoa's voice was very near, behind me: "You always have to watch your back in this country." I spun to her and she said, "Didn't they teach you that?"

"If you'd wanted me then, you could have had me," I said, not even intending a double meaning, thinking only of her coming up behind me, this admittedly myterious Vietnamese woman, and shoving a knife between my ribs.

But this was one of the two times that she spoke English to me. She looked at me for a moment in silence and then she drew a deep breath and said, "I do want you."

I had sense enough not to banter about her bluntness. I had just a little trouble drawing a breath at this, much less shaping my breath into words, but my face was already speaking to her, I think. She looked closely at me and smiled and returned to Vietnamese, "This seems to be a happy man."

"Yes," I rasped.

"Walk with me across that field behind you."

I did. We walked with a wide space between us and we did not speak, both of us thinking of the black-toothed man and his notebook, perhaps, but at the trees Hoa turned us up the line and we moved along the verge of the plantation toward the distant water tower and as we did, she came nearer to me and said, "I love the trees. It makes Father furious, but I go out with the tap crew sometimes and I cut them."

She was very close to me now and I could smell her hair, even though the talk of the trees made me aware of a faintly musky smell from the plantation and I glanced down the passing rows, the trees' shafts rose high and they seemed naked, all of them stripped of lower limbs and laid bare, and the spongy, dank smell seemed to come from them, but it was Hoa's hair that was the strongest smell and it made my hands stir and my groin stir and I said, perhaps with a niggling little nervousness, "You cut the trees?"

"It doesn't hurt them," she said, veering slightly into me, her shoulder touching my arm and her head bending near in a gesture that seemed consciously intimate. "It's a very delicate cut and then their juices flow, very slowly, a sweet, white flow."

"Where are we going?" I asked.

"You'll see," she said.

Her shoulder pulled very slightly away from my arm and I touched her hand, turned my own hand and took hers and she intertwined her fingers in mine. "If you cut too lightly," she said, "the hidden tubes will fail and the tree will not give. If you cut too deep, it won't heal and one day it will die."

Hoa let go of my hand and slipped her arm around my waist. I glanced over my shoulder and the workers' village was far away and I looked ahead and the water tower was close now. It was a two-story wood platform with a roof and a waist-high wall surrounding its tank. It looked very much like the guard tower where Betty and Jane had come to us, and they were only lately dead, dead not more than a few weeks, and I turned my face slightly and touched Hoa's hair with my cheek and she pulled me closer until our hips ground together as we moved and I glanced over her to the rising of the trees and their gray barks showed the scars of all the delicate cuts and I thought of Betty and Jane splashing barefoot in the dark through the stream, slipping into our camp, and I looked hard into the trees now and though it was still daytime, I thought of the VC moving out there, thought this not with fear but with a sense of portent about these trees that gave Hoa their juice in the day and by night hid the men who would kill me.

"Are we going into the trees?" I asked.

"No," she said. "Up there." And she nodded to the water tower and we came to the ladder and she started up first and I followed and the VC were here each night, there were lights, the black-toothed man had said, none of the workers came to the tower anymore, even by day, but I climbed and this was a sensation that I never did quite get over in Vietnam. When I learned where the VC had recently been and then found myself in the same place—passing through the same stretch of road, standing in the same grove of trees, stepping into the same village shack as these men who were hair-triggered to shoot me dead—at those times I always felt a quick butt-pucker of fear, sometimes even more than that, like now, like passing up a narrow stairway that the coarse and quiet feet of these men had slipped up last night and would seek out once more in just a few hours, now my fear was more, was a faint quaking all through me, all through, that wouldn't stop, but I kept climbing and part of the quaking was fear and part if it, maybe the part that kept it going, was desire, because Hoa's feet were before my eyes, her shoes were like little slippers with the toes covered by brocade peacocks and her heels were bare and they were smooth and bulbous and her foot lifted and I could see a flash of the soft wrinkles of her instep and then her foot was gone and after a flurry of black silk the other foot was there, the double hollow of her long ankle and the lift of the soft round bulb of her heel and the instep and it was gone and then I had her other foot again. These were the images that made me tremble inside but also the quick, hidden men's eyes and those quiet, repellent feet of theirs, men's feet; I shook my head sharply to clear it, to close my ears that I realized were straining now to hear the whisper of running in the trees behind me. I wanted only the whispering of the softest place of a woman's sex and I lifted my eyes to the roll of Hoa's hips, to the ripple of black silk between her thighs, and it was there that I would bend to listen and we were up the ladder at last, and the platform was dim with the late-afternoon shadows and the wood smelled of mildew and faintly of cigarettes, though there was nothing on the floor up here, it was all clean and I knew it was true, what the old man had said, I knew the VC were here every night because it was all too clean and Hoa moved away from me and turned and leaned back against the wooden water tank and she lifted her face and she was very beautiful, her eyes deep behind her Asian fold and her lips were wide and they smiled that really smart smile of hers and her hair lay in a great cascade down her right shoulder and over her breast and it occurs to me now that I should have feared her. That first time we were alone together, there in the water tower, I should have feared that she was one of them. She could well have been, a smart woman rebelling against her wealthy father and in sympathy with the workers and who came so easily to this place that everyone else at the plantation feared. I could have looked at her smile and taken one step toward her and her gaze could have slid away over my shoulder and her smile could have turned ironic as I felt a rifle barrel in my back and the low, sharp command to lie down with my hands behind my head.

But I wasn't stupid in Vietnam, I was afraid much of the time and I was careful and I wasn't stupid and I can understand now that I must have known enough to fear her in that afternoon edging on to twilight in that water tower alone by the trees, but I did not care. There was no jasmine smell, only mildew and old cigarette smoke, but I could remember the smell of Hoa's hair, I could summon it back just looking at her pressed against the water tank and her smile waiting for me and all the secrets of her flesh just moments from my hands and my eyes, and the thing I feared the most in the world was that she would say, Wait. That she would say, Perhaps I've been too hasty, we shouldn't do this. That was the fearful part of the trembling that persisted in me, that the great privilege of touching this new woman would be taken away. So I moved to her and we touched our lips once, twice, lightly, and then the third time, they touched and held and opened and Hoa's tongue slipped softly into my mouth and the only thing that cut through my desire for her was the soft padding of Jane's bare feet in the dark, but that was very brief, and though Hoa drew her hands down my sides and to my belt as we kissed, I did not give her a chance to move, I kissed her beneath the chin and then on the throat and then I dropped softly to my knees and she whispered, "I knew you would love me," and I pulled her pantaloons down and she was naked beneath them and there was only a soft little lick of hair in the pinch of her legs and I gently spread her open and I memorized the track of her at once and drew my face near and followed her with the tip of my tongue, a rising edge up and around and around again and down the other edge and then to an inner fold and I moved my head with my tongue, like following the cadence of a waltz, and she grew wet and I slid down a bit and she opened wider, spreading her legs, and my tongue entered her and my face grew wet and there was no smell at all now, no smell from the trees or from the tower but no smell from her either, I realized, she tasted like rainwater and later she drew me up by the ears and kissed my face and I turned her and I could see only the tops of the trees and only the quick jungle birds could hide there and I laid her down in the shadows on the wood planks and she said, "No," when I began to unbuckle my belt and she drew up and did this herself and I wanted her to see me, this hidden part of me, I was hard and I was glad she wanted to touch me with her eyes first and when I was free, prickling in that first splash of air, she said, "Oh my. It's lovely."

This was important. It has always been important. I start off talking about religion, about these religious women, and

Hoa hasn't shown it yet but she will, and when I tell you that what she said is important I mean it was like somebody saying to a Catholic—a real Catholic, one for whom every movement, every word of the Mass signifies those cosmic things they're supposed to, signifies them in the Catholic's hands and feet and knees and groin and blood and bones—like saying to that Catholic who fucking *feels* what it means, "The blood of Christ," or saying "The body of Christ," or saying "Your sins are forgiven." It's lovely. Your penis is lovely. My penis is changing all the time, clenching and lolling and sleeping and coiling and quickening and yearning and when it yearns it becomes my blood and it becomes my body and it becomes my sins and it becomes my sweetest secret gentleness and it fills and hardens and rises with the feeling that I'm totally present there, that all of me is drawing into this farthest yearning tip of me and it *is* me and I yearn, Ira yearns, all of Ira yearns as he is transubstantiated into the head of his penis, he yearns for the pouting pink labial complexities of this woman, this one woman, this particular woman who is there, who is all drawn into that deep soft well and he can place all of him in all of her and when he goes in, though he thinks he is all there already, he finds, always to his surprise, that there is more of him to arrive and it does, it flows there in a ceaselessly nerve-jangling stream, blocked though for a time, blocked and backing up and filling and there is only a great bloating self and a ravishing awareness of this woman, these eyes, these nipples touching him, erect, and these hands, not his hands, these slender women's hands grasping him hard and pressing all of what he is deeper into her and he can hear her voice, the tiniest waveform nuances of this voice, crying to him and every ridge and fold of her deepest flesh is gripping him, soft and soft and he is enormous now and full of a great stream rushing but not rushing, not moving yet, not until every tiny shred of what he is is caught up and carried along and then he rushes free, Ira rushes, I rush, I rush and rush, all of me, all of Ira, all of me into this woman, this one woman, this one woman now, and I flow and she fills and she is all of me now and I am all of her and the cut is deep, the cut is very deep and I flow quickly and I do not care how deep the cut is, I press to make it deeper and I do not care if I will heal.

I laid my head on Fiona's belly to listen to the baby churn inside her and she touched my upturned cheek very gently with her fingertips and she said, "Ira, I find that I can't carry this baby and lie. I've had many men in my life. Many many, Ira." Her fingers closed into a fist and lay heavily there on my cheek with the confession, with the effort to declare this thing but then not let all the men back in. "You never lied about that," I said. "I figured. It makes no difference to me." I meant this to reassure her, but the fist tightened and began to quake and then it was gone and she said nothing and the baby was very quiet at that moment. He was so still I suddenly thought he was dead.

I put any thought of Fiona aside and I just listened harder for the child, and when I say that I thought *he* was dead, I do not mean to say that we knew the sex of the child or even that I had an instinct about its being a boy, and this just made it worse, I feared that I could not picture this child clearly enough to will it back to life. I listened hard and then I sensed a movement, my upward cheek burned from the memory of her fisted hand and the cheek on Fiona's belly sensed a deep stirring, and Fiona rushed back into me and I lifted my head, turned my face to my wife and her face was hard and she said, "It makes a difference to me. Just because I'll be distracted by my child, don't think you can bring all the ghosts back."

And it may seem odd, but at that moment I knew we would have a son. Still trembling a little from that crazy notion that the baby had died, and with Fiona speaking of the many many men, I knew with my occasionally absolute faith in irony that there was another man inside her even then. My little man. I waited until a few days later, so there was no connection at all with the declaration about her past, to tell her what I had decided. We were in a grocery store and she was studying the label on a can of soup and I was keeping my eyes in our cart because I knew there was a female of some sort coming this way and I didn't want a little side glance to cause a big argument tonight. Her jealousy continued to roil in her and this instinctive blinkering was part of my public attachment to Fiona now. So I was studying the folds of a lettuce and it was clearly the pussy of a round, green woman; a lovely, very complicated, round green woman and Fiona said, low, "Goddamn artificial color," and she slammed the can back onto the shelf. I looked up at her and she glared at me as if I was trying to persuade her to buy the soup.

"I'm not going to poison my baby," she said.

"It's a boy," I said, and as soon as the words were out, I regretted them. I wished it could remain my own little secret.

But she said, "I already know that."

"You know?"

"I know when there's a man inside me," she said.

She must have seen something happen to my face. For me to say that our son was in a sexual place was a nice little irony; for her to say it, I really doubted that it was a thought anymore, and you had to *think* to be ironic, it had to be primarily a thought, you had to be on the outside. I was afraid that this was a close-up, no-backing-off-from-it feeling for Fiona. She looked at my face and misread it.

She lifted her hand, palmed it at me to stop any misunderstanding. "The doctor hasn't had to do any tests. He doesn't know what the baby is." And now she put her hand down and leaned toward me a little and someone passed behind us—the woman I'd sensed, no doubt, because Fiona glared at her a little bit and waited until she was gone and then she spoke softly. "But *I* know."

In the doctor's office the following week, my son's heartbeat filled the room. The doctor plugged his stethoscope into an amplifier and he said, "Great new toy," and he put it on Fiona's bare belly right below her navel, and I'd been kissing her navel every night now, it was beginning to dilate and I was touching little tucks of it with my tongue that I'd never touched before, and the silver disk of the stethoscope landed there and suddenly the room was full of a great staticky churning sound, this was from a world far away that no man had ever seen, a methane sea on the planet Jupiter, and overriding the sound of the sea was a manic two-beat rush, like standing at the train track as the express races through, the track clack, that sound, and maybe it wasn't from Jupiter, but where it was from was strange enough, mystery enough, and my son was there right now and though he was tiny still I could hear his heart and it was a human sound now, he was swimming inside of Fiona, and when we got home that afternoon, she sat me down. She said, "This is important. I feel very strongly about this. I love your cock, you know. I love it. But it will be a scary thing for our son. You can't put yourself inside me now, not until he's born."

There would be no arguing about this, I knew. I sat back and I looked across our little living room and out the open door onto the balcony where she'd told me we had to go to church, and across the street the warehouse windows were so dark with dirt that they were opaque in the daylight. A car honked furiously somewhere nearby.

"There's still plenty of sex without that," she said, though her voice was full of negotiation, not passion.

"Okay," I said. We'd had one argument since she'd gotten pregnant. Just a week or two after the news; she wasn't even three months along. There was an old photo of me that she'd found in a book. I was maybe a junior in college and I was on a Florida beach and I was all alone in the picture, sitting on a towel on the sand in my swimsuit and next to me, very small really, almost out of the frame, was a pair of sandals. They had—and in the three-by-five print, this was very hard to see, though with careful study it could be done—the sandals had a leather flower next to each buckle. They were a woman's sandals. When Fiona found the photo, I was standing on our balcony, leaning out to watch the sky bleed its way into night. Though if that sounds like I was in a dark mood, seeing a bloody sunset, it's maybe just how the sunset seems in my memory. At the time, I was pretty happy. Fiona was visible through the window over my shoulder. She was sitting in our overstuffed chair, her legs tucked sideways beneath her, her bare toes peeking out around the armrest, and she was reading a book I'd been trying to get her to read for a long time, since we still talked about art, since she was still working at the gallery, though we talked less and less now about all of that. I'd given her a dog-eared, mustard-colored paperback of Collingwood's "Principles of Art," one of the handful of my college books that I'd never let go of, and she'd said just a few minutes ago, looking up with a slow nod of her head, "This is good, Ira," and she blew me a kiss. That's when I stepped out onto the balcony and the sunset flared down at the end of the street and I stood with my hands at my sides and I drifted in this space for Fiona and me, the sculpted womb of art, the walls fresco, the air about us pointillist, no anger here, no pain, no jealousy, and then I heard a little bark of pain and a whack behind me—the book flung against the wall, I later realized—and Fiona was beside me on the balcony with the photo.

"Who is she?" she asked, struggling with her voice to keep it low.

"Who?"

"The sandals," she said.

She thrust the photo into my hand and I looked and it took me a while to figure out what she meant. The sandals were very small in the photo and the leather flowers were smaller and it was the flowers that made me remember a woman I'd known for a week in Florida, a woman who said she sunned not for the tan but for the long soft kiss of heat from the part of the universe that wasn't human, and she accepted my kisses too and when we made love it always seemed as if there was a grain of sand or two involved, even when we went back to the motel room and we showered and showered, and we ended up pretty sore, her pussy and my penis, so the last night we were together we had lovely sex just lightly tonguing the hurt places and blowing on each other there and putting Vaseline on, rubbing and rubbing, softly but for a long gentle time, and she had a low-pitched voice, like the rasp of a cat's tongue and when she felt goofy or baffled or surprised she would cross her eyes.

Fiona waited, her eyes fixed on my face as I bent to the photo. I wanted simply to sit her down and tell her the truth, if that's what *she* wanted, but she did not. She desperately desired this feeling rising in her to go away and the truth would only give it a human shape and form and then it would never leave her and so I again willed the false words out. "I don't understand what I'm supposed to see here."

"Don't play games with me, Ira," she said, her voice running out of breath even in those few words. "That's a woman's sandals on the sand next to you."

"That means nothing."

"Did you put that photo in the book on purpose? You don't like going to church so you think you can make me stumble bad, right away, then we'd just stop?" She was talking very loud and I looked down and a man in a suit passing by glanced up.

"You don't have to look at some woman in the street," Fiona cried. "It's me you need to think about."

"If I wanted to make you stumble, this is a little too goddamn subtle, don't you think?"

"Is it? I'm here making a jealous monster of myself with you, aren't I? It's very easy. You know me real well. You can be subtle with me."

"That photo's been in there probably six or seven years. I forgot it."

"Did *she* read that book?"

"No."

"She took the photo, didn't she."

"I don't even know who you've got in your head."

"It's *your* head I'm trying . . . Oh shit." The curse was suddenly soft. Fiona staggered back and leaned against the door frame. "Oh shit."

I flashed hot, a sensation just like the ones Fiona had complained of the past few nights, but mine was from terror. She was holding her stomach and she'd gone white. "What?" I said.

"We can't do this. Not while I'm pregnant. We're going to kill our child if we do this."

"What's happening? Are you in pain?"

She did not speak for a long moment. But it didn't seem as if she was listening to her body; she seemed already to have the answer to my question and was just putting it off. Then she said, "No. Not this time. Not yet."

I still had the photo in my hand and I held it up before her face and I tore it once, again, and again. "Eight little pieces," I said and I turned and tossed them off the balcony.

She said nothing. She eased around the doorway, as if she were standing on a precipice, and she moved inside. We said nothing more until that night, lying in the dark. I could not bring myself to run the lies out of my mouth anymore and so I let the silence alone. Then finally she moved near me and I felt her breath on the side of my face and she said, "Please, Ira. Please. When you remember your ghosts, you make me remember mine."

"I wish that gave you joy," I said.

"Joy from that?" she said. "There is only one God, and He gave his only begotten son to die for me."

That was the one argument we'd had since her pregnancy and so when she said that I could not enter her until our son was born, I looked out the balcony door and then back to Fiona and I said, "He's worth that."

And he was. He was worth what Fiona asked and he was worth whatever I had to do to avoid upsetting Fiona and he was worth far more and at that moment I may have had a faint premonition that this feeling would be tested fully one day, but maybe not. I loved my son already and I began to speak to him, now and then. This was a Vietnamese tradition, and I learned about it from a woman I'd spent only one night with. I met her in a bar and she had short hair and a sharp-edged little laugh that seemed a conscious thing, like her bobbed hair. When a Vietnamese woman wanted to show her liberated modernism, she did it the same way American women did in the twenties, by cutting her long hair short. And the laugh set her apart, too. This woman—I can't remember her name because she told me only a Western name that I never believed and so never remembered—this woman took me down an alley and through a back door and up a flight of winding metal stairs to a dimly lit corridor of cubicles. There were a dozen of them sectioned off by wooden partitions not much taller than me and well short of the copper tile ceiling. She took my hand in the corridor and I tagged along in her firm grasp and each cubicle was filled from side to side and front to back with a mattress and each half-open plywood door showed a woman, one painting her toenails, one reading a paper, one with her future spread out before her on little Chinese cards. We passed an empty compartment and in the next, two women were together, one in her black lace bra, the other behind her rubbing eucalyptus oil into the back of her neck with a coin. Another compartment was closed and two voices blurred and then separated as I went by: a heavy American male voice was panting and crying out "Little darlin', little darlin', my little darlin' " and a reedy woman voice was crying in Vietnamese, "You pig, you pig, you monkey's ass."

My bob-haired woman smiled a quick, conspiratorial smile at me and raised an eyebrow, knowing I understood. "When we are making love, we always tell the truth," she said and then she reached up and gently pinched my cheek. "Only you will understand." We were near the end of the corridor now, and she stopped and opened a door and we stripped quickly in the cubicle and she had a long scar stretching between her navel and the fringe of her pubic hair and it was very white and wrinkled like an instep and at some point I kissed the scar, ran my tongue down it, and she gently placed her hand on the back of my head when I did that and when we were done and slick with my sperm she said, "For seven thousand piastres a month I can rent this room and then you can come to me every night. I will never leave this place and I will wait for you." As soon as the words were out of her mouth, she laughed that same sharp laugh, as if she had just realized that after vowing the truth, the first thing she said after making love was a lie.

"If you never leave, how will you eat?" I asked with elaborate wonder, letting her know that I understood her laugh.

She said, "If you are in love, you don't need to eat. I will drink water and eat love." Then she gently tweaked my nose and we lay down together and said no more, but she did hold me close, though strictly speaking, her work was done. We lay like this for a long while and I may have dozed because when I heard singing, it was with a lazy kind of surprise and I turned my head toward the sound, which came from far away, it seemed, and my woman of the bobbed hair was still entwined with me and she said, "That's Miss Xa singing to her unborn child." There was no sharp laugh at this, no trace of a sneer in her voice. I turned my face to her and she said, "That's the way of the Vietnamese. We can speak to our children in our wombs."

"Do you have a child?" I asked.

"Yes."

"Did you speak to your child in your womb?"

"No," she said, and she took my nose between her thumb and forefinger and tweaked it once more, but this time very slowly and gently. "I should have," she said.

So during the months when I could not enter Fiona's body, I spoke a few times to my son. The first time, Fiona didn't even think about it, it was such a natural little extension of my trying to feel him move. I put my hand on Fiona's belly and I said, "Come on, my little guy. Give us a kick." Fiona smiled at this. I went on, "Your mother says it's all right. Give her a sharp little kick in there, okay?"

"Be careful," Fiona said, though she made herself laugh.

"Okay, my son. Take it easy on her. Just think about where you are. I want you to remember it all and tell me everything about it. You've got eyes in there where I have to move blind." I envied him at that moment, though I knew he'd never remember. Fiona was right, wasn't she, in telling me not to come inside her while our son was there? But not because it would frighten or confuse him. That wasn't it and she knew it. It was because carrying this little male inside her was the ultimate sex act, surely. A male life entirely inside her, joined at the belly, and he was so deep inside that the fluids flowed the other way. It was her fluids rushing into him. I lowered my voice, like it was just between him and me, and I said, "You remember everything. We'll talk when you get out."

"Stop this now," Fiona said.

I did stop it, but I spoke to him again, softly, in the night, while Fiona slept heavily and could not hear. "My son," I said. "Maybe this is when it all starts, our yearning. Maybe this is the best fuck you will ever have and you'll spend the rest of your life trying to get this back. Maybe I'm crazy, talking like this to you. If I really believed you could hear me, I should be saying the things a child should hear. I should speak only of innocent things, furry animals and sweet things to eat and fire trucks and holding your mommy's hand walking down a street and rushing down a slide into the sand, but maybe all that's a little bit of transubstantiation, too, when you get down to it, the embrace of furry things and the taste of sweet things and things that go fast and make you cry out like a siren and linking fingers to move through the smells and sounds of the street and rushing through a slick groove into a soft fall: maybe this is how your memory will come to you, not quite presenting itself for what it is but in the guise of what we can all think of as a child's innocence. And Mommy will rub you there and powder you there and of course there will be nothing in her mind like that but maybe you'll remember, little man. Maybe all of it will make you remember bumping around inside that fleshy room that was warm with the flow of her blood and was the deepest well of her sex that anyone could ever touch."

Some of those words sounded only in my head, but I did whisper some of them, too, I drew near her belly and I spoke some of those words aloud in the dark and Fiona breathed heavily in her sleep, whistling softly at times, and when I finished I listened to her breathing and she seemed very far away, a mystery that I could never begin to understand and I put my hand gently on her stomach to feel for my son and I really did wish he would remember. I needed help to love this woman, I knew. I was trembling now about the future. Fiona was sleeping in the bed and I was awake and beside her and I had awakened in the night many times before and the covers had been sloughed off us and Fiona was naked and she was luminous even in the dim light and she was florid with faint smells, her bath soap and her pussy smell and her sweat and her damp hair, and she was moaning from her dreams and whenever this happened, I touched her and she quieted at once, and though my penis had stirred at the sight of her in the dark and at the smell of her, when I touched her and she grew quiet and I knew that her bad dream had ceased with my touch, it was this that made the stirring in my penis turn to clear, lifting purpose. But now, now when I whispered in the dark to the unborn like a Vietnamese bargirl, now when Fiona was sleeping in the bed and I was awake, I suddenly and sharply realized there was someone else here too and it was my limbs that stirred and it was I who moaned softly, as if I was having a bad dream.

I spoke to him again the next night, and it was the last time. "I love you," I said to him, and some of the words were only in my head as I bent near his mother and gently moved the sheet away from her and let her nakedness shine in the dark, and some of these words I whispered to him very softly. I said, "I love you as much as a man can love something that he can't even imagine. I try to feel you in the crook of my arm, swaddled in a blanket, or under my hands in your bathwater and you're kicking and cooing and I can imagine some baby or other but I know it's not you, I know you are very specific and unimaginable because of that. Does the pain in your mother alarm you already, my son? It alarms me and I'm on the outside. Are you drinking it in from her? Is it flowing in the cord that binds the two of you? Can you sense her dreams in the blood you share with her? *I'm* afraid. I will tell you that now, mostly not believing that you can hear me. I'm afraid that I can never really touch her pain. I'm afraid that her pain will get worse, in spite of your love." And whatever else I whispered to Fiona's naked belly as I dreamed of the baby inside, I know this part was sounded only in my head: I'm afraid that I will someday want to leave her. I'm afraid I will do that. And I'm afraid that I won't.

This was after the ban on my entering her, after one night the following week when I moved down between her legs and touched her with my tongue and she gripped my head with both her hands and drew me up firmly. She looked me in the eyes. Something was changing. I knew that from her voice, though I was not inside her and would not be inside her again for months yet to come. *Something was changing. I looked Ira in the face and I understood how much I had only recently needed that look he was giving me, the same look as when he came and he told me I was all right. But not now. I didn't even need his tongue. This surprised me. I was naked to the spill of light from the window, I knew, but I was not naked at all. I'd left the surface of my skin, gone away. I'd receded like a tide and reshaped beyond all that Ira or anyone else could see and this was a very nice thing, this was very nice, they had only the flat puddled former shoreline and it stretched far out to sea and I was beyond some reef out there with new breakers on a new shore and no one could get to it. That's how it felt. I was deep inside my skin and I was filled already with my little man and he whispered to me what my shape was and where my real skin was and that was enough for now. And Ira came up beside me on the bed and he was very far away but he was speaking and I could hear him like I could hear a gull cry from a very great distance over the water and he needed something and I looked at his face and if I worked hard at seeing, I could gauge that it was very close, Ira's face, and this was my Ira, after all, my sweet Ira who was trying so hard to do the right thing for me and I understood him, all right, I did love him and I did remember that I could make him happy, You want to make me happy, don't you? You love me, don't you? I take care of you, don't I? I could smell smoke when he said this. He smoked cigars that he kept in the inner pocket of his tweed suit and he would pull one out and it always seemed as big as my arm, but he didn't have one now. That wasn't the smoke I could smell. Maybe it was still in my room. The curtains and the walls and the rugs and my clothes were all new, but maybe the smell of the smoke from the fire had just hidden itself somewhere and waited and when everything was new it came back again and would never go away, and he said, You want to make me happy, don't you, my sweet child? And I knew I was confused. I sat up and I put my hand on my belly and though there was not even a stone skip of a movement, I knew he was in there, my child was in there, my own child, a child who had never been on planet Earth before, and I was very close to him. And I looked around the room and I worked hard to smell for smoke and there was none. And I looked out the window and the sky was smudged with city light, New York City, and I turned and it was Ira beside me, also sitting now and asking what was wrong and it was Ira and no one else. Sweet Ira Holloway. I looked down and Ira's penis was poking its head up like a sleepy child awakened from a dream and I put my hand on him there, I ringed the shaft and it always surprised me a little how warm he was to the touch and I slid my hand up to the cuff of him and I could feel him growing in my hand and Ira lay back down with a sigh. Okay. Okay. I was looking out the window again and I could feel him growing and my hand suddenly felt small, suddenly seemed too small for him, like a child's hand, and now I could smell smoke once more, though the city has fires, too, it didn't have to be my house, it could be a trash can out there, some street person keeping warm, his hands over the fire, though it was August and Ira's penis grew and grew and it was forcing my fingers apart, my fingertips did not touch because my hand is too small for this thing, like a child's hand, and I try to see the light against the sky out there as the fire that I smell, somewhere out there in New York City, a warehouse somewhere or maybe it's Macy's or Bloomingdale's and not a house at all, there are no real houses in the city, but I hear a man sigh, a quavering sigh and my head jerks around like somebody else has come into the room and the light from the window is bright enough that I can see my hand clearly and I can see this surprising part of him, this surprising part that is so big I can't get my hand around it, not like taking the middle finger he offers me when we walk together to the store for candy and I ask him what should I do now and my hand stops and he says don't stop and this part of him feels like it's alive, like it has its own life separate from either of us and I start to cry and he says what is it and this thing I'm holding is listening to what we both say and I am trembling and I say, He knows.*

Fiona jerked her hand away even as I gathered beneath it and she clambered away from me and off the far edge of the bed and she stepped to the window. "What is it?" I said, rising to one elbow.

"He knows," she said.

"Who knows?"

She turned to me like I'd said something very wrong and she seemed about to speak, but then she paused, a little head-snap pause like she'd just awakened and for a moment didn't recognize the room. Then she sagged a little and turned back to the window.

I waited for a long moment and when it didn't seem as if she would say any more, I repeated my question softly. "Who knows?"

"Our son knows."

"He knows what you were doing?" I said.

"Please," she said, and I was smart enough not to press it.

I lay back down and I was still erect and waving in the dark like an anemone at the bottom of an empty sea.

So it didn't surprise me when the next morning Fiona was scraping toast and she said, very casually, "Ira, I know you love me."

"Yes," I said.

"I think sometimes you should just walk out the door. Run as far away from me as you can."

This did surprise me a little bit. I was ready for the request I figured she was building up to, but this was the wrong way to do it and at that moment I was prepared to risk her anger. I said, "For Christ's sake, Fiona, you're pregnant with our child."

She flinched and, to my surprise, softened. She stopped scraping the toast. "Of course. You're stuck now."

"I'm not stuck. That's not how I meant it."

"I sound like such a terrible fool sometimes, Ira. You haven't forgotten why you loved me, have you?" She pulled her hands away from the sink, turned to me and I went to her and held her because I hadn't forgotten and because her very struggle made me love her, I knew, and she squeezed me tight, the toast shedding crumbs down the back of my neck, the knife she was using waving free somewhere back there too.

That night in our little bedroom she turned the overhead light on and then the light by the bed and she looked around as if to see if there were any more lamps and when she saw that there weren't, she shrugged off her satin gown and she was naked there and she let me look at her. She stood and waited for me to take her in and she was very pale, though it was the summer. She always kept herself in the shade and she wore a large floppy hat everywhere and it sagged over her face sometimes and she would touch the brim lightly, as if she were posing for one of the Impressionists that she loved. And now her whiteness was a little startling, for she hadn't stood clearly before me, naked, in a few months, and this was a pretty rare sight, really, even through my range of memories. I always vowed to ask a woman I loved to walk just a few steps away from me when she was naked and turn and let me take her nakedness in whole, not just focusing on a part at a time. But I rarely remembered to do that. I would get caught up in the close-ups and in the smelling and touching and tasting and that was the wholeness that usually took precedence, and that was fine, of course, but I loved when my lover would stand before me like this and it was a kinesthetic thing, I guess, all the little tendons and joints and all the little places where all my muscles were stitched in to the rest of me, all of this felt her before me and I was whole and exposed just like her, and I could feel the width of her shoulders and the dangle of her arms and the curve of her sides and the bloom of her hips and I could feel her pubic hair as a texture sprouting amidst my own and her nipples cried to mine to touch at the tips and this was how it was on that night and in addition I could see that her nipples had darkened just a little and her breasts had thickened and just above the pale lily pad of her pubic hair was a visible bulge and my son was no longer than my finger yet, but he was waiting and maybe even listening and Fiona was very beautiful and I said so. "That's just the sort of body I'd want my son to be inside," I said.

She smiled quickly, like an act of bravery at a sharp twist of pain. And now I realized that I'd been so caught up in looking at Fiona that I could not see her. I could not see the tight grip of her mouth and the concentrated set of her eyes, and she lowered her face briefly now and even as I realized that all of this—the lights, her nakedness—was an act of her will, she crossed quickly to the bed and stripped off my pajama bottoms and she sat beside me and took my penis in her hand and she held it tight, like it was the hand of a child that had just strayed too close to the street. I already understood the night before, I think. Much of it, at least. I had expected the next thing this morning, when instead, she embraced me with her toast in her hand and won me once more with her own sudden self-awareness. She hung on to me now and pumped her hand up and down me again and again and after some moments of that she glanced over to confirm the perception of her hand and it was true, I was not hard. "What's wrong with you?" she demanded.

"Nothing. It's all right."

"It's not all right. It's me, isn't it." But the anger in this, the old anger of self-doubt, had disappeared even before the words were out. She began to weep softly. "The problem's with my hand," she said. "It's not you. It's me."

I lifted her hand from my penis and I turned and I kissed her palm. It felt cold, though the night was warm, cold and damp and I kissed her again there, right in the middle of her life line. I said, "So let's just wait on it all. We won't have any sex at all until our child is born and you've rested up and you feel okay again."

She took her hand from mine and laid her palm against my cheek. Its coolness felt very good now. "I'll make it up to you," she said and she smiled that crooked smile of hers and a week or two later she was fired from her job at the gallery. Fired or she quit, I never did get it quite straight. There was an exhibit coming in of pussies done on enormous canvases in phosphorescent paint. Fiona said she didn't want to have any part of it. I don't know if she said anything to her boss about the child inside her not understanding. Maybe he wasn't an issue here. Maybe it was just the Catholic Church. We went to Mass every week now and we did not miss and I would mumble through the hymns and say nothing during the responses and Fiona would dig her elbow in my ribs whenever I tried to sneak my butt back to my seat in that long stretch on our knees when the priest was preparing the wine and bread. But when I came home one night she was sitting on the couch still wearing her navy skirt and her white blouse with a big bow at the throat, the outfit she often wore to the gallery, and her feet were up on the coffee table like they were sore, and she told me she wasn't at the gallery anymore and she told me why. The pussies were painted horizontally so they seemed at first glance to be mouths and they had various expressions on them, downturned in petulant grimaces, she said, upturned in fatuous smiles. She said, "I couldn't be part of hanging these things. I couldn't live with myself. There wasn't any real art after people began to have doubts about God, anyway. Martin Luther killed Art as well as the Church."

"Right," I said and I stepped out onto the balcony where even the exhaust from the street below seemed a bit of a relief.

"You're angry," she eventually called out to me. "Because I'm no longer contributing."

I waited a while, staring at a terra-cotta lion roaring silently from the warehouse facade directly across from me. I wasn't angry. I was nursing a bit of a void in me, really, not feeling much of anything. All I could sense was that things were turning a bit strange on me and I just wanted to stand there and do nothing but smell the cabs and listen to the scuffle of feet below and stare at the lion. But Fiona's mind was whirring away and she said, "You're angry because I brought up the Church. Martin Luther and the death of Art. Right? You're a little scared about that sudden leap to religion, aren't you?"

It hadn't occurred to me, but she was probably right. I turned and leaned back against the railing and all I could see through the door were Fiona's stockinged feet thrown up on the coffee table and I thought she might as well have had her shoes on, her feet were sexless. Her stockings were thick and nearly opaque and the color of a teenager who's lathered on too much pimple cover-up. I hated those stockings and I loved Fiona coming up with that idea of my being afraid of her conversational leaps to religion, because as long as she could come up with something like that, she would never go too far, and all this went through me really slowly and it was so muted that it made me wonder what the hell was happening inside me. Fiona had been so preoccupying for me, the sex of her, her pussy was whispering all the time, speaking in tongues, languages no one had ever heard, inspired, and I'd been listening carefully for a long long time, it seemed, and now there was nothing, no sound, a pair of sexless feet on the coffee table, no touching now, and I was the one unborn, that was this mutedness, I was not really there yet. It will be all right, I thought. I will go out and do my work and I will wait to be born back into the world of the whispering once more.

But it didn't work out that way. The next morning I was in my charcoal gray suit and my powder blue tie and I had my briefcase in my right hand and my Times tucked under my left arm and I was walking to the subway and a woman passed me and she was moving quickly and she was thin-faced and her spring-wheat hair flowed behind her and she was braless under her T-shirt and her breasts moved like they were sullen, indecisive, first a nod yes and then a gentle shake of their heads no and then a nod again and the woman was gone but the movement of her breasts continued in me, yes and no, yes and no, and by the time I'd taken five more strides and was on the top step at the station on Fourteenth and Sixth I was already hard.

I stopped and I turned and I stepped back into the center of the sidewalk and the woman was gone but, of course, there was another almost upon me and she was dressed in a navy blue suit with wide lapels and a skirt that showed just the quick flash of her knees as she moved and she passed me and the suit had a faint gray pinstripe and she had beads of sweat on her upper lip, a fine mouth and sweat above it and she smelled of something not the least bit flowery, a firm hand gesture of a perfume making a really intelligent point, something sweet really but almost astringent, and she was gone down the subway steps and I staggered and leaned against the handrail and then I went down, too, and the woman in the suit was gone but a woman the color of teakwood passed me and her hair was in cornrows, stitched tight on her head but dangling then to her shoulders in long locks like a bead curtain and she turned her face to me as I hesitated at the bottom of the stairs and she smiled a sweet, easy smile and she was gone even as she pushed up from me in my mind, her hands on my chest and her curtain falling before her face and to anyone watching me closely I must have seemed mad for I suddenly and without apparent reason shook my head sharply and I said, "Not now. Turn it off, for Christ's sake." I said this aloud and I shook my head again and it still wasn't clear and my erection had not gone away and I rolled my head and looked at the ceiling and to anyone watching I was obviously a New York subway madman, in spite of my charcoal gray suit and powder blue tie and who the hell knew what was in that briefcase.

Sometimes—and it doesn't necessarily have anything to do

with times of stress, as perhaps it did to some extent that day in August before my son was born—sometimes I can become a little overwhelmed by the vast chorus that sings all around me, all the women, their throats throbbing in an Ode to Joy. Not a chorus, though. The voices don't blend together into one, they remain themselves, each different, each singing alone to me in a sunlit room with clean sheets and all the time in the world. But when there are many of them singing at once, then it's sometimes too much for me to take in. And it always seems that no one else is noticing when it all fills me up so full that I have trouble appearing sane. I was in Zurich again just last year. Rebecca wasn't there. I knew where Rebecca was and I was far away from that place. I was in Zurich and a business associate told me to go to the Utoquay, and I did. It was a floating wooden bathing pavilion on the bank of the Limmat River and it was a place where the women of Zurich went to sunbathe topless. I changed into my swimsuit and went up onto the upper deck and I strolled in this Swiss garden of nipples and it was very difficult for me to breathe, though it was a very strange place, really, like so many strange places around Europe in recent years, a place with single sunbathers, of course, but also husbands and wives together and boyfriends and girlfriends together and fellow workers together, men and women, and all the women come and they sit in the sun and they pull the tops of their suits down and their nipples are naked and there is always an air of quiet around the place, the quiet of elaborate casualness and everyone here is trying to turn nipples into elbows or wrists. There's no presumption of a secret about this place on their bodies and perhaps if you grow up with this, then it's true; if you can see a woman's nipples as readily as her knuckles or her knees, then everybody can be as rigorously nonchalant as they all seemed to be loung-ing on the wood planks that summer day beneath a pallid Swiss sun.

But for me, this was much too strong, all of this. For me,

even a woman's elbows or wrists or knuckles or knees can knock me down with desire. So all of these nipples made me spread my towel quickly and sit on the deck because I was afraid my erection would soon pop out of my spandex suit. And I crossed my legs to hide my ardor and I leaned back on my elbows and to my left were nipples the color of brick and they seemed permanently erect, their owner apparently asleep, her forearm flung over her eyes and her brick red nipples erect though the sun was warm, and perhaps it was her dream, perhaps her nipples were yielding in her dream to the lips of a man who loved her. And across the way a woman with nipples nearly as large as the palms of my hands was lying on her back and she put her finger in her navel and then the finger slid out and up her skin, drawing a line from her navel to her throat and then around her breast and down again and this was a very casual gesture, as idle and calm as the lapping of the water over the edge of the pavilion, and to her right were three women on their stomachs, side by side, and the bottoms of their feet were very white in the insteps but the balls of their feet and their heels and the outer rim of flesh running in between were much darker, the color of a ripe tangerine, a parenthesis of tangerine and there were these three sets of parentheses and the message spoken aside in each one was so incidental as to have disappeared, and that's what it all seemed up here, there were men scattered across the deck and they were reading newspapers or dozing or lying with their eyes shaded and a few were speaking to the women with them but their eyes never once dropped from the faces, never once acknowledged the secret tips of all these lovely breasts wrinkling into erection just below eye level or smoothing and spreading into quiescence.

And beside me to the other side was a woman who had been lying on her stomach with her face turned away when I sat down and she was very small, really, though she did not seem it at first glance because she clearly had powerful legs, not heavy with muscle but solid and strongly shaped, and now she sat up. Her hair was short and though she was not more than thirty or so, her feet were angled in sharply at the joint below the big toes and I knew these were an athlete's feet, a tumbler's feet, working feet, and though I never did find this out from her, I am certain even now that I was right, and I could imagine her springing up to hang on rings and her triceps going hard as she pulled up and lifted these fine, working feet and tucked them as she rose, and now that she was sitting up beside me, her breasts seemed as strong as the rest of her, stretching straight as if they were holding a ring pose before a panel of judges and the nipples were prickled with bumps, as if she'd just been told thrilling news but only her nipples really knew about it and the gooseflesh came only here. She took an orange from her bag and she dug both thumbs into it and a sharp smell of the fruit brought my eyes up from her nipples to her face and she turned her gray eyes to me and she smiled and offered the orange. I said thank you and she took off a section and gave it to me and we tried briefly to speak but she spoke only Swiss German and Italian and I spoke neither and so we shrugged at each other and I ate the orange and kissed my fingertips and flared them before my mouth to tell her it was good and she laughed.

We shared the orange and now it was I who was not looking at her nipples and perhaps I understood, because it was my glance that would be the gesture of exposure for her, but if I could not look, then why were her breasts bare before me? If she thought that I did not wish to look, wouldn't that make her a little sad? This was a form of her hidden self, wasn't it? But no longer. That had to be part of this whole thing. The new elbows and knees. But already I was loving the angle of her toes and the cords of her calves, so how could I not love her nipples, and yet I was sitting here and she was feeding me slices from the orange that she'd dug her thumbs into and I wanted to take her thumbs into my mouth and kiss the juices away but we could only look at each other's eyes with her nipples just a glance down.

And when the orange was finished, she turned to her bag again and took out suntan lotion and she began to rub her feet and her legs and her tummy and her arms and her breasts. She sat beside me and she rubbed her breasts and her eyes were on her work and I could look again and her nipples smoothed out a bit, though some of their soft roughness remained, and they glistened now and she smiled again at me, catching me, I think, in my stare at her breasts but she did not show any sign of that, and she lay down on her stomach and her face was turned toward me, though her eyes were closed. This was the dumbest, simplest approach of all, but I touched her arm and she opened her eyes and I motioned that I could rub lotion on her back if she wished and she nodded and said "Thank you" in heavy English and I rubbed her back and her skin was very soft though I could feel the power of her, too, beneath my hands, and as I rubbed I studied the nearly invisible fuzz that ran down the indent of her spine and I rubbed her shoulders and her arms—those lovely gymnast's triceps—and I rubbed her sturdy ribs and I brushed the sides of her breasts with my fingertips and she opened her eyes and smiled at me. And when there was nothing else obvious to cover with lotion, I put some on my fingertip and I rubbed the place behind her ear. She lifted up at this in surprise, but I pointed to the sun and frowned and touched the place again behind her ear and she laughed and she lay back down.

We did not speak again. She slept and sunned and I sat and watched her and after a while she turned onto her back and I memorized her nipples—the iron clay red of them, the thumb and forefinger circle size of them, the little V gash of their tips. And this was all thrilling to me, of course. But what stirred me the most, after a time, was the rise and fall of her midriff. Her breathing seemed lovely to me. Just that, just the rise and fall of her breathing made me love her and yearn to speak with her and learn how she used this wonderful body of hers to tumble and to soar. She lay there with her breasts naked and she was breathing. She was alive. I felt a great tenderness nibbling in my own breast and I knew I would never be able to touch her but it was all right, if that was the way it was to be, because I could sit in the sunlight and watch her breathe.

The rapture of all the nakedness around me finally focused on the soft fuzz of this midriff rising and falling, a living woman, softly sleeping beside me, a woman who had filled me with a smile and I wanted very badly to touch her, to enter her, and Vietnamese words were running compulsively through my head, words of love, words of gentle supplication, dumbly confused about why they weren't being spoken, thinking that their exoticism was universal, and I lay back and looked at the sky and I felt the heat on my face and still the Vietnamese words murmured away in me, Can we touch each other this night, You are as beautiful as a fairy princess, I want very much to hold you until the sun rises. I thought in Vietnamese, I love your crooked feet and I love your muscles and I love your bumpy nipples. And I looked to my right and she was on her stomach and her face was turned from me again. And I looked to my left and the brick red nipples were still erect. And I looked at the sky again and I thought of Rebecca, where my thoughts should have naturally gone some time ago, but they did not. I had never been in this place with Rebecca. I don't think she'd ever come here, because she felt the outward press of her flesh at all times and I'd been telling her for a long while that she did not look fat but she could never believe it. Still, this was her city and this was her sky and this was her muted sunlight and Rebecca's big toes also angled in, but very faintly, and she said it was because she loved to walk like a duck when she was young, when her feet were still growing and impressionable, though I never believed that this would affect the shape of her feet. I would hold her foot in my hand and show her how slight this turn in her toes was and I would tell her it was *her* foot, after all, and I loved her feet so much that I didn't even like her painting her toenails because I loved the pink naturalness of them and the nail polish just seemed like a layer of clothing. And her skin in places was almost translucent and I could see the blue veins. She came from the tennis court in that first meeting in America and she whistled in surprise at seeing me, actually whistled, and she came to me and she drew her wrist across her forehead and I wanted to stop the wrist before it nudged against her little flared tennis skirt and wiped the sweat away. I liked her sweat and her whistling. I wanted to take her wrist and kiss her sweat in appreciation for the little shadow sex cry she had made whenever she hit the ball. And she had no makeup on and I was looking closely at her face and her lips were naked, the way I'd loved them as the morning wore on in the office in Zurich, and on her left cheek, just at the curve of her jaw, in spite of a little color in her face from the late-spring sun, there was a white lucency to her skin and I saw a faint blue vein and it stunned me, really, it was a special kind of nakedness, I was seeing inside her body, and she said, "Not so close a scrutiny please, Mr. Holloway. I look a mess."

I said, "You are a very beautiful mess, Miss Mueller."

Fiona's skin was often translucent, too. I walked to the subway and was overwhelmed by the welter of women about me and I walked on the deck of the pavilion at the Utoquay and was overwhelmed, but there it all came down at last to a woman breathing, just watching her breathe, and why couldn't it be that way with Fiona? We could no longer touch because of the baby and she would sometimes nap in the afternoon and once with our window air conditioner broken on a warm day that September, she lay on the bed naked and I came in and her skin was very white and there was something juking around in my balls like it was trying to run in circles but there was always something trying to stop it and it had to duck and dodge.

I leaned against the wall and looked at Fiona from a little distance: the lift of her belly, the drape of her left arm off the bed and her right arm laid over her eyes to block the light. Her left leg was drawn up slightly and her right leg was angled on its side so that the bottom of her bare foot lay beneath the arc of her other leg. Very lovely, really. And her skin was as white as sun glare beneath the open window. And I wanted to be content with this. I wanted to live for the rest of these months content with the tiny appreciations of her. The rise and fall of her breath, like a naked tumbler in the midst of all the naked secretaries and naked clerks and naked schoolteachers and naked house fraus and naked lawyers. But I already knew much more of Fiona. Maybe that was the problem. And I was jumpy now around her. I know I make you jumpy, she would say to me. I understand, she would say. I talk crazy sometimes, she would say, and that would sound so sensible and self-aware that I would hold her close but she would keep her lips closed in her kiss and I almost would remind her that she was not carrying our son in her mouth and she would say, You know how easily you turn me on, just as if she knew my thoughts, always as if she knew exactly my thoughts about her. But whatever was happening inside me as I watched her sleeping naked in the sunlight, her white skin seemed suddenly as white as the skin of a woman who rushed back to me from a bright noontime in Saigon. I was walking back from the Honeysuckle and the soft touch of Miss Hue's lips lingered on my penis, which slept now and dreamed its child's dreams. I smelled diesel fuel before I saw anything. The street was quiet and I wondered about the smell and then I was past the corner and suddenly in view of the circular fountain just down from the Saigon city hall. Black smoke was starting up there, as if from inside the plume of water, not much above the trees yet, and I stopped and I concentrated and I could see the smoke was from the other side of the fountain and now my mind turned odd and it seemed for a moment that the street had somehow gaped open and the fires from the center of the earth were escaping. But there had already been an immolation at the circle, a few weeks ago, a veteran with half a dozen children who was unhappy about his pension, and I began to run and as I ran I smelled flesh burning.

When I passed through the light spray of the fountain, the smoke was billowing and dark, and when I came out of the water and was on the far side of the fountain, it was a woman this time, I felt the heat from her body on my face and arms and I stopped and she was five more strides away and she was on fire. A Vietnamese MP jeep had arrived and a man had an extinguisher and was pushing his feet closer to her and leaning his body back and he had not sprayed her yet and a lash of the smoke cleared her face for a moment and she was young and her eyes were closed as if she was waiting to be kissed and then there was a swirl, white foam, black smoke, and a burning in my eyes and I turned away and her face lingered in me and her lips and I waited and I looked and the smoke was thin now and her blouse and pantaloons were burned mostly away and her face had been dark, a peasant girl's face, a girl walking with bare feet in the dust of a country path and lashing at a water buffalo with a reed and she could have been the older sister of the young Buddhist farmer woman I'd loved with my eyes in the back-alley room where I'd crouched and ate and listened to the father speak of the Perfume River. The face of the burning woman was dark, her naked body would've been dark if I'd laid her down last night and loved her enough to make her change her mind about doing this thing today. And where her clothes had burned away, there were some patches of much darker skin, charred from the flames, but more than that, but more, most of her body there where her clothes were gone was now a dazzling white, pure white and slick, and her dark peasant's skin had been burned away and there was this other skin beneath, and she seemed unutterably naked, and I wept then, the smoke was still swarming invisibly in my eyes but I knew my own tears, I knew I wept from loss, this fragile woman was crumpling now, falling to the side, and I wept from desire, from a vision of a nakedness I dared not touch but that I yearned to touch, to touch and then to say, Is this what you wanted me to see? Is this the skin you asked the flames to show? How could you know that I would come to you just in time? How could you know that I would see this secret skin of yours and love you for it? She was crumpled now and she gave off a smoke as white as her skin and I even stepped toward her, my hands and my arms yearning to take her up, but the police were here and bodies came in between ours and I could not move to her and I turned and drifted away like the smoke and I knew that it would have been impossible to take her up, that my hands would only hurt her, and I continued to weep.

And it was the white of this skin that I saw on the bed beneath our open window on the Sunday in the September before my son was born. Fiona was naked there in a way that I could not touch. Even with my eyes, and I turned away.

I wish this voice that I hear now were other than it is. I yearn for sweet Fiona and the brief, sharp plunge of her sweet child into the world. But instead, in the birth, I hear all that ravaged her: *I told Ira to get the hell out. I didn't give a fuck anymore about the fucking Lamaze classes. Pant pant blow, he was telling me, just like they'd taught. "Pant pant blow it out your ass," I said to him, and I felt bad about it even at the time, really, but what was in the front of my head and what was in my mouth were nothing I had any control over. I was in a bed in a fucking hospital and the ice glare from outside was re-flecting on the ceiling and these student doctors had been coming in for an hour sticking their fingers up me for practice and I told them to get the fuck out, too, and now I was contracting and the pain was clotted between my navel and the top of my muff and then the pain was bleeding all around and spouting* halfway up my spine and back down, but that was all it was, for a time, just the great squeeze they'd all told me about, and I was looking at the shapes of sun on the white acoustic ceiling, the fucking tiles up there defying me to cry out, ready to muffle me, and then I realized what was really happening and that's when I told Ira to leave and he looked at me like he'd been waiting for this and he said "Are you sure?" and I just nodded at him, sharply, like I wasn't going to waste any more words on him and he left and any strangers who put their hands on me after that didn't really matter, it was like they weren't there at all. Somebody was fucking my brains out. Like Ira felt inside me sometimes, in a way, my thick-cocked Ira, but more than that, much more, this was the one you dream about, I was being fucked and I was filled up and he wasn't going to take it out of me till I came and came and that's what these contractions were, I was full of some man and I was heading for the big one, all the squeezing was just the crawl to the edge. And this whole thing was running backward. The big deal for the man is putting it in, but this cock was just there, an immaculate erection, and the big deal for me was going to be when it came out. I didn't know it right away but these were thoughts I would regret, these were dangerous impressions because the sunlight blurred up there on the ceiling and somebody was measuring me and somebody else said something and I wasn't there, I was panting and blowing without even trying because somebody's hands had me around the pelvis and this motherfucker was squeezing so hard I was sure I was going to split open and my cunt was gaping and there was this huge thing in me and it didn't fit—that was real clear—it didn't fit and somebody took my hand, my hand must've been waving around and somebody took it for a moment and I wanted it to be Ira but I'd sent him away and then the sun splashes were moving and the ceiling opened up above me and I was gliding down a corridor and maybe the hand was still holding mine and maybe it wasn't but it was too late, and it was trees and blue sky above me and I wanted to miss all the cracks on the sidewalk but he had my hand and he was going too fast and I watched above me instead and then I was in my room with the smell of smoke and my eyes were clenched shut and it struck me hard now: no wonder this cock was too big in me, no fucking wonder, I was only a fucking child. Then my legs were lifted and held and the pain of him came running together, came from all around my hips and my ass and my thighs and it all vortexed down to my cunt and now I thought he'd crawled all the way in and was fucking his way out, he'd spread me wide, my peach-fuzz pussy, spread me until I was ripping up the middle, but just before I split in two he crawled all the way in, tweed suit, leather buttons, watch fob, wing tip shoes kicking and wiggling in, and now he'd turned around inside me and his cock was coming out the other way. And he was crowning, his one slit of an eye looking out of me, and I was screaming, I knew, I could hear myself screaming and I knew this would piss him off real bad and I tried to stop and then I thought of my baby and I couldn't picture him and I didn't want this all to get fucked up because of somebody who was dead already, dead and dead and goddamn his eyes and the Pope said there was no such thing as a soul dying then coming back in a different body, there was no such thing at all, this was my new baby coming but then why was this cock crowning and stretching out and at the base of it a flower bloom of boxer shorts and his tweed fly unbuttoned all but the top button except for his cock stretching out, he looked like he was ready for the office, all except that part of him that could never fit in me, surely it never did fit, surely it never really happened because it never could, I would sit up when my room was empty and I'd look at that part of me and I'd look at my hand and I'd guess how many fingers it would take to be like that part of him and it was my whole hand, more, and I'd fist my hand and put it there at this opening into me and already it would never fit and that's why I was splitting open now, split-

ting open and flaring with the pain and he lifted one tweedy knee and he pushed it out of my cunt and then the wing tip appeared and his shine was ruined, spread with my blood, and he'd be pissed about that and he was climbing out of me, rushing now, you're a nasty little girl, you know, you little fucking bitch, but I love you anyway, no matter what, why else would I put this secret part of me inside you?

It was all fucked up for Fiona. I know that for a fact, though at the time all I really knew was at the last minute she wanted to do this thing on her own. She said to me, "Get out of here now. I've changed my mind. This is private." And this was between her gasping and her eyes digging into me when they weren't squeezed shut from the pain, and I made sure, I asked her if she was sure, and the flash of her eyes was all the answer I needed and I stepped out of the room without a look back and I went down to the waiting room and I was glad it was empty and I was glad there was a window and I went to it and stood looking onto the roof of the next wing: a cyclone fence around a cluster of piping and cowling and a plume of steam and all of it melting its way out of the overnight ice on the wide table of the roof and beyond, brick facades, water tanks, glass buildings, all silent, I could hear the click of the clock on the wall behind me and a distant nasal voice over the loud-speaker, briefly, then only the clock, then not even the clock, just the silence of the steam and the glint of midday sun on the ice and there was a time when I would spend weeks on the road and I would rent a car if I had several clients in a two- or three-state area and I'd stay each night in a motel on some interstate somewhere and I would stand at my window after I checked in and it was late afternoon and there was this silence outside, a whisk from the interstate and then silence and then another whisk and the highway sounds only put a little frame around this silence at the center, the empty pool quaking in the fading light, the jumble of deck chairs, the motionless witch grass beyond the parking lot. And I knew how it would feel, this great inertness, except for one thing, I knew how like death this was, this empty room smelling of disinfectant and mildew and this empty pool and this craggy verge of land along an interstate, how like death except that there might be a woman in the lounge or a woman at the Kmart or a woman in the office I would go to in the morning or a woman at a local bar or a woman sweeping her front porch, the whisk of her broom the only sound on the street I walk down, and she looks at me and I look at her and she has something about her that is beautiful, the tiniest thing, and she is a mystery, she is hidden and she is unique and I love her already.

Not that it ever really happened like that, with me out walking in a tract of ranch houses in a strange town and a woman with her hair pinned up and wearing jeans and a ragged man's dress shirt with the sleeves rolled and she's barefoot and sweeping her porch and I'm passing by and I stop, I can't help but stop because I can see from here the deep hollow of her throat and the darkness of her brow and the great whispering wideness of her eyes and she knows instantly what I'm feeling and I know instantly that her answer is yes and my hand rests only briefly on the gatepost and all she does is straighten slightly and I come to her and we go inside and we kiss then without a word and the eaves are humming, it's early in the fall and the wind in the plains west of Chicago is still warm and the eaves hum and I know how terrible that sound is for her when she is alone here in this house, how she grinds her teeth at the whisking of her broom or the clattering of dishes in her sink but when those sounds stop there is just this humming in the eaves and it is the same as the sound of traffic on the interstate from my motel room and though it didn't happen before her house with me walking by and her sweeping, I did make love to the woman with the deep hollow in her throat and she had a splash of ginger brown, a birthmark the size of my hand, between her breasts and she couldn't look at me when she knew I was seeing this for the first time and I thought it was beautiful and I told her that and I explained how it was just color, a secret of her flesh, a lovely color that promised a taste and I kissed her there and I licked her there and it was flesh, as soft as the rest of her, softer, and I told her I could taste it, ginger, and I told her this color between her breasts made the pink of her nipples blush and I did not meet this woman by walking her street and her straightening from her sweeping but at a bar the night before and she was a little drunk and she said that she didn't want to be drunk when we made love and she insisted that I come to her house the next morning and that was how I found her and it was like that little fantasy of mine about walking along a strange street, and I played it out and so did she because she was sweeping when I arrived. She'd had her own fantasy all that time about a man coming along the street, even as her eaves hummed on and told her how she was maybe dead already, but now it was just like she'd imagined it, a man coming along and seeing her and he was somebody she knew instinctively that she could take into her body and feel good about it and here he was and there I was, as she'd asked, and we looked at each other and I put my hand on the gatepost and kept it there for a moment, trembling at the mystery of her, and she straightened up and leaned on her broom and she laid one bare foot on top of the other and waited for me.

She did not let me slide out of her after we'd both come and that was a sweet thing and I told her what a good idea and we lay very still and I could hear her whisper to me, though she said nothing, *Listen, though the wind has stopped you can hear the house ticking and there's a child crying somewhere very far away and these sounds are as deadly as the hum in the eaves, I know the danger of them. And the thrill of you is this: with your penis inside me, these sounds are transformed, in just the way you tell me my birthmark makes my nipples glow, these sounds heighten our secret, these sounds of deadly blandness are suddenly as good as foghorns from a bay and the rain sputtering at our window. You fill me up and your taste is in my mouth and we are slick with one sweat and I am alive and our feet are still in sunlight and there is still some time left for us, I am alive for another hour. But when you have to come out of me and I have to wash your juice from my thighs because my husband will be home this night and when the pasta pot is boiling, I will collapse again in the center of me, collapse from the weight of these days, and the sound of that will be tiny, a whisk and a hum and I'll be dead.* She spoke to me a little about her husband and he refused to let her work and even with the kids in school he didn't want her to have to worry about a thing, the stupid son of a bitch, and she was smart, my lady with the ginger splash, she was smart and I wanted to tell her the usual stuff, to leave, to search for herself in a job, and I think I said a few things like that, and I meant it, the man made me real mad, though if I'd stopped and thought about it, I would have felt like a hypocrite because I was here with his wife, after all, and is that a better kind of guy than the one who has it in his head that he's supposed to take care of his wife or he doesn't love her well enough? But I didn't know in the bar that she was married until after I'd fallen in love with the hollow of her throat and she was happy to be loved and she loved me, as well, within those tight little boundaries that two people in a bar wordlessly negotiate, and for all my anger at him, the husband wasn't actually real to me, but the idea of him made me very angry and yes, he was the worse of the two kinds of guys, I was making love to his wife because she wanted that and she wanted that because she knew that it wasn't just a misguided sense of love that was at work in him but the exercise of power over her, the fear of her being smarter and more competent than he was in the very things that kept the center of *him* from collapsing. She talked about all of that and this was after I had stayed inside her long enough that I grew hard again and we made love again and she pulled my face down to her birthmark when she came and then the shadows had crawled off the bed and were approaching the array of photos on the dresser, all of them of children and there were two photo frames lying facedown.

Then she and I showered together, but it was very quick, she was distracted now because she had to pick up her children from school. But she talked about all of that, about her husband and finding herself and having a career, and I loved her and she was very smart and I knew she would understand if I told her that it made no difference, that even when she had all those things that had been denied her, the commonplace sounds still spoke of death and you still imagined a street in a strange town where two people look at each other and understand instantly that the answer is yes and it is the mystery of what is to come from that, of the sight and taste and smell and sound and feel of these secret, embodied selves, that turns us away, for a time, from the abyss. I knew she would understand but I couldn't bring myself to say it.

And I couldn't bring myself to think it now, standing before the window of the hospital, waiting for the birth of my son. I'd avoided this thought once before, of course—as most people do—at the time of my marriage. Fiona had a lifetime's worth of mystery to her, I must have felt. And maybe she did. But maybe it was the mystery behind the humming of the eaves that she carried around with her. Maybe her pussy would have to hold a million turnings, a thousand shades of color, maybe I would have to slip cock and hips and thighs and knees and chest and head and all inside her, I would have to disappear completely inside, to comprehend the shape of who she was and if I couldn't do that, then it was just the same as no one, the same as lying alone with the shadows crawling slowly down the bed and the eaves humming and the house ticking and children crying somewhere far away or standing by a motel window with the cars hissing past. Except there's nobody out there at all, no stranger waiting at all, because you're married and from the body beside you comes only silence and the steam from the hospital roof thrashed now and the hollow of her throat had a bandage, she rose from behind the vast, clean desktop and she smelled of citrus and there was an adhesive bandage in the hollow of her throat and she turned before me and led me down a corridor and the billow of her hair made my hands restless but I was thinking about her throat, about the wound that was there, unseen, and I wanted to kiss it and I thought about it for as long as I spoke with the man she left me with, the man who made radar detectors, and the steam from the roofs behind him became my movement inside her, though I never did kiss her wound and I never did plunge my hands into her hair and after I went into the black onyx bathroom and thought about Miss Hue and I came out again and finished my business with the man and I went out of the office, the woman was gone, another woman was there and she wore heavy glasses and was twirling a lock of hair with her forefinger and the radar man was at my elbow anyway and he was holding the glass door open for me and her wound healed soon after, I'm sure, though no one could have cared about it the way I did and now someone was behind me saying my name and I turned and she had white wings in her hair, a nurse's cap, and she was saying my name again and she was very pale with thin brows and a thin, soft mouth and she said, "You have a son, Mr. Holloway."

"I know," I said.

She smiled at this and she led me down a corridor and into a room with an empty bed near the door and in the far bed was Fiona, propped up, and in the glare from the window her head was ringed with fire, her hair splayed on the pillow, and I came to her and she turned her eyes on me and they seemed very sad and she was sweating and her mouth flattened and stretched and I tried to take this as a smile. The nurse who brought me here moved past me toward the door and she said something about the baby and Fiona said to me, very low, "He hurt me," and I said, "He didn't mean to," and she looked at me so oddly that I realized I didn't know who she was talking about.

"Did they give you something?" I said.

"What? A drug?"

"Yes."

"Am I incoherent?"

"I'm not sure."

Now her mouth actually lifted a little.

"Are you smiling?" I asked.

"No."

"Are you unhappy about the baby?"

"No."

"Are you happy, though there's no smile?"

Fiona let her head fall to the side and her gaze went out the window. She said, "I tried to think of the saints. I tried to think of Mary. But where the hell was she? She was just a woman."

"Are you in pain?"

"No." She turned her face back to me as if it took all of her strength. "And yes, I'm happy about the baby, though there's no smile. This wasn't easy for me, Ira."

Now there was a stirring behind me and I half-turned and the nurse brushed past and there was something in her arms and the nurse bent to Fiona and I drew near and now there was a face below Fiona's and it was tiny and it struck me that this was like some cosmic blind date, me and this little guy, and we were linked now, matched and that was that, once and for all, he was tiny and pinched and his hair was dark but his eyes were blue and his mouth was wide and doing the same thing that Fiona's mouth was doing a few moments ago, stretching and flattening and not smiling, it was too early to smile, he was too recently part of this woman, sharing her blood and her dreams and he was pretty grim, it seemed to me, but even as that struck me about him I knew I would never leave him and I reached out without hesitation and Fiona said, "What?" but I didn't stop, my hand came out and touched his cheek very softly and his face turned to my touch and his mouth began to suck at the air, he knew I would nourish him but neither of us knew quite how it worked.

And Fiona clasped him close and she said, "John."

This was the first I'd heard of the name. Fiona raised her face to me and waited for my question. I just looked at her and after a moment she said, "He was the only one who wrote of Jesus forgiving the adulteress."

"John Holloway," I said, trying to hear if it was right.

"Don't worry, Ira," Fiona said. "My mood will pass. I'll be okay. Just let me name him John."

I said all right, but it never quite was. It sounded too adult, right from the start. And I couldn't bring myself to call him Johnny, which wasn't the name of a child either, for me; Johnny was some guy with a toupee. But John it was, and in some ways, he was indeed an adult very nearly from the start. His hand grasping my forefinger there in the hospital room was the hand of an adult. I expected the little nubby fingers of a child, and those did come later, but when he was born, my son had a man's hands in miniature, the fingers and nails long and tapered and these were hands you see in monochrome holding a hoe handle in the dust bowl or caught on the AP wire gesturing at a burning building. This hand grasping my finger knew a great deal right away, knew it from that crazed womb, and though the hands soon changed, for a time, to the bland chubbiness of childhood, it seemed as if my son knew from the first where he was headed. And, of course, it wasn't really this odd little foreshadowing of the hands that made him an adult. All newborns have that, I think. It was our life together, his and mine, that Fiona began right away to create for us.

But the story I am driven to tell is not about John, really. This landscape of the women in my life, this place where I live, is not a place of fathers and sons. It's not even a place for a son who is eight and already is sharply critical of the boys in his class who torment the girls, a son who ducks his head and grins at the mention of a particular girl he walks with to our corner each day after school, who will in just a slippery quick few years be old enough to hide his own precious hand, scented forever with its first touch of a woman, and then soon after will be old enough to see for himself the glance of a woman in a passing pickup truck or subway train, old enough to lie down in a room in a house with a woman who whispers to him, who uncovers her secret flesh for him and makes the pounding of the pulse in his ears so loud that he can't even hear the hum of the eaves. He will have his own landscape and I will be out of place in it, just as, ultimately, he is out of place in mine.

And yet I must speak first of this dream, a dream that I dream still, but it is always just the way it really happened. John is starting to run to me across the wide grassy slope stretching from the water to where I'm standing, at the edge of the bike path, the observatory behind me, and I know it's there, its bone white dome cracked open, ready for the night, and maybe the glance I'd given it a few moments before is what makes me sensitive to the sky but I see the shadow of the airplane right away, when it is still out over the sound. John is running and he is not yet three years old and running is still the most joyous thing he can imagine and he is laughing, he was laughing already as he'd run away from me for the fourth time, run to the center of this grassy slope and he was laughing even with his back to me, his legs thrashing away almost too fast for the rest of him, always threatening to run out from under him, and he was laughing, the seat of his pants smudged with grass and his hair lighter now than when he was born, somewhere be-tween mine and Fiona's, the color of chestnuts and this color was his own, my little guy's own, and that's what I was calling him then, Little Guy, I was always trying to find something other than John, and I called him Little Guy every time that I dreamed about these few moments, I'd say, "Hey, little guy, that's far enough" and he'd turn and he'd pause and that's when I would always see the shadow of the plane, just like when it really happened. I saw the shadow even before I saw what was making it, though the plane itself was low. Little Guy began to run and he was laughing and that was the game. He'd run away from me and then he'd run back laughing and I'd open my arms to him and he knew I'd catch him up and lift him and hold him as high as I could, his legs still kicking, as if he was swimming to a distant surface, up to where the eye in the crack in the dome would look, and his laugh wriggled in my hands and I'd hold him aloft for a long moment and then lower him very slowly and his legs would stop and his laugh would stop and he'd grow very quiet as I lowered him and then, when we were face-to-face, he would kiss me on the tip of the nose, a big smack of a little boy kiss, and I'd thank him very much and he'd start laughing and kicking his legs again till he was soon on the ground and running away. And this was a favorite game. We always found a park or a large grassy space some-where far out on a branch of the Long Island Rail Road, which was his other great joy at this time, riding the trains endlessly with me on Saturdays, and we'd played the game three times already on this day and the observatory was a bonus—he loved domes, too, my little guy—and on the fourth time we played, I saw the shadow of the twin-engined plane, its props buzzing over the laughter and I could see the shadow rippling across the water behind my little guy, pursuing him, and he could not see it and just as the real moments played themselves over and over in my dreams, so did the bottom-of-the-sea drag of my limbs, like in dreams, come upon me in the real moments. I was rigorous with dread. The shadow was rushing across the sound and my son was running and waiting for my arms to rise to him and he was still dozens of strides away and the shadow leaped onto the sward now and was very wide and very dark and the two engines stretched forward, rushing at my child who was impossibly small before me and I could not draw a breath and I could not seem to lift my arms and my little guy was laughing louder still, thinking I was adding to our game, teasing him with my stiffness, building the suspense of when my arms would open to him and even as I thrashed inside in fear I understood how absolute was his trust: he did not doubt that my arms would open to him and I would save him, even from the things he did not know to fear, even from the dark shape that rushed at him from behind. And I could not cry his adult's name and I could not cry a pet name and so I cried, "Son!" fearing for him and loving him and the shadow crashed over him and then over me and I heard the engines hammering above me now and then away and he was still running and I grabbed him up but I did not lift him, I clutched him close and he grew very still and he put his arms around my neck and his head on my shoulder and I heard him sucking there faintly, not his thumb, he'd cured himself of that but he sucked very softly at the air and he did not question why the game ended this way. He knew I had my reasons.

And my reasons had become Fiona. My sweet Fiona. She, of all people. I floated the bar of Ivory soap between her breasts and she laughed and the sunlight was all around us, falling from the ceiling, and nothing had happened yet between us, nothing but an eccentric meeting on the street and a day at Coney Island and a lunch and one afternoon of touching and my penis was still sleepy from the first grasp of her and she laughed. I know she laughed when the soap nudged her between her breasts, I can grow still even now and I can move across this landscape inside me to a certain place and once again I can climb the dark stairway full of the smells of life on Avenue C, salsa and old piss and wet wood and rutting roaches, and Fiona is beside me and she holds my hand and I want to take her away from all this, that old line runs through my head, but at the same time all the fetid cityness of the stairway makes her even sexier, makes all that will come even keener, makes the bed we lie in and the foxed shade at the window and the sounds outside in the street as sensually vivid as her scimitar navel and we go upstairs and into her apartment and we make love and we bathe in her wooden tub and she laughs and I wish to the God she finally began so ardently to pursue that it had always been like that for her, like when she'd just found a new man and all she could see, still, was that he desired her and she could laugh, and she had a landscape of her own inside her and all the men who had touched her lived there and I wish her landscape was like mine, even though I realize that part of what I have to figure out is what this place inside me means and if I can live there anymore, but if Fiona could've visited those men over and over when she'd needed and they could've whispered to her and she could've loved them again, then maybe she would've been all right. But that was impossible, of course. Taken one at a time, their love held her in the present. But when the men moved together in her, the love she had for them was the link that carried her back inexorably to the first man who lifted her in a burning house and touched her and carried her away. A man I have grabbed by the throat on that staircase a hundred times in my mind and thrown into the fire and I myself have carried Fiona down the steps with her clinging to me like the little girl at the Coney Island Cyclone clinging to her father. I would gladly give up all my adult touching of Fiona to have held her sexlessly in my arms as a father just that once and cast the man from her life before he could scatter her mind and heart like the sparks rising from the burning house and I have walked a hundred times away from the child Fiona and into the dark and she did not know who I was and I did not look back but I knew she would be whole forever. And I want to hold her now—desperately want to hold her—in that moment when she laughed and leaned her head back and let her hair fall out of the tub behind her and let her tea rose red nipples rise up from the water.

But her nipples were different when I turned away from the ice glint and the steaming rooftops and I followed the nurse down the corridor. I followed the nurse and I had not seen Fiona's nipples in a few months. She said she was shy about the bloat of her body and I argued with her about that but she touched her belly and said in a desperate voice not to argue and I stopped and so I did not see her nipples changing. I followed the nurse down the corridor and I saw the fine spray of her hair at the nape of her neck, softly unruly hair refusing to be knotted up under her cap, refusing to let me believe the tight thinness of her mouth. And then I was with Fiona and then the baby was there and he suddenly became John and then Fiona was opening her gown at the chest and the nurse was helping her and neither woman was looking at me and John was trying to figure out this mumbly yearning in his lips, he was waiting for something he didn't quite know yet to want, the first touch of a woman's nipple, and Fiona's right breast was bare now and it was an odd little reaction, I know, but my chest cinched at the sight of her, a bizarre little squeeze of fear, and the reason was her nipple, not because it wasn't beautiful, because it was, but because it was as if it wasn't hers, the tea rose red was now much darker, henna now, a burnt henna, and this nipple was larger and it was erect and oblivious to me and my boy didn't sense it yet, his eyes still strained darkly at the ceiling and his mouth muttered wordlessly and this was a very beautiful nipple and of course I understood why it was different but I looked at the sharp line of Fiona's profile and I tried to shake this feeling but it clung to me, this feeling that she was gone, Fiona was gone, and this was an imposter and the face turned to me now and her eyes narrowed and I think she wanted me to turn away, wanted to keep her body hidden still, but I shook my head no, very slightly, and the eyes widened and then softened and then cast their gaze down very

briefly in apology and she turned her profile to me again and
she smiled down at our baby and the fear was gone from me
and it was Fiona's nipple, I realized, though I guess I'd been
right to be afraid. Because the nipples knew. Her nipples knew
that something drastic had happened, and they always kept a
dark cast to them, even when it was I who once more began
to suck at them, even then they were different and so was
Fiona, though not different so much as simply darkened, Fiona
engorged and darkened and erect and bruised now in a way
that would not fade. It began moments later. Fiona touched
John's cheek with her nipple and he turned at once to her,
clear now about what to do, and he took her in his mouth and
began to suck and the nurse smiled at us both and left us and
I did not move, did not breathe for a long moment, and Fiona's
face was angled down and for a brief time it was the little scene
that I had always expected and I think that even she had expected and yet I could not breathe and I was right, for soon
her smile grew tight and then it disappeared and then she
looked up at me suddenly and she whispered, "Does he like
me?"

*And Ira stood there with his mouth gaping like he didn't
understand that this was the only question a mother can ask,
really, after you figure out your child isn't in trouble himself,
after you count his fingers and his toes and you check to see,
when they tell you it's a boy, you check to see if he's got his
penis, and maybe I should've done all that, though I did do it
the next day all right, and I'm not an evil person just because
I didn't check all those things right away. If he didn't have all
his parts, the doctor would have been there right along with
the nurse explaining it all and so if the first thing I decide to
do is let him suck at me, then it doesn't mean I'm selfish or
anything, I wanted to give him something, after all. And then
it's natural to want to know if he likes you. I touched his cheek
with my nipple like they said I should do and maybe that felt
a little funny, how tender that felt, how separate from actually*

feeding him and a spot of my milk glistened there on his cheek as he turned, glistened like the ice outside, and then he took my nipple in his mouth and the pull was so soft and he was so tiny and there was this pull, pull, and I've got pretty breasts, I've always had pretty breasts and they were different now but not in a bad way, they were bigger now and I liked my darker nipples, though I didn't want to show them to Ira because I had my little man inside me and I thought Ira might like these nipples, too, he liked everything about my body, my sweet Ira, any little thing and sometimes when I thought I'd caught him in a lie about that, about something that he said he liked but he didn't really, he could always persuade me finally. He was still with me, wasn't he? He was standing right there, though the look on his face was pissing me off. It's a perfectly reasonable question for a mother, whether he likes me, because John was sucking away there and my cunt was so beat-up it didn't know what the hell was going on but any woman who's having her nipples sucked is going to feel a little bit of something no matter if it's a man or a leech or a bathroom plunger or even a baby and that doesn't mean a thing about me and it's the only thing a mother can ask, really, because it's a lie if they say you already know. What you know is you're beat-up with love for the baby, you're stretched and ripped and battered with love for the baby and now he's sucking at your tit and he doesn't even look up and you know that it could be anybody's tit there, he could have been carried off to the wrong room and stuck in anybody's arms and if she'd touched her nipple to his cheek he'd turn his head and open his mouth and start to mindlessly suck there and I don't blame him for that, don't get me wrong, he's a baby and his head is mostly empty and he can't even really see yet and he's only thinking about staying alive now and he's got to suck at something to do that, but what I'm saying is that just because he's at my particular nipple doesn't mean he has any feelings for me. All that he knows is my insides, is the deep well behind my cunt, is my blood, is *this whole ocean of me inside there where he's been swimming for nine months and he's got to have some real strong ideas about who I am and maybe they're going to sink away from the surface of his memory by the time he can really think and talk, but they're still going to be there, and at that moment when he first takes my nipple in his mouth I know that he knows, right then I'm clearer to him than to anybody who's ever tried to crawl into me from the outside and so I want somebody to tell me the answer to this perfectly reasonable question. But the baby isn't saying and he can't even raise his eyes and look at me and he's stuck anyway, this is the tit they gave him and he knows he better treat it right no matter what he thinks, and Ira isn't even saying, he's just standing there gaping, though now he's working at it, trying to make his face behave and find something reassuring to say, and on the one hand I love him for this, for trying hard to help me even when he doesn't understand that I'm not crazy and on the other hand I hate him for this, for not admitting that he's frightened and repulsed and then getting the hell out because, unlike John, he's not stuck with this tit.*

"Of course he likes you," I say. "He loves you."

Now it's Fiona's turn to struggle with her face. She stretches me a thin smile and I think she's about to let it go at that, but at the last moment before looking away, she says, "And so do you, right?"

"Right," I say and I intend to say it firmly but it comes out as a whisper.

She picks up on that instantly and with that first little slither of anger going through her words she says, "You're all husky with emotion, right?"

"This is a very emotional moment," I say and I nod clearly to the baby and Fiona looks down and she stares at him for one beat, two, and then she softens, she brings a hand up and gently passes it over his head and she says, with something that sounds like tenderness, "He's got your hair."

And the next day we swaddled him up and we passed through the hiss of automatic doors and we paused on the sidewalk and it had turned suddenly mild overnight in the middle of this January and the ice and snow had gone moist and the traffic slushed before us and a cab horn barked as it passed and another car swerved away from it and a thick-armed ambulance attendant at the curb folding a stretcher jerked his head to the street and cried out, "Quiet zone, motherfucker," and the doors hissed again behind us and somewhere inside, far off, a woman's voice began to wail and four men in leather and studs separated and moved around us two on each side and then reformed and stopped and shuffled their biker boots on the pavement looking one way and then another and there was a hammering in the sky and over the broken line of rooftops a news helicopter eased by and there was a clutching at shoulders among the four men and they went to the right and the attendant moved toward us with the stretcher battering-rammed in his arms and his head was turned to watch the men in leather and he was muttering something and coming straight for us and then his head jerked to us and he swerved and passed by and the door hissed once more and the woman's wail went on and there was a siren now somewhere out in the streets and the air smelled of exhaust and cordite and I linger with all of this because Fiona said, "The city makes me real nervous now."

We'd already been looking for a bigger apartment, delayed only by Fiona's having become very picky all of a sudden. I figured now I knew why. "Do you want to leave Manhattan?" I asked, and if she did want to leave, I found myself ready to do it right away. The baby was in her arms but the approaching stretcher, swerving at last even as my mouth was too slow to shape a word of warning, had started a thing in my head that I would fight for years, the impulse to sometimes shape images of harm to my son, the thousand ways of his vulnerability not just making me alert but filling me with vignettes, clear and insistent and usually unstoppable, of little scenes of disaster, like the metal foot bar of the stretcher crushing the soft skull of our baby and Fiona falling backward, the child sliding away in the melting ice, dead. And Fiona made her declaration and I asked the question whose answer I knew even from each gritty rasp of a breath I drew here on the sidewalk and I have to admit that I'd always liked the smell of the city in some odd way when it was just me and the next woman on the subway or on the street corner but now I knew that the baby's lungs were filling with the same thing and I looked at Fiona and she still had not answered my question and didn't seem about to. "Let's think about it," I said.

We all three slept that night in our one bedroom, the boy in a crib in the glow of a night-light and Fiona and I in our bed and I was awake most of the time, and when I say that images of harm came to me I don't mean to say that it was constant or even very frequent but I never did quite lose a sense of my son as part of me, part of my own body and my own blood, lying outside of me, and though sometimes that seized me as an exposure to harm, mostly it was a gentle sensation of reassurance, the opposite of harm, really. I lay awake on that night and even the faint panting of the unknown that was beside me, the inscrutable quickening I sensed in Fiona, could not bother me with John across the room. I was lying there in my own body and I was somewhere else at the same time and I could go down into the subway tomorrow and fall in the path of a train or I could go back to war and end up dead among the rubber trees or Fiona could take a turn next to me in the bed, one that I never saw coming, and she could rise up on her knees and draw near me and with quick hands cut open my chest with a kitchen knife to look for all the other women she knew were there and none of any of that could obliterate me now, not really, not fully, not at all, and I lay on the bed and I listened hard to hear John Holloway breathe and sometimes I thought I could, his breath cutting clearly through the sound of Fiona sighing and panting and hissing and moaning softly beside me and I prayed that she was asleep and I think she was most of the time and I knew her body was hurting and was tired and before we'd gone to bed that night she'd taken John into the bedroom and closed the door against me and in my mind I could see her open her dress and this was as clear to me as an image of harm coming to my son and I could see her brooding nipple touch his cheek and his face turn to it and take it in his mouth and I turned away from the door and I crossed the room and then I crossed to the balcony door and I rested my forehead there and it burned from the cold glass and the door to the bedroom opened, too soon, much too soon, and when I faced Fiona she was standing in the center of the living room with John in her arms and her dress was closed, buttoned one button off, an empty hole lifted against her throat, and she said, "You have to go out and get bottles now. I'll write down what I want."

I did not say anything, though I wanted to tell her that she was wrong, that he liked her, but then I realized it wasn't that simple, maybe. Maybe she thought he liked her too much and maybe that was what bothered her, his sucking at her nipple and her feeling her pussy stirring and a son is too much like a father maybe and all this was coming to me now not in her voice but in some other way and I wondered if I was cut off from her forever, but I wasn't, her voice would come back but not right then because my son was in the room too and he was the one I was most worried about in these thoughts because I didn't know to what cliff edge the switchbacks of her mind would lead and he was in her arms and I wanted to grab him away but I knew—how rightly and strongly I instinctively knew—that it wouldn't be easy. She was holding him tight against her and all I could do right then was go out and get what she wanted.

When I returned, John was crying and I heard him from the hallway and I fumbled at the lock trying to hurry and a fear spanked across my thoughts like some ragged cat in a car's headlights and this was a familiar animal already and the key wouldn't turn at first and when it did and the door was open, Fiona was standing right there in my face, John wailing in her arms, and she said real low but with conscious control, "What took you?"

I didn't say anything and in fact nothing had delayed me, I'd made good time to the all-night pharmacy, but I did not answer and Fiona disappeared anyway, returning John to his crib and then whisking back past me and snatching the package of bottles and formula from my arms. I drifted into the living room and shed my coat on the floor and I sat on our overstuffed chair and I figured it was my last moment of comfort for the night. Fiona was blaming me for something now and I waited as John continued to cry and I wanted to go in to him but I dared not at that moment and she banged around the kitchen, hurrying the formula, and then she disappeared into the bedroom with a bottle and she closed the door as if she were going to show her tits and I turned my face to the window and all I could see in the reflected light there was myself, my own figure sitting on the chair, arms laid out on the rests, and I could see that I was just waiting for the trouble to begin. John stopped crying and after a long while, the bedroom door opened and Fiona stepped out and she crossed the floor and stood before me and I looked up at her and I wondered how she was going to handle this because I didn't think she would want to wake the baby with an argument. But her face surprised me.

It was stricken, all right. But not with anger, as I'd expected. Her mouth was soft and it even parted slightly for a moment as if to address the surprise on my own face but then stopped and turned into an indulgent little smile. And this smile, as casual and easy as it seemed, happened even as her eyes had fixed me in the chair and maybe it was the shadow of the room lit only by a stand-up lamp at the couch, but the blue of her eyes, normally a blue as pale as the ribbon of morning sky over our street, had darkened, like her nipples had darkened, it seemed suddenly to me, but they were upon me and they were dark, cobalt, but they were soft in a way, too, I did not fear them at that moment. She looked at me for a long time and I waited and she was very beautiful, whoever she was, whoever this darkened Fiona was, and finally her hands moved to the front of her dress, a plain, long-pleated dress the color of a sidewalk, and she went down the row of buttons and opened the dress to her navel and pulled it off her shoulders and let it fall to her waist and her breasts were naked for me now, after all these months, and they were like the breasts of a different woman, a dark-nippled woman, a new woman with new secrets and Fiona said, "It will be a few more days before you can get inside me."

I expected her to say more, but then it seemed as if she was waiting for an answer. "Okay," I said.

"I'm still hurting there."

"I understand."

"Look at me now," she said.

"I am."

"Look at me the way only you have ever looked at me, Ira."

This sounded a little ominous but I think I was already giving her what she wanted anyway, naturally, because her words were very distant and the nipples before me were charming strangers and I was taking them in with an awareness of not much else at all in the world but the willing gaze of these breasts and she said, "I'm sorry for going away from you for a while, Ira. But I'm here now." And her hands moved to her hips and pressed the dress over the curve of them and it fell at her feet and she was naked and instantly I could smell the rich wetness of her and she said, "Show me that you want inside."

I looked up at her eyes and they were no longer soft but they weren't angry either and they weren't passionate exactly, though they wouldn't let me go from their waiting and I pre-

sumed they were waiting for a sign of my wanting to be inside
her even though I couldn't be there tonight, and if I couldn't
slip inside her I at least could touch her body, kiss her gently
all over, and that would show her that I wanted inside her and
I made a move to rise up to let my hands seek her out and she
put her own hands up to stop me. I fell back into the chair
and she stepped out of the crumpled dress at her feet and
backed off a little ways. "Show me," she said.

I obviously didn't understand and her hands fluttered in
impatience. "Come on, Ira. Think. How is it that a man's body
shows its desire? That's what I want to see."

I was acting a little simple-minded now in the oddness of
all this. I didn't say anything but instinctively glanced down
to my crotch. "Yes," Fiona said drawing the word out as if to
a child. "Show me."

I knew that beneath my jeans I was erect, until a moment
ago wonderfully so, thankfully so, after many weeks of discon-
nection from Fiona, and the erection was persisting, I thought,
but this new thing now, this test of my desire, was a little
distracting and I knew I better get out of those jeans fast. Which
I did. I unzipped, and since she hadn't let me stand up a
moment ago I assumed she wanted me to stay where I was and
I peeled the jeans and my shorts off together and I tried to
shake the new compulsion behind Fiona's words and I raised
my eyes only as far as Fiona's weary pussy and it didn't show
any signs of her ordeal from this distance, her fine fluffy red
splash of hair was as I remembered—it had not darkened—
and I could see the upper nip of her lips even though she was
standing with her legs together and all of this was enough to
clear my head and block any distraction in my penis and then
I looked at Fiona's face and her eyes were upon me and they
weren't pleased yet, as I thought they might be, and she
stepped closer and she knelt before me and she drew her face
near to my penis but I did not expect her to touch me, not
yet, this was an approach as if to something you're not sure is

real. Fiona was checking to see that my erection was not some kind of a trick, an illusion: that was my clear impression. My penis waved in the air like a man still very much alive but in the midst of drowning and this was his sign, his arm lifted above the water while his face was below and out of sight and blind to the world now and he wondered if he was going to die or be saved, and at the last moment Fiona reached out her hand and grasped me there and I knew I would be saved, at least this night, and she stroked me, she held me in both her hands and she pulled and pulled at me and then she let go and she moved back and she stretched herself out on her back on the deep pile of our rug, her face and breasts in the circle of lamplight and I was invited, I knew, and I rose and stripped off my clothes and she watched from the floor but her eyes never left my penis until I knelt beside her and kissed her on the mouth, a kiss she returned distractedly, and on her throat, a kiss she sighed about, and between her breasts, a kiss she whispered a soft yes for and then I felt her hands grasping my head and she led me sideways to her right breast and she said please and she let go of me and I drew my head back to see this lovely new nipple clearly and it was a dark red now, even in the light, the color of the scab of a flesh wound, and the areola was sharp-edged and the very tip of her nipple was wet with milk and the color of her milk surprised me. It was a pale blue. There was a drop of blue milk on her nipple and again she whispered please and I bent to her and I touched her nipple with my tongue and then her hands were on my head again, gently pressing me, and I kissed her nipple, enclosed it and she said suck and I did and her milk was thin and very sweet, as sweet as if that color of blue had a taste, the color of a high sky or of her eyes before all this began, and I sucked her milk and she stroked my head and then after a time she lifted my head and she looked at me and she said I love you and I said nothing, though that seems a dangerous thing, as I think of it now, and I did love her still at that moment but her milk was on my lips and I wasn't sure who I was to her, exactly, and I didn't say I love you in return but she didn't seem to notice, she said let me touch you and I rose up on my knees and she took my penis in her hands and she tugged at me till I was alongside her, over her breasts, and she pulled me and pulled, watching carefully all the while, and then I said I was close and she took one hand away and lifted up on that elbow and she said this is ours and she touched the tip of my penis with the tip of her nipple just as I rushed out to her and rushed and she held me very steady there against her, governing our confluence.

And the next evening she said, "Show me." She shushed me at the door and I was in my suit and my tie and camel hair overcoat and I had my leather briefcase at the end of my arm and she opened the door at the first sound of my key in the lock and she held up a finger to her lips and she took my briefcase and drew me into the apartment and she was wearing a long flannel robe and her hair was still damp from washing and she whispered that the baby was sleeping and she had candles burning and she opened my coat and she opened her robe and she was naked underneath except for a pair of milk blue over-the-calf socks and the socks were wonderful to me because they made the rest of her even more naked somehow and she said, "Show me."

I looked at her, the question surprising me, though it was vivid from last night and I knew what she meant. She said, "You remember."

"Yes," I said, and the socks had already done it, the socks accenting the absence of everything else, and I opened my pants and she did the zipper herself and that helped even more and she stripped off my pants and crouched before me and she whispered yes to my erection, Yes, she said, It's you Ira and this is how you see me as I am, and she touched me with her mouth but she did not engulf me as she had always done, she sucked at me but just at the tip, she sucked and sucked and did nothing else and I leaned back against the door and she sucked at the tip of me steadily, as if she were feeding herself there and eventually she drank and in those moments I looked down at the top of her head, the soft falling of her hair from her naked part and she seemed very small below me, and very far away.

That night we both stood by John as he slept and I slipped my arm around her but she gripped the edge of the crib and she said, "We have to leave the city. I want a house far away, either Jersey or the Island." Things were going well for me at the agency and I had a GI Bill loan to take and it was 1972 and houses were still pretty cheap. We could get out of the city and buy one but Fiona had always loved the city for its art, the only art worth thinking about was in the city, that's what she'd always said, and though she left the gallery over the pussy exhibition, I still had it in my mind that she might work again. But she hated the commuter trains and if she wanted to be that far out of the city, I suspected that she'd made another decision, as well. I couldn't quite ask this directly, but I didn't need to. I said, "Would you be okay out there?"

And Fiona said, "Do you mean will I never work again?"

I was suddenly caught. I smiled at her as lovingly as I possibly could and said, "You're scary sometimes, how you can read me." She returned the smile. "John seems like a full-time thing for a few years at least, don't you think?"

"If that's what you want."

"It is," she said, but her smile faded. "And there's the Church."

"Yes. The Church."

"The city is no place for our baby." She let go one of her grips on the crib and touched my arm.

"You're probably right."

"You won't mind the train?" she asked, but her hand had gone back to the crib rail.

"No."

There was no more discussion; from just that, it was finally decided. The next day was Saturday and I awoke to her indent in the bed beside me and nothing more and when I stepped bleary into the other room she was sitting with the baby, who was taking a bottle in her arms, and beside her on the couch was a pile of newspaper clippings that she nodded me to. The dates ran back several months and the three on the top all had to do with a little town on the North Shore of Long Island, Seaview, a couple of square miles full of Victorian homes on Long Island Sound.

And that day we found a place and the next day we went back to make sure and the realtor gave us the key this time and said go and look, get acquainted privately, and it was a little gingerbread place with a wide front porch and a widow's walk upstairs and wavy glass and John was asleep in his carrier and Fiona set him in the center of the living room floor and led me through the dining room and through the kitchen and out to a glassed-in mini-greenhouse of a back porch that was actually warm in the sunlight on this not-too-cold-anyway January day and there was a high privet hedge around the yard and a trio of oversized sugar maples and I was thinking about all the goddamn leaves to rake when she said, "Show me."

This was before we touched, except for our fingertips as she led me, before she showed me any naked part of her, this was when I was still thinking about this house and the Long Island Rail Road and raking leaves and all of that and I turned to her and she was waiting. "Are you going to get involved in this?" I asked.

She was standing there in her leather jacket, tight at the waist, and she was wearing a tweed skirt and sleek boots and she looked very nice but she was bundled up, her muffler was still clutching her throat, and this was a reasonable question, I thought, unless she'd really gone over some edge now and the proofs she desperately needed from me were impossible.

Her eyes narrowed at my question, but then her head snapped a little and she looked around for a moment as if she was getting her bearings and then she looked back to me. I touched my throat with my forefinger and then twirled my finger around. Her hand rose and found the scarf and she sort of smiled and she pulled it away from her, dropped it to the floor, and she stared down at herself, at her heavily clothed body, and I guess she understood what I was talking about. She looked at me again and she smiled a little foot shuffle of a smile and she unzipped her jacket slowly and by the time she could wait no longer for me to show her, I was ready. Her breasts were bare beneath the open jacket and all the rest was still clothed but thankfully that was enough on that Sunday morning in Seaview for me to show her that I wanted inside her, and this time she let me in, her tweed skirt pulled up and her boots lop-eared beside us and her panties balled and thrown into an empty flowerpot on the window shelf and us on the floor, improbably carpeted wall-to-wall in spite of all the trellises and hanging hooks and seedling boxes. She let me inside her with protests of careful careful, she was very sore and very tired in there, she said, but she was very wet and it turned out to be all right and I didn't move much at all I just holstered myself and she hummed a little and I say holstered because she hummed "The Streets of Laredo" and when I asked her why, she had no idea. Nice. Odd and nice. But there was an edge to all of this that made me nervous. Even as we lay on the floor of what was clearly going to be our house and made love there for the first time in the pallid warmth of the January sun, even while I was still preserving my readiness, remaining stretched hard inside her, I was nervous about what was happening.

And the next night, in the city, the decision about the house already made, I said to her, "Can I feed John his bottle?" I was leaning in the pass-through between our dining alcove and the kitchen and she was on the other side, at the sink, fixing the formula. I asked the question and she kept working, her back to me, and she didn't seem to hear, though I knew that she did. I'd waited until the water was off and I said it clearly. Her arms were moving, doing whatever it was she was doing, and she didn't make a sound. Not even in my head. I waited and finally I said, "Did you hear?"

Her arms stopped and she waited a moment and turned to me and she said, "You understand why this is tough to decide?"

"I guess so."

"I feel guilty about not breast-feeding."

"I never questioned that decision."

"This is one reason why I love you, Ira. Why we can be together."

These are not the kind of memories I usually keep. They belong to me but they are from a different place in me, across some painted sea. But I have to go through all of this: this is a reminder to myself, something I can't forget. But I want to slip away now. I love my son and I love just about all the women I've ever known or seen or imagined and these two things were about to clash and now that I am thirty-five years old and I find a place alone and I begin to speak, as I do now, as I begin to move through this landscape in me, I don't want to go farther than the boundaries of my passion or of this oddly cumulative joy I have from all the women in this place, I want to slip away into some open field there and lie down and all around me in the high grass I can sense women, all of them lying here just like I am and they are naked and they are waiting for me, each of them, but I look at the sky first and it is the color of Fiona's milk. I have to deal with things that are not of this place. But I am in the field now and first, I will listen to just one. Just one woman first who is whispering off to my left and I can turn my head from the sky and she is asleep on the commuter train. In the facing seats by the partition next to the door I sit with my right knee touching hers and she is across from me and one seat over and she has dusky skin and a cleft in her chin and lovely dark eyebrows and her eyes are large and closed without a wrinkle, the faint track clack has put her to sleep and she is dreaming, I can see her eyes moving beneath her lids and her lips part just a little and she has a large mouth, a thin face, really, but her mouth is large and very beautiful and I am conscious of our knees touching and I want very much to slip inside her without her waking, to slip inside and meet her for the first time in her dream and her eyes follow me across a field and her mouth parts to speak to me, to call me to her, and the sky in her dream is very bright and the palest of blues and she wants to touch me so badly that she has no strength in her voice and can only whisper, which she does, her lips part just a little and she whispers to me and to her surprise I hear and I turn and I come to her and she says, "I told myself, If he can hear me whisper to him on this bright day across this field when I can't even find my voice, if he can hear me anyway, then I want him to make love to me."

I watched her carefully on the train, memorizing her, and she woke with a start after a time and she looked at her watch and even as she did, a voice came over the loudspeaker and said "Mineola" and she smiled and then stretched her eyes wide open to put her dream aside and she gathered up her purse and a Bloomingdale's bag at her feet and she glanced at me once before she rose and I said, "That is a remarkable talent." She looked surprised, but only for a moment. I didn't have to explain what I meant because she smiled a sudden little whoop of a smile at me and she said, "It was pure luck."

"If I see you again, I'll nudge you for Mineola."

"I'd be in your debt," she said and then she rose and she was gone and this was perhaps six months after Fiona and John and I had moved to Seaview and I was conscious of having just fallen in love with another woman, however briefly, though I was rushing home on the Long Island Rail Road to my wife and our infant son.

So I chose the wrong woman in the grass. This one has brought me right back to Fiona turning around at the sink and giving me one of those little declarations of fidelity of hers that always sounded like a warning. She loved me and decided we could remain together because I never questioned her decision to stop breast-feeding on the first night home. I said, "Look, if you feel like giving him his bottle, that's okay with me."

"It's not that simple."

"I know it's not."

She smiled her crooked smile and lowered her eyes and she said, "Why do you put up with me?"

She'd asked me this, or something like it, a number of times before. Always when I was just about to entertain a thought that was perhaps related to it: how can I ever hope to love her enough to quiet the hatred she has for herself? And yes, there was some deep irritation at times, but I took Fiona's odd intensities and spiky moods as part of her complexity. I didn't like those things for themselves. It should be clear by now that those things aren't what attract me to anybody. But Fiona had more secrets in her than any woman I'd known. And they promised to yield to me not only through our talk—we could still talk splendidly, about art and people and the city and all of that—but also through her flesh, her lovely flesh and through my own yearning flesh and she always knew when to drop out of her seeming madness and look at herself and share my growing irritation. Then there were three of us. Me and the Fiona that I despaired at and the Fiona that had suddenly appeared beside me and laid her head on my shoulder and slipped her arm around my waist and shared my mood at this other woman. And all this was usually behind whatever answer I muttered at her question. I'm not putting up with you. I love you. It's okay, Fiona. Come here and let me hold you, Fiona. Whatever. But on that night when I first wanted to feed John, she asked the question and I found myself rushed by a shadow, like across a grassy slope, and this was the first time. I looked to the door of the bedroom and the baby was in there and he was vulnerable and I felt this rushing in me, a hot, foul rushing like a tube of air before a subway train, and I looked back quickly to Fiona, quickly so I wouldn't betray this thought, wouldn't let her see how her question had a new answer, as if she didn't already know, as if she didn't know that things were different now, very different.

Fiona waited for an answer. "I'm not putting up with you, Fiona," I said, making it as sweet as possible. "I love you."

She nodded at this. Then she thought for a moment more and said, "I'm glad John will be close to his father. He needs that."

So I went into the bedroom and I sat in the glow of a night-light and I held my son in my arms and he sucked at the bottle and he was so light that my arms could not feel any pressure at all after a while and he was quiet, except for the faint sucking, and except for his eyes, dark in the dim light, and his eyes were voluble to me, saying milk is from you, too; saying I knew that you would come to me; saying listen to the quiet from the other room, listen to the darkness of it. And he was right, she was brooding in there, and I held him tight against my chest, and the lightness of him, the fragility, became part of me there and he sucked and sucked and the bottle nipple popped away and he was moving his lips as if to speak to me, as if to tell me what he knew of the woman in the other room before he would forget who she really was, and I bent near and listened but no son ever told a father those things; if he could tell me what a woman was, he could have just as readily told me if there was a God. He strove to speak, strove hard and his arms and legs began to move in the effort, and when I knew it was futile, I gave him this nipple that was no one's and he turned to it and sucked.

And Fiona sucked that night, sucked deep on me, and she had not asked this time for me to show her but had decided to check on her own and she waited till we were in bed and till I was half asleep and she had told me weeks before, when she was still pregnant, that she didn't think we should make love in the same room with the baby but now she was breaking her rule, for she burrowed down under the covers and tugged my pajama bottoms off me and it was very sudden and I knew she was checking on my readiness but it was dark and at least she touched me before deciding if I wanted her and I leapt to her quickly and she sucked away, invisible to me, and maybe she didn't think she was breaking her rule, because if anyone were to step into the room at that moment, it was as if I was lying in the bed alone, I was on my side, the covers tucked in my armpit and my face turned toward the trickle of streetlight at the window. And in some way it *felt* as if I was alone. There was something happening in another part of my body but it might as well have been another part of the world, like the evening news, the war still going on, B-52s striking the Ho Chi Minh Trail today and all the talk flowing on in Paris, and I had some connection to all of that but it was very far away, talk from the tube, and that's how this was, me up there watching the streetlight and Fiona somewhere far away working on something that was only distantly connected to me and I was aware for a time of my son, breathing undetectably across the room, and I was far from him too, I suddenly felt, I was outside the window there dumbly emanating from a streetlamp in the winter night and I grew afraid, afraid of myself, afraid of pulling away from him, but not to abandon him to Fiona, not to that, instead I feared that I would stay with him and yet try to make everything seem all right to him, make him think that the world was benign, that this woman—who sucked at me out of his sight—was not frightening at all, not in any way, I feared that all the things that would happen between the three of us in the years ahead—I had some dark prescience about them already—would seem to my son to be the way love is.

And I thought of my own father, because I could see that he did this to me for many years. He told me that my mother was right about love and about women and about sex, and later, when she was dead, he and I met twice a year and I slept in my old room and listened to the trains somewhere out there beyond the mill still picking up momentum every night rolling out of St. Louis and heading for Chicago and there was never a woman in the house, never a trace of one, just the spread of photos of my mother on the mantel, and even when she was dead he agreed with her and he would talk sometimes after we'd drunk a few beers and watched the late news and he would explain her as he always had and he never even spoke of another woman and he was faithful to her and he said once— when a midsummer night was so cool that we put on sweaters and sat in the yard and even the mosquitoes were groggy with the chill and we lingered and he had more beers than usual— he said in a general way that he could have married again but it was all the same, and I said what was all the same, and that was as far as I ever went to challenge him, and he said that women are all the same, ask any man, that's why some men go to bed with all the women they can, because women are all the same and a woman just wears off right away and a man can take any other woman and have the same thing, and he said that he himself sees this about the way women are and so he can just as easily have no one. I did not answer and he must have figured I was misapplying all of this. All except your mother, he said, his hand finding my shoulder and gripping it hard, as if I'd just disagreed with her and made her cry and he was coming in from the other room to protect her feelings. So I said he was right, she wasn't like other women, thinking that was what he wanted to hear. But then he said she was very *much* like other women in the things she believed. Her whole generation had troubles with certain things in modern life. How could she understand what a man wanted to feel like with a woman, he asked, since everyone she knew was ignorant of that. I may have heard a yearning beneath his words even then, something that didn't make sense if he really believed that women were all alike to the touch. But he shivered and rose, and without another word he disappeared to his room for the night, and I never pressed him for anything else because I couldn't speak to him of the things that really mattered to me, and what mattered was the women, what mattered was the tiniest detail of each woman, and though men have always talked with each other about women and I have done some of that, I have never spoken to any man about this, not the things I'm saying here, not in this way, though now I can see that there is no other way to speak of all this, not for me, and I have never spoken with a woman like this either, except perhaps with tongue and palm and penis, and I pressed the thought of my father away by listening now, as I lay watching the streetlight, listening closely to hear if my son was breathing, if he had stopped breathing, and then he sighed in his sleep. My son sighed and my father was dead by now, dead the year before, and he never saw his grandson, never knew of his conception, never met Fiona, though he might have, but when I flew back for the last watch at his bedside, she and I decided it was best not to complicate his mind at that moment. He didn't even know about her.

And I flew back and sat with him and he died when I was down the hall making a phone call and Fiona was saying, "You take care of him, okay? I know you don't talk together much but he still needs you." Meanwhile he was newly dead and I didn't know it and as I walked back to the room I thought about the last time I'd seen him in the hospital, a few days after his quadruple bypass, and there was something new for him to live with, the nightmares, the doctor said there'd been wild nightmares so far and they would continue and he tried to explain them to me. "I'm a rational man," he said, "and this flies a little bit in the face of that, but I've seen this over and over, these dreams. I suspect that the body knows what's just happened, that it had to go onto a machine for a while, that it lost control over itself in some absolute way. On a cellular level I'm talking about. I think the body knows in its very cells that it lost control and it makes these dreams."

And after this, I went in to my father and he had just awakened from one of the dreams and he was panting from the ordeal of it. I sat beside him. I didn't know if I should ask about it, so I kept quiet. But he looked at me and he said, "Something terrible was happening."

"In your dream?" I asked, and he looked away from me at this, he looked toward the window as if he was trying to figure it out. "It's a bad dream," I said. "The doctor said that's normal."

"The open hearth," he said and I remembered the place in the mill. He'd showed me once. He'd taken me up on a catwalk and we watched the great fire of the furnaces below us and I was a little boy and I clung to him and he held me tight and the air all around us thrashed like a flame, invisibly but I could feel the hot shiver and lift and shake of it, and I looked down in the great roiling core of the fire and this was what my father had seen in his dream, I thought, and it seemed right, somehow. But then he said, "Cold. Cold inside it." And I thought of the machine that kept him alive and there was no fire to it, not like the fire his cells sensed about themselves, and again I thought I understood. And then he said, "There were women." He looked at me, took care to fix me with his eyes, though they were jaundiced and puffy with weariness. I was surprised, of course, to know there were women in this dream. I shut off any more thoughts about where the dream came from and I waited. "Inside the hearth," he said. "I knew some of their faces. Some I didn't."

Still I waited for him to say more. I couldn't even begin to shape a question anyway. But his eyes drifted from me, out the window again. We were on the top floor of St. Mary's Hospital, where I was born, and the window had been dulled toward translucence by the gritty air, and I followed my father's gaze over the crests of maple trees and the tar-shingle roofs of shotgun houses to the stacks of the mill's North Plant. Were these women he'd made love to, or had failed to? Or did it have anything to do with that at all? Finally I thought to say, "Was Mom there?"

My father's face rumpled and returned to me. "Please," he said, and the word squeezed out of him slowly, as a real plea. "When I'm dead. Don't hate her."

"You never needed to protect her from that," I said, trying to be gentle about it, trying to make it a reassurance and not a reproach.

He did not register the words on his face but instead looked back to the window. His mind was far from the dream now, I assumed. And it probably was. He was looking at the plant where he'd spent much of his life, even after his wife was dead. He watched for a long while and I would have thought he'd fallen asleep except I could see that his eyes were open. I finally stopped waiting and looked out to the mill stacks. They were empty. The tips of them were cut against the sky and there wasn't even a shimmer there of invisible gas. When I was growing up, the North Plant of Wabash Steel never was silent. There was always smoke. Even on Christmas mornings you could look toward the North Plant and there would be great storm clouds of red smoke rolling up and drifting off toward the river. But now there was nothing going on. Later, there would be changes down there. They would computerize the hot strip and the smoke would go gutless, would lose its color. Then the hard times would come and they'd lay off and shut down and start up again. But when I sat with my father and he was dying, the mill was still working full shifts and the smoke was still red but on this weekday afternoon there was nothing out there and it must have been a cycle of maintenance or something but my father could see no rush of smoke from the stacks out there and I wondered if that had shaped his dream, it had been that and not sex after all. But the cold furnaces were full of women. I wanted to make him speak of his dream, make him tell me if he ever made love to anyone but my mother. I squared around to him, ready to press for this in spite of the great cut in his chest. But he was asleep now. His face was still turned to the window but his eyes were closed.

And as I came back from the phone, this little scene raced through me and when I'd left the room to call Fiona, he'd been resting, his face turned slightly toward the window but not far enough to see and the night out there was glossed by the reflected light from beside his bed. I'd switched the light off before I went to the phone in case he should wake while I was gone and want to see the mill out there, a faint constellation beyond the dark trees, a scattering of lights and a red glow. As important as women were to me, I never did learn a thing about the women in the cold furnace. I never learned a thing as important as that about my father. When I turned into the doorway, there were people in white around my father's bed and I knew he was dead and the landscape of his women, even if it held the living flesh of only my mother, had sunk now beneath a dark sea. And so had my mother's landscape, she'd surely had one that at least held my father in it and I leaned against the door frame and I wept for them both, for my mother too, I wished for her a fine field beneath a bright sky and her own nakedness there, a nakedness that she found beautiful, surprising to her perhaps but unquestionably beautiful, and I was vaguely aware that I was coming now. I could hear Fiona's faint throat sighs and I was conscious now of her mouth on me, but I was still far away, I was still alone, I was still afraid of making some dreadful and fundamental mistake with my son.

And so we moved to Seaview and Fiona stripped the wood floors of our little Victorian house and refinished them and she put tiny-bladed blinds at the windows and no curtains and the furniture she bought was chrome and leather and there was very little of it, she let the wood floors shine there empty, rugless, nothing to break the great glint of them, and for a time she put up art that she'd had in storage for years. There were two big oils of New York street people, portraits full of detail, every stain and every torn thread on their clothes, every whisker stub and liver spot on their faces and hands, and they were sitting, a man on a standpipe with his legs pulled almost primly together and a heavyset woman on a bench but seen slightly from above, one hand on a thigh and one on her lap, like Picasso's portrait of Stein, and there was another oil of a woman rising from the sea, a roiling, stormy sea, and she was wearing a business suit and her face was painted like a whore and her long hair was on fire, bursting into flames at the tips as if from its exposure to the air, and another oil of a great blaze over a city skyline but not seeming to come from anywhere precisely, just overarching it all, and the flames modulated here and there into tongues, long sharp-tipped tongues lapping at the sky and they were as red and yearning as the flames. And a series of pencil drawings on construction paper, the range of bright colors from any schoolchild's satchel, but the drawings were very faint, barely visible, not just on the fern green and the royal blue sheets but even on the lemon drop yellow and the crystal gray, so faint that across the room the pencil strokes weren't visible at all, there seemed to be only framed rectangles of color, but very near, especially in the flat angle of morning light through the living room window, the faces were visible, children's faces, all little girls, all suggested with very few lines to indicate the shape of a jaw, the fall of hair, but around the eyes were details, lazy lids or widening, lifts of eyebrows or furrowing, the faces showed strong feeling but you had to keep looking very hard for them not to disappear again into these blocks of color ready for scissors and paste.

And I want now, after saying this much, to drift away. The only linear movement of time I feel comfortable with is the progression of things from the moment I ease inside a woman until we have collapsed into each other and even then I hold back and hold back, reluctant to relinquish her soft thereness even to my release. So it is painful for me now to consider the straighter story of Fiona from those first few nights in Seaview to some moment many months later. What I really want is to follow the Fiona of that soft thereness I just invoked, the Fiona that lives still in my landscape of women. It's these women— all of them—who whisper in me, specific women waiting to show their faces in the block of color. But I also want to press on about the story of this one woman, of Fiona. If only to give myself a free mind for the others. And to understand. Did Fiona see those girl faces in the drawings as struggling to hold their shapes or trying to fade away into invisibility?

I don't know how long it took. A few months. No. More. John was about eighteen months old and he was talking and Fiona had been working tirelessly with him. I'd come home, jittering in my teeth and fingertips still from the Long Island Rail Road and she would be on the floor with him, words written out on index cards and strung all around the floor, a train of words and John was speaking them, putting them together and laughing and he would leap up and he would always thank Fiona for the words and she would smile and say he was very welcome and he would put his arms around her neck and kiss her on the cheek and then he would run to me, his stockinged feet sliding out from under him on the naked wood floor, and I would lift him and shake him and hold him and Fiona would smile up at us from the floor, her feet bare and her hair tousled, and she would say, each night, "He's a genius, you know. He can read them all," and the train would coil around and around Fiona. And she and I would go upstairs at night and every night Fiona asked for me to show her, sometimes with the specific words and sometimes just with a look and sometimes with a coil of arms around me from behind and this was every night, every night, though she did stop wanting me to make love to her during her period, when she would grow very quiet and I would rest and wonder at all of this, and surely I must have been slow to show her some nights in that first eighteen months, but maybe not or maybe she clenched back her pain at it for a while.

Slow. When John was about eighteen months old, I rocked him to sleep one night and this was in his upstairs bedroom, just across the hall from ours. I slipped into our room and the intercom was locked to transmit on the night table by John's bed and it hissed softly into the receiver beside ours. Fiona was sitting on the bed with her back to me and leaning slightly in the direction of our intercom. In all the static she tried every night to pick up his breathing. Her hair was getting long and I liked it that way, in long curls, and she was wearing a dark sweatshirt and the bedclothes were bunched up and hiding her from the waistband down.

I was tired. I was very tired. Did she know what she was about to start? *You blind fool, of course I didn't know. Haven't I earned that much from you, even in your memories? I sat on the side of the bed that night and I wasn't aware of a thing except that I was naked from the waist down and I knew you couldn't see that. I sat with my legs a little spread and whenever I really needed to know about myself, that always focused me real fast, the touch of air on me, the faint smell of me from being covered up all day, faint but distinct, it always seemed to me, and though you made it seem that my cunt was a pleasure to you at all times, I never got over the conviction that you were lying about that little smell when the panties first came off after a day of me walking around and I don't care how much I washed after that, it seemed like that was the real smell of me, unguarded, unprepared, and that night you're talking about, I knew that the love had to happen right away, no waiting, nothing, or all the lies would crumble away and I'd know the thing was true that I feared all along. This was all battering around in me even as I was bending to listen to my son, and I wasn't even trying to hear him, my head was full of all this and something else was going on, too, the touch of the air on me, the touch of the air on my cunt and that was another kind of focus, on my nakedness, I could feel the air as a tiny zip of nakedness going down this crack of me and I was starting to gather there already, I was lining up there, all up and down my labia: me, my blood there, and my body there, all of it, I was becoming that doorway now, my blood and my body and my sins and my strength too, my fuck-this-I'm-nobody's-fucking-daughter strength, and my nipples burning and my head falling back and feeling my hair hang long and it's all there crowding around the opening of me and my cunt is weeping, though I don't know if it's in happiness or sadness, and it's me there, it's all of me, and it gets so crowded that everything that's gathered rushes inside and I am very large now, a doorway still but a vast space just inside as well, a vast empty space, and the rush inside is a little show for the penis that will touch all of this, harden to it and touch it and weep to it in happiness, weep with me in happiness over the beauty of me, I make a little show of how to rush in, just like this. Harden, I say, and follow all the little shreds of me inside here. And it might seem that the smell of me and the nakedness of me—a thing of my evil and a thing of my happiness—would be at war with each other and one of them would win and eventually that was true, but not right away, not until there was a man, not until I stood up and Ira could see that I was naked. Till then my evil and my happiness hung in balance and I heard Ira behind me and I was ready and I was afraid now, I leaned to the intercom and I listened for the sound of life, breathing, a sigh, a rustle of limbs settling into sleep, something, but I couldn't hear a thing and I knew it was because I was listening to myself and my breath had stopped and my body had stopped and I yearned now, that's all, and if Ira thinks he knows about yearning, he's full of shit, he's just a dilettante in yearning and I rose up and my legs were quaking and I was dripping now with the weeping of my cunt and I turned to Ira and he looked at me and I was breathing again but it was fast, it was too fast, and my cunt was flung open and there was no time, I knew, no time except for Ira to open his pants and leap for me, leap to stop me up before I spilled out, before everything that had gathered inside me splashed at my feet and I should have ripped this carpet up long before this, I was distracted by downstairs and putting up my paintings which I hated now anyway and this was the room I had to polish and simplify and now it was too late, if Ira didn't come to me quick I would make a great dark stain on this rug and that would be me and I would sleep next to it for the rest of my life. And this was sort of how it was going in my head when Ira looked at me with what I knew at once was fear and I guess I'd seen the look before, but goddamn it I'm sorry, Ira, you have to love me this much, you have to learn to love me this much or I can't make it, and he said, "Fiona?" in some pathetic little wimp voice like he thought it was my face that was showing something dangerous. I moved my legs, I made them move, and I was going to do this much, at least, I couldn't let him hold this against me, too, I wouldn't let him make me out as evil so I moved my legs and I circled the bed and I was naked from the waist down, for Christ's sake—forgive me father, for I have sinned, I have taken your son's name in vain and for this I am contrite and ask forgiveness—and I came to Ira and I stood very near to him but this was a mistake I suddenly realized because he could smell me and then I knew I was in trouble and he said to me, "Please be patient for just a bit," and I said, "A bit? How big a fucking bit?" This was a relevant question. This was the only question except for one other that occurred to me right away. "Patient for what?" And I had to know. I couldn't wait. He was wearing sweatpants and I knew it was easy to know and I could know just by looking because Ira is big when he wants to be but I couldn't leave any room for doubt and I thought this would help him anyway and I reached forward and my hand was trembling so much I made a fool of me, a goddamn fool, and I touched him there where he could save me and he was soft, he was mushy with hate for me. "Darling," he said, drawing it out in a plaint and there was nothing doing in my hand, and this terrible*

*truth had happened all at once, all on one night, all the truth
came out and after this I knew I would accept lies again, I'd
have to accept Ira's lies because I had no choice, but I'd never
be able to turn away from the truth again. And so I squeezed
the thing in my hand that had turned against me, a quick
squeeze of fuck-you-you-disgust-me-anyway, and I won't start
worrying about that squeeze because it wasn't hard enough to
make him cry out or double over or any phony dramatic shit
like that, he just flinched and I let go and I told him that I
understood how things are and I told him how he didn't have
to pretend anymore and that should make him happy because
as elaborately as he'd spun that big lie out, it must have taken
a lot out of him, and I told him how he should just go ahead
and leave me and my son to ourselves if he really felt like that
and I was being real clear, I thought, very rational about all
of this, very mature and rational and not evil at all—that was
the surprising thing, I didn't feel evil at all even though Ira
had just done what he could to convince me that I was. And
yet. And yet. I found myself on my feet in the middle of the
bed, staggering around in the middle of the bed, trying to pace
there, I think, but not doing a very efficient job of it and finding
it a little odd and then I found myself in a room with light
coming from below and the lamp was on its side and the shade
was off and the bulb was naked and hot and clean and it caught
me for a moment but then I saw books scattered on the floor
and I recognized one of them as a book I was reading just the
night before, a book from the nightstand, and my face was wet
and I dragged my wrist over my cheeks and I expected blood,
for some reason, but it was froth and I'd stopped speaking for
my wrist to pass by but I was speaking again now and it was
about how he could just go ahead and leave if he wanted, right
now for instance, and I was suddenly conscious of the froth
again and it was me, it was from me speaking, and I stopped
and wiped my mouth again and I looked at my wrist and I*

said, "I'm frothing at the mouth," and I looked at Ira and he was a little disheveled and there were three thin scratches on his left cheek, long parallel lines running down, and I said, "Does it mean you're crazy if you froth at the mouth?" and I said that real soft, I think, I could barely hear myself and Ira was offering me a hand to climb down from the bed and I felt tired, very tired, and I took his hand and inside I was saying to him, Lie to me now. Please lie. And Ira said, "You're not crazy, Fiona. And I don't hate you. I love you. Let's go to bed and sleep." And I said, "You still have to make love to me. There's no other way." But I said that soft, like when I asked if I was crazy. And I stepped down and I lay down and I closed my eyes and I waited for him and he was touching me and kissing me and I kept my eyes closed, assuming he was ready right away, assuming everything was like before and eventually he was inside me and he was hard, all right, but I'd vacated those premises quite a while ago and it was good that he was in me but I was all alone.

When Fiona went a little crazy that night, I found myself oddly detached. We'd been through these things before. But when it was just the people through the walls or upstairs or in the street below or all around us in a restaurant or a museum or Central Park—because some of the arguments had a public part, never quite as bad as the private but noticeable nonetheless—when it was just strangers to overhear us, my only concern was for Fiona, to get her through it, to take away the pain. But now I was keenly conscious of John in the other room, the hiss of the intercom played clearly behind Fiona's loudest cries, and ironically I couldn't let go of her own words, an early little shrug of an admission about why she might be embracing Catholicism once again; she quoted the old saying of the Church: Give me the child till he is seven years old and you can never remove these beliefs from him. Part of me was in his room, listening to all of this in the dark, in half sleep, in the drastic dilation of an infant's mind and heart. I heard a catechism of madness.

I am conscious of my penis sometimes when a faint shudder runs through it like a sigh, and I think: this part is me. My penis is more me than anything else. It is the gathering and the thrumming of me. When I love a woman and I rise to her, all of me goes into that part and it fills with blood and it thereby conjures itself from flesh into bone and that's all of me—blood, flesh, and bone—in one gesture. And that's how I am when I'm ready to make love, but the changing always astonishes me, the movement of my penis from small and rucked to great and smooth, all from the flow inside me, the tidal flow drawn by the woman before me as if she were the moon drawing the sea in me; stronger, a stellar pull, the force of a star, and I never thought I would have to worry about any of this, it was always so powerful in me, but when John was only eighteen months old and suddenly Fiona's sanity and my son's sanity and my own, too, perhaps, depended on my penis never ebbing, never, always rising to her without hesitation, I began to doubt. I showered the next morning, after that first night of Fiona's new need, and I was aware that my cheek stung—but that was my own fault, really; the flash of her nails was meant for my forearms, as it had before, in other arguments, but this time I did not offer my arms and instead ducked a bit and it was a mistake, where she caught me, one she regretted right away, I think, because she cried out as if it were she who had been hurt. So I held the washcloth softly against my cheek and then I thought of my penis. I cupped myself, and flaccid now, loose in the hot flow of water, I fit mostly in my hand and there was a weariness in me and I thought of the night to come and for the first time in my life I doubted.

There are so many details that accumulated to make all of this happen the way it did. I want to open my hand now in this memory and let go of my slack penis and move from that shower back to the real home in my head and rest inside of a woman, the first one who creeps softly back to me, stealing into my darkness, and she is barely past twenty and I am a decade older and the room we are in has no window but a long, glinting wood table and I know only by my watch that it is dark outside, nearly tilting, as we are, into the winter solstice, and they'd spoken in the morning about an ice storm and the place is too hot and her hair is long and fine and the color of the winter sunlight and it is pulled back and there is a bow at the crown of her head and we are alone and the company files are scattered before us and her steno pad is down now and she has been talking for a long time about the man who lives with her and who makes her feel like a fool and she speaks about this with such a fine sharp edge to her mind that it is easy for me to love her and for her to love me because of my comforting words which she knows are true and then the room goes dark and there is nothing, we are blind, we are now only sound and smell and touch and we know at once that we must hold each other very close and when I slip into her on the great, hard surface of the table I know that I will never see her naked but I know, too, that if I could see, I would never feel the soft grip of her quite so clearly, and later that night in my motel I know to turn off the light and to run my fingers along my penis and smell the dampness of her, still there, and in the dark it is rich and sweet.

But let me say the things that need to be said. I could not persuade Fiona to go for some sort of professional help—I dared not even try—because before she'd met me she had been in therapy for seven years, starting in her midteens, and the doctor later made the front page of the New York Post and I was with Fiona and she saw his face there one evening and she stopped at it and I didn't even realize for a while that something big was happening in her, and she took up the paper and she stared at the man and the headline was about a Dr. Feelgood and she looked at it for a long time and when the guy selling papers said Hey lady, she snapped out of it and carefully put the paper back and she took me by the arm and walked me quickly away. I asked what was wrong and she said, "One of the reasons I love you, Ira, is that you have never mentioned psychiatry to me."

This was when we were still in the city and before we had a baby and when she just seemed excessively jealous, that's all, and you could make an allowance for that with anybody, it seemed to me. And we walked on and it was chilly out but she hadn't taken a jacket and I put my arm around her and she was shivering and she said, "I'm going to tell you this once, and then I will never mention it again. And please don't you mention it either."

"Okay," I said.

And she told me she had been this doctor's patient for seven years and his therapy was to try to drag up a bunch of stuff from the past—she expected that much, but it didn't seem to do any good just on its own—and at the same time he put her on speed. He put her on speed after the first month and for the rest of the seven years she was on speed and that was his therapy and it was all a crock of shit anyway, she said, and she loved me because I had never been in therapy and it was like such a thing didn't even exist for me and she had no confidence in any of that and could never have and that was the last time the subject would ever come up between us. And by now she was trembling so badly she could hardly walk and I knew it wasn't just from the cold and I held her close and that didn't calm her even a little bit.

So when things got very bad then, when John was eighteen months old, there wasn't an obvious solution. For a week or so it was all right. She'd just come off a period and the next night she gave me maybe twenty seconds. I was okay. I was hard for her just in time—I could sense the trouble rising again, but I was okay. I made it and we were fine and she rolled me over on my back and spiked her arms straight at each side of my head and she let her long hair hang softly into my face and she smiled but about a week later, after seven straight nights of orgasm since her period, I didn't make it in the twenty seconds and maybe that night she didn't even give me that long. But the fury happened again: about three hours of struggle, the door closed, the intercom hissing, Fiona raging and frothing at the mouth. And I tried to shut down my mind, the part of it that put things together, associations. This had nothing to do with our intimacy, nothing at all, I insisted to myself, even though she was naked, even though it was in her lovely nakedness that she flew about the room, her hands ravenous with frustration, clawing at my arms, finding books, the lamp, the pictures on the wall, only framed photos in this room and she felt free to fling them: the Chrysler Building eagles flew across our room, a grain elevator in Nebraska was uprooted and careened off the ceiling. And it was in her sweet nakedness that she did all of this and it was in her nakedness that she squeezed all tone out of her voice, made the sound of metal brake shoe on metal subway wheel but forced that sound into words and they said that she and her son would just disappear if I hated her so. Always she linked herself and our son. Always she summoned up the threat of my little guy caught up in these frantic arms and clutched to that naked breast and stolen away into Fiona's dark night, though only once, in the third of these arguments, or maybe the fourth, did she actually make a move toward the door as if to go wake John. I knew that this was a place I had to draw a line and I stepped and blocked the door and I said, very low but she was listening, "I won't let you do that, Fiona." She hesitated and I said, "You show him this side of you and *he* will hate you. I won't let that happen." That's how I put it, and when I heard that, I shuddered a little, as if it were my father speaking. But I knew that wasn't how I meant it. I knew that was for Fiona's benefit. It wasn't to preserve his love for her; it was to protect his inchoate mind and heart from the image of this chaos. Fiona's first spasm of reaction to my declaration was a lift of the hands as if to go for my throat and she hissed "Fucking bastard" but then the hands seemed to rethink all this. Her face was contorted with her words but the hands hesitated and then grabbed at each side of her head and pressed hard and she spun away and the argument continued with no more moves to the door.

And there was always contrition the next day and I always accepted it. These middle-of-the-night furies always began with time running out on my penis and this happened about once a week and then after a few months it was about twice a week and I took a walk in the dark with John and it was a cool night and we were wearing matching sweatshirts I'd picked up on Fourteenth Street and he had a watch cap and he pulled the cap down over his eyes and staggered around in the park, the leaves wet and the streetlights between the pin oaks sucking a little mist to them, and he walked around in the dark chortling and he kept telling me to go off, and then he would find me from my voice. We played this for a long while and then he gave me the cap and he told me to do it, to cover my eyes and find him. I don't know quite why I chose that moment to ask him, maybe it was this game of moving in the dark, but I knelt before him and told him okay but I wanted to ask him a question. He was talking pretty well and had been for some months now. He knew the alphabet by one year old. Fiona was filling him with words and he loved it; this was a wonderful game for him. We were in a pale splash of streetlight and I said, "John, when you go to sleep. Do you wake up?"

He cocked his head at me. I had an odd feeling that he heard me posing some wild new possibility in the world to him. As if he thought he was awake but he wasn't. Or that he might *not* wake up. Quickly I said, "I mean *when* do you wake up?"

"Morning," he said.

"What wakes you up?"

He pursed his lips at this. This was his face when I asked

him what he thought was a good question. He liked me to ask him things that made him ponder his senses. But he had trouble with this one, at last. "I don't know," he said.

"You know 'dream'?"

"Dream?"

"Do you see things when you sleep?"

"I don't know."

"You think about that next time you wake up, okay?"

"Okay."

"Do you ever hear people talking loud in the night?"

"Put on your hat," he said and he took the watch cap from my hand and placed it on my head.

"John," I said in my pay-attention voice. He looked at me steadily. "Do you hear loud talking in the night?"

"No," he said and he was only a little over two years old and he was a very smart kid, very smart—scary smart, if you want to know the truth of it—but I couldn't believe that there was any guile in him; I had to believe that he was telling me the truth. I put my hand on his shoulder and he was tiny beneath my hand, tiny and so fragile in bone, it seemed to me at that moment, that I was afraid to squeeze him there in appreciation as I wanted to do for fear he would crumble. He shook free and stepped in closer and took both his hands and pulled the watch cap down over my eyes and I waved my arms and demanded to know who put out the lights and he laughed loud and I heard him dash off and then call to me from far away. I stood up and he called again, and blind and wobbly I made my way toward him.

But about Fiona's contrition. I believed that John was not hearing us. He told me so that night and I'd always assumed it. So I could always say to her with sincerity: "Forget it, Fiona."

And on that night, after John reassured me and we played our game and we walked home—me with the watch cap still blinding me and he leading me by the hand until we were at our front door and he was full of pride at guiding me home safely—and after he went to bed and Fiona and I sat talking about the day—a small fire at Penn Station, ten new words for John—and after we went up to bed and this turned into a night when I didn't respond fast enough and Fiona thrashed beneath the presumption of my hatred toward her and after this went on for two or three hours and then we finally made compromised love, weary and hoarse and weepy, and we went to sleep, after all of that, the next morning she clung to me with wordless tears and that evening she put John in his room with his Lego blocks and his books and she took me to the glassed-in porch filled now with plants and flowers and she sat me down on the floor in the place where we made love for the first time in this house, though she never referred to it, and she sat down opposite me and she said, "I am a monster, Ira."

"You're not a monster, Fiona."

"Don't argue with me, Ira. If you don't agree I'm a monster, I'll rip your fucking head off." For a moment this sounded like a declaration completely devoid of irony. But she watched my face closely and then I could see her recoil slightly with the shock that I was taking her seriously. "My God," she said. "I was trying to be funny. Was that a plausible thing I said? Could you believe I'd say that for real?"

I shrugged. She'd said as bad or worse in some of our nights, though now I just shrugged and kept quiet.

"Of course," she said. "Of course you could believe it. I don't even remember most of what I say when I get like that, Ira. But I *know* it's terrible." She paused now and she waited for me to answer. Not to deny this. I knew she wasn't looking to minimize what she'd done. Quite the contrary. She said, low, "It *is* terrible what I do, isn't it."

"It passes. It's from all the fear you have. All the bad feelings about yourself." I hated these conversations. I sounded like a fool. If she'd lost her faith in analysis, my pale little psychoplatitudes were eventually just going to anger her, I feared.

She was weeping now. Her head was bowed and she was

trembling with the weeping. I tried to lift my hand to touch her, to comfort her, but I had no strength to do that. I tried to speak a word or two. Just her name, even. But my mind had shut down. We sat like that for a minute, perhaps two. I kept saying to myself, Now. Now. Just touch her. Just say a word to reassure her. But I could not, even though this weakness that was upon me was from pity and I wanted very much to do something to make her feel all right. Then her crying finally snubbed to a stop and she lifted her head and she said, "I'm sorry, my sweet Ira."

"It's okay. Please just forget it."

"I won't always be like this. I know what I need to do." She paused only very briefly to lean forward and squeeze my hands, which were drooped between my crossed legs. I knew right away to be glad that she didn't pause very long; I didn't want a chance to ponder this announcement. She caught my eyes and fixed on them and she leaned a little forward and said, "There's a God in heaven. He loves the miserable sinner. And He gave me something to do, and it was right under my nose all along."

So Fiona got up and she went into the kitchen, which was next to the glassed porch, and she dialed the phone—a short dialing; information, I knew, because she never picked up the book, though it was right next to the phone. And I heard her say, "Give me the rectory number for Our Lady of Sorrows Catholic Church, Seaview."

This was the church we'd gone to every Sunday since we'd moved here. It was down by the water and it had an old priest with white hair yellowed over the ears like a dog had pissed in snow and his knuckles were the same yellow, this from nicotine, I knew, because he smelled of old smoke when he came along the rail and offered the body of Christ. But now she called this priest. Father Zieglitz. And she asked if she could come down to the rectory right then. She needed to confess. Face-to-face. Right away. She could not risk a death in the night. She really felt she had to do this. There was a string of these little persuasions; Father Zieglitz was obviously reluctant. She knew that God had brought her to Seaview and it just took a while to understand why. "You're very special to me, Father. I know you understand. I know you've been blessed," she said. I was still sitting among the plants with my legs folded together. I waited and there was silence in the kitchen and then Fiona said, "You're a saint. Thank you." The phone was down and Fiona was in the doorway. I looked up at her and her hair was ringed with the glare of the kitchen ceiling light. "The answer doesn't lie between you and me, Ira. That's where I've made my mistake. I'm sorry. I've ex-pected too much from you."

I smiled up at her and nodded a reassurance. But this new direction made me nervous right away. Then I overrode that. If she had lost her faith in psychiatry, then let her go to its ancient precursor, the Catholic confessional. Fine. "I'll be back," she said.

"I'll be here," I said.

And she rushed out of the house and I heard the car and she squealed the tires in this dead-calm Victorian neighborhood and a dog barked somewhere, very far away, and I stayed where I was, sitting on the floor where Fiona and I had made love and I wondered if she was right, if there was a God who gave a shit about all of this. If I believed that, in the way Fiona meant it, I would have said a prayer at that moment. I would have learned at last from the great sighing mutters from the parishioners of Our Lady of Sorrows, their prayers in the Mass, and if I could have said a prayer, maybe Fiona would have had some spiritual help as she tore around corners and down the bluff road and along the shore of the sound and into the smoky presence of God's priest to speak her sins and receive the yellow-knuckled tracing of a cross and with it, forgiveness and peace. Was that how the infinite was expressed on the planet Earth? I leaned forward and closed my eyes and what I needed was a woman to touch and to love and she was Vietnamese and she was young and she was the enemy, a real live Viet Cong, a cook she said, forced into service, but the Vietnamese intelligence captain had told us privately that he was sure she was more, much more, a political cadre at the very least, a shrewd and ruthless VC who worked to proselytize the women in the villages all over the province and target the resisters for assassination. I could smell the sea. I was on loan to the Australians here in Phuoc Tuy province, a goodwill exchange program between Allied armies, and I could smell the South China Sea, though the room was small and close and we were in the middle of a salt flat and the Australian who brought me here was sweating off the curried eggs and sausages of the Aussie base-camp breakfast and the Vietnamese officer was pacing up and down in front of the woman and stirring up the dust on the floor and smoking one Salem after another and still I could smell the sea from beyond the mountains. She was sitting in a straight-backed chair in the middle of the floor and she was scared, though the captain was still talking pretty mildly, was still letting her tell her cover story without challenging it very seriously. Her eyes had the ancient fold, the fold that all babies have in the womb, I'm told—we are all Oriental in our private sea—but her eyes were very large and they were full of tears and one tear eased out and traced a line in the otherwise-invisible dust on her cheek and her skin was dusky and I knew it was very soft and I knew she had the lush long hair I loved but she had it all wound into a bun on the top of her head. The captain asked her now, letting his skepticism show, how it was that she went about her duties as the simple cook she claimed to be. She had a pale blue cloth in her hand and she was wringing it and she smiled a little now, quickly, but it was hard to understand, whether it was the nervous smile of a peasant girl caught up innocently in all this or whether it was an ironic smile, a smile at all our suspicions that she knew were correct and that she would never admit. She smiled and there was a moment in those eyes—I was looking at them closely because they were beautiful, not because of a suspicion; I would never have looked this closely at them if I was simply suspicious—but there was a moment in her beautiful eyes when she turned hard, knowing that things were going to get rough, her beautiful eyes went hard and she let one, quick, fuck-you-all glance rise to the captain and then she quickly brought the cloth to her face, covered the smile as if it might be showing too much and she let her eyes go blank and move to the window beside the closed door. And suddenly I knew that in another place, out on the highway at dusk with a market basket on her head and me passing by in a jeep, she would be a very dangerous woman.

I followed her eyes to the window and outside was the long, low wing of the holding cells and behind one of those iron doors was a windowless concrete cubicle where she would lie down tonight and close those dangerous eyes and in the silence that the captain left for her to implicate herself, the paddle fan whisked overhead and she kept her eyes out there and I knew that if she expected to have a chance here, she should be telling lies by now, she should be saying *something* and I wanted to prompt her, tell her to imagine food, imagine cooking rice for VC platoons and just start talking about it, but now I wondered if the fuck-you smile meant she was giving it all up, meant she knew that whatever she said, it wouldn't be believed and the end would be the same anyway.

For the first time, with a frantic little scrabble in my chest, I considered what that end might be. This wasn't the Aussie's prisoner. We were here as a professional courtesy and also because they thought I might be able at some point to speak with her in my fluent Vietnamese and surprise her with it, throw her off guard. In spite of our little forays into the countryside looking for the spoor of VC among the rubber trees, all we really were working with at our own camp were rumors of mortar attacks on the Bien Hoa air base that we did up in spot reports. I was in quite a different place now. And she was beautiful to me. Her hands were strong and they both worked hard at the cloth before her face. I desperately wanted her to speak, to explain herself. I must have seemed about to speak myself because the Vietnamese captain caught my eye and gave me a little shake of the head as if to say, Not yet. The gesture was very familiar, comradely, even conspiratorial, and it made me focus on this woman and I wanted her to know that the captain was wrong, that I wasn't actually part of this, all I wanted was to go somewhere with her alone, quiet, to drive across the salt flats with her and she would undo her hair and let it blow in the rush of air and we would drive through the low mountains with only occasional, languorous, wait-just-a-little-while smiles, and we would go down to the South China Sea and we would stop at the beach and walk along the surf and talk of her family and of America and of the great birds—flashes of red and yellow—rising from the trees and dashing west, away from us, and we would talk of the sea and how we both have always loved it from opposite sides of the world and we would sit together in the shade and talk some more and eat mangoes and doze and then we would finally feel so full of all that we knew about each other that we would turn to the great mysteries between us and we would touch and we would join.

But of course my yearning for her meant nothing. I was in fact part of this thing that was going on. I was the enemy to her. Simply that. And if she were not a prisoner now and if I were to walk that beach alone, drawn as I was by the romance of the South China Sea, and if I were to sit in the shade and think of all the women in the world, then this one, this woman I'd never seen with the blue cloth in her pocket, might well have slipped silently from the trees behind me and blown the back of my head away and that would be that. Still, she was very beautiful hiding her mouth with her cloth. And I turned from the captain. I crossed the room to the door and kept my back to the questioning and the man's voice rising and growing shrill and I stopped hearing the Vietnamese in my head. I tried to think in English about what I would say or what I would do if things got out of hand behind me.

And on the floor of the glassed porch in Seaview, New York, with Fiona's begonias and spider plants and African violets leaning over me, I tried to snap out of this, tried to think of some other woman if I could, a woman I could be alone with now without complications, and the intercom was hissing in the kitchen and I wondered who Fiona would be when she returned and still the air smelled of the South China Sea and the captain suddenly appeared beside me and he said to me in English, "Time for you talking now. Do what you like. She is sure VC."

And the Aussie was just behind me and he said, "You want me to go out, too, mate? Or should I play the muscle?"

I turned to them and I was ready to tell them both to go to hell, but the captain misinterpreted my look and he said, "If you talk, do not turn your back. But she has no weapon. I strip her myself and search." And a faint little man-to-man smile curled across his face at this and I had no words now, I was surprised by a feeling that should have been no surprise but I didn't want it, not at all, and all this was taking too long and I groped around for words to say and all I could come up with was "Leave me."

They did and I turned to her. She had said her name was Gio. The Vietnamese word for the wind. Her blue cloth was in her lap now and her hands were there too but they were still. Her head was bowed. And I was still wobbly with jealousy. The shrill-voiced captain had stripped her and searched her and his eyes and his hands had touched her body and it wasn't as if I wanted to touch her the way he had—I wanted only to love her and my love for her had nothing to do with power and it had nothing to do with anger and I could never move to her, could never touch her, could never look upon her nakedness, without her yes, without her sweet yes—but I could not shake this feeling either, could not help but wish to take the edge of a knife and scrape her memory from the captain's skin, could not help but wish for that secret of her myself, a secret that could never find expression—never—in a sly smile to another man.

"Were you born on a windy night?" I asked her.

Her face rose and she could not believe that I was speaking Vietnamese and more than that, much more than that, she could not believe what I'd just guessed about her. And she said, "Yes." She who had kept silent though it imperiled her life to do so said yes to me about this. And then she said, "What are you?"

I thought to tell her that I was a man who loved her. But that would frighten her and she might not speak again or it would frighten her and she might offer herself from fear and I could bear neither of those things and I said nothing. I waited.

Finally she said, "My mother heard the wind all through her labor."

"From the sea?"

"Yes. . . . What are you?"

A chair was against the wall near the door and I took it and brought it before her and I sat and our knees did not quite touch and I said, "Tell me one thing you can remember from your childhood. Something from when the wind was blowing and you could smell it clearly."

Now she narrowed her eyes at me.

I knew I'd made a mistake. "Please," I said. "I may sound mad to you, but I am not in your country because I like this war. I don't care about these men I am with. If I could think of a way to get you out of here, right now, I would do it."

She turned her face sharply away. She looked out the window again and I feared I'd lost her.

I said, "When I was a child, I would go sometimes with my parents to the top of a great . . ." I did not know the Vietnamese word for an Indian mound. "A great pile of earth made by people from many years ago. I could see all around me and I always wanted to go and stand near the edge and my mother would never let me, but she loved the air on the top of this earth and so she brought us there perhaps once a year. I would stand in the middle and lift my face and I felt as if I was part of the sky, and the clouds were moving and I was very conscious of the wind. I liked to think that the same wind that moved the clouds moved over me."

Gio looked at me once again, but her face was still knitted tight in suspicion. I sat back in my chair and I said no more. I just looked at her face. I tried to memorize her face, though on the floor of the room in Seaview it was only her eyes that I could see very clearly, her large, deep-folded Asian eyes and they gradually softened and her brow unfurrowed and grew smooth and she said, softly, "You speak our language like my brother."

"Not a brother," I said and I said this softly, too, and having said this much, I knew not to move, not even to lean forward to her now.

She thought about this for a time. Her face was still placid, but I knew she was trying to understand what she'd just heard. Finally, her hand went to the top button of her blouse and I said, "No."

She stopped. Her fingers were curled lightly near her throat and I yearned for this hand to touch me, the fingers were long but the nails were nubbed close, these were working hands, these were the hands of a jungle fighter, hands with a memory in their palms of a weapon, the heft of it, the smooth heat of it, but her hands were gentle in the stillness of this moment and I regretted the word I'd spoken, regretted it instantly, but it was all that I could say and the regret was for losing her, the regret was for losing her from before I'd first seen her, and I knew if she were to lunge for my throat at that moment, lay her hands on me to kill me, I would not have the strength even to lift my arms in a last, ironic embrace. But her hand lingered there near her button and I thought to say yes. I animated my limbs now to the lie that she wanted me, that this gesture had nothing to do with the fear for her life that burned beneath her lovely, placid face and she really wanted me, it took only this little for her to fall in love with me and she really did want this for herself. But it was a lie and I knew it was a lie and I said, "A memory is all I ask."

Her hand fell and she angled her head slightly to the side and she looked at me very briefly in that hint you have sometimes when you love a woman and can never touch her, the hint that you both know there was some alternate turning, never reached or missed forever but clearly understood to have been there, clearly and wordlessly understood between you both, a turning where you and she could have lifted and opened and joined and clutched softly and known everything about each other and no one else could ever have known those two things at once, ever. And that's what I saw in her look and that's what I heard in her words when she said, "I was very young but I already understood about my name and there was a storm coming in off the sea. It was night and our house was of thatch and it was like having no house at all, the storm came in hard and blew through it and the flame of the kerosene lamp was bending over almost flat. This was a wind, too, I suddenly realized. My older sisters and brothers were very frightened and I could see fear even in the faces of my parents. But I was very calm. It was my name. This was me. I knew I had this great, strong thing inside me, too."

Gio fell silent and there was just the swish of the paddle fan overhead and it could have been that she chose this memory to tell me that she foresaw her future as a revolutionary, but she spoke all of this to me and she didn't have to do that, she was moved to speak in the most unlikely way, given who I was, and if she really had used my odd request simply to convey a covert political statement, then there would never have been the softness in her eyes, and that was most certainly there, she looked at me closely and her eyes were wide and soft and her voice was soft, too, and when she finished, she lowered her face at once. This was not the gesture of a proud freedom fighter who had just told this slightly lunatic American that she and her cause would prevail. The strength she recognized as a child was more personal than that. It was surely even a glimpse of nascent passion, the passion of her future womanhood, fulfilled in spite of the preoccupation of politics and war, and if it wasn't her passion that she was thinking of, she would not have looked down at her hands after saying this and then angled her bowed head slightly to the side, a sweetly coy gesture, it clearly seemed, and she would not have twisted at the blue cloth and then finally raised her face to me once more with her eyes still gentle.

I was breathless now with all this. I was sure that I was right. And I was sure that she was a woman quick to the expression of her passion and my own passion was quick in me now, quick and soft-seeming as napalm. But still, I knew the terrible fear in her and the power I unavoidably held over her in this place and I knew that I could not ask for what I yearned now so keenly for, I could not even put my hand over hers and wait for her hand to turn upward, to grasp mine, because that would begin what I wanted in every way except for the way that it would then seem, as if it were not her own desire. But if I did nothing, if I sat as still as I was now sitting before her and made no movement and said nothing and kept my face still, not even asking with my eyes, and if then she were to raise her hand once more to the top button on her blouse, then I would say, You don't have to do this, if you do this, it must be for you. And if then she would say, I want you—say it in whatever way she wished, with her mouth or with her eyes or with the tips of her fingers never hesitating and undoing the top button and the next and the next—then I would have gathered all of myself into the furthest leaping tip of me and

I would have leaned deeply into this strong wind, I would have placed all that I was inside her and listened to her and felt her rushing all around me and the clouds would have blown before her forever over that landscape where I live.

But I stop now. Now in my thirty-sixth year. I stop because I must face this about myself. If a woman wants me, if there are no lies or coercions between us, if there is no persuasion other than the implicit persuasion of our two ontological whisperings and our two inclinations to listen, if a woman wants me like that, then I must say yes to that and it has always been that way for me, from the first glimmerings of my sex, from Karen Granger's first yes, yes here are the bones of my feet, and it is that way for me even still, even as I speak one word of all this after another, I must say yes to a woman who wants me and who wants me to want her and that moment eventually came even with Sam, the wife of the guy at the public-relations firm, the hostess of the dinner party who fondled her long blond hair and laid a strand of it beneath her nose and pushed up her lip to hold it there and whose eyes slid my way even as I stared at this odd little, lovely little gesture and everyone else was talking and distracted—even Fiona was or I surely would have heard about this silent exchange between Sam and me in the argument that very night, if it had been observed— and Sam looked at me and she lifted her eyebrows at me and I don't remember if this was before or after she posed the hypothetical about a woman coming naked out of a shower and confronting a strange man and she having only a washrag to cover herself, but this little lift of the eyebrows seems in retrospect to have something of that same quality, of her being caught naked and not really caring. She knew I was watching this habit of hers and she said with her eyes that I was seeing something intimate but she didn't care, since it was me.

Not that anything came of this at that point. As I said the last time I thought of Sam, there are little things you do to mute your response to a woman you want but you shouldn't want because of reasons that have nothing to do with the two of you. Another man in love with her, for instance, a man she's made a commitment to. So you make yourself look away. You don't say anything. There is no persuasion. You love this woman but you care about the other man by the passivity you preserve with regard to your passion. The passion chooses you. The love chooses you. All you have to resist it is your breathless passivity.

And I pushed away from the dinner table that night in careful preservation of that passivity and I wobbled down the hallway and into the bathroom and I closed the door and I slipped the bolt and this was a time when the only formal impediment was another man in Sam's life, when no promises had yet been spoken between Fiona and me. It's true that I loved Fiona, loved her already as richly and powerfully as I would later. But if Sam had come and knocked softly at the bathroom door and whispered, Ira, please open the door for a moment, then I would have unlocked the door—even though I had slipped the bolt deliberately—and I would have opened the door, and even though I would not lift my arms to her right away I would look her in the eyes and if she said yes there, if she whispered again, not just with her eyes but in spoken words, I have to touch you, Ira, I have to see who you really are in that secret place of yours, then I would have had to take Sam into my arms, even on that night, even though I did love Fiona already and even though Sam was married. I would have been unable to make a different choice, even if some rational, loyal, honest, omnisciently considerate and caring part of me said it was wrong. Because I loved Sam, too, and if it wasn't in the same way as I loved Fiona, if it might seem to some rigorously rational and honest and loyal and considerate and caring outside observer that it was a lesser love, not worthy of the name even and certainly not worthy of expression, and more than that, if it seemed that it was a love that was forever preempted because somebody else already loved me at that moment, I have no answer for that except all that I've already said in this story of

mine and all that still remains to be said. I can't reason this
thing out. That's always the big mistake, trying to believe these
things yield to reason. And as far as my friend Harry is concerned, all I can say is that I did everything I was capable of
to avoid this, but ultimately it was Sam's choice, as well. I'm
not happy with all that. Really I'm not. For the sake of Fiona
and Harry and the structures of society and the cornerstone
of Western civilization or whatever else might be at stake here,
I'm not happy with this. I'm not happy either at having to keep
that kind of secret. But I struggle always, *always*, with that
other unhappiness: the vision of a universe where love is something you get one of, where this other yearning, if you have
it, is never to be expressed fully, after a certain point, and if
you do, there are dreadful secrets to keep.

But I didn't mean to get off on this now, or maybe ever in
these terms. I wait on the floor of our glassed-in porch in
Seaview as Fiona confesses her sins to the yellow-knuckled
priest and that's where I veer off and I end up talking like this
about sex and love, talking in the abstract, reasoning it all out,
but no man ever reasoned himself into love or out of it. No
woman, either. I sat on the floor with the smell of potting soil
all around me and I thought of Sam then, briefly, still never
having touched her, I thought of her after Gio, I bolted the
door of Sam's bathroom behind me and I leaned for a moment
on the basin and I was breathless and the soap here was something heavily perfumed, unfamiliar, and I stepped to the bowl
and I opened my fly and took myself into my hand to piss and
I was in the little room where she was naked every day and
the soap she used filled me up until I turned my face to the
window, which was open a few inches to the night, and there
was a plant in a little pot on the sill and the leaves were gouged
with red and now I could smell the potting soil and it smelled
like a summer night and there was a slow drip from the tub
behind me where Sam had that very morning slipped into the
water and lathered her breasts and her legs and her pussy and

I leaned forward against the wall, erect now in my hand and unable to piss.

And it was several years later that I did indeed open a door to Sam, the door to my office and Harry was somewhere uptown with a client, and this was a year or a little more after that night of confession in Seaview, and Sam said "Ira" and I said "Sam" and I was standing there with my tie askew and my sleeves rolled up and I was writing some little ode to a hand-held calculator and a lot had happened that I should speak of but I won't now, I won't, I will stand before Sam and I will say, as I did then, "Sam, would you do something for me, since Harry is not here in the office to think I'm a crazy son of a bitch for asking?" and she said, "What?" and I said, "Would you take a lock of your hair and make a mustache of it?" and she said, "Aren't you afraid that *I'll* think you're a crazy son of a bitch?"

And, of course, what I'd said wasn't really a seductive thing. At least I didn't think of it that way. But it also was. It came from my desire for her, after all, but it was also crazy enough that I guess I figured she would never get turned on by it. It still seemed to me as if I was being passive. She didn't wait for me to answer. She separated a lock from the long drape of her hair and she put it under her nose and pushed up her lip and I said, "Thanks, Sam. That's all I need."

But she dropped the hair at once and she cocked her head at me. "No it's not, Ira," she said.

I held very still. I waited and I felt my hands yearning and so I softly slipped them into my pants pockets and it was not lost on me that I'd been communicating with her somehow. And that was not passive at all, if you wanted to get down to it. Sam was speaking inside my head, even as I stood before her: *What's the pose now, Ira Holloway? You aren't taking me into your arms, you're hiding your hands from me, you're trying to put it off on me. What kind of nonsense is that, Ira? You reached straight out and touched my elbow when you found me standing before your door and I know what you'll say, that you're a toucher with all people, that you touch Harry's elbow just the same way whenever you meet him and there's nothing sexual about it at all, but no man whose eyes soften the way yours do when they look at me and whose hand is so gentle in its touch on my arm and whose shoulders lift ever so slightly when I fall suddenly into thought and raise my chin and turn my profile to him, a profile I know myself to be very pretty, no man like that is going to get away with thinking he's not constantly whispering in my ear I love you I want you. And I can't help but think that maybe you love me more than anyone else, even on the very little evidence you have of who I am. So when you suddenly ask me to do something with my body that I always do and that I'm put off by myself because it's a silly little ugly little nervous habit and you ask me to do it as if it delights you, as if it's a sweet and sexy and pretty thing, then you have to understand that you've already taken me into your arms and kissed me. Kissed me in a way that makes me understand it's just me, me alone, you're kissing. That's a feeling I don't get very often. I am too pretty for that, if you want to know the truth of it. I walk in the street and I get two kinds of looks, the look that strips me naked, hard, right away, what a fuckable cunt of a woman just like the one who passed by a moment ago and just like all the others, and the look that hits me hard across the face and throws me to the ground and kicks me in the ribs, wanting to kick me between the legs but holding back because any touch there, any touch, would be unthinkable, and I'm not talking about just the hard hats stripping me and just the fish-on-the-lapels knocking me down, I can see the slick smiles and the big hellos and the hey-sweet-ladies and the haven't-we-met-befores stripping me too and making me just like all the rest they've stripped and even if they were to touch me in physical ways that you'd think were the deepest possible, they'd never have a clue about me, never even walk on the same planet with me, and I can see the thin mouths and the sharp shifts of the eyes and the pulse at the temples knocking me down too and it doesn't even have to do with religion, at least that's a clear cause that has nothing to do with me, but worse are the ones where whatever it is that I look like makes them angry and they don't know why, they just feel a swell of anger when they see me, and both kinds are the same in a way, both want so bad to be part of something they see as beautiful but they can't, they can't, and it hurts them bad, it makes them grab and grab and never hold anything or it makes them look away and tremble and hate and both kinds are all alone and I know that and I guess I should pity all of them, the poor sons of bitches, but it makes things real difficult for me, every goddamn day of my life. And so, Ira, if you touch my elbow and I know that it's my elbow you're touching and I look in your eyes and they're seeing me and you ask me to do this thing with my hair that for me is a nattering little voice in me going, You're a foolish thing an empty thing how do you expect anybody to see anything in you, and you clearly love it, Ira, your eyes are telling me that, then how can you put your hands in your pockets at a moment like this and act like you haven't started this whole thing?*

And of course she's right. And now I have to face what it was that I was doing. I was in love with Samantha, just as I am in love with so many others. I was married to Fiona, and I still loved her, too, though things had changed even more for us at the moment Sam stood before me at my office door, and I haven't gotten to that, those months following the night Fiona went to confess, but that's maybe on purpose because no matter what she'd done, I was still married to her and Sam was still married to Harry and I don't want to portray myself in any way but a truthful way, I'm doing the best that I can to tell the truth, I'm trying as much as is possible to speak what happens inside me and what I do, and I can't hide behind this passivity shit anymore, I guess, though it is also true that I still waited before Sam and it is true that part of me was saying,

If I wait just a little bit longer it will pass; you've already brought it this far but you can wait just a little longer and maybe those things you have so much trouble controlling will just get confused because nothing is going on and they'll burrow back inside.

So when Sam said that my seeing her put her hair on her upper lip was not all I needed, I kept my hands in my pockets—feeling like a hypocrite, yes, feeling like a coward, yes, but I kept them there—and I said, "I'm trying to figure all that out."

She wrinkled her brow and I knew I was hurting her and if it wasn't in the same way the others hurt her, then that just made it worse. And, to be honest, Sam stood before me and I looked at her upper lip, left naked by the lock of hair falling away, and there was a mustache of faint blond fuzz there and I knew that her habit had something to do with that, covering up the one part of her that she did not feel feminine about, and the tenderness I felt for her at this sucked my hands from my pockets and all the pretty posing I'd always watched her do and all the sharp-edged talk and her mind and her heart, all the complications there, and the voice of her in my head, all of Sam, all of her, was kissable in that moment right there, right on her faint blond mustache, her mustache that I could clearly see was beautiful, and so I bent to her and she lifted her face and her lips parted to return my kiss but I said softly, "Wait," and she closed her mouth, her brow knitting again, and I bent nearer and I kissed her upper lip, drew my tongue along her lip, feeling the soft brush of the fuzz all along, and she sighed a pretty, almost inaudible sigh but it rippled through her body and I felt the slip of her breath on my tongue and then we made love.

And I could not imagine this happening, my making love to Sam, when I sat on the floor waiting for Fiona to return, though I thought of Sam then and yearned for her, and once it did happen I could not imagine it happening only once, not by my choice, though it did, only once and it was because of me. For when Fiona came home that night she was very happy, or seemed on the surface to be. She came and I had not moved and she did not notice that I had not moved though it had been an hour or more and she came and sat beside me and she said, "It worked, Ira. Like they said it would, I confessed and I was forgiven, this saint of a priest put up with me, put up with my hysterics in the booth and I think I may have put my toe through the paneling in there or something because I was kicking it when I talked and I didn't even know it until he said what's that noise, what's happening do you think? That's when I understood and I stopped and I said not to worry it wasn't the king's men come to martyr him, he was a saint already and didn't need that, and he didn't laugh and then I confessed even saying that, because it was a stupid thing to say, and he forgave me for that too and the good thing was I couldn't even see him, they have an old-fashioned confessional booth there and I just sat sideways and there was this wall between us and you knew that it could never fall down. He couldn't see me and he couldn't touch me and he forgave me. I'm going on, aren't I?"

With this she stopped and waited for me to answer. I looked at her and in spite of her words her face seemed very calm, her eyes were steady on me. "You're excited," I said.

"Yes," she said. "Yes I am, Ira. Ira you've got to go to confession."

"Me?"

"Of course you. It's a sacrament. If it works for me, it works for you."

"I don't know."

Her hand came out and grasped my arm, hard. "You want me to survive in this life, don't you, Ira? You want me to have a chance in the next one, don't you?"

I had no real answer for that, of course, except yes, though the conclusions that would flow from that premise scared the hell out of me.

"If these things are true," she said, "these sacraments, this Church, then they have to be true absolutely. You follow that, don't you?"

"Yes."

"God and His son and heaven and hell and the things the Church can do about all that, these things by their very nature can't be optional, now can they? They're either true and they work or they're lies and they don't."

I was trying to hear her voice inside me at that moment, trying hard, the voice that came to me, I knew, from the deep connection of sex, her pussy voice whispering to me, but I had nothing in my head, just these perfectly logical words, spoken in an uninflected, firm voice, and so I tried to focus on her face, on the wide mouth moving now because it was also the mouth that held me inside, held the head of my penis so often when I was entirely present there, when all of me had collected there, but her mouth was in shadow and I could hear the words, going on now, though I did not answer her.

"If they're lies and they don't work," she was saying, "then I don't know what I can do except die, except just disappear somehow from the planet Earth. Are you following this, Ira? But they're *not* lies, that's what I know from tonight. The Church is right. I'd been hoping this was true for months but now I know it's true because tonight I was forgiven. You're not going to take that away from me, are you? If I were to live with a husband and a son who didn't completely under-stand that these things were absolutely true, then how am I supposed to survive that? If you aren't with me on this, then either you're right and I'm a fucking fool and I'm lost or you're wrong and then I've got to think that the man I love and the child I love are going to hell. Tell me how that's going to work, Ira? Tell me."

I was breathing fast, I realized, panting softly, and Gio was before me and I wanted her very badly, wanted to take her in my arms and kiss her all along the fold of her Asian eyes and

I wanted to lift her and let her put her arms around me and her head on my shoulder and I wanted to walk out the door with her and into the afternoon sun and down the road, past the interrogation cells, and she would keep her eyes closed and her face against my chest and I would walk to my jeep and place her gently inside and I would drive away and the Aussie and the Vietnamese captain would come running, astonished, but I would be accelerating and they would be far away, blurred in the dust cloud behind me and she would be safe then, she would be safe and then it would be all right for her to open her blouse and strip off her clothes and I would run after her naked into a paddy and we would fall laughing into the water among the green shoots of the rice. But I could not do that, I knew, and so I leaned near her and I said, "Talk to me some more. Please. Tell me about the strong wind in you." I loved her and I wanted to hear her voice and I wanted to think about her strength.

But then a terrible thing happened. She confessed. She looked at me and her chest heaved once, as if she'd given up some hard struggle, and she looked out the window and said, "I was meant to fight for the people and for the expulsion of all imperialists from our country." And though she spoke of the thing in her that she knew was strong, this was a gentle little sigh of a confession, as if she expected me to touch her cheek and tell her I understood.

But I was afraid for her. "Why are you saying this to me?" I said and it wasn't a question at all, the rebuke of it was clear in my voice.

She looked at me and smiled. "You sound like my oldest brother when you talk."

"Oh Christ," I said and her hands were quiet in her lap and I put mine over hers and then I pulled them back because I was lifting strongly to her, I would soon take her into my arms but I knew that this was a moment when my love for her, if it was as real as my penis insisted it was, had a more important immediate expression. "I wasn't trying to make you confess," I said.

"I know that. That's why I could tell you."

"So you won't say it again. Okay?"

Her brow furrowed and I wanted to let my hand go out and smooth it away but what I had to do was harder than that, I knew.

"Please," I said. "You have to understand what's going on here."

"Do you think I'm a fool?" she said, though her rebuke was soft-edged. "I know what's going on."

"Then don't say these things again. You're a cook. You don't know about anything but cooking rice."

"I'm tired," she said. "This has all been very hard for me and I'm very tired. It was time to say these things and get it over with." And Gio looked away from me again and I was instantly aware of the smell of the sea, coming from beyond the mountains, and the smell had faded from my attention for a time but now it came rolling back into me and I knew it was because Gio was smelling it at that moment, I was inside her skin in that moment and I sensed what she sensed and then I saw Betty's face from my dreams, her mouth on my penis and her eyes rolling back and she was dying and if I had not loved her, if I had not been part of her coming to the tower to prostitute herself, would she have lived? And the answer was no, she would still have done what she did and there were always others to offer themselves to her but they did not love her and I did, I loved Betty and I loved Gio but she was going to die, too, I realized, die soon, die from this confession of hers that she could finally bring herself to speak because of me, because I loved her and the first time was always the hardest and she needed someone who would be gentle with her the first time and I was gentle because I loved her and so she gave herself to me, gave me this confession and gave me her life, and I didn't know it would be like that, I didn't know

I would make it easier for her now to give these things again, to others, to the men who did not love her and who would kill her and she lifted the blue cloth to her face now, blocked out the sea and the sunlight and she began to quake slightly, she was weeping.

And I said, "Gio, stop. You've got to keep fighting. Look at me."

The quaking ceased. But she kept her face covered.

I said, "I'm one of those imperialists. Look at my face. I'm an American. You can't talk that way to me. I would kill you. You know that. You never said those things. You never said anything at all. I'm going to tell them that. Please. You're a goddamn cook."

And still she did not look at me, and then I couldn't bear to look at her. I rose and I walked away to the window and I stood at the window of the glassed-in porch in Seaview and Fiona said, "You walk away from me? Is that your answer? Is that how it's going to work?"

"Do I have to give you an answer right this minute?" I said without turning and I could hear her jump up. And she was right, of course. It was like my pausing to count the women I'd made love to. If I stopped and counted, then they were still alive inside me, they were all there and it took time to sort them all out. I had to say two, I had to say three, I had to say that's all there ever was but she was the only one. She was right behind me, I knew, I could feel her there but she wasn't making a sound and I needed time to think and there was something else now, there was a cleft hoof pressing into the center of my chest and I suddenly knew what it was and it was her inclusion of John in this whole thing: how could she bear it if her husband *and her son* didn't agree with these cosmic truths that she depended on in order to live? I needed time and so I turned to her and I was right, she was there, I had to rear back to keep from bumping her over and she was rigid before me, her face lifted, waiting, and when I pressed back against the window, there was more to it than I'd expected, there was this much more: I didn't want to touch her at all, I didn't want to touch her in the slightest way, I knew that some part of me now had to begin to fight this or I would die.

This story is not about my son. It should already be clear from what I've said that I loved him from the very first, loved him more than I could ever have imagined I would. I still dream about him running across the grass with the shadow of the plane silently pursuing him. I dream about all that and I wake in a sweat even now that he is no longer a child, now that he is becoming a young man. But what it is I'm trying to do with these words is to understand the yearning in me that never stops. That and also to capture forever the landscape inside me, capture it as if in the wild swirl of color of the Van Goghs that Fiona pondered on that afternoon when we first made love, her face lifted to the sunlight. And I'm trying also to figure out how to live from this moment on.

This is not really about my son, but my love for him will shape my story for a time like a star curves space and time around it. It was John in my mind when I pressed back against the window and faced Fiona's logic and I could hear the static on the intercom in the kitchen, and my little guy was hiding in that sound, he was sleeping somewhere above me and he was still untouched by all of this and for now all I knew to do to keep it that way was to say to Fiona, as I did, "I will confess." She closed her eyes softly in relief at this and pressed forward and laid her head on my chest and she felt like Fiona and she smelled like Fiona and she made a faint exhalation of contentment that was also Fiona, I realized, realized for the first time that this was a sound I'd heard often from her but only at that moment did I consciously recognize it, I recognized it at the very same moment when also for the first time I could find no impulse in me to embrace her, me, Ira Holloway, who lives on a planet full of women who, even as strangers, if they were to embrace me, would instantly open my eyes to them, would show me their lovely particularities and would move my body and my mind and my heart to love them. And yet, though this woman with her head on my chest felt like the Fiona whom I already loved—loved still, even then, really—though she felt like her and smelled like her and sounded in that faint exhalation of breath like her, my arms refused to lift to her, I did not feel any desire for her. There had always been passing moments when I was not inclined to let my abiding desire for her be expressed, of course. In the midst of one of her rages, for instance, in the midst of a public grimness that would lead to a rage, but that was always a temporary withdrawal, I knew, like having a headache or being too tired and it *never* happened when she was being loving herself and I *never* sensed the absence of the desire to desire her. This feeling as she held me now was something else. I stood with her arms around me and her head on my chest and I did not feel even the possibility of desire for her. Not tonight, certainly, and beyond that I had no idea what my feeling would be. And surely this wasn't a thing that happened all of a sudden. But it felt like it. All of a sudden. On the night she said I had to confess. And perhaps that was it. She wanted my confession, and though it was not a confession I would make to her and I would never speak it even to a priest, even when I went to the church and she was beside me, her hand hooked in my arm and smiling at me with motherly encouragement, and she knelt in the pew to pray as I went into the booth, not even then did I think to confess this thing aloud. But to myself there, with Fiona's arms around me, I confessed it to myself. Forgive me Ira for I have sinned, I have failed to maintain my passion for a woman, in spite of hers for me.

And Fiona said, "Let's go upstairs now. I want to make love with you for the first time without guilt."

Was that really possible for her that night? Had the Church really given her the peace she sought? If I had been able to follow her up the stairs and make love to her at once, smoothly, as I had done hundreds of times before, if I had whispered to her as she came, You are beautiful, my Fiona, and now God has made you whole, if I had whispered that and she could see before her a life with her husband and son at her side in the church where the creator of the universe could touch her and tell her she was okay, she was forgiven, she was worth the breath she drew, if I could have done just those few things on that night, would it all have turned out differently? If I could have done it, I would. Not that I could have been content with the-husband-and-the-son-at-her-side part of it, if it meant my embracing forever as true whatever beliefs she found useful to her. And particularly not if it meant being part, even by my silent complicity, of the effort to shape John's mind to those same beliefs. Surely Fiona and I were already doomed on that night as I climbed the stairs behind her barely able to lift one leg after another even if I could have willed my body to want her again, want her right then. I don't like to think that after all I'd done to try to convince Fiona she was both loved by me and worth her own love, that I had a chance to make it all okay for her and all I needed to do was have one more goddamn erection, a thing that has always come so easily and naturally to me, all my life. But I was slack on the stairs, slack and dead in the center of me, and I followed her into the bedroom and I glanced once across the hall at the closed door of my son's room and I felt the sudden scrabble of panic in me because I had to keep that door closed to what was about to happen and a great chasm of future years cracked open before me and by the time I was in the bedroom and Fiona was turning to me and pulling off her sweater, I had gone one step too far and I was poised over that darkness and there was no way to call my step back and her sweater was gone in a breathtaking second and so was her blouse and so was her bra, and her nipples were still beautiful, I suppose—of course they were—but they meant nothing to me, absolutely nothing, and she knew instantly.

"Oh dear God," she said and it sounded like a real prayer.

I had no reply. I had already managed to close our bedroom door behind me and for that I was grateful because now I could not move.

Fiona crossed her arms on her breasts, covering her nipples, and she closed her eyes and I think she was waiting, just as I was, to see what she would do. I was on the verge of challenging her: if the Catholic vision of the universe that she expected John and me to build our own lives around was so absolutely true and it had totally captivated her in the confessional on this night, shouldn't it be effective for at least an hour, shouldn't it be able to keep her whole before the mere silence of my cock? A silence that she had no reason to believe was anything but temporary? Could my cock so easily overcome the Church and its sacraments? Her arms jumped away from her body and spread wide and exposed her nipples again and then her hands leapt back at her breasts, clawing at them, and I was finally able to move, I was before her and I grabbed her hands away and there were three parallel slash lines down each breast and she was very strong now and fighting to free her hands and she spit in my face and she cried out, cried wordlessly at first and then cried words about how I'd wanted this all along, wanted to take away any real peace she might have, wanted to make her sin and sin and sin and never be forgiven and if I was going to do this, she would take John and disappear and never divorce me because divorce was a sin, the Church taught that and the Church taught that the child must grow up in the faith, the child must have faith or he too would be damned just as she was, just as I wanted her to be, but if she had to burn in hell then she would do it alone if need be, she would never let her child burn there too.

I held on tight to her hands and I let these words flare past me and the word God is like the word pussy or the word cunt, full of sound and connotation that are ridiculously far from the thing you're trying to name, and the word prayer, too, and if I tell you that I said a prayer to God right then, you have to realize that it had nothing to do with anything Fiona understood about all that or anything the Roman Catholic Church or any other church understood, but it is an interesting irony that even as I recoiled in some deep place from Fiona because of God and prayer, I prayed to God to give me some way to survive this life that I'd been led to, survive without offering my only son up to sacrifice. I said this prayer not in words in my head but as a kind of focused resistance to the thrashing that threatened to seize my limbs and my voice and make me thump and wail and accuse just like Fiona, just like her, and then we'd both be lost, we'd all three be lost and then I was given this: Fiona struggled still to free her hands and I was about to let them go and fist my own and she dipped her head and I saw Gio, I turned from the window after walking away from her confession and she was sitting in the chair and the blue cloth was coming down from her face and her head dipped and Fiona said I am a dead woman and Gio said nothing but I knew she was a dead woman and their two heads were angled just so, just exactly so and I moved to Gio and I cupped my hand and gently brought it forward and I touched my fingertips very lightly to the point of her chin and she let me raise her face and she looked up at me with a look of a woman who was holding my penis in her mouth and I shuddered and she felt it through my fingertips and she took my cupped hand and lifted it and kissed my palm. I took Fiona's wrist and I lifted it and I kissed it on the spot of her pulse and Gio kissed my wrist there too and I pulled her up to me and I held my two women then, brought them to me and they felt desperately fragile in my arms but I held them close, afraid I might crush their bones but unable to hold back my strength, angry with Gio that she would confess, angry with Fiona that she would confess, and I kissed them and I undressed them, holding the kiss but moving their hands, helping out with the slip of cloth that bared the sweet pouting of their pussies and I felt their feet moving about mine, kicking off the cloth crumpled there and I carried them both to the bed there in Seaview and I laid them down in it and they were breathing heavily already before I lay down beside them, before I touched the part of them that smelled like the sea and I knew that the heavy drag of their breathing was only partly from their own feelings like mine, the yearning to join hard flesh to soft, soft to hard, and as for the rest of it, the dark draw of the death they sensed was near, I could not touch that and it made me yearn even more to be inside them.

And that was what I was given when I myself came to a thing in me that felt like death and when I said something that amounted to a prayer and it got me through that moment and it gave me something to do thereafter but it became a disturbing thing really quickly. I loved the women who lived in me but they were uniquely themselves, they lived in that landscape together but when I encountered them, they were solely who they were and they were no one else and when I was with a woman in this other life we all recognize, in the now, then I was with that woman and that woman alone and that was the only way a new woman could begin to live inside me and even though I had already been with Fiona many times like that, when it was only her, it disturbed me now that she had to disappear when I was making love to her, had to, could not be there, and that was so, that was certifiably so, I drove Fiona to her fits and her confessions three or four times, in the few weeks that followed, by trying to go back, by trying to be with her alone when I made love to her, by saying to myself, Enough, enough, this is Fiona, this woman with the rosary now in her hand and with the missal and with the lowered face and quaking chest who kneels waiting for the confessional and with the full eyes and gaunt radiance who emerges nodding yes, yes, I am whole once more, this is Fiona, I said to myself, and I said, This is my wife and I must find a way to make love to her so she does not go mad and maybe if I loved her enough, then the other things, the cosmic truths, would sit easily in her and she would not expect me to believe it all, would not desperately shape our son to believe it all. And so I tried three or four times to make love to her without reference to the women in my head and it never worked, it never ever worked again that way. I always had to find a woman from inside me— someone from the past, someone I saw in the street that day or on the train—and that would be the woman my flesh filled for, yearned for, as I entered Fiona. And the worst thing was that Fiona began to affect the others, she began to linger just on the edge of my memories, even when I was alone, even when I was sitting on the commuter train maybe a month later and I rested my cheek against the window and it was snowing outside and it was dark already though I knew it was still early in the evening and we raced through Queens and I saw the lit windows and I could see some woman moving there in a window, just briefly, a woman with long hair shaking it down and when I saw that woman and began to yearn toward her, Fiona was there too, she was beneath me, waiting to be part of the moment. I closed my eyes, as if I could block Fiona out that way, and I watched the image from just moments ago, the shaking of long hair and the snow falling between us, I focused only on that, and for a time it was just as it had always been and I was with that new woman there, listening to the steam pipes clank and glancing into the dark at the blur of train windows out there, then they were gone and I could smell her hair and this was the sort of connection that I wanted, one woman at a time inside me, for summoned by the passing image in Queens was a woman once in winter, a Chicago winter, and I did not know her name, I met her in a bar on Rush Street and this was long ago, many winters ago, I was still in college, and she was maybe thirty-five to my twenty, maybe forty, a beautiful forty and this thought is only in retrospect, at the time she was solely a woman to me, solely a beautiful woman with hair corded long down her back and she took me to her apartment and it was dark in the room and it was snowing outside and we were near the El tracks and the trains passed every twenty minutes at that time of night, slowed for a curve just outside and whined past and I lay on her bed and watched the flash of lit windows go by and the snowflakes flickering in the train lights and she rose up on her knees beside me and lifted her face and shook down her hair which she had loosened to make love to me and her hair was black and it was profuse and it smelled like sheets dried in the sun and even with the memory of all that on the Long Island Rail Road train, even with my eyes closed and resisting any other intrusion, even having not thought of this woman for years much less used her to make me erect for my religious wife, I felt Fiona's breath on my face, heard her panting, nasal now to my ear, nasal and thin and preoccupied, and I wanted only the woman from the bar and I was hard even there on the train and she felt me touch her hair and she looked over her shoulder as the El train raced away and the room grew as quiet as the snow and I could see her smile in the dim light and then she looked down and saw my newest erection and she whispered, Boys, and Fiona whispered, My boy, and she jumped up from the bed with my sperm on her thighs and she'd heard something in the static that worried her and she was gone and this had happened just last night and not with the woman in Chicago, not her at all, but now there was Fiona slipping out from under my memory of the bed in the dark in the winter by the El and I opened my eyes to the train car and I shuddered a little bit at the thought of my sperm on Fiona and that had been new, that had been a bizarre new reaction, the shudder, and I laid my head back and I needed to deal with this in some other way. I would keep my long-haired woman from the bar out of Fiona's bed and all the women from my abiding landscape, as well, I would try to choose others, others that I had to sacrifice for this thing, the woman across the aisle, for instance, dozing, her face turned this way, her chin cleft and her eyes large, large enough for me to see them moving in her dream, and I would bring her face into my mind tonight and she would wake and we would watch each other and then get off at the next station and that might help, letting the woman do this thing that would be tainted by the touching of Fiona before she became important to me, but already I was afraid that there was a limit to all of this.

But for now all I knew is that I'd used Gio again last night and I'd done that several times already and it was a mistake. I couldn't do that again, even though I'd always summoned up the same scene as on the night of the first confession, the night it all began, the night I began making love with women in my head so that I could seem to make love to Fiona. I used the same scene of Gio looking up and then kissing the palm of my hand and then my making love to her on the floor of the in-terrogation room and that was a lie, the scene was a lie. In fact I turned to the window and Gio was quiet behind me and the Australian captain saw me in the window and he was standing with the Vietnamese interrogator by a jeep in the square and the Aussie flipped up his chin to ask if it was time for them to come back and I did not have sense enough to shake my head no, I simply turned my back to him and I faced Gio once more and the blue cloth was coming down from her face and her head dipped and she said nothing but I knew she was a dead woman. But I did not go to her and touch her chin and lift her face and I did not make love to her though I wonder if I had whether I could have persuaded her to live. Instead I just repeated the empty words I'd said before about her needing to lie to these other men now, and it wasn't enough. I knew, even as I spoke those words, that what she really needed was to be touched, what she needed was to have a connection to this world she was ready to leave. But I did nothing and then the two men were at the door and she looked up at them and she looked at me and I was about to announce that she knew nothing, that she was innocent, those words were shaping in my mouth and I think Gio knew it and she said in English, "Fuck you all."

And the Aussie and the Vietnamese interrogator looked at me with a glance like I'd done a good thing, I'd provoked her this far at least and they knew that she was done for, and they didn't even realize the half of it. I pressed past them and outside and I walked heavy-footed to the jeep and waited sweating in the sun and the Aussie was with me shortly and he slapped me on the back and he asked didn't I want to see the rest— she was about to open up in there thanks to me and I said no I'd seen enough and he said, Right mate I kind of respect the bastards myself, and then we drove off. I left the Australians at the end of that week and before I went, I asked the Aussie officer if he'd heard what happened to the young woman. He hadn't and when I got back to Homestead I was ready a dozen times to write the man and find out more, but I didn't. On the first night that I used Gio to make love with Fiona, I lay beside my wife afterward and she had turned on her back without a word and she was still very unhappy and I looked at the ceiling and Gio was dead, I knew, long dead, she'd been sucked dry of all she could say and it would never be enough and whatever they wanted to know after that—where the COSVN headquarters was, when the next big offensive would take place, how long Ho Chi Minh's dick was, whatever—if she didn't know those things, they'd do her in, one way or another, they'd end up killing her and it was what she was ready for and Fiona said next to me, "I've got to go back now, you know. I couldn't have even one full hour of grace before I had to go back."

"Go back where?" I asked, though I guess I knew, if I'd been willing to think about it for even a few seconds, but I wasn't willing, Gio was dead and I wasn't willing at all and I guess I went on from that night to use her again and again, making love to her in my mind to keep this other woman whole, as a kind of sympathetic magic, as if it would bring Gio back from where I knew she had to be.

"Confession," Fiona hissed.

"Isn't that the point," I said, "that you can keep doing it? You don't run out of chances?"

Fiona rolled onto her other side, facing me, and propped her head up on her hand. I thought I was in trouble again but she said, "That's good, Ira. That's good." Then the suspicion returned. "If you really mean it."

"I really mean it," I said.

"But you're going to try to help me in all this, aren't you?" She brought her face close to mine and I held myself still, stifled the impulse to recoil from her. And the next day was Saturday and she caught John and me in the backyard and he was walking me around the yard and he was naming the things he saw, just as Fiona and I had named things for him all his life. He held my hand and led me around and he said, pointing to a tree stump at the corner of the fence, "See, Daddy, this is a frixnack."

"Yes?" I said. "Yes? Is that what it is?"

"Can you say that, Daddy? Frixnack."

"Frixnack."

"Good," he said, and then he took me to a stack of wooden tomato-plant spikes and he said, "See? These are wibbles."

"Wibbles," I said.

"Yes," he said. "Good."

And Fiona was in the back door and she said, "It's time to go to Mass. We have confession."

John looked up at me for an explanation. This was Saturday, he knew, the day we had together without interference and we had gone to Mass only on Sunday mornings before this and he always sat on my lap and combed the missal for words he knew, trying to whisper them to me when he found them only to be shushed by Fiona. "They have church on Saturday too," I said to him.

He nodded gravely but turned to the stack of spikes. "I've got wibbles to fix on Saturdays."

I crouched beside him and I began something that would last for years, that would sustain us both for years. "My little guy," I said, very low. "We have to have a little secret now."

He turned to me avidly.

"Mommy needs to do some things in the church and we have to go along. Okay? It's important for Mommy and we can't say no. Not ever. But you and I will have some secrets about all of that. Just you and me. Okay?" I did not plan these words. I would have been afraid, if I had planned them, that it was too early. If John ever let on to Fiona that he and I had something hidden from her on these matters of her survival, then things would go very bad very fast.

But John looked at me closely and then looked at Fiona in the doorway and she was brooding there already, she was grim and waiting to go seek her absolution and John had seen this in her already, he'd asked me once what was wrong with Mommy and I'd said she was worried, and he looked at her now and he said, "Just you and me?"

"Yes."

"What's one secret?"

I flailed about for something to begin. Something small, but not trivial. If this was going to work, he had to understand it was important. And John was special. He was already special and he was going to have to be special all his child's life, I knew. "Mommy's sadness," I said. "She has to go to a place at the church and talk with a priest about that, and you'll see me go in there too. But I'm not really there for the same reason as Mommy."

John cocked his head at this.

"I'll tell you more some other time. Some of the secrets will also be puzzles."

I was still crouched beside him and he sidled closer and put his arm around my shoulder and he whispered, "Okay," and I nearly wept. My eyes filled quickly but the secret behind the tears would be too puzzling to explain to him for many years and I worked to hold them back. Then Fiona said, "What's going on? What are you talking about? It's time to go," and her voice wiped the tears away and I rose with my son beside me and we crossed the lawn.

And we went to church and to confession and it wasn't just Fiona and me, with her hand hooked in my arm, and the fetid motherliness of her there was not just for me but was for our son as well, and we climbed the steps into the white clapboard matron of Our Lady of the Sorrows and the place smelled of the wood pews and wood beams, the fiber-deep musty smell of wood a hundred and fifty years dead, and Fiona was bent to John and explaining God and sin and redemption and this would go on and she would never weary of it and it was like the string of words on the index cards that she'd been teaching him since before he even decided to walk. Like me, she never acknowledged how young he was, and though he clearly had special gifts from birth, maybe the most important thing that made him a prodigy was that he was never treated as anything else, he was made to see all that was going on around him sooner than most other children, and he did seem always to hear, he did seem always to understand so much, and this specialness of him scared me and never stopped scaring me, not for years, because Fiona was constantly teaching him an institutionally religious way of understanding the universe and I could not take for granted that he would sort it all out for himself, that if he was destined for a religious belief, it would be truly his own; I was afraid that at the heart of it, it would just be Fiona and her madness putting the universe on index cards and him accepting it with no more choice about the matter than he had for the cards for cat and dog and umbrella and run and jump—the yellow-knuckled priest had even used the old saying in a homily, straight, sincere, hopeful, without irony, that all the Church needed was to have the child till he was seven years old and you could never take him away after that—and we moved beneath the vault of the ceiling and I knew—as it was intended—that the lift of it was supposed to catch you in the chest and lift you with it and I saw John glance up a couple of times at it, as he always did when he came in here, and it was working on him, I feared, working on him, shaping him beyond his own will, his own self, and then we were kneeling in a pew and Fiona said, "I'll go first," and she looked at John and said, "That's the confessional I was telling you about," and she nodded to the double-doored booth and its wood facade had a wide grain, great dripping teardrops of wood grain and she rose and crossed herself and she disappeared into the left-hand door and a red light went on over it like it was dangerous in there, like there was radiation, and John watched her go in and then I was given a little sign. He got up from his knees where Fiona had put him, down deep in the shadow of the pews, and he climbed up on the seat and put his arm around me again and he nodded toward the place where his mother had disappeared and he said, "That's the muckyfussal I was telling you about."

"So that's it," I whispered back.

"Yes," he said. "And always remember to go like this when you're in there." And John touched the forefinger and middle finger of his right hand first to his forehead—I thought briefly that he would make the sign of the cross Fiona had drilled him on just moments ago—but then the two fingers went to his nose and then to his chin and then down to his belly—right onto the belly button, I realized—and he made a little quacking sound, very solemnly, this last from a game he and I played together before sleep. The quack button.

"Can you do that?" he asked.

"I can, but it will be one of our secrets and we can't let anyone see it."

He looked around at the scattering of elderly women mumbling rosaries and he said, "Okay. You do it in there," and he nodded toward the muckyfussal and I had reason to hope from all of this that I had a chance with him if I could just stay near.

And soon Fiona was beside us, kneeling for her rosaries of penance, her prayers to the Virgin Mary, and she was already a little uneasy about that part of it, I think, because she didn't seem to notice that John was no longer kneeling but was standing beside me in the pew and there would be years ahead when she couldn't tolerate that, the very position of our knees and our butts in these pews being a test of our acceptance or rejection of the truths she needed to make her whole. But Mary made her uneasy.

I sensed that very early on, though it was a long time before she would speak of it at all. The woman in this religion made Fiona very uneasy and it would cause her a great deal of pain for a time. She would talk to me about the doctrines, explain how clear it all was, how crazy she was not to have seen it all along, since she grew up in the Church, but she told me only as much as I needed to know to be at her side and to appear to agree with it all and she never spoke the painful words aloud—perhaps she couldn't have even if she'd wanted to— but I heard them anyway: *I don't know what she's doing there so often in the center of things. This Mary. This mother. I didn't come to this thing for a mother. A mother isn't what I need. I know what I need. I know who it was that God offered. The Church says that, too, and I'm trying to keep this all straight, but it seems hard to reconcile this thing. It's Him up there on the cross. His eyes are big and deep and they fall to us in pain. The cross right outside the confessional booth, on the south wall. The eyes there. He's the one who understands. His hands are nailed down and He can't touch me but I can touch Him and if I do, I'm cured. That's the deal. But the priest says, Ask the Holy Mother for help. Pray these rosary prayers to the Holy Mother and she will intercede for you with her son. And I say to the priest how about some more prayers to the son, and the priest says the heavenly father sent Mary to us at Lourdes and at Fatima to encourage us, to give us faith in this faithless age, and this is your penance for your sins, to pray these rosaries to our Blessed Mother. And I'm squirming around in the booth and I'm trying to be obedient but it's not easy and I'm trying to see God looking around heaven in 1917 or whenever it was at Fatima and He says, This faithless age needs some faith so I'm going to create this miraculous appearance to some Portuguese children and I've got to figure out who to send. And He looks around and He sees Jesus, who you'd think would be the logical choice in that situation, but God says no, you had a shot at it, my son, and the world is still faithless, let's let your fucking mother give it a try. Forgive me, Father, for I have sinned. I have let God call Mary a fucking mother and I know she never did fuck and so I have told this lie, mea culpa, mea maxima culpa, but she missed her big chance like any fucking mother and what I want to know was where was she when the house was burning down, and the answer is that she was out in the street saving her own ass and we always ate dinner at a big cherrywood table and my father's hand would come over to me and it would pinch my shoulder when I said something cute or it would touch my cheek and my mother was far away, down at the other end and she was cutting her meat into such neat pieces, such tiny neat pieces, that she had to concentrate very hard on that and later, a few fucking years later, when the night would come and my father would wave me to him and put me on his lap and kiss me good night and he would wink at me to let me know it was okay, I wouldn't be alone tonight, she was across the room and she was easing her needle through a stitch and her forefinger came up and wound round and the needle waited*

*to pull out and she did this over and over and she bent near
and she could not see any fucking thing but this needle going
in and coming out and my father was too big for her, too,
maybe, and he was too messy for her and she leapt up from
the table when a water glass went over and her lap was wet
and she cried out as if in pain as if in terrible pain and she
would not let herself be wet there and I was the one who'd
have to pay for that, mother of purity, mother of virginity,
mother of sorrows, and I'm sorry, I say to the priest, and I
want to say to him, I'm sorry but I can't pray to my fuckless
mother, but instead I say, I'm sorry but I've just sinned again,
I've been willful and disobedient and I've lied and the priest
answers, You are forgiven go and sin no more and say five
rosaries and a hundred Hail Marys and three Lord's Prayers,
and I say okay I say thank you Father and maybe a year later
I say to Ira, Let's go to this place tonight, it's a Wednesday-
night prayer meeting and don't be shocked, I say, because it's
not Catholic, but there's truth there, it's important and Ira
does that thing with his brow, the brow I used to love so much
but I can't look at anymore, I can't look at it when I'm making
love with him because it makes me think of the times when I
say something that I know is true, something that it's been
crazy for me to miss all these years and now that I know it, it
will help me, it will make me well, but his brow does a thing,
a quick little furrowing in the middle, just for a moment and
he tries to keep it from me but I can see it, I can notice all the
little things, all the tiny sloppy little things that can drive a
woman crazy and he does it when I tell him about the prayer
meeting, but we go, the three of us, and it's a brick building
and it's Full Gospel, it says on the sign, and there are three
or four of these people around us at once when we walk in
and John lets go of my hand and the women in front of me
have great rolls of hair on the top of their heads and hair nets
over them and I know that if they let the hair down it would
reach to their cracks and it's because of the Bible, they say,*

when I remark on what wonderful hair they all seem to have, the Bible says not to cut your hair, and this is complicated enough, I think, to have to be concerned with that, I have trouble with that, and John has slipped past them and they watch him go by and they smile at him and he stands in the doorway of the sanctuary and it's a plain little place and I'm afraid John will say something, my sweet little John who already seems so holy, who seems so much like a little priest in the making, and I know that's what I want for him, as soon as I think that, I want him to be a priest, and I want to accept it all, I need to accept it all, but I have no feeling for the Mother of God stuff, never will, I know, and I look around at these smiling faces and I am being swept along into the sanctuary and I look up and the cross over the altar is empty and I don't know what to think of this right away. John is lagging behind, grabbing onto Ira now, and I stop and turn and watch them and they are both taking in the place and I love them very much at that moment because I can see they aren't at home here, they are clinging to each other and they are so much at ease in the Catholic church but not here and they have such good instincts, I believe that, they have such good instincts, they're such good Catholics and now I've brought them to this place because of my own sins, because I am sinning against God by not accepting the woman He chose for veneration, but it's hard, it's very hard, when I hold the rosary beads in my hands, I don't feel right, these beads want to take over the center of things and this is how I see it, this is why I have come back to the church: human beings were born to worship. We have no choice in that matter. Everyone worships something. I mean by worship that we put something in the center of us. We have to, to make a decision about anything. Do I get up in the morning and go in to the bathroom or do I lie in the bed all day and into the night and the next day and on and on until I am too weak to live and if I go to the bathroom, do I brush my teeth or cut my throat and then do I go out and do this with my life or something else and do I speak to people in this or that sort of way and do I go to bed with this man or that or no man at all and do I try to get ahead or do I just get by, do I try to change things around me or do I turn my face away, and all that and more, everything, has to go back to something inside and whatever that is, inside there, the decisions are made because of it and that's worship, that's the only way to see it, even if all that's in there is the reflex to grab what you can and keep your body alive for another day, that's still worship, that's still something at the center, and if ancient Egypt worshiped cats, well I've known a few cat worshipers in Manhattan and there are plenty more in the city who I don't know but they've all got cats in the center of them, you find out what makes them happiest and what can make them saddest, what quickens them and what quiets them, what it is that they bend all the rest of their lives around, and it's cats. A woman at the gallery found love late in life, a sweet man, really, good and gentle and sweet, and he was allergic to her cat and they married and the cat stayed and the man's lungs filled and never emptied, he spent his life with her miserable in his body and the shots he took to fix it hurt like hell and didn't help and one year passed and two and it went on like this and the cat finally died and the woman wanted to let it be but someone gave her a kitten and she had to take it, could not refuse this little life, and the man stayed with her and she worshiped cats and he worshiped her and if there is, in fact, a sentience behind the universe, what we call God, then you've got a big problem with worshiping cats or football or money or fame or sex or anything else. If there is a God, then it's Him you have to worship, you can't put anything less at the center because He will come to you and find you and you won't even realize that there is smoke all around you, you've been fast asleep and there is smoke all around you and you haven't been seeing far enough, you've been lying there and you had no idea what was beyond and you have to pay for that, finally, and it's just as well if God comes and plucks you away from there, puts His hands upon you and plucks you away because behind all that smoke are the flames and it is hell, you understand, the flames of hell, and if you just lie there thinking that your bed is the whole universe, if you can't see anything beyond and sometimes somebody comes to your bed and puts his face in your cunt and you make him happy, that's all well and good, but there are flames out there in the smoke and somebody much more powerful waiting, waiting, and if you don't go to Him on your own, He'll come and snatch you up and carry you away with Him and at that point He might be really pissed. Rightly so. He created you, after all. And you gave yourself to a cat or a cut of beef or a few lousy bucks or a tongue in your cunt or a cock and He's the only one who should get that deep inside you, only Him. And I look at the empty cross over the altar and I stop cold, right there in the aisle, and I say something about it, not to the women with the long, rolled hair that are all around me, but just to myself, under my breath, and they must hear me because they pick up on it right away and they say, We worship Christ resurrected here, He has come down from the cross for us, and I say, He is still on the cross as long as we sin, we have to see Him and touch Him because we are still hurting Him, and I turn around and I say to Ira and John, I'm sorry, I've made a mistake, and I put my hands on them and I turn them around and we go out and I pray to be obedient, though I know that out there in the smoke the mother is really just looking out for herself like all the rest of us, but I can confess to the priest any anger at her, over and over, and I can just kind of stay out of her way the other times because I know why I'm in the Catholic Church and I turn my face on my pillow and I wait for His hands, open to them now, ready for them.

And on that late Saturday afternoon I confessed, I went into the booth to do the little routine and as I sat down and the panel door slid open on the priest's side of the screen, I was struck by the fact that my life was none of this man's goddamn business. It was in this that the Catholics were making a big mistake, I think, in not having women priests, at least for the men, at least for me in those years. That would have made things a little better. My life is certainly the business of any woman I love and I would love the women priests, I know, many of them, the young ones breaching from awkward youth and falling into corpulence and devotion, the older ones growing weary and growing deeply, quietly worried about what it is that they're doing, but all of them with their soft hands offering the wafer to my yearning tongue. But it was always a man on the other side of the screen and because my life was no man's business, I made up some sins for him—lies to my colleagues, shady business dealings, a great long public oath placing the names of God and Jesus and several of the saints in an obscene context—and these he forgave me for and he asked if there weren't any others, any sins of the flesh, and I did not say fuck you Father I said no Father the flesh is no problem for me and he said I was a man who was blessed and I said I often feel that way and I knew that until very recently this was true, I was blessed, and I still was, in some ways, because the great gentleness of the flesh of women was alive in my own landscape, the gentleness and the peace these women give that passeth all understanding, a peace that is of themselves and also is of far more, far more, since the Church has me thinking in these terms anyway, a peace from the sweet wet center of the universe and maybe the Church was right about God being love, for me, yes, perceivable here in women, and perhaps I sound overheated to you now, neoreligious even, caught up in the very terms that I was forced to assume with Fiona and that have now trapped me unawares. But that's the problem before me. I cannot shake the conviction that all that preoccupies me is important in some drastic way. And I get caught between one part of the world that has turned the whisper of our flesh into religious revulsion and fearful circumscription and the other part of the world that has turned it into secular commodity and trivial consumption. If I sometimes speak in a way that seems overextended, sentimental even, then it's because I am struggling with the same problem I have with naming these parts that I love—the parts that are neither pussy nor cunt, neither rump nor ass. No matter. This is how I am and I can speak only for myself, myself and—I feel this very strongly—for a woman I love as well, when I am near her, when I am listening to her, when I am joined to her.

All of which is to say that I feel suddenly stripped of words. No. That speaks of sex and nakedness. I am suddenly *clothed* with words, layers and layers until I can't even imagine being naked again. I come up to a stretch of years in my life when all the words that I'd need to speak of the daily tremblings and sweats and soft barks in empty elevators after women who have just stepped out or on subway platforms or in planes and hotel rooms, all the words I'd need to speak of all this would wrap this story up into sexless silence. But some things have to be said. I was nearly dead for six years and something has to be said about that.

A critical night was the night when I was on the train heading for Seaview and it was snowing, the night I thought of the woman in Chicago. It was a late snow. It was past the middle of March. It was snowing and I vowed not to think of Gio again when I made love to Fiona, and that night she was full of talk about the Stations of the Cross that she'd done that day and she'd explained the Stations to John and he'd listened very carefully, she said, very carefully and he'd even patted her on the hand and said that it was a good thing she was doing this and I kept my face straight and I·thought I'd have to tell him tomorrow not to make it so clear that he and I knew she needed these things she believed. Tomorrow was Saturday and we would bundle up and go off to the park and lie beneath the trees and flap our arms and make snow angels and we would talk some more about how strange it was that the stars were so far away and then Fiona and I went upstairs and I closed the door and I began to think of the woman sleeping on the train and it didn't work and then I relented and I thought of Gio and it didn't work and by now it was way too late and Fiona was already alternately weeping and flailing at me, and her body once seemed so beautiful to me and seemed beautiful still in odd moments, but only sexless moments, when she came in from a shower in the morning and she was hurrying to get ready for early-morning Mass, but now her body took on the shape and color of her rage, she danced her rage and her fear and I wanted to help but I couldn't, I was slack in the cock and weak in the limbs and her body had no shape and color apart from these things I could not love and could not cure and I had come last night after intense focus on Gio once again and I'd come the night before from Xau and the night before from a woman I'd met at the office who had lovely great gray eyes and who was darkly quiet always now because she was only a month back at work after having her left breast removed and I knew that if I could go with her to some quiet place and we could lie with windows open to the sea and I could undress her very gently, then I could convince her that she was still beautiful, I could kiss her all the length of her scar and I could love her and she was in me again that night when I'd failed with thoughts of the woman sleeping on the train and of Gio and even as Fiona flew about the room I thought of the gray-eyed woman and I began to quake because I knew I could never touch this woman, not in the flesh, I knew now what I had to do because it was the coming that had made it impossible this night, after I would come a few nights in a row—however many it was, four, five—eventually there was an inevitable slowness in responding and I knew that with this distance now between Fiona and me, between my yearning and her body, an orgasm one night could easily mean one of these terrible scenes the next, one of these scenes that were going on for hours now.

And on that night, I finally seemed to respond to Fiona, I finally made love to the gray-eyed woman in my head but I dared not come, and I did not, and the next morning I was up early to take my son out of this house and when we were sitting in the car he pulled off his watch cap and I stopped the car sharply and bent to him and in his dark hair I saw a flash of pale tea rose red and I looked and he said what is it and I said sit still and I drew a long strand of Fiona's hair from his and then another and I remembered her brushing his hair just before we left and she used her own hairbrush and I don't know why this bothered me so much but it did. I ran my fingers through his hair over and over, looking for her hair lurking there and he sat still for it, he sat patiently with the car idling just outside our driveway and I found one more of her hairs and I pulled it free and rubbed it off against the edge of the car seat, rubbed my fingers hard there. I was panting, I found, panting and I was trembling and the next day was Sunday and we went to church and I could barely breathe in the place and on Monday I went to a lawyer.

And it was 1974 and it was the state of New York and he said that in the year 1974 in the state of New York if Fiona was not committable and if she was able to go into a courtroom and make herself seem loving and capable, there was no chance whatsoever of my getting custody of John if I sought a divorce and I staggered out of the lawyer's office and I called a man I worked with and he suggested another lawyer, a woman, and I went to this woman and she sat before a wall of leather-bound books and she had entered the room with her nostrils flared and her nose was thin and very lovely and she was small and wiry-powerful and she cut any delicacy of mine short right away by saying that she was not a religious woman and I didn't have to mince words, she understood the dangers I saw and agreed with them, and then she told me that in 1974 in the state of New York I didn't have a chance, really, I would have to make a choice.

And I went home that night and the paintings were all down from the walls, the street people and the woman in the business suit rising from the sea and all the faint little girl faces struggling to stay visible in the blocks of color, all of them, were gone and in one of the spaces, over the living room couch, was a triptych of Jesus in the manger and Jesus on the cross and Jesus appearing after his death on the road to Mary Magdalene and in another space, where the little girls had clustered on a side wall of the living room, there was a dark wood crucifix with a pewter Christ upon it and it looked very small there and the nails were all around it where the girls had hung and Fiona came into the room and I turned my face to her and she said, "You look terrible. Are you sick?"

"Yes," I said. "Maybe."

She came to me and laid one hand on my shoulder and brushed the hair back off my forehead and she put her palm against me and she said, "You feel cool, but you shouldn't take any chance. I'll make it all right. I'll help you." And she said this low, said it softly, and there was a faint tremor in her voice of love for me, and I was holding very still, trying not to recoil from her hand on my forehead and I knew what the choice was that the woman had posed to me without ever naming it, without saying any more and without me saying any more, the woman who was beautiful to me equally because of the thin nose that flared again as she spoke of the choice and because of the quick cut of her mind and the silence she let me have after that, the silence that I could see she respected and she said to me, You're a very smart man, Mr. Holloway, your son must be special, and I said nothing but nodded to her, loving her for how smart she was and wishing to take her in my arms and knowing right then that the choice was getting worse the longer I thought about it.

I let Fiona feel my forehead and I waited and she said, "You get sick so rarely. I don't want you to suffer but I am happy to be able to take care of you. You take care of me every day, every minute." And she took her hand away and laid her head on my chest and I made my arms go up and hold her and I looked to the stairs and she knew what I was thinking. "He's upstairs with things to show you. Do you think you're contagious?"

I looked at her. "No."

"He needs you."

"I know," I said and I moved away, climbed the stairs as heavily as if I was following my wife up to bed, and I stood at the door to John's room and he had not heard me and I listened and he was humming softly and I looked through the crack in the door and he had laid four of his books open before him and this was the game he'd started with me, trying to get me to guess why these four books were open to these particular pages—a rabbit somewhere on each, the word ball, a father in each, which is what it was when we'd played last night—and his face was lowered, he was studying the four books and he was humming a tune from Sesame Street and his hair was dark and his eyes were blue and he had his mother's wide thin mouth stretched now in thought and I pulled back from the door for a moment, I pressed myself against the wall and this was the choice I had to make: I would go now to find a different life for myself and let my son live much of his life alone with Fiona, with Fiona and with no one to tell him that women are beautiful and the more you know about them the more beautiful they are, to tell him that he will one day be able to figure the universe out for himself, not only be able to but *have* to, no matter where that leads him, he would be alone with Fiona and with a self in him that she would create with all her passion and smartness. A terrible self. That was one choice and the other was for me to stay and to stay and to live two lives with my son, one to keep Fiona sane and one to whisper to my son all the things that I felt deeply were true. To stay and to lose the fullest moment of my sexuality: to stay and never to come, never dare to come for as long as she continued to need my penis inside her every night to stay alive. There was no other way, I understood. My son hummed behind this half-open door and he waited for me and I had no choice at all.

And that night Fiona laid me down in the bed and patted the pillows into a hollow for my head and fed me soup and told me to sleep and the next night I thought about a woman who passed me on the street and my penis rose and I entered this woman, entered Fiona, and after a time I wrinkled my brow and cried out and it was real, the cry, it was a rush of pain even as my penis held back, and Fiona clutched me hard and she had me look in her eyes, though I did not see them, and as it turned out she did not know one bodily fluid from another, or did not let herself know, did not care as long as my penis rose to her and entered her, and whenever her period began, I masturbated the first night, thinking of someone who mattered to me, someone from the landscape inside me, and I dared not masturbate even a second night in a row because I had to be ready for when Fiona wanted me, near the end of her period, still bleeding some, happy to remind me of this thing that was ours alone and I would cry out and my eyes would roll back, in rapture, she must have thought because she let me avoid her own eyes in this way, my eyes would roll back in what she took to be rapture but it was not. It was not.

A little over a year later, South Vietnam fell. It was clear for quite a while that it was going to happen, but I was too absorbed with my own life to give it much thought. I had lived a little more than a year from the night of the late snow, and the regimen I'd foreseen as necessary had proved to be true. I dared not let my semen go if I wished to keep our family from flying apart and it came finally to pass that I dared not let myself love even the women in my head except on the night of Fiona's first blood each month or I would begin to quake, and so I did not think very much of the women I'd loved in

South Vietnam as the end drew near for their country. But on the last day of April 1975, it was all over and the newspapers were full of the story and I went home and I entered Fiona and I removed myself from Fiona and just afterward she climbed from the bed and knelt before a crucifix on the wall and prayed, as was her custom, and when she had gotten back into bed and the room was dark, I lay still and empty until her breathing was steady with sleep and only then did I think of Hoa. I thought of all the others, too, briefly. I could see them in that field in the place where I live, the field that once had a sky the color of Fiona's milk but now the color was different, it had darkened, Fiona's milk had run dry and the blue of the sky was dark, the color of the South China Sea where the fishing boats nodded and yearned after the American warships, yearned with their decks full of women I loved and women I missed loving, and Hoa was near me, lying in the grass, watching the sky, and the others who had let me inside them, who let me love them, who let me fill and rush for them, rush with all that I am into them, they were across this field, they moved in a languorous file at the tree line beneath the sky the blue of the South China Sea. And I turned my face toward Hoa's sigh.

She was beside me in Saigon and she had driven into the city to see me after I'd been transferred, after she'd wept softly with me in the water tower in the hot afternoon when I'd come to tell her I was leaving Homestead. A few weeks later she came to the city and she said she'd meet me on the veranda of the Continental Plaza Hotel and I sat there beneath the paddle fans and everything was slow where I sat, the scattering of American journalists and embassy men in their Asian walking suits and the officers in their starched khakis with the great moons of sweat under their arms were all drinking slow, some with Vietnamese girlfriends wearing their ao dais but no one saying a word and all of them turning slow eyes from each other to the street and eventually back again, and the kitchen cats were lolling under the tables, their tails curling and uncurling slow, and everything out in the street was fast, the open xich-lo cabs buzzing past trailing plumes of dark smoke, the Hondas weaving and circling with the Saigon cowboys, their cigarette packs rolled into their T-shirt sleeves, and the young women were walking by with brisk steps, the front and back panels of their ao dais fluttering about their legs, fans held beside their faces to keep the sun away. I saw Hoa's Citroën circle the square before me and a few minutes later she appeared on the veranda and she was dressed still in the black pantaloons and drab green blouse of the peasants but she was very beautiful and it was this, as much as the way she was dressed, that left a wake of slow-turning heads behind her.

She sat beside me and she said, "I'll wait to kiss you in private. When I start, we won't stop."

And I said, "Your feelings are still strong," and I didn't mean it to make her think of her Buddhism, but she turned to me as if I'd rebuked her and that had to be from the Buddha's warning about desire leading to unhappiness. I wanted to take the words back, but she said, "I desire you too much, Ira."

Then we went to a room in a hotel by the river and we were up high, the top floor, and the balcony doors were open and we looked to the east, over the trees and past the sprawl of shanties and out into the flat paddyland and we lay down and the fan moved slowly above us and we slid together and we made love sweating till the sheets were soaked and when we were done Hoa brewed me hot tea and I sweat some more and once when I moved to wipe the sweat from my brow she said, "Don't. It will make you feel cool," and then she thought for a moment and she leaned forward and licked the sweat from me there and I said, "You will make me feel warm," and she licked the sweat from my cheeks and from my neck and I licked the sweat from between her breasts and down the long stretch of her arms and we made love again, and I think now—now as I speak this—of Rebecca coming in from tennis just yesterday here in the hotel in Puerto Vallarta—Rebecca; yes—and there was a tennis pro and Rebecca played while I drowsed with our beachside doors open to the late afternoon and she came in and she was sweating and I told her, "Don't," as she took up a towel and I drew her to the bed and I laid her down and I licked the sweat from her forehead and her cheek and I went to the hollow of her throat but before I could lick the sweat from her there she said, "No, Ira, please." And I stopped and lifted my face to her and she smiled and kissed the tip of my nose and she said, "I don't feel pretty right now, not my sweat" and I said, "Even your sweat is pretty to me," and she flinched a little, as if she'd just been struck by an idea, as if she'd just figured me out, and she said, "Then it must be all of me that you taste in it," and I said, "Even this little hesitation," and earlier, in the morning, the blonde in the shop with the towel knotted at her hip had padded past me in her bare feet and I'd thought of Karen Granger and she was still humming softly in my head, waiting for me to show her what I never did show her, the bones of my feet, and I licked the sweat from Hoa's feet, the toes long and slim and the second toes longest of all and I licked the faintly wrinkled bottoms of each of her toes, the second toes first and then all the others, and Hoa sighed and this was after we'd come, this sweat was from us, from our making love, and the paddle fan whisked overhead and I lay in the bed beside Fiona who was sleeping deep now, not stir-ring, her breath no longer audible, and I thought of the endings of things, the fall of the Republic of South Vietnam, where women I'd made love to were huddled or scattered in fear, the ending of things, of feelings, but so few of my feelings ever ended, ever really ended, they live even now, even as I put one word after another, and the next time I saw Hoa she said to rent the same hotel room and wait for her there and I stood on the balcony and the river was busy with sampans and gun-boats and the customs launches all bobbed in line along the quay and I looked far east and the South China Sea was out there invisible but it was part of me already, from a beach in Vung Tau where the Aussies dropped me one afternoon and I stretched and dozed and I woke and I hunkered into the surf and watched a fishing boat out on the line of the horizon, its sail a dark crescent moon verging in the east, and I looked down to the street a dozen stories below and a Citroën pulled up to the curb and I knew it was Hoa who got out, though I had every reason to doubt that it was her. This woman was not driving but got out of the backseat even as a man in a uniform, a chauffeur, circled the car to open the door for her, and she waved him away, and this woman was wearing an ao dai, and all of that should have made me miss who it was from up here, not seeing a face, but I sensed the height and angle of Hoa and then she even raised her face to me and yes, it was Hoa, and she was wearing her hair long down her back and the chauffeur was getting into the car and then pulling away and she was looking up at me and waiting, as if she were waiting for me to leap now, leap into her arms, but her face went down and she disappeared into the hotel and I turned and stayed on the balcony and I waited. I had left the door ajar and she came in without knocking and she was beside me and we faced the horizon where the sea was invisible and she said, "Ira, you are Vietnamese to me, you are as dear to me as the dearest of my ancestors."

I did not like the sound of this. I said, "I've never seen you in an ao dai."

She looked down at the ao dai she wore. "My father loves me like this." And she continued to study herself: the jade green silk fit her tight at the throat and at her breasts and clung to her along her sides and held her about the waist and then separated into two loose panels, front and back, falling to her ankles and beneath the panels she wore white silk pantaloons and on her feet were high heels the same jade color and the shoes were cut low enough to show the cleavage of her toes. She sensed my breathlessness, I think, for she raised her face and she closed her eyes and she said, "You make me crazy, too, you know."

"Is it crazy?" I asked, knowing I was pushing this thing.

"Yes," she said right away, firmly. "I have certain beliefs, Ira. Even when I am deliberately pulling away from them, I know that they are still there."

I turned away and draped my arms over the balcony and leaned a little out over the empty space that plucked at me faintly. Inside I was already falling, as if my body had gone up and over and into the void and now everything inside was pressing upward, bloating my chest and my throat and my face and my head, everything was resisting the fall that was happening, was scrambling up away from it. I said nothing.

She touched my arm, very lightly. "You can know this: No man made me feel as strongly as you."

"Aren't you saying, then, that no man was more dangerous to your Buddhist soul?" I looked at her and her eyes were steady on me.

She smiled. "I would think you'd like that."

"No," I said. "I don't like that at all."

"Would you have had me desire you less?"

I didn't have an answer for that at the time. And on the night that South Vietnam fell and I remembered all this, I turned my face to Fiona's quiet form beside me in the bed. Soul is a word like the word pussy or the word cunt. Worse. But whatever it is that the word soul is getting at, my desire, I know, is tied up in it, both my soul and the woman's. I couldn't say anything to Hoa about that, though. I still couldn't, not even if I could play that scene over again this very afternoon on some hotel balcony looking east over some river full of fishing boats and with a beautiful, religious woman who desired me standing beside me to say good-bye, I still wouldn't have an answer. Except maybe all the words I've said so far. And then she would simply think that I was mad, or if she were truly religious, she would think even worse of me. But I took

Hoa in my arms and kissed her and she was gone already, she had found that Buddhist core of her and was sitting back there with her legs crossed and her fingertips looped and she was chanting something secret to herself and I wasn't even there. I let go of her and at least her eyes were filled with tears, just like mine, and she said "Good-bye" and this she said in English and then she was gone and I did not linger beside the balcony, I went in and closed the doors and I suppose the answer was no. No, I wouldn't have wished her to desire me less, even if a lesser desire would put us naked together in the bed at that moment. And for me to desire her any less would be to worship cats. And now she was in danger somewhere, hiding in the water tower, her plantation overrun, or out in the South China Sea. Maybe she was on one of those last helicopters, her father's connections getting them out at last. Or maybe she was one of the VC and was triumphant now. But for me, she was lying in the grass next to me, lying there and looking at a sky the color of the South China Sea and I stretched out my hand to her and our fingertips touched and this was not the first day of Fiona's blood and I could not still the quaking of my cock and I had to struggle to keep myself inert there in the bed, keep myself from turning to Fiona and dragging her face to me with a hard hand and lifting her by the throat and throwing her across the room, even as she wished to do to me two or three times a month when even with the ragged hunger of my come-less cock and the desperate inventiveness of my imagination with some woman from the office or the street or the train, I still failed to rise to her quickly enough.

And I did struggle, I turned on my side, put my back to her, and I knew how I'd had to pay for three nights in a row after I'd made love to Sam in my office. Sweet Sam. We joined very softly lying on my leather couch and when I slipped inside her she was easy from the first touch, wide and deep and softer than the fuzz on her lip and she said my name at the first touch of the tip of me on the opening of her and she sucked me through and she said, "Ira," once, very softly, and one of her hands cupped the back of my head and it stayed there the whole time as if I were a baby she held carefully in her arms and my head needed constant cradling and I asked her to open her eyes when I came and she did and we watched each other and I loved Sam very much. And when we had lain for a long while blurred together, I thought to ask her if I could see her standing naked before me, if I could memorize the look of her, and after a moment of thought she said yes and we untangled and she rose and she moved a few steps away and she turned and her sun yellow hair licked up from between her legs and the hair was soft and thin and her lips were visible there, the upper edge of her lips where the place was that I wished even then to pluck at once more with my mouth, the small hard yearning place, and I looked at her face and when I did, she smiled but she could hold the smile for only a moment before she put her hand there and covered it, covered her eyes, as if she had stepped from the shower and I was a stranger and she had a washrag and if I could not see her face, then it would do me no good to see the rest, and I said to her, "It's Ira," and her hand hesitated and then came down and she nodded at me and the smile returned only now it was slow in shaping, as if each increment of it had a specific impression of me attached to it, as if there were stations of this smile and each one was a contemplation of her growing love for me, and this was what I had to give up, *I* did, *I* had to stop it, *I* had to say, No, I can't, we have to stop, and I called Sam to somehow tell her this and we met at a bar in the West Village and then we walked, walked without purpose for a while and we ended up at the Hudson River and we sat on a bollard on a pier and there was the smell of dead fish and cordite in the air and I told her the whole story, exactly the way it was, and I showed her the scratches on my arms from the three nights that I could not bring myself to make love to Fiona no matter how much I tried. My cock had said, Fuck you both I'm happy with Sam thank you very much, and Sam began to weep, though she turned her face away a little so I could not see, and she did not touch me, though her hands wanted to rise from her lap, I sensed, wanted to rise and move to me, but they did not and she understood how much I loved John and she did not say a word to suggest that I was wrong to do this and I loved her even more for that and we kissed a last time and on the fourth night I was able to convince Fiona I loved her, my cock knew that Sam was gone and was pissed at that but allowed the old, unfocused yearning to happen again, and I made love in my mind to a woman from the street with tired eyes, sad tired eyes and skin the color of nutmeg, and I did not use Sam, I never used Sam, and a few months later Harry left the firm and went to the West Coast and Sam went with him and I lay in bed on the night when South Vietnam fell and I wept as quietly as I could and all that kept me from going mad that night was a feeling on my skin. But it wasn't the touch of a woman, it wasn't the imprint of sex, it was the touch of my son, his taking my right hand that night on our walk around the block, his slipping his hand into mine and it was still there in my palm, and in the other palm, too, he took my left hand on the way back, he always wanted me to walk on the street side so he could peer into the yards and watch the lit windows going by, and his hands were imprinted on both my palms and I lay in the bed and wept and I drew my hands near my face and I concentrated on my son.

And this helped in the worst moments. Helped me bear the pain but did not lessen it even a little bit. And when I went out of town alone on a business trip I had two very strong and conflicting feelings. I was anxious for John and I would leave him only after a careful talk the night before about our secrets and, as he grew older, about why it was that Mommy acted the way she did, never telling him about the burning house, the hands from the smoke, only telling him that she had a difficult time, that she was not loved and her mother and father were both dead. I added details as the years went on and he was ready to understand more and more, and just a few months ago, when I knew he would understand, when he was ready to understand, I told him in gentle, slightly circumspect terms, about what I'd come to realize was the sexual abuse of Fiona's childhood and he said yes. Quietly. Yes, he said, and he said he understood how that would damage her. And that was all of it. We sat silently together for a long time, I think, and it made me a little sad to realize how mature he was, and that's how it was whenever I went away. I put my faith in all that we said to each other on the street on our night walks in Seaview, and in the hollow beneath the low-hanging mimosa in our backyard where we would go and sit in the smell of earth, and in the reading corner of his room with the intercom turned off, and on the Long Island Rail Road and New York City subways in his year or so of obsession with riding trains, and he always understood why Fiona needed to believe the things she did and why we needed to make her think we believed those things also and why he would have to choose his own beliefs independent of that someday, and then I'd go away on my trips and he was always there on the palms of my hands when I turned my thoughts to him, his voice was always in my head whenever I needed it, and still I would worry about Fiona's zeal, her logic, but I would also feel free for a time, not free to actually make love to a woman because I knew from Sam how intolerable that would be, but at least I could watch more closely and think more openly and it was about two years after Sam, I believe, that I went to Zurich for the first time and I heard Rebecca whistling the "Ode to Joy" and I worked near her and watched the bright poppy red of her lipstick fade and fade until her lips were naked and I could not touch her but I thought of her that night in my hotel room and I touched myself but it was a closed loop, as it always was that way, and it was better than not coming at all but afterward I keened softly into the dark of the room and counted my age once more till John would be eighteen and an adult and Fiona could no longer seek control of him, and I was thirty-two years old in that Zurich hotel room and it did not help to count the years because I would be forty-five and though I understood that thirty-two was still young, forty-five did not seem it, and so I rose up and paced the room in the dark and even having let my semen go did not give me any peace now, not even for ten minutes, as it sometimes did, but I had thought of Rebecca's naked lips and all that the coming did was make me yearn even more for their touch.

Then I saw her playing tennis and it was maybe six months later and this was on Long Island and I was on no trip at all: Fiona waited for me to return that night. I was visiting the estate of the owner of the Swiss company who'd hired us and I did not expect to see Rebecca's naked lips again or her tassel-kissed ankles or the wrist passing over her forehead to wipe the sweat away or the faint blue veins on the curve of her jaw and when she saw me taking her in and she said, Not so close a scrutiny please, Mr. Holloway, I look a mess, and I said, You are a very beautiful mess, Miss Mueller, I did not plan to go any farther than that, I dared not go any farther than that, I was ready to give the images of Rebecca Mueller up to the savage and hungry god of Fiona's need. But Rebecca said, "Have you finished your business with Mr. Ritter yet?"

"No," I said. "I'm just walking the grounds while he takes a few calls."

"Then I have time to make myself not so much a mess for you?"

"Please, I don't think you're . . ."

"You have to trust me on that, Mr. Holloway. I know when I am a mess."

"All right. Yes. You have time."

And she went off and I went back in to Mr. Ritter and when the business was done, she was waiting out on the lawn, standing out in the open, facing into the stiff breeze from the ocean, her hands clasped behind her back, and she was wearing a white sundress and her arms and shoulders were naked and she was barefoot and Ritter said, "Oh, Rebecca, why don't you show Ira the beach," and she turned around to face us. She did not move but stretched out her hand toward me, though I was far away from her. "Come on," she said.

I went down to her and we walked into the breeze, along the ten-foot privets which smelled very sweet, very strong, though they showed no flowers, and down narrow stone steps in a break in the hedges and we stepped into a great sucking white sand beach and before us was an ocean horizon high enough at first glance to look like a tidal wave coming in. I stopped and retreated to the steps and took off my shoes and socks and she watched me. "You have good feet," she said.

"I do?"

"Yes. I hate a man with little feet. It makes him feel precarious all his life and that does bad things to his personality."

I sat with my shoes and socks in my hands and pondered this for a moment but Rebecca wouldn't allow it. "Put them down and let's walk," she said and she offered a hand to pull me up.

And so we walked and it was the first that I'd seen of her shoulders and I was afraid to get too close, and speaking of this now it seems bizarre to me that I should have averted my eyes, kept them out to sea or fixed on the detritus of the beach, anywhere but on Rebecca's shoulders, but not bizarre at all, really, just a measure of my life with Fiona at that time, a week earlier I had failed her in that critical first half minute—she gave me half a minute now at least—but I'd had a wet dream the night before and now I was in trouble and Fiona was naked already and she backpedaled her way quickly up against the wall before any of the sounds of her rage began and I was lying at the foot of the bed and she spread her legs wide to me and she pounded her pussy once with her fist and then again and she cried, How ugly this must be to you, and for the first time in my life it was true and I scrambled back, too, off the bed and back to the far wall, protesting with my words all the way but she could not be blind to the direction I was heading, and it was true, for the first time in my life a pussy seemed ugly to me—just this one, of course, only this specific one, and for one of the reasons that every other pussy I'd ever seen was beautiful, that it held in its form the secret self of the woman and this was indeed Fiona's secret self now and part of that self was this bondage, and I pressed against the wall and I thought of Xau and her little place around the corner from the bar where she hustled Saigon Teas and took men home so that she could survive and I thought of all the kisses she'd given me the first time we were together, the ones before she loved me in return, the ones from the first time I was inside her, and later I never asked her how she did it, never asked what had been in her mind that first time, what she'd felt then, but it was easier for her, of course, she could will her legs open for whatever man she'd decided to go with and if she wasn't wet, he could ignore that, but I had kissed Xau down there, kissed her deep and long and that had made her wet and maybe that had already begun to make her want me in return, I loved her already, sensing the sadness in her over her father, though I didn't know it was that, I loved her already for the secret pain in her that she struggled to live through, loved her for the way she touched only my hand to ask if I wanted to go with her and I thought of Xau as I pressed away from Fiona, I longed for whatever trick she might know to teach me to go through this, but I had to show the woman before me that I wanted her, I could not simply lie down and open my legs as she was doing now and she pounded her pussy once again and I cried out for her to stop and I knew I should cross the room then and kiss her there, pull her back down on the bed and lay her out and kiss her there but I could not, she was right, this pussy was ugly and it was the first time I'd ever felt that and it scared the hell out of me and I had to do whatever was necessary never to feel this again and that meant I kept my eyes out to sea while I walked beside Rebecca because if I let myself fall more deeply in love with her I was afraid I could not face Fiona tonight and in my mind, I stopped on a street in Seaview. I never did this in life but in my mind I stopped in the dark on some street in Seaview and I squared John around and I said to him, Can you really ask this of me, my son? Is this something you have a right to expect of me? But even in my mind he looked up, waiting, and I knew he was ready to say to his daddy to go on, save yourself, he'd do what he could to be the un-buffered son of Fiona Price Holloway, and sometime in the months of his recent passion for trains he and I had stood on a West Village subway platform waiting for the A train and he had let go of my hand and I let him go and I didn't think about it, I was reading an ad on the clock hanging on the platform, an ad taken out by some guy who worked on Madison Avenue and wanted to find a nice woman to date and he was tired of the singles bars and so he made this ad for himself and I was thinking about that and I felt the dank stirring of air that meant a train was coming and I turned and John was very close to the edge of the platform, leaning out looking, and I clenched and lunged and pulled him back, though the train was still far away, but I knew at that moment that if it had been necessary for me to leap onto the track and throw John up to the platform and then turn and face my death beneath the wheels of a New York subway, I would do that for him, gladly, and so how could I not do this, how could I ever turn him to face me in the dark after telling him all the secrets there, after arranging a life that I felt gave him a chance for wholeness, and say to him I'd had enough of this, it was too painful to go on.

And so I kept my eyes out to sea and Rebecca must have been saying things that I'd not heard. She nudged me a little. "Ira?"

I looked in her direction but only a glance and then I returned to the horizon. "I'm sorry. The ocean always distracts me."

"I've been thinking about what you said about women who whistle."

"That I like them?"

"Yes. I get very self-conscious now when I do it."

"I'm sorry," I said, and having troubled her, I had to turn to her for this. But I did not look at her shoulders or the ruffled gape of bodice of her dress, I kept my eyes on hers, the blue of her eyes that seemed to churn, though of course it did not, the color of her eyes was fixed and steady but there seemed a vortex there and I felt it as a faint tugging at me. Her eyes were narrowed a little bit in amusement. This had not been a real complaint. I said, "Are you afraid you'll inadvertently seduce all the men who think like me?"

"I wonder if any other man in the world thinks like you, really."

"I don't know. I bet there are others."

"I know very little about you, Ira."

"I have a son," I said and I looked back out to sea. It was wrinkled like the instep of a woman's foot.

And Rebecca asked me all the questions about a son, how old, does he go to school, what's he like, and I answered her in the blandest way possible and she whistled at his intelligence and called him a genius and she said, "Does he get that from you?" And I knew what was next and I was ready now to end this thing for myself in the most obvious way. It was all in the phrasing, in the tone of voice. I did not wear a wedding band, had never worn one; this was something that Fiona in her jealousy never asked for and I think I knew why, I think I knew why Fiona had said in a voice firm enough to hold back a trembling that she did not believe in men wearing wedding rings, she said that long ago, when we first began to speak of marriage, and she never took it back and I knew from that, much later, that her father had worn a wedding band. But my naked hand had led Rebecca to follow this particular line of small talk and now I said, "Maybe from me. Maybe from my wife." This was a very difficult thing for me to say and I looked at Rebecca to watch her read the subtext. I knew she would do that and I heard Rebecca's voice for the first time then, I think, just a whisper of it, but thinking now about that walk along the beach I can hear it from the moment even more clearly: *Now why has he let me go this far? This is so unlike me, really. I know the impression I make. I whistle, yes. I take charge. And all that puts a comfortable distance between most men and me. And if I don't sense something special about Ira Holloway, I would have trouble now because I'd be angry at him and not know how to express it. If he said, "Maybe from his mother," and so made me ask another question or even two or three—he could have delayed telling me that he is presently married for at least two more questions and maybe three— then I would understand that there is trouble there, that he is in a troubled marriage. But to go straight to "my wife" means that this is a truly married man and I had no idea of that in Zurich or up at the tennis courts. Especially at the tennis courts when he caught me in a very vulnerable moment, when I was very conscious of my being in my body and it being a little weary, and he can look at me in a way that surprises me, as if he's really seeing me. So when he refers immediately to his wife, I look at him and my face and throat are hot suddenly. I suppose I am indeed angry because it is very unlike me to seem to be coming on to a man—the way I suddenly fear I seem to be doing—but I do sense something special in him and I don't have a clue where that's coming from in me nor do I have a clue what it is about Ira that's leading me to do this. But I just turn my face away and we walk for a time in silence. All the while, I'm trying to figure out a way to get us out of this. I need to find small talk now, but I am always ironic in small talk and irony would lead me at once to bring whatever just happened out in the open, and I don't think I want that. If he believes he can see something in me with my whistling, then I wish he'd figure out the predicament he's put me in and*

do something about it himself. He should talk about his won-
derful marriage, at least, about his lovely all-American wife
just like my sweetly foolish American mother. That's the part
of me, I suppose, that he's touching, and I walk along beside
him wishing—academically, though, dispassionately—that
there was just a little bit more of my Swiss German father in
me so that I could simply dismiss him and go about the business
of my life. And of course I understand the irony of that. The
very dispassionateness of that thought is every bit Papa.

I knew I'd hurt her. Even before her voice grew strong and
full in me, I understood that much. I made her assume I was
offering intimacy and then I made her seek confirmation and
then I seemed to tell her it was impossible, and behind the
assuredness of her I knew there was a deep reticence and I
loved each of those things in her already and I loved them both
existing together and this was why I was fighting so hard to
keep from touching her. If I were to make love to her, if I were
to come with her, then I would be lost before Fiona and then
John would be lost. But with every step we took in silence on
the beach I sensed more strongly the thoughtful chaos I'd
wrought in her and I looked at her now, looked at her near
shoulder and it was a little square and full and showed no trace
of her collarbone, either beneath the arm loop of her dress
or on the top of her shoulder and even the morning color in
her face from playing tennis had begun to fade and she was
cloister white and her shoulder was very beautiful and she felt
me watching her but she did not look at me and I stretched
and crackled inside like the breaker sweeping beneath our
feet and finally I said, "I don't know much about you either,
Rebecca. But I'm sorry if I've confused you today. I didn't
mean it."

She looked at me. "I'm tempted, you know, to play dumb
now and make you explain what you're referring to."

"That would be really awkward for me. Not that you should
spare me. I deserve it."

"I'm not like this, usually," she said.

I'd explained how I was living once already, to Sam. But I'd known Sam a long time, I'd already made love to Sam, Sam knew Fiona, for Christ's sake, but I'd confessed to Sam and Sam had absolved me and I would make it clear—as I *had* to, I thought, to preserve my own sanity and Fiona's and John's, too—I would make it clear to Rebecca that I was not trying to go to bed with her, *could* not, really, that this story of my life was offered in explanation, as complex as it might seem, for why I had made her feel awkward. And that was true, in a way, but it was also bullshit. I wanted to be close to Rebecca, as close as I could get, and these words I would speak were a kind of intimacy, a kind of lovemaking, I knew, and I began to tell her who I was and who Fiona was and what she and I and my son had come to. *This was a surprise to me at first, when Ira Holloway began to talk about these private things. He'd been around the office in Zurich for about a week and now I'd met him again and it had all been business, really. Not that I was blind to his flirting. I am never blind to that sort of thing in men and it always puzzles me. How desperately insecure they all must be to do this so compulsively. It's not me inspiring the attention. It's something about them that looks inward, something that can't even recognize a specific woman there before them. I watch the flirting seize men when almost any woman comes into their presence. A woman, of course, within a certain range of physical attractiveness. The men do it to anyone and so not only is it not just me inspiring it, it's never me. That's the effect. It's never any of us. It's just them and their own problem, whatever that is. I don't even exist. Papa was an exception and so he unconsciously taught me to see it this way. He was the manager of a department store and I would go and hang around with him and he'd show me every-thing about the store and whenever we'd meet a woman—a customer or a salesclerk or a rep for a line of perfume or dresses, any woman—he would stiffen and nod his head a little*

*and speak in the most careful and formal ways, very respectful,
and he would always seem to know something about each of
the clerks and he would say, "Greta, is your mother better?"
or "Marie, do you miss Geneva very much?" All of the women
were in love with my father for this, I think. For the very
reason that he was not going all soft-edged and breathy and
complimentary or, on the other hand, clenched and tough and
wry. He would do everything but click his heels and tip his hat
to them in respect. That's what he would do, my papa, and
that seemed to me to be so different and so much better than
all these other men who were always on the make. It seemed
like that for years. It seems like that, in some part of me, even
now. Even at this very moment as Ira is trying to figure out
his life and I can speak in him because of it and I can carry
him wherever I want and I can think out my own life, if I wish,
and Papa seemed just the way a man should be for a woman.
I was maybe eight years old and he showed me the storerooms
where clipboards hung at each junction along the rows of metal
shelves and we went up and down looking at the stock, looking
at the clipboards, and it all seemed wonderful in its logic, and
then we passed through a room full of mannequins and they
were all naked and all the women had the same big eyes, I
recognized them by their eyes, the women from the fourth floor
where they wore the latest tweeds and furs, and here they were
naked and my father took my hand as we passed through this
place, he was pulling me faster than I wanted to go. I wanted
to look at the bodies of these women, though they seemed
strange to me even then. The women had breasts but they had
no nipples. And between their legs it was smooth and slick and
there was no opening at all there, but my father was pulling
me hard and I looked up to him and his eyes were on the far
door, he did not look right or left and I understood this as
part of his respect for women. And he would talk of respect.
We would always end up on the roof, at noon, with our lunch
spread around us. This was the last thing we would do when-*

ever I would spend the morning with him. We would go up on the roof of the store and he would say to me, "Rebecca, you must always respect yourself. Take care to do that. You must think how it is you are inside and act that way, and if you like the logical things and the strong things and the quiet things, then you be that way. Do you understand?"

Did I understand? In many ways I did. In ways that I could never have spoken of in those years. Of course I wanted to be like Papa and he was telling me that it was all right to be like him even if I knew already that the world expected me to be more like the woman living in the center of my life rather than the man. And this was another way that I understood what he was saying. I would go home from the store and my mother would flutter through the house at the sound of the front door, I could hear the beat of her fragile wings from far away and I would wait for her because the few times I'd tried to make it to the stairway to go upstairs and consider my morning in quiet, she would catch me with her words as I was halfway up and I would turn and look down the steps to her and she would be curls and ruffles quaking at the bottom, not daring to take a step up to me there but waiting only with her stricken face for me to go down to her and give her the embrace she wanted, an embrace I would be very happy to give if only I could just go first upstairs and sit in quiet and not be forced to bring my feelings to the surface right there and then. Papa knew me somehow, knew about the quiet things, the feelings that did not have to flow at once to the surface, knew about the logical things. And he would arrive home and my mother would fly to him and she would alight before him and not come near till his coat and his hat were hung and he would turn to her and she would hold very still but I was always aware that this stillness was the stillness of a great flying rush that went equally in two opposite directions. Papa would kiss her then, bending to her from the waist, and her left hand would always rise and touch the point of his right shoulder and not long after my first passage through the room full of mannequins I saw my mother in her bedroom. I came into the room and she was standing before the mirror and she turned to me and she was naked and her breasts quaked in the turning and she was not smooth and slick and empty but lush with color and shapes and fur and she put both her hands over her face and I said, "I'm sorry, Mama," and I backed out of the room and inside me I clicked my heels and tipped my hat and bowed to Mama and she was just from her bath and was choosing her wardrobe and we all live in bodies, mamas and daughters and everyone else, too, but a little later it was not so quiet or logical in me and she seemed very interesting, I looked at myself and I was flat still and pucker-nippled and only barely fuzzed and Mama was very interesting beneath the fluttering of her wings and I wanted that too, I was grateful to her for this glimpse, and it wouldn't be until I was thirty that I ever really asked myself what it was inside my mother, what it was between Mama and my father. And maybe that isn't so strange. I would sit with my father on the roof of the department store and before me was the jagged rip of the Alps against the sky and he gave me things and he withheld things and sometimes he did both things at once, and it's not so strange, when what you're given is good, to concentrate only on that for a long long time. What I might otherwise reject as not Rebecca was opened to me by my father and he sat and I sat then in the strong, logical silence of that lesson and we watched the sky and we ate together and I felt very close to him though we said almost nothing more and I realize I felt very far from my mother though it was neither strong nor logical to keep my mind and heart silent about who she might be.

And I must admit that my first reactions to Ira Holloway's confession came from all of this. What kind of creature was this? From my experience he sounded at times like a man elaborately on the make, flirting in some bizarre and extravagant way but flirting nonetheless without any sense of who I was.

Surely he didn't give a damn about who I was for him to tell me these extraordinary things after only a week of working near me, exchanging ironic small talk with me, and then he saw me playing tennis and now he was telling me about this life he'd found himself in. He had no idea how I might react and surely that meant he didn't care. If the story worked to seduce me, fine; if not, he'd try it on someone else. But on the other hand this was real feeling going on here, this was a man who wasn't silent and wasn't trying to look strong and wasn't clinging to his logic and that was something I had to take into account. We walked along the shore and we did not touch. Ira was a toucher. In Zurich he would touch my wrist, my shoulder, he would lay his hand on mine when he spoke, and this was another of those things that you usually understand as a man trying to find his way into your bed, but I couldn't shake the feeling that he was trying to comprehend me when he did this, he was memorizing me even, understanding the exact breadth of my wrist, the curve of my shoulder as he touched me, and though I still felt he wanted to take me to bed, it seemed to be Rebecca Mueller he wanted to take to bed, not this thing in himself. But when we walked along the shore that day he did not touch me at all.

I am a rational woman and I tend not to believe in intuition, not that I don't have it at times, but I don't trust it. I had an intuition about Ira, about how he was seeing me and about who he might be, and eventually it made me fretful that he'd stopped touching me. Even as the rational part of me concluded that this was a good sign about him, his not touching me during his story; he was letting me know why he was telling me all of this, not because I might be encouraged to take him into my bed—there were much simpler ways to try to do that—but because this was the only way for him to truly be there with me, by speaking about this strange life of his openly, by showing me his feelings, giving them life in his words. There was something of my father in me that still recoiled from this, I think.

For a while Ira seemed nearly mad, speaking of all this so openly. But he was not touching me with his hand as he spoke, not even letting his shoulder touch mine as we idly veered in and out of the breakers as we walked, and then he was telling me things even more private, telling me how he must make love to this woman who seemed so sad to me, sad and real to me, and Ira was telling me that he had only a very little bit of time to respond to her, physically respond, he said, and of course I was led to see him in my mind and this is what was so strange about all of this, I suppose. He spoke of his penis and of course anyone hearing a story has pictures springing automatically into her head and so in a way it was as if Ira had unexpectedly disrobed before me. This was when I thought him a little mad but he was not touching me and I could see his son sleeping in the other room and dreaming his child's dreams and I could see this man desperately trying to preserve that and I could hear his love for his wife—Ira made it clear that he had always loved this woman and I believed him about that—and I knew how terribly his wife was suffering and so I did not think him mad for long and I wished he would in fact touch me once to make a point, touch my elbow or lay his hand on mine. I would take his hand—I could do that, just for the moment, just for sharing these feelings with me—but he did not touch me and I felt a churning begin in me about that, like the moment near our feet, played over and over, when the waves rushed back from the beach and clashed with the next waves coming in. Like that, two wet and tumbling things in me colliding: one thing was the feeling of a friend now who had been given a special confidence and could suffer with three people who were trapped in a pain that I could not touch, and one thing was the feeling of—who? of Rebecca, my mother's daughter, perhaps, of Rebecca of this body and heart—the feeling of Rebecca who was yearning in her fingertips and in her nipples for the touch of this strange man who seemed not to be strong but who seemed very strong because of that, and who seemed not to be rational but made sense because of that, and who was not quiet but gave me a feeling of quietude even as he spoke on and on, and that quiet in me said to take his hand, but I did not.

And after a time he told me about a woman named Sam and the way he lived now in his body and this should have been the strangest thing of all, the images that this man who had known me for so little time was putting in my mind of his semen, of his penis inside his wife and the ultimate quiet it kept there, the quiet of things withheld, but it did not seem strange by then, it seemed logical, it seemed a very logical thing that Ira was doing and he was suffering for it, I knew, and he could not make love to me, I knew, though now I knew that he wanted to very much and now I knew that it was all right, that I wanted that, too, though I could never look at this feeling with my logic and make anything of it.

And we turned and went back along the beach and he said that he felt pretty stupid and I told him that he shouldn't feel that way, that he must think about his son, and I said to him that it was very strange for me but very nice that I could find such a good mother in a man and he stopped and turned to me and smiled and he was clearly pleased by this notion and then I said, "It's the making physical love that's the problem for you, isn't it? You can let me hold you for a few moments? You can just kiss me now, can't you?" And that was a logical point that he instantly took up.

And I kissed Rebecca for the first time, kissed those lips that by now had slowly stripped the poppy red away and were naked and they were large and they opened gently and I touched her tongue with mine and she was a little tentative there, shy, happy to be touched but not quite ready to touch me in return, not of her own will, but happy still to have me upon her and I drew Rebecca close and there have been many women I've loved, many, and some of them I loved without ever touching, like the waitress who left the impression of her fingertips on a wine bottle, the woman with corkscrew curls on the passing subway, the Vietnamese woman jangling her bracelet on the language tape, a woman I never touched and never saw, either. And I loved them and many more like them and I love them still and it might seem that it was all right, after all, that I never touched them, that I never lay naked with them and plucked at their nipples and slid inside them and clung with them in the sweetness of our sweat, and it's true that I love them anyway and they are alive in me still in spite of our never making love, but part of the peace I have about letting those fingertips fade from the bottle and the subway pass on and the tape run out is the rich and surprising possibility of life on this planet, that sometime perhaps I will be on a fast train in a strange country and a landscape of rice paddies and palm trees or of salt flats and gray mountains or of triple canopy forests mounting to a hot sky is blurring past me and I look away from the window and I am alone and she is there across the way and her fingertips lie still in sleep or her corkscrew curls fall across her face as she bends to a book or her bracelet jangles as she draws a weary wrist across her forehead and by the twilight we are in love and by the rising of the moon in a room open to the night we join the secrets of our flesh wetly together. That is part of the reason this landscape lives so insistently inside me. It is the life of the past, it is the undying life of all the intimacies I have been blessed with in these thirty-five years, but it is also the cry of the train in the summer night, the cry as I'd heard it lying with my hand in the sweetest, softest place on Amanda's body, the cry that said there was a future before me, there was a future full of women I would love, women I would yearn for and leap with and rise to and give to and give and give and dream with and that was what had always quickened me, what had given me this keen presence in the world. And when I kissed Rebecca and when I touched the tip of her tongue and when I held her close with her lips naked and her feet bare and her hands pressed tight against my back and when I bent hard in the covered center of me straining to touch her deepest whispering place, I knew that it was impossible to draw closer to her than this, and then I could not sense a future at all, the cry of the train stopped, the sky went black, the hum of the horizon ceased, and I must have made some sort of sound at this, for Rebecca whispered, "What? What is it?" and I had no answer for her, I had no answer for myself, I dragged a breath into my body, and another, and it was all I could manage just to do this.

And Ira and I held each other very close and after he made a little sound, like the release of a spent wave, the holding changed somehow, became more formal, and that would be more like me, to make it like that, and I wondered if it was I who was responsible, if I had changed things. Perhaps it wasn't me, nor Ira either, really. Perhaps it was the sound that he made, it was just the farthest natural reach of that wave. So we gently disentangled and we began to walk back along the beach and just to make sure it wasn't me, I consciously took his hand and we entwined our fingers and we walked mostly in silence. When the great wall of Mr. Ritter's privet hedges appeared up ahead, Ira slowed and then he stopped and we were still holding hands and he looked briefly out to sea. Then he said, "I wish I could see you again," and it came out not as a request but as a regret for something that was impossible.

I understood why he thought it was impossible and it had nothing to do with my being in Zurich, but I realized that I hadn't told him something relevant. "I've been transferred to New York," I said.

Ira looked at me and his eyes seemed more gray now than blue and I knew that I'd just made things more difficult for him. "If you just want to talk," I said. "If saying all this to me has made it easier for you, you can do that again if you like."

"Has it been all right, my speaking like this to you?"

For a moment I was puzzled. It seemed to me as if I'd just answered this question. But he waited for something more and then I understood what it was. "Yes," I said. "I like your voice very much, Ira. I feel close to you, listening to your voice."

"That's how I feel about you now," he said. "Even when you aren't speaking."

We walked on in silence after that, and I knew what he meant.

I wasn't sure I'd ever see Ira again. Or hear his voice, except in my head, except in my dreams, and for a week, two weeks, three, I did hear him there and nowhere else. I could hear Ira's voice from the beach and the more I heard it, the more familiar it became and the stranger it became. Both things at once. My father told me a story once, up on the roof of the department store. I could see the jagged run of Alps from there and if I looked to the southwest and then followed the mountains east across the horizon, I would end up at the two great spires of the cathedral, the Grossmünster, topped with pale green domes, a place once Catholic and in the sixteenth century turned Protestant. It was here that the Swiss reformer Zwingli urged priests to take wives, as he himself had done, and he died for that, and these two tall, green-tipped spires always drew my eyes from the mountains and I didn't know any of this history of the place then and finally one noontime my father watched me as I quietly considered the place and he spoke of it. But he went back to the early Catholic martyrs who are the patron saints of Zurich: Felix, Regula, and Experantius. "This is what the Cathedral means," he said to me. "In the third century, the three saints came to Turicum, which is what they called Zurich then, and they tried to convert us to Roman Catholic Christianity. This was not easy and finally the Roman governor of the region took Felix and Regula and Experantius and plunged them into boiling oil and then made them drink molten lead. But this did not move them. They refused to renounce their faith. Then the governor had them beheaded. But still the three martyrs did not die. They picked up their heads and they carried them to the place where the cathedral now stands, and they dug their own graves and buried themselves there." I think I replied to that, "But it isn't Catholic anymore, is it?" and my father laughed in approval and I was very pleased. I think I replied that, but perhaps it's only in my memory over the years that I have come to please him at that moment. But this was a surprising story from my father, in its way, and his voice has remained clear in me all of this time and Ira's displaced even that voice for a time, as I waited and wondered and then doubted if he would call. I could hear Ira speaking as we walked along the beach and I dreamed once that I was beside him and he was telling me of the secret times with his son—and this was true, this was in my dream just as he'd told me on the beach—Ira and John were sitting beneath a mimosa tree in the backyard and Fiona was moving as a shadow among the plants on the back porch and Ira whispered to his son, "If God did send a son and he did die to give us some idea about the way the world was and you could get that idea from eating this little wafer, then he would give it to anyone who wanted it, whether they were Catholic or not, wouldn't he?" and his son whispered, "He would give it to anyone, even Sammy Gold who isn't Catholic and who hits me on the shoulder whenever I go near him" and Ira said, "That's right. If all that was true, then I think you're right," and I looked at Ira to smile and nod at this little example of his secret talks with his son and I could see only the ocean on Ira's shoulders, the stretch left and right of the ocean as wide as the Alps and Ira's head was gone and I stopped short and I scrambled back away from him and Ira went on a few steps and he was walking firmly but he was headless and then he stopped and turned and his head was cradled in his arm and he asked, "What is it, Rebecca? Don't you understand?"

I woke up with no answer to that question. All I knew was

that I thought of Ira Holloway often in those three weeks and my hand was on the phone in my office a dozen times and I'd begun to move up through the marketing department and there was always some good reason to call our public-relations counsel but I knew quite well that it was Ira himself who drew my hand to the phone and it was Ira too that stopped me there, would not let me pick the phone up to dial. If he and I were to touch voices again, it would have to be his choice. And then one day there was a pink memo slip on my desk and his name was on it and I called him back. I just wanted to thank you for listening to me on the beach, he said. That meant a lot to me. It's okay, I said. I was happy to. Any time. And then we chatted a little bit, idly, and I could sense his struggle, I could hear the voice beneath the voice that was speaking, and he was saying Rebecca is waiting for me to ask to see her again. It's in the soft edge of her words. It's in her patience now with this sudden silence between us. The phone is hissing softly and neither of us feels compelled to fill this moment with words. We are comfortable together even with silence on a telephone and I want to see her but I also want to touch her and enter her and last night I found my way into Fiona only at the very last moment and if I had not, if I had made love to Rebecca and diminished the blind hungriness in my flesh and thereby failed to rise quickly enough for Fiona, there would have been a whole new realm of secrets to create for John because while I was inside Fiona's body John knocked at our door and Fiona pulled back sharply and scrambled up and threw the bedclothes over me and pulled her ankle-length nightgown on and if I had not entered Fiona quickly enough on this night, John would have found us in the first wild moments of a fight over sex and I was happy not to try to explain that to him at five years old. He woke from a bad dream and he was seeking me, I think, but Fiona opened the door and knelt to him and she touched his cheek and then she held him and she told him it was only a dream, he was good and he was loved and he could always overcome any dream and she nearly wept with tenderness for him and this touched me so that I could feel Fiona very briefly on my skin. And it's through Rebecca's voice that I can see this now about myself on that night, it's through Rebecca's voice in me—sweet, clearheaded Rebecca—I could feel Fiona on my chest and on the tip of my penis and she was lying on her side next to me in the sagging bed in the walk-up in the East Village and she watched her fingertips trace the lines of my face and beyond her I could see the great shaft of sunlight pouring down into the kitchen and the smell of Fiona's sex was as rich as the smell of the summer nights before I'd ever touched a woman and down in the street there was the sudden running whoop of children and then their laughter and Fiona's fingertips paused on my lips and she lifted her eyes and looked past me and she smiled at the sound and then she looked me carefully in the eyes and this was very early on, perhaps the first afternoon we made love, before anything, before even her first twinge of jealousy, before everything, and I loved her and she was looking at me with that faint smile on her lips at the sound of children and I knew that we would create someone between us. I could not imagine who our child would be but I knew that this much would come from us, and I'm sure she was thinking the same thing and we said nothing, we watched each other for a long time and then finally she closed her eyes and laid her head down to sleep and to dream and I remembered all of this with a soft rush as I watched her kneeling before John and holding him and he was looking at me over her shoulder and his face was still, unmoved now by his bad dream but unmoved by his mother's love as well, and even as I felt the quick tongue kiss of this memory of the Fiona I loved, I saw the phone-hiss silence of that moment between Fiona and John and I wanted it to be some other way, I shrank back from this thing I was doing. I motioned for him to put his arms around her and he nodded a little bit and he did this. He lifted his arms and returned her embrace and I was flushed now with regret. But once, I'd tried something else; I'd sat Fiona down, just the two of us, and I started out by gently asking, What if there's something about the Church that I really can't quite accept, and she said, Well what might that be? and she began to rub her knees, both hands and both knees, a quick, hard-pressing rub, and she was struggling to keep her voice steady and before I could answer her, before I could find even some little thing to start with, she said, You think you're smart enough to make up your own religion, do you? You think you can invent your own God and destroy mine? And that was that. And I lay in the bed and watched my son bring his arms up to hold his mother and I wondered at what price he was making this gesture for her and Fiona held him close and her smile lingered in me with the smell of her sweet pussy and the motes of dust floating in the sun from the skylight and then Fiona said to John, "You'll get dreams that seem like good dreams, too, and you have to fight them as hard as these bad dreams. The devil brings them both. We'll talk about all of that sometime. The devil wants you to get caught up living in this world and forget about heaven. That's where your only true life is." And her smile and her scent and the sun falling beside our wooden tub all vanished and John was looking at me and I put my forefinger to my lips and shook my head no and John made the faintest nod of his head to show me he understood. *And so the morning after, Ira called me and he sat with me in this silence on the phone and he felt no pressure to speak. He knew I was good for him, didn't he? He didn't need empty words from me. I just had to sit there and send this feeling to him in the silence, and that might not have been logical but it wasn't silly and fluttering and prattling either. Then he said that his regret on the beach was his being so self-absorbed. He wanted to know how life was for me in New York after Zurich, and I said I was okay, and we spoke in small ways for a time and I told him how it was that I got to work, using the subway, and he* told me that his son was presently passionate about trains and subways and the two of them came into the city every Saturday, catching a morning train from Seaview and arriving in Penn Station and then riding subways all day long, all the lettered trains and all the numbered trains. When he said this, there was another pause and I waited to see if he would invite me to meet them at Penn Station. I knew this was on his mind, but nothing was spoken and finally I asked how long he had been doing this. He said over a year and I said, "Ira, forget the difficulties of sex. This is the greatest sacrifice you have made for your son, that you should commute every weekday into Manhattan and then on Saturdays ride the trains again."

He laughed and we spoke in small ways some more and then I had a pressing call coming in from Switzerland and I hated to tell him good-bye but I did. I called him back later in the day, but he was gone, he was out of the office and out of town for a few days. Perhaps if I had gotten through to him on the phone that afternoon or even the next day, I would never have done what I did. One thing led to another after that, but I don't think he ever would have chanced a meeting with me if I myself had seemed willing to keep the telephone between us. And if I'd been willing to keep a telephone between us, we would surely have passed from each other's life long ago. But that Saturday morning I woke and I did not think about it, I took a cab to Penn Station and going down the steps to the platform of the midmorning train from Seaview I felt suddenly very fragile, as if all my bones were bird-hollow and would break with one misstep. I felt I might crumble even from the dank press of the urinary air but I went down the steps and along the platform and then there was the quick, knife-blade slip of the train and the flash of windows, people rising, and the train hissed to a stop. And I thought that this was a logical thing for me to do, really, since I found myself drawn to this man: I would see for myself if Ira had a relationship with his son that was consistent with the rest of his story. What I did *not have was an excuse for being there. Then I thought I was spared anyway. I did not see them in the first flow of passengers and I was ready to turn away and that surely would have been that, but then, three cars down from where I stood, a dark-haired child stepped off the train and his arm was raised behind him and he was holding a hand and the hand emerged and the arm and the man and it was Ira and when the boy had his father on the platform he stopped him and turned to him and opened a map and Ira crouched before him and they began to point at the map and trace long lines on it with their fingertips and their heads leaned very near to each other and Ira's hair was long and soft and black and the boy's hair was cut closer and I could see even from where I stood that its darkness was mitigated, there was a reddish cast to it, and I wanted very much at that moment to touch Ira's head, to keep him crouched there and to touch his hair, but even as I felt that, I snapped into a warm-cheeked consciousness of my presumption. There was no logic to this at all. I'd already come to believe Ira. I tried to move myself now, make my legs work to turn me and carry me quickly up the steps before Ira saw me, but Ira put his arm around John now, pulled him close and the boy put his arm around his father and I found myself working not at movement but breath, I was breathless at this embrace and I stood on the sidewalk in front of the terminal at the airport and my father bowed a little at the waist and his hand came forward to me and I wanted to brush it aside and put my arms around him but I could not myself initiate that, it would be a presumption and it would be illogical, for an embrace means something only if both desire it, and I put my hand in his and he shook it once, twice, firmly, and he smiled and his eyes were full as I left Switzerland to live in New York and I knew what all of that meant, that he was proud of me, but still I could go breathless before this image of Ira and his son embracing and I knew I shouldn't be here, I could not myself initiate this either. I turned my back to them even as I saw Ira rising from* beside his son and I took a step and another and I wanted to escape unseen and I wanted to hear his voice and I took another step and I was at the foot of the platform staircase and then Ira said, "Rebecca?"

I stopped and turned to him and wanting to hear his voice made all of the other considerations disappear. I didn't even try to think up an excuse for being there as Ira and his son approached. John was busy folding his map as he walked and he glanced at me only briefly but Ira held me unblinking with his eyes, his eyes that were blue like the sky west of Zurich, beyond the mountains there in those few minutes when the sun is nearly gone and night is near. I was held by his eyes and they made me feel not the least bit in need of an excuse, and for me to dote so on the color of them struck me as some sort of indicator. I was falling in love with him, I reasoned. I also reasoned that I should be scared as hell about that. But I wasn't. Ira was here now and I was breathing just as if I had done what I should have done, run up the steps before he even saw me, and he said, "Rebecca, you've come. I'm glad. I want you to meet John." And at this, his boy raised his eyes from the map and they were just the same eyes, blue with the darkening of night, and Ira said to him, "This is a business friend of mine, John. Her name is Rebecca Mueller." And at this, John stepped foward and put his hand out for me and he was five years old and he was no higher than my navel and he was full of secrets from this life he led with his father and he stuck his hand out to me and he said, "Pleased to meet you," and I took his hand and he shook it once, twice, firmly, and I said, "My pleasure, John," and I found myself still breathless.

John let go of my hand and turned to his father. "Let's get Rebecca's opinion on our route."

I glanced at Ira and his eyes fixed on mine. I was still waiting for things to slow down inside but his eyes were so soft upon me I could not put words or thoughts together clearly and I *was happy when John threw himself onto the second step of the staircase and said, "Sit here next to me, Rebecca."*

I did, and he explained the decision they had to make to get to Stillwell Avenue Coney Island, involving the F train and the D train and the A train and he wanted to make as many transfers as he could, there were a bunch of stations he wanted to see, and he talked very fast, his head bowed over the map, and the easy, quick-flowing matter-of-factness of his voice and the touch of his hand on my wrist to make a point made it seem as if he'd known me all his life, and once when John paused to find a spot on the map, the place in Brooklyn where he'd change from the A to the F, I looked up at Ira and he was watching his son and if his eyes reminded me of a nearly nighttime sky, the night there came on with sweet reassurance, I wanted this look to turn to me, this look in Ira's eyes as he watched his son bent over his subway map, and then it did, then as if he stood by the cribside of our own son and I had just whispered Ira's name to come away now and let the boy sleep, he held his gaze for a moment more on the child and then he turned it to me, he turned the tenderness of these eyes to me, linked all three of us together in just this easy movement of his eyes. I knew that my own eyes were nakedly loving now. Ira could surely see it. "What do you think?" John said. I held my gaze for a moment more on the man and then I looked to his son with the same tenderness Ira had just given me and I reaffirmed this link, though I knew that I would have very little of it in the years to come, this was one secret that John could not share, I would see almost nothing of this child that I also loved and I looked at his map for a few moments, working logically back and forth between Penn Station and the great tangle of lines in the center of Brooklyn, trying to find something for John, and then I said, "Have you considered the 2 or the 3 Train to Atlantic Avenue?" His head snapped down and even as he checked this out he said, "Oh my gosh. Oh my gosh. That's good Rebecca. We can change for the N train there. The N to Stillwell Avenue Coney Island. Rebecca's good, Dad."

When John spoke her name to me, said she was good, I found I couldn't look at Rebecca anymore. Not on that day. I did, of course, but she knew there was a strain in me all of a sudden. And, of course, she understood. She put her arm around John and gave him a squeeze and said she was glad she could be of help but she had to go. John asked me if she could ride the route with us. But she didn't look at me. She'd already peeked at my face, right after John's compliment, and she knew I was struggling with all this now, and she just crouched before my son and she said she was sorry but she had some things to do. And then she gave him a kiss on the cheek, which he cocked his head at after it was done, and she went quickly up the stairs. John watched her go. Then he carefully folded his map and put it in his back pocket and after he'd done all of that, he said, "Nice lady. I hope she's not a Catholic."

John and I talked for a while—not for the first time—about how he could not assume anything about any other Catholic just because his mother acted a certain way. He understood that, he said, but he still seemed relieved when I told him that Rebecca was not a Catholic. "And since she's not a Catholic," I said, "it's best not to mention her to Mommy. We'd be expected to convert her." John nodded his head grimly and that was an end to the discussion. I knew he would say nothing, but I knew, too, that all this was very dangerous. Still, I called Rebecca on Monday morning and she was very sorry she had presumed to show up at the train station and I said I was glad she did and we should have lunch, we should go somewhere just as we would do anyway, given our business relationship, and have lunch.

And it's not difficult for anyone listening to my words to anticipate that after our lunch, Rebecca would become important in my life. That much should be clear by now. I've spoken only of her for too long. It's not easy, trying to tell all of this in a way that is true to what deeply moves in me, what whispers to me, moment to vivid moment, telling me that I am alive in a special place and there is something behind all this, something unseen and unheard directly but approachable, accessible through the tumescent joy and tenderness of sex in me, and whenever it seems that all this has come to be focused on one woman or even on this voice I speak with, whenever it seems at last that the great synthesizing vision I seem to be chasing has just found its full expression in Fiona or in Hoa or in Rebecca or in me speaking in this voice of mine, then I know it's stopped being true. If I go to that lunch, say, and from that, Rebecca becomes The Great Love Of My Life, the woman who better than anyone I've ever known cares about me, opens to me, touches my own outward reaching self, who receives, more fully than anyone else, my love, my own richly detailed and even, ultimately, in some ways, selfless regard, if all that is so, it does not change the part of me that, for instance, reads in the newspaper this very morning—on the same beach in the same canvas chair where I read yesterday about X rays— that after more than five years of Communist rule Saigon still seems much the way it did during the war and I become efflorescent with love and not even for Hoa, at that particular moment, not even for a woman of Saigon but I fly away from Vietnam on leave and I land in Bangkok and I check into a hotel on the Chao Phraya River and I have only nine days and there is the trembling of gnostic yearning in me now and I sit only briefly to gather myself on the back veranda of my hotel and I watch the river and the women with their flat-topped conical straw hats pole by in their canal skiffs and I rise and I go out into the street and I find a massage parlor, slick and new like all of the center of this city, and the foyer is dim and plush and a man meets me and smiles and my first impulse is to speak Vietnamese but that's another country now and he shows me around the corner into a corridor and one wall is a vast window and behind it on three levels of carpeted platform are women in white minidresses and they are lounging there with pillows, watching television and doing their nails and talking and dozing, and each has a number on her sleeve and the man says that they see only a mirror on their side, take my time, choose the woman I want and he is sure that she will want me too, and I lean against the window, flatten my palms there, feel my breath come back warmly to me, and I am weak with love for them all and I know that I will never decide if I look at even a few of them closely, and so I let my eyes fall on a woman on the upper level hugging her legs to her, her chin on her right knee, her head angled a little to the side and her eyes closed, a pose of reverie, and the number 61 is on her sleeve and I tell her number to the man. He steps inside with two towels on his arm and the women stir but number 61 does not, she dreams on, and he speaks and she opens her eyes and they are very beautiful, these eyes, dreamy still, and she comes down the level and takes the towels and I meet her at the door and she smiles at me and her skin is curry brown and her eyes are still very slightly closed, as they will remain, like a silent-movie queen, and she takes me upstairs and into a room with mahogany paneling and a dresser and a couch and a steam machine and a tub and a massage bed and music coming in, poky Tijuana brass, this guy's in love with you, and when the door is closed, number 61 turns to me and she says, "You just want rubdown?"

I say, "No. Do you just want to give a rubdown?"

The question surprises her and her heavy eyes open wide very briefly and she looks at me carefully then and she smiles and says, "No. I think I want love with you. You good-face man."

"Your name is not 61."

She laughed. "No. You want me telling you my name?"

"That's what love is," I say. "You know these things about each other."

"You name?"

"Ira Holloway."

She tries my name on her tongue, skipping the Holloway quickly, rolling the Ira around a couple of times with pretty good results. Then she says, "Mr. Ira, my name Kesree."

"Kesree." I repeat it softly and she smiles.

Then she looks suddenly away, across the room. "Two hundred baht extra. Okay?"

"Okay," I say and then Kesree's eyes come back to me and she picks up the smile from my saying her name and she undresses me and she puts me in the tub and she begins to lather me with soap that smells like mangoes and she works her way down my chest and then she whistles at the gathered fullness of my penis, she whistles softly and leans to me and kisses me lightly once on the lips and she nods at my erection and says, "This come from you know my name?" and I say yes and then she rinses me and leads me to the table and she wants me to lie on my face and she touches my penis for the first time, holds me to point downward so I can lie flat, and already each part of her echoes all the others, her hand has become her heavy-lidded eyes, has become her whistle, has become her reverie behind the two-way mirror, and this touch of her hand thrills me almost to the point of taking her in my arms right away but instead I let her lay me flat on the table and she slips from her dress quickly and she sits on me and I feel the soft fur kiss of her pussy on the small of my back and she rubs my shoulders softly for a time and then when her hand comes near my turned face I catch it with my hand and bring it to my lips and I kiss each fingertip and I hear her breath snag at this gesture and she rises up and then we lie side by side and she considers my face very carefully and we don't touch for those moments at all, I simply kissed her fingertips and now she wants a little time to figure me out and I wait and then she kisses me lightly on the lips, an invitation, and I lay her on her back and I kiss all the dusky rises and falls and planes of her, I hold her henna nipples in my lips and tongue the tips of them—and they are on my tongue now, even as I speak, even as I remember her, the tips of her nipples are still shadowed on my tongue—and after touching every part of her with my tongue, every pore, I end at her pussy and she is splashing with love there, there is no massage-girl trick in the world to fake this rich flow of love and she arches her back and I touch as deeply as I can inside her with my tongue and her soft depths squeeze my tongue even now, even as I remember, and I drink her again and I taste the warm, musky flow of her and I love her for her little joke that wasn't a joke, that knowing her name made my penis fill for her even before her first touch or her first real kiss, and I touch her deep and I drink her and I am faint with love for her and she is sighing over and over and over and finally she lifts at the hips and I press deeper and she shudders and cries out and I slide my tongue up to the little yearning tip at the top pinch of her pussy and I can feel its hard upward yearning and I wonder if she gathers there as I do in my own late-day shadow of this place and I lift my eyes and she cries out louder now with my tongue on this spot that has no name sweet enough to speak and she covers her face with her hands pressing at her eyes and then she draws her hands down her cheeks and she sighs now and her hips fall and go slack and I kiss her pussy once more, gently, and her hands are on my head and she draws me up to look at her. Her eyes are wide now and they swarm at mine and she says, "Why?" and I know what she's asking and I understand that if I use the word love, it will make the wrong kind of sense to her, I will turn into a kind of man she's seen before and she already realizes I'm not like that or she wouldn't be asking the question and so I say, "I can see how beautiful you are." She has her own way around the cheap use of words—even in this foreign language of English—so she says, "I like you," and she says this with the stretched vowels of a real discovery and she pulls me to her and kisses me deep and *when I kiss him*

I can taste my own pussy on his mouth and because it is on his mouth and because he drank me there and because he found me beautiful, I can taste how good it is: mild curry and coconut milk, tree bark, wet earth in my father's field. I know from his mouth that I am so beautiful I can simply be myself, and nothing I say or do can change the taste of me.

And I meet Kesree on her day off and we walk in the streets and we pass the Grand Palace with its great white crenelated wall and rapier spires and fluted towers and in a parade field nearby there is a weekend market and a throng of stalls have been thrown up with silks and fruits and fish and radios and pots and straw hats and rugs and steaming soups and we watch a snake charmer grab his cobra by the neck and pry open its mouth with a knife to show the fangs to all of us in the circle around him and a trickle of blood comes from the animal's mouth and the man casts the snake down and it rises up spreading its hood and Kesree takes my arm and moves me away and we enter a temple's walls and we are surrounded by the vision of a universe filled with a profusion of bits of bright color and great upswooping curves and bells quaking in the distance and a high brassy woman sound of chanting believers, and we move beneath red glaze snake-scaled roofs and at the peaks the faces of the snakes appear and rear high into the hot sky, and these are the snakes, Kesree whispers, who wished to be Buddhas, and we slip from our shoes and pass into the temple and we kneel on red mats with the chanting voices all about us and I glance at Kesree's toes lined sweetly up behind her as she genuflects far forward and I bend now too and before us is the emerald Buddha, high in a spotlit glass case rising from levels of flowers and food and statues and smoking incense and all about us on the walls are monkey warriors and demons battling and Kesree bows and prays and I bow and taste her still on my tongue and I feel her folded body next to mine and then we go out and when we are in a deserted turning of the temple grounds, she draws me to her and we kiss and a bell murmurs somewhere nearby and I keep my eyes open as I kiss her and our embrace is an upswoop of color here and we go out and suddenly she says, "Burmese destroy many beautiful temples of Thailand. I hate Burmese. All Thai people think that. Burmese come many times and hurt our country. There is one big pagoda in Burma made of gold and all that gold is from Thai Buddhas. I remember my other lives sometimes. One life I live before, I go to heaven. I remember that. I am in heaven and I see no Burmese there." And with this, she puts her arm around me and lays her head against my arm, and that night she stays with me in my hotel room and she wants to do this for no money, she says, and I open the window to the sounds of the night, the distant murmuring of the temple bells, laughter somewhere out on the hotel grounds, even the soft slip of the river. I listen for that sound, certain that I can hear the river sliding through its banks, and then I move to Kesree naked on our bed and she says, "Drink Kesree again," and I do, she opens her legs and I lick all the faintly darkened flesh ringing her pussy and then I drink her deeply and I realize at last that she shared her hatred for the Burmese with me today as an act of love and I was sorry for her hatred when she told me, I wished she didn't have it, and I am sorry still, as I drink her, and I am sorry now as I speak, but I felt even closer to her when I realized why she spoke, she tasted even sweeter for this intimacy, though I knew I would love a Burmese woman who hated the Thais and I would love a Cambodian woman and a Chinese woman who hated the Vietnamese and I already loved Hoa, who hated the Cambodians, and I already loved Xau, who hated the Chinese, and they all felt they hated in order to protect the ones they loved and they wanted to protect me too with these warnings about others and they held me close and I ached for all of them and I loved all of them and I suppose I sounded at times with Rebecca as if I hated Fiona, but I never did, really, and Rebecca did take the intimacy of my sharing these feelings to be a reflection of my love for her, and it was, and she sat with me in a Thai restaurant in Times Square at that first lunch and I spoke to her for a while about the Thai spices, how the basil in her chicken was good but it was a substitute for something else in Thailand that was even better and in the middle of the small talk I spoke suddenly, as Kesree had spoken suddenly, of the difficulties of the previous night, the fright of John at the door of our bedroom, and Rebecca put her hand on mine.

And this is how Rebecca and I made love with each other on that day, a way that we found with very few words spoken about it. After the lunch, she simply said, "Let's go someplace private," and I said, "Yes," and we hailed a cab and she gave the driver an address on Riverside Drive and my fear of letting go to her remained *but I knew what he feared and I knew already that he loved me and that he even loved small parts of me as perfect little microcosms of all of me, so I reasoned that there were things that we could do that would make us closer, that would bind us together in the way I desired and the way he desired but that would not make his other life impossible* and I looked once at Rebecca's face, which she turned to me, knowing my thoughts, whispering to me silently, and she had not refreshed her lipstick, her lips were as naked as they were when I first loved her in Zurich, and then I turned my eyes to the quick flash of Broadway shops as we dashed uptown and I vaguely shaped in my head the Götterdämmerung of the coming evening in Seaview and I did not say no, I did not say stop the cab, though I thought that my son would surely be involved, *and this was the moment I still wish to think about, there was no better moment than this: Ira sat next to me in the cab and he held my hand the whole way to my apartment and he did not say no, he did not say stop the cab, though I knew that when we were alone if I said that I must have him inside my body he would have to say yes, he loved me enough to risk even the delicate balance of his life in Seaview, even that, even with his son involved. He held my hand*

and he looked once at my face, his eyes going to my lips and I immediately wished I'd put my lipstick on in the restaurant, though he would tell me on that very afternoon about the nakedness of my lips and I was glad not to know it in the cab because I was maintaining a delicate balance as well, one of mind and heart. This act of love seemed even an act of passion, and it was to a certain degree, but it was more than anything an act of love, which is perhaps even more uncontrolled and unreasonable than any act of passion, and if I'd known my nakedness before this glance of his, if I'd thought of my lips there in the cab, perhaps my mind would have prevailed and I would have said no, for I was struggling to gather my heart's courage against the logic of that no even then, I was arguing with my father even then and at last I left him fuming in the study and I climbed the stairs, up the foot-faded flowers of the carpeted stairs, and I knocked softly at my mother's door and I wondered, as I always did since the time I'd seen her after her bath, if she would be naked and she said come in and I did and I closed the door behind me and I went to her and I was sixteen, I think, and she was sitting at her dressing table and she was not naked but she had only a light gown on and she was naked beneath that and I went to her and I wanted to go out with a boy and my father had said no and she said she could do nothing but she held me close and she smelled of sandalwood and gardenia and I could feel her nakedness beneath her gown and she seemed so vulnerable, weeping for me but unable to help, and I felt naked in the cab with Ira, and my own perfume smelled of those same things, as it always has, of sandalwood and gardenia, and I turned my face from Ira and I concentrated on the smell of me, I lifted my wrist to my face and smelled my mother's smell and it gave me courage now and we drove on in silence and I held her hand and there was that sweet thrashing of anticipation that had begun in me, like the guttering of a flame in a dark room, and I tried to keep the flame small, keep its dipping and flaring soft, contained,* because I did not know what shapes and textures and tastes of this woman I would actually be able to bend to, to hear the deep-space whisper from, we might still just go and sit in a quiet room and talk some more or just be silent together— that would be lovely too—but the flame-thrash in me was the possibility of more, was the true life in me—that's what I'm coming to know in all of this—and in the cab I could only hang back in the dark, watch the flame from a distance, and then we were in an elevator and we rose together and we kept our hands entwined and then she fretted with her key at the lock and I could see the faint quaking in her hand and we were through the door and in each other's arms and her body was pressed full against mine and *I could feel him through our clothes, the great rising urgency of him, and it took my breath away, from desire and also from despair—suddenly I could not figure out how this might work, I could only anticipate either sexless talk, which was no longer tolerable, I knew, or a full loosing of all this, which he believed would make things impossible for him at home, and about that I was convinced he was right, from all he'd told me, the logic of that was inescapable, but I did not say no, I did not pull away, and he is no fool, he knew the risks and he did not say no, he did not pull away*—we pressed together and I kissed her and our mouths opened at once to each other and I touched the tip of her tongue with mine and when we were on the beach her tongue was shy and I expected that again now, even though she'd brought me here, but it was not, her tongue slid forward to meet mine and they rubbed together, leaned heavily and rubbed there with the languor of cats after a nap, and I was trembling with gratitude at all this and I was trembling with fear and she seemed to want to make love with me. And this much I know already, this much I've said already and it's true and the more I speak, the more nakedly true it becomes to me: if a woman asks me to love her, to touch all that's unseen in her, to listen to her faintest voice, I cannot turn away from that, I cannot withhold my hands my mouth my own unseen body my own unheard voice and Rebecca was asking now and *I did not know what to do with him now that our tongues were touching, and part of my mind was trying to work this problem out and his tongue moved beneath the tip of mine and he gently lifted me there and then he touched that thin front edge of skin beneath, slid down to the root of my tongue, and this was a surprising little thing and very nice and when he stopped that, began to move somewhere else, I pulled gently away and kissed him briefly on the lips to show him there was nothing wrong, and I said, "All I have to do is say yes to you and you would jeopardize everything."*

He did not hesitate even for a breath. "Yes," he said.

"For the same reason you would say yes, I can't let you," I said.

He nodded. And then I laid my head on his shoulder and we held each other for a long time until our hearts slowed and I whispered to him, "You know that I want to, very much, even though I will not say yes."

"I know," I said and I trembled to press her now, to ask her to say yes because I knew that she would but John was clinging to my hand, was leading me blind in the dark, and I would not let go of him and I said nothing though I could not even draw a breath now before Rebecca I was so clenched with desire for her.

"What if you visited me here now and then," she said. "We can sit together. We can touch hands. We can speak in low voices with the shades drawn. I will whistle Beethoven for you."

"With naked lips," I said.

"Yes." She took her head from my shoulder, leaned back just far enough to look me steadily in the eyes and everything in me went slack, I was slump-shouldered in love for this woman whose delft blue eyes fixed on mine and I could not speak but I knew there was no more fear in this for me and then I knew I had to offer it back because I loved her more with each moment of her eyes not moving, her brow smoothed and waiting, her body smelling of flowers and trees and willing to yield its dark earth-root love smells to me and neither of us saying yes, and I said, "If you're doing this from love, then it will be bad for you."

I already knew it was from love and I knew I loved her, too, and if I'd reasoned it out as she had, the thing that I should have done from love at that moment was say no to her, I should have kissed her once more and then disappeared, and eventually I did say to her, "I don't know what I can offer you. There are years of this ahead." And I did say to her, "Tell me to go."

"You don't want that," she said.

"No."

"I don't either."

This was the only reality then: Rebecca and I at the same moment stopped the words and came together once more and pressed into each other and opened our mouths but only as a brief link to the previous embrace, a little oh-yes-this-was-where-we-were kind of touch of the tongue and then we separated and she took my hand and kissed my knuckles and she drew me into her living room and we looked around the room to find a place and I sat her on an old claw-footed overstuffed chair and I sat on the footstool before her and we linked our hands in her lap and we spoke for a while, about Zurich, about Wabash, and her lips were naked and she sang the "Ode to Joy" softly to me in German and her cat came and rubbed against me and horns honked in a distant street and there were footsteps in the hall that came and went and there was a ticking clock somewhere in another room and we often lapsed into silence, Rebecca and I, we sat together, she and I, twice a week for more than two years and there were many hours of silence, many, and there was never a stirring of even a hand in uneasiness at this, we were easy in our silence and we each listened for the breath of the other and sometimes we would bend near, she sliding forward on her chair and we would bring our faces close and I would feel her breath on my cheek and she would feel my breath on hers and I would kiss the tip of her nose and she would kiss the cleft of my chin and we would study each other's hands and there was a faint fuzz there on her knuckles, the color of the pallid Swiss sunlight, and I knew there was a soft sargasso struck with this same sunlight there between her legs, hidden always, yearning for me but hidden and she would hear the snag of my breath at these thoughts and she would take my hands to her face and kiss them and I would yearn, of course, yearn till I wanted to cry out in this room and this would go on for more than two years but as far as Rebecca and I knew there was a decade or more to go and I yearned to bend to her and put my mouth against her secret lips and speak to them and listen to them whisper and open my own secret self to her, enter her and cry out to her inside, but I held very still, I did not move, for that moment I yearned for was a leap of self, nothing less, and there were women forever alive within me because of more muted moments of intimacy than that, so I knew that I could never come with Rebecca and then rise from her bed and go out and lie down with Fiona and pretend, for Fiona was now a woman I did not love, not in that way. Love, yes, to wish wholeness for, to wish peace for, but not to love in the way that would have me gather my self into tens of thousands of fragments and dash them into the dark, a little echo of the moment when the universe was a tiny testicle full of everything and all of history waited for its own leap in order to begin.

Is it crazy, thinking of all this on that scale? The Church thinks not, that's clear. The Church that has put itself in the business of figuring out the universe has always known that its greatest rival in those matters is the ravishing focus of our bodies. For myself, I'm just trying to understand why my life is so powerfully compelled by soft touching, joined flesh, complex parts of a self unseen.

And I went out of this hotel in Puerto Vallarta this morning, alone, and I put my room key in my pocket and I was held briefly by the image of this woman I love sleeping in the bed upstairs: Rebecca, her hair splayed on the pillow. And down at the end of the long drive there was a pothole and a road crew had a cauldron mixing tar and with the smell of tar a girl rides past me on her bike and she has long russet hair and she is barefoot and I am ten years old and I stand beneath the horse chestnut tree in my yard and watch her go by and it is early summer, school is out and all the summer lies ahead, and somewhere in the direction she's heading, a street is being resurfaced and the smell of tar is in the air and I run to my bike and I race after her, watching the lift of her hair behind her and she is willow thin and her bare heels rise and fall and rise and fall and the smell of tar grows stronger and she turns at the corner and I turn and ahead the street is slick black and at the far end the dump truck has just whooshed into emptiness and stops in a cloud of gravel dust and I've been thinking all along about how to overtake her, how to speak to her, and miraculously she stops ahead and gets off and nudges her kickstand down with the ball of her pretty foot and already I have the instinct from this moment of enchantment looking at her summer-bare feet to follow the line from her instep up her ankle up her leg to the sweet subtlety of her knee to her thigh and then to vague thoughts of things that are still as secret to me as the origin of the universe. And she is moving to the straight edge of fresh tar.

I pedal up and I stop and I say, We're stuck. She turns to me and she has a long, thin face and her eyes are russet too and very large and she brushes a lock of her hair back from her cheek and she looks at me for what feels like a very long time, deciding something that I suddenly wish I had not encouraged. But then she smiles, and in that smile the smell of tar is rendered sweet to me forever, and she says, I wanted to stop. And she crouches beside the tar and she stretches out her hand and scoops a little dollop of it onto her fingers and without standing up, without making a show of it for me, without the slightest pause, she brings her hand to her face and takes the tar into her mouth and begins to chew it. I feel my eyes bug at this, but she is not looking and I quickly smooth out my face and say, Is it good to chew? Yes, she says, and she rises and chews for a time, concentrating on it as if she were trying to guess its vintage, and she does not ask me to join her and at the time I'm grateful for that and I do not volunteer, though for a few days afterward I am hard on myself for not doing this thing also, not showing my connection with her at once, and I blame my aversion to licorice and what a dumb thing that would be to lose this wonderful girl for the rest of my summer just because I hate licorice so much and I replay the rest of that little scene over and over trying to rewrite its ending but it always goes the same way, just as it really did. She chews with calm contemplation for a long while and I stand and watch her without speaking, without moving, carefully subduing even my breath so as not to disturb her, and finally she stops and lifts her hand to her mouth and takes out the ball of tar and she holds it up and I look at it in wonder and it is slick and wet and it is the blackest thing I've ever seen and I think of the inside of her mouth and then she tosses it away and moves silently to her bike and I know I have missed a chance, I know she was waiting for me to get off my bike and join her in this and when I did, she would have told me her name and would have asked me to ride with her and now I am lost as she lifts the kickstand on her bike with her bare foot and her toes are long and the nails are painted pink and she gets onto her bike and at least I have the presence of mind to say, I'm Ira Holloway, what's your name? And she says, Karen Granger, and then without a pause she pedals away.

And this very morning, as I strolled into the Mexican street, it was Karen Granger who filled me up and I stopped and she was still showing herself to me. I realized for the first time that even as Karen was in a place in her life that led her to pedal across town to find road tar to chew she was also carefully painting her toenails, and I loved her even more, loved the sweet complexity of her, and I have not spoken of Fiona for a long while now, I realize, not really spoken of her, not summoned her up and looked at her or touched her or smelled her or tasted her, not spoken of the Fiona who is still alive somewhere in me, the Fiona who stood in a column of sunlight and spoke of Vincent Van Gogh and then took me into her body while children laughed in the streets and pigeons dashed past our window and I gathered inside her body and I died there—the words so often sound wrong about the body parts and the things they do, but that's how the Elizabethans spoke of that moment, to die in a woman's lap, to die, and the sound of it is right, and they understood the immensity of that letting go, and they all believed—even the greatest intellectuals among them—that there was another life after death, a richer life, and so to die was to seek rebirth, to seek a vast life impossible without that death—and I died in Fiona many many times and I came back to life each time and it was true that I was altered, each time altered, and if I stopped loving her in such a way that I could no longer die inside her, she still had shaped me forever, for I knew her, and that was the way the Elizabethans, in their wisdom, spoke of the whole act: to know. To make love is all right but to *know* is the real truth of the touching, and I knew Fiona and I do not want to say any more now.

I wander from the hotel and the street buzzes with motorbikes and taxis and I want to say no more. I circle the hotel and I slip along a shadowed path of bougainvillea and down to the beach and I look out to the far horizon, wrinkled like the instep of Karen's foot, and I try to place myself out there, far away from these words, and I want to say no more about any of this, I want to remain unknown even to myself, I want to take all of these words back and never speak them and when Karen comes to me this morning I stand on the beach and I weep for her and so many things are behind those tears that I want only to hold her and not speak, not like this, certainly, not even speak to her in our embrace but just offer my naked-ness to Karen Granger and receive her nakedness in return. And yet I must carry this to some conclusion.

Not long ago, late this summer, John went through a little rush of growth, he was only eight and it didn't make him seem on the verge of adulthood to my eye, far from it, but he lost some baby plumpness and he seemed tall when he moved with his peers in the school yard and it struck Fiona, I know, that things were changing in him and this spoke of other changes that were pretty near, really, and one evening the three of us were hunched quietly over soup at dinner and I felt John brood-ing over the long grace Fiona had said, moving from the soup to our sins to our place as perpetual children in this evil world and we ate in silence after that and Fiona was watching John and then abruptly she rose and came to him and he looked up and my hands turned hard and I pushed back just a little from the table but she came to him softly and the hand that she brought to his face did not make him flinch because it was clearly driven by some cryptic gentleness and she touched his cheek with her fingertips and she ran them in a circle there and then to his upper lip and he frowned and then pulled back, and she whispered, "Sorry," but her voice was jagged and she was sorry not for this vaguely odd thing she'd done, though it was in her mind to apologize for that. Rather—and I understood all this later—she was sorry because one day there would ap-pear on that lip the first signs of being a man and this was the thought she'd had, all at once, over the soup, with her mind on our perpetual childhood and John sitting there, clearly growing, in refutation.

And this was the summer he'd begun to pursue roller coasters with the single-mindedness he'd once given the subways and they frightened Fiona and she never went with us as we ranged into Connecticut and New Jersey and upstate New York looking for coasters and it was okay with her, I think, because they were a child's thing and then in August John found a brochure for an old playland with a beach and a wooden coaster, a relic of the twenties, on a Jersey lake, out far past the refineries and the tank farms, out in the Highlands, almost to the Delaware Gap, a long drive for us, we wouldn't be back till midnight, and he and I would talk, as we always did on these trips, we would talk about this world we lived on the edge of and he could see everything clearly in spite of the motions we went through now for Fiona, Mass every morning with the old women with lace laid on their heads and rosaries dangling from their fists, he could even see the old women clearly and the night before we were to go to Jersey, he said, "Mrs. Minetti looks very sad to me. She says all those rosaries but it never takes away her sour face." Fiona came into the room to tell him good night at that moment and he and I shushed each other with a brief locking of eyes and I thought of bringing up Mrs. Minetti the next day on the drive, to let him talk that out a little, but almost the first thing Fiona said after we'd fallen silent was "I want to go with you tomorrow."

This was what John and I had come to in these five years of our secret life: he was sitting on his bed in a T-shirt and the boxer shorts he liked to sleep in, his back against the wall and the playland brochure unfolded before him, and I was sitting on the edge of the bed, turned now away from him at Fiona's presence in the room. She'd made her declaration and she waited in the center of the floor and there seemed to be a meekness about her, something tractable. It seemed to be in her hands, crumpled together before her, and in her feet, she was barefoot and I did not want to look at her feet closely, not in an intimate way, not her pussy and not her feet either and not the fuzz on her forearm or the whorl of her ear when she put her hair up, but I did look at her closely all the time in another way, in order to read her mood, her pain, and her right foot was angled up and the toes were curled back out of sight and the foot fell a little to the side and then righted itself and then fell again, waiting, and even to the careful eye these things might be seen as a readiness to be talked out of her request, but as John and I didn't answer at once and the silence stretched on, Fiona's chin began to lift slowly and her head was steady and her eyes were steady on us even as her hands and her feet made little-girl, please-may-I gestures, but I knew from her eyes that this was not negotiable and I also knew how disappointed John was, I'd heard his faint suck of breath when she said this thing and he was thinking now about all the reasons he could offer to discourage her from going and I turned back to him, I wanted to signal him that we shouldn't push this, but either he read me instantly, just from the turning, or he'd already seen what I saw in his mother, and he said, "Sure, Mom. Bring your swimsuit. They've got a neat beach, too." He looked at me after this and again all we needed to say we said with the brief locking of our eyes and I wonder if he felt a little rush from what had just happened, as I did, the little glide-and-swoop-and-glide-again feeling of expertise; at least there was that feeling we could share when the dance of just the right few words carried us around her pain and her rage.

"Is that okay with you, Ira?" she asked.

I turned to her at once. "Of course," I said.

She nodded faintly at me, a heavy-lidded nod as if she were very sleepy and I'd just told her to put out the light. Then she roused herself a bit and she said, "Can I have a little time alone with John?"

The question, of course, was rhetorical, but she never failed to ask it. I would often have the last word at night with John, though she allowed it only because she thought the two of us prayed together and she liked that, but some nights she had her own concerns that she wanted to put to her god with her hand clutching her son's, and John would keep his head bowed and his eyes squeezed shut, and the next day it would always be the first thing he wanted to vent off, he would tell me about her impassioned pleading with Christ and I could hear far more than even he, *Please, I ask my Jesus there in the presence of this boy child that came from my body, please Jesus come into my heart and into the heart of my son and let him live on this planet without the terrible distractions that would draw him away from you and from your heavenly father whom you were sent to embody, whom you actually became, incarnate, in that great mystery, the mystery of how you became God made flesh, became the sentience behind everything, became the man who waits and breathes softly and watches and judges behind everything, and no one can really picture God and that's something God was aware of and that's why He sent a man, He sent this man and He became this man, He became this beautiful man hanging on a cross, became you sweet Jesus, and I look at the sculpture of you, the image made of your bloody body that hangs in the church in the dim shadows of the arch beside the confessionals and I look up at you there, the slick whiteness of thighs and chest and arms gouged deep by the forces of this world, and I am overcome with tenderness.* But I have never told John about the voice of his mother that I can hear so strongly inside me, and I wonder if this will be his gift, too, someday, to hear the voices of the women he loves, and I wish that for him. Before I say the rest of what I have to say, I must give voice to that devout wish, that when my son grows up and loves a woman he loves her enough to listen for her deepest voice, to find her deepest pain and her deepest joy and her deepest strength and then love her for those things. But with his mother he dealt with her prayers over him in his room by humming soundlessly in his head, that's what he told me when

I asked how he felt at those moments, he used to listen to her but he soon understood that what she said over and over was coming from the same pain that caused her to do all the other things she did and he decided he did not need to hear these prayers, they frightened him a little and he finally decided he didn't have to listen and he found that he could hum in his head and then it was all right. And I was always somewhere downstairs pacing during this—I could never sit still when these last words before sleeping were spoken to John, and I prayed, too, in a way, I focused my fearful love for both of them and asked without sureness of a hearer that no harm would come to my son.

And on this particular night when John was eight—just eight years old—Fiona came down the stairs and she seemed very calm. She grabbed the knob at the bottom of the banister and she held on and stretched there, almost swung there as if on a gatepost, a girlish, first-day-of-spring gesture with a placid face, her wide mouth quiet, faintly smiling if anything, and she said, "He's a good boy. I can trust that."

I was—and I regretted it at once—standing across the living room and I was beside, I suddenly realized, the crucifix hanging on the wall, and Fiona looked at me and said, "Kneel and pray with me now," and I knew this wouldn't have happened if I hadn't been standing there, it wasn't part of her routine, but I was caught and I knew I could not say no to this, and she came to me and took my hand and turned me around and we knelt there before the crucifix and I was glad to realize that she meant for us to pray silently. Away from the bedroom I had won her trust enough that she would let me have my own prayer at a moment like this, and I bowed my head and I could not hear her voice inside me, as I might have expected, I only felt her body folded nearby and I'd already said whatever it was I had to say and I began to hum in my head. I hummed the "Ode to Joy" and Rebecca's breath was upon my face.

But the next morning I grew suddenly fearful of what had

happened the night before. I knew in hindsight to distrust Fiona's calm mood. John was tight-jawed at breakfast and I realized that it wasn't simply because Fiona was going with us. He'd reconciled himself to that immediately the night before. He'd had far worse challenges than that. We sat at the kitchen table and the morning sun was pressing in at the window over the sink and there was a moment right after John sat down across from me that Fiona was rinsing out a glass, she was filling it and draining it and filling it over and over, and her shadow was on my son and his jaw was tight and he lifted his eyes and he told me by a quick narrowing of them and then a steady fix on me that something was wrong, but Fiona was whistling suddenly at the sink, she was blocking the sunlight and her shadow hovered over John and she was whistling now and I wondered if she had ever whistled before. I didn't think so and I had a foolish little pinch of fear that she'd somehow read Rebecca's image on my hands and she was whistling to let me know, but she couldn't have done that, she could not even read the true hearts of her husband and son, she just whistled tunelessly as she rinsed the glass again and again and I kept my eyes on John who after a few moments shook his head faintly no, to tell me there was nothing to be done for now, we'd have to put the problem aside, and then suddenly the sunlight was upon him and he flinched a little and turned his face away and Fiona was beside me and I did not look up at her, for John's head was lit up from the splash of sunlight from the kitchen window and my breath caught at the redness of his hair, at the veining of red in the black of his hair, and Fiona was standing over me and I made myself look up at her and she had the glass in her hand and she said, "I'm very happy this morning, Ira. I'm very happy," and in the car none of us spoke except finally Fiona, who insisted on sitting in the back so as not to disturb the two of us in any way, said, "How beautiful this is," as we droned through the rise and fall of forests of white oak and red oak and chestnut, the sky cut at that moment by a ridgetop with the trees stunted at the crest from ice storms that were unimaginable on this hot morning. "I'm glad you came," I said. "Yes," John said, turning around in his seat, "me too," though I could hear the force of his will in this, much more than usual. "You're both a blessing from God," Fiona said, and she rolled her window down and I turned the air conditioner off and touched my rearview mirror to see her and she angled her face into the open window and her hair thrashed behind her like a flame.

The park was on the shore of a glacial lake in the midst of the highlands and we walked through a great basket-handle stone arch rimmed with painted plaster clown faces and the midway popped with pellet guns and sparked and thumped with bumper cars and everything was shrouded in trees and it was cool here and up ahead the lake flickered with the high sun and off to the right the coaster rose humpbacked from a stand of red maples and John was leaning that way already but Fiona stopped us and she took a deep breath and she turned her face to me and she was smiling a smile that was stretched as far as it would go and it was as if she'd just rounded a corner on a city street and she'd smiled at an old man with a broom out of sight there and the smile was still on her face as she happened on to me and I collapsed inside with tenderness over her, once again, after all of this, I collapsed inside and I was very happy that she was moved to smile this smile, I was happy for the day before us and she had even brought her swimsuit with her, I knew, and there was a blanket rolled under her arm and we would walk into the water to our waists, to our chests, to our chins, we would float there together and perhaps hold each other beneath the water, out of sight, and she would say nothing of all that she had brought between us, she would disappear beneath the water and come up and she would be the woman she once was and I would lie with her on the beach and so I told John to go ahead and ride the coaster, I'd sit with his mother on the beach for a while first, and he always trusted my reading of her and he took this as something I saw that she needed to keep her on balance and he nodded briefly at me and slipped away and Fiona watched him go and her smile remained but faded just a little at the edges into a smile that I, too, could have for him, a smile of how, in just a few short years, he was to separate from me in some drastic way. This was natural. And I took Fiona's hand and we walked past the barkers and the spinning wheels and falling metal ducks and we took our shoes off and I watched her do this, briefly, watched the lift of her foot behind her and the shoe slip off and her instep rippled whitely and she wiggled her toes, sweetly, and I prayed now again, prayed that she would say nothing but just walk with me and sit with me and lie with me and the air smelled of fresh water, not like the sea but like a roaring summer rain that had passed now and was still hanging on the trees, the air smelled of that and of August honeysuckle and of charcoal fire and of cotton candy and Fiona spread the blanket.

We sat and watched the lake and soon I closed my eyes to the sun-flash chop of the water and the slide of sails out there. I closed my eyes and I lay back and I touched the back of Fiona's hand, she was still sitting and was braced against this hand and I put my fingertips on the faint rise of the veins there and I felt a sweet nibble of desire at this and I wondered how long this feeling would last. And then she said, "It's the color of your eyes."

I did not respond for a moment, stricken as I was with thankfulness. I kept my fingertrips on her hand and I lay there, understanding that she was looking at the lake and seeing me, seeing me perhaps on a city street before anything else had come between us and she came around the corner and she looked at my eyes and she loved me at once, just from that, I became part of her landscape with that first look and perhaps I am part of the landscapes of all the women I've loved. I knew them and that was the point of the touching, to know, and that was my abiding desire, to know. But the desire was also to be *known*. My bones, my nakedness, my deepest self laid bare to a woman. To be known by her.

"The lake," she said.

I sat up beside her now and she turned her face to me, looked into my eyes. "It's true," she said.

"Yours are lighter," I said. "They're the color of your milk. When you nursed John, your milk."

Her brow furrowed briefly and I stiffened from my mistake. She'd taken him from her breast right away. This was a bad thing for her. More guilt. I wanted to say something to make it right, but it would only make it worse. But then the furrow smoothed and it seemed to be all right. "I don't remember that color," she said, and her voice was soft, there was no pain there at all.

"You were very beautiful during all of that," I said.

She turned her hand, took mine and intertwined our fingers and lifted them to her lips and kissed my fingertips. I leaned my head against hers, smelled her hair, the sweetness of her hair that swept away fresh water and honeysuckle and smoke and filled me and I felt the quickness of my breath. I wanted to say, It's okay now, Fiona. You can let go of all these desperate things you've clung to for a decade. If I can love you like this, love you still, then any loving god would too, even without the rituals. You're afraid of what's in your center and surely it's not been God at all but these ways of the Church instead. Let them go now. I wanted to say these things but I kept quiet and she moved her head just a little to cover my face with her hair and when her kisses on my fingertips slowed finally to a stop and she let go of me, I lifted my arm and I put it around her, cupping her far shoulder in my hand, and I began to hum softly, in my head. An ode to joy.

We sat like that for a time, and she was breathing quickly too. I felt it in her shoulder, I heard the quick slip of it even above the plash of waves and the buzz of a boat out on the lake and the chain creak and knife slide of the roller coaster off in the maple trees, carrying John, I knew, and I was sad not to be there with him on this first try of a new coaster but I was glad to be holding Fiona, glad to be really holding her for the first time in a very long time. Let it all go, I wanted to say to her, but I knew not to say it, knew that she was very delicately balanced now, knew that any implied doubts about all those absolutes might still devastate her, knew that if she was ever to let any of that go, it wouldn't be from any persuasion of mine.

I was content to hold Fiona Price. I was content to sit beneath this sky the color of the milk of her nipples and I was with her beside this lake and I was with her, too, in the quickest center of me, sitting beneath a sky of that same color, a woman-milk sky awash over the landscape where this finite mind and body of mine knew that something important pulsed in me and in all things. I was in both places now. Fiona was in both places now. She would always be. And she sighed a ragged little sigh because her heart was beating furiously and she said, "I wonder if there was a time when I could have been an artist. I can see things a certain way, you know."

"Like Van Gogh," I said, not trying to make conversation about art but trying to place her in the fall of sunlight in the kitchen of her fifth floor walk-up with the wooden tub.

"Maybe too much like him. Maybe that's why I never tried."

I woke to her words now. "Not at all. You'd certainly have your own vision."

"Perhaps."

"And why do you say, 'there was a time'? You can still do it. Artists can start late. It's not gymnastics."

She pulled back from me a little bit and looked at me closely. There were tears in her eyes and I thought I'd made another mistake, I'd pushed too hard for this and she saw it for what it was in my mind, an alternative to the religion. But she wasn't angry. The tears just came and crouched there in her and her mouth did not grow hard and she did not bark or thrash or raise her hands to strike at me. She just sat very still and the tears clotted in her and did not fall and then she leaned to me and kissed me once, very softly, very simply, on the lips. "I'm going to change into my suit now," she said. "Why don't you go ride the coaster with John. He loves you a lot, you know."

I leaned to her and I was already hard, I realized, hard without thinking of anyone else, hard simply from these words of my wife, from her sudden mood, from the quiet *thereness* of her that I hadn't felt in years, not in years of that time we all claim to live in together, and not even in that inner time of my own that clings to all the women I've loved, that ticks softly in Fiona's hair her navel her eyes her tongue her lips her pussy her feet her shoulders. In that time of my own I had not been with her for years, she had long ago risen from beside me in the field where all the women of my life lie in the tall grass and moved off down the slope and disappeared into the trees, years ago, alone, and now she'd come back, sloughing off the shadows of the wood like water, she was inside me again, and she was here before me as well, beside this lake in New Jersey with my son rushing down a steep slope in the trees and he would be a man someday and I leaned to Fiona and kissed her in return, I kissed her and parted her mouth a little with my own and touched the soft inside of her lower lip with the tip of my tongue and even before that, even before the kiss, I was already hard, I realized, but what I did not realize was that before the kiss and during the kiss and after the kiss I did not hear Fiona's voice, even as some great sea change had come upon her I could not hear the speaking of it from inside her, I was hearing only the rush and the cries from the coaster and she said to go to him and I rose and she smiled up at me and raised her hand to me and I took it and she pulled on me, I held firm and she lifted herself by my hand, and when she was standing she whispered, "Go on now," and I went off.

I found my son in a dappled patch of sunlight by the entry gate to the coaster and the place smelled of old wood and mildew and faintly of grease and of the burning smell of quick steel on steel, and he was perched up on the slat fence that led to the turnstile and the shadows of the leaves of the maple trees quaked on his face and his chest and he looked up at me as I came to him and he did not smile. "Is it okay?" I said. "Is it any good?"

"I didn't go yet," he said.

"I had to be with her at that moment. One of those times."

"I know," he said. "That's okay."

"I'm glad you waited, though," I said and I was, but I was also beginning to press him gently at times to separate from me a little bit. I knew he would need to learn to do that.

"I wanted to talk to you first," he said and he slid off the fence and he moved a little away, drawing me with him, and I realized at once what had been on his mind the whole trip— whatever had tightened his jaw at the breakfast table, something I'd tried to set aside in my mind as just another thing like all the things we'd handled together so far.

But he took me off to one of the trees and he leaned against it and his voice quaked a little. "She said some things last night."

I braced my palm against the tree and waited. He looked away. Usually our talk was very easy about all of this. We'd done this for a long time. But he didn't look at me now and I thought of her fingertips on his cheek, his lip, and I knew. "What did she say?" I asked, trying to keep even the slightest pinch of concern out of it.

John looked back to me quickly and his eyes would not hold on me, he bowed his head.

"She told me there was only one hope for me when I died, one hope that I would not burn in hell." He hesitated after this, but just for a moment. His chest lifted and he rolled all the words out quickly now. "She said I should begin now to think of being a priest. It's the only safe way, she said. To be a priest and be pure. I don't have to be a priest, do I?"

I squared around before him and opened my arms and he climbed me and hooked his legs around me and I held him close, his head on my shoulder. "No, my little guy," I said. "You know you're going to choose your own life. She's gone way too far now." And she had, it would get worse, I knew, and there was a limit, I also knew, to how much I could protect him from the damage of all the words she might say as his body shaped into manhood.

I held him, a child still, just a baby boy, and I looked down a clear corridor of sight between the edge of the stand of maples and the back of the midway and I could see the lake and floating there were bright scraps of my brief scene with Fiona, like the flakes of sun on the chop of the water, and I could not draw a breath. I felt the touch of her lips in that kiss on the beach, the touch of the flesh of my Fiona of Avenue C. But that Fiona was gone. She was dead and reborn as a new creature, as the believers would say of her. She was somewhere nearby at that moment and she was naked, she was in a corner of the changing room and she smelled mildew and concrete and popcorn and she heard the boat drone from the lake and the distant laughter from down the beach, just as I was hearing these things, and if I had not come up to the coaster, if I had drawn my mouth from hers and helped her stand and then if I had followed her up the beach and watched her go into the changing room and if I had waited for a moment and a moment more and if I had waited until no one was looking and there was no sound inside except for the tiny sounds of Fiona, the slip of cloth, and if then I'd stepped into the doorway and her back was to me and she was naked and her skin was dazzling white, as if it were the rapture and she was about to ascend into heaven, and if I'd stood before the vision of her and if all that I am rushed into the center of my body, into the tip of my body, and I lifted to her and she felt a prickling on her skin from the nape of her neck down the indent of her spine to the cleft of her bottom and down the sweet cheeks of her and down her thighs and the backs of her knees and her ankles and it was like a cool breeze had come through but it wasn't a breeze it was my eyes upon her and if she'd heard my breathing then and she turned around very slowly and she saw me in the doorway and there I was with my dark pompadour and my Wally Moon eyebrows and my eyes that she should have expected to be dark too but they weren't, they were blue, and she could see that what was in those eyes was no anger at all, nothing like that, it was only love, she knew I loved her she knew I could see her as no one else had ever seen her and if she'd believed me if she could always have believed me, if she could have believed me forever, believed that I loved her and she was worth loving, worth it more than anyone was worth it, and if she did not cover her face she did not say anything but she stood there and her body opened to me every pore opened and she knew she was in love with me because all her pussy hairs had jumped up and because there was a freshet there beneath them, a rush of water, the sweet river that I would move to and enter and seem to drown in and then come up out of and be changed, if all that had happened this day, then maybe it would have been all right for all three of us, father son and wife lover mother sacrament holy ghost, all right for us. But as I stood there following my son's eyes to the lake I thought of her nakedness and she was far away, far far away, beyond my touch, and I did not know what to do, I could not think of a thing anymore and I said to John, "We have to love her," thinking, We can't let ourselves begin to hate her.

"Okay," he said softly.

And then he climbed down out of my arms and we went through the turnstile and onto the wooden waiting platform, dim in the shadows, and there was a smell of burning and the coaster slid before us and we sat in the front of the front car

and the iron bar came down to hold us in and then we rolled
into the shadows of the trees and then we rose up, blinking
into the sunlight, the chain had caught us and was dragging
us toward the top of the hill and the treetops fell slowly away
and we were looking into the milk blue sky and I was wrong.
I was wrong ever to imagine that loving Fiona would be enough
for her or enough for me either. And this I understood now,
even as I speak this: I was wrong to think that I could come
to understand myself with any words except the words that
yearn the way my body yearns, my body and all else that I am,
all signified in my body through the whisper of grace, and I
stand in a column of sunlight in the center of that very floor
where Fiona once stood, the building long since rubble and
the sunlight coming through skylight glass long since burst into
shreds and gathered with all the brick and wood and dumped
in a hole in the Meadowlands, but it's there that I stand now
and I lift my face to the sunlight and I wonder about that sky,
about its vastness and its agitation and I fly apart I am broken
sweetly into bits of pigment and I swirl out there around the
sun, broken down and flung out there because I have loved
all the women in my life and I love all the women I meet even
now and I tremble before the future and all the women to come
and I will love them all and each of them claims me each of
them holds all of me, takes the great rush of all of me into
them, and I crested the hill and I gripped the bar hard so that
I would not fly away and I saw the lake, saw the whole great
curve of the water and Fiona was entering the water even then,
she was wading into the water and her feet were gone and the
calves of her legs were gone and at the top of the hill there
was a moment when everything stopped and it was very quiet,
the clanking of the chains fell away and the sound of the wind
fell away and the sound of my heart fell away and I floated
between the earth and the sky and I knew that I would rush
into Rebecca as I had always yearned to do, in that place without
sound I heard her breathing and I was happy for that and it

was true, the prophecy of that moment, for a month later—
just one month after that moment floating with my son above
the lake—I am in a hotel room in Puerto Vallarta and Rebecca's
eyes are full of tears the blue of her eyes have darkened to
lake water from the tears and they are complicated tears but
I am naked and she is naked and I move to kiss the tears and
the car begins to fall I can hear nothing still but I look down
the track and my son's hand moves against mine on the bar
and *I move deeper in, the water rising to my knees and to my
thighs and the sun is very bright and I pray to God to take
this brightness away and He does He gives me the soft shadows
of His church and it's like walking into church, into this water
that rises to me, and I don't need a mother, that's one thing
wrong with the Catholic Church, and I can think this without
calling her names and I realize that and I am grateful for that
because I am still holding my own, I'm not sinning so very bad
right now and the other thing that's wrong with the Catholic
Church is that we're baptized as little babies and I can't remember the moment and it's something that I envy in the
churches with the empty crosses, they wait until you're old
enough to know what's going on and I wish I had a memory
of the moment I wish I had gone down into the water and felt
all the sins being washed away and I come up and I am clean
I am a new creature in Christ and the water is cold on me as
I move it rises up my legs and I start to tingle a little there,
in the place between my legs, in the place that I shiver at now,
the place that whispers to me to come away, into the smoke
and into the fire, and I wish it would shut up, just shut
up, and I wade harder, push against the water and go deeper in
and that part of me is covered now, underwater, and maybe
when I come out it will be changed or maybe it will just disappear, I love the nuns, I love their starched nothingness, and
they wear wedding rings and they are married to Jesus, they
are the brides of Christ, and my hands are underwater now
and something bumps me softly and I look down and the shape*

is dim but I can see a fish, a little fish and it plucks at my
wedding ring with its mouth and I feel so tender inside at this,
the little fish nibbling at the shine of my ring, and he knows
who I am and I say I love you and Rebecca's tears are on my
lips and she says, I love you, and I say it too and I have said
it all along and I have said it with every touch and every breath
on her cheek and she has always known that and the question
now is what does that mean we'll do, when the tears are gone,
and they are on my lips tasting like the sea and I kiss the lids
of her eyes and I feel the touch of her nipples, visible to me
at last, surprising in their redness, the color of raspberry, swirl-
ing into hardness with the touch of my tongue, fading in their
penumbra to a faint blush and a blue trace of veins, visible
there in the translucence of her skin, the deep secret of the
flow of her blood, and I try to put all thoughts away for now I
want only to die in her and to know her and to be known by
her and I've said to her several times in these two years that
I couldn't promise what the future would be and she has said
to me each time I'm a big girl don't treat me like I'm stupid
it's the one thing that will always make me angry at you even
though I know you're trying to be honest and I say I'm sorry
and it passes and there is no need to do that now, we do not
want any coyness here, no sweet choices, no words at all, we
know this is the time when I will rush into her and it will be
all right and the sun is coming through the balcony window
and the bay is vast and the color of jade and the room smells
of sandalwood and gardenia and already of her wet riverbank
pussy smell and this time I can go inside her and I do, without
any other touch or kiss, and we smile at this, we look each
other in the eyes and we smile and her soft grip squeezes all
the thoughts away and that is in our smiles and I do not move
for a long time inside her and I wait there and I begin to gather
I am up to my chest in the water and every tiny hair on my
body lifts, every pore tightens toward the faith of some release
and my eyes are still kept dim the water rises around me but

I am also in the church and before me in the faint haze of the morning's incense I can see Him on the cross, my sweet Jesus scattered with wounds like stars and I come nearer and His skin glows in the dim light, as if this is the moment of His ascension, His skin is so white that my own skin grows tighter still, so tight that it feels as if it will pull away from me and I will show a deeper nakedness, a self that is dazzling white as if I had never left that bed in my burning house as if my father never came and I never left and the flames had come to me instead and burned me burned this visible skin away and I was left white and beautiful and I move to the foot of this cross and I look up and His skin is white like that and gouged deep and bleeding and there is a sudden spot of warmth on my cheek and another on my forehead and it is His blood falling and I look at His face turned to the side, the ragged line of His bone black beard and the stretch of His mouth in pain, the even teeth, He is very beautiful, He is a beautiful man and his eyes are dark and they turn to me, all the rest of Him is absolutely still, just as He has been every day at Mass, but now His eyes move to me and He looks at me and I stagger back and I feel His blood on my face and I lift my hand, extend my fingertips, and I touch the spot of blood on my head and I bring it down and I do not even look at it I put my fingertips to my tongue and He tastes like the sea, warm and viscous, and I have tasted this taste before on my tongue many times I have smeared this taste around and around my nipple and then up my chest to my lips and I tremble and His hands turn now and pull free and his eyes have fixed me and they are beautiful and they are terrible and I feel the cool banding of my wedding ring and it is this hand which is lifted to my mouth and His feet pull free and He slides softly down, the eyes descend but do not let me go they just grow larger and He is falling, I think, He has leapt from somewhere above and is falling to His death His eyes are looking into my eyes and then sliding down to my breasts, quickly, and this time I act, I reach out and catch Him and He does not fall and His arms are around me and I am naked, a miracle, I am made naked and the statues are all wrong, they crucified Him naked and there was no cloth there to hide Him and all the crosses in all the churches in the world should tell the truth of it He was naked there and I feel Him against me the gouges in His flesh mouthing my arms my side my breasts my thighs and against the puddling center of me I feel the rise of that part of Him that the churches lie about, the part that was in fact naked to the world, His sweet cock, wounded too, gouged and thorned and wounded and alive now once more for me alive and I am His bride He is a man and He loves me and it's all right I am loved and that means that love exists at the distant center of the universe because we're too stupid to make something like this up and I say I love you and Rebecca says I love you and the movement begins, the wave swells along my skin and with a tide of shadows beneath it that goes bone-deep, memory-deep, like dreams that I cannot remember but I know are there and I know are very strong and though these images do not lift to the surface of my mind they move beneath my skin as part of this rush of tightness that comes from eyes and thighs and feet and hands and from the small of my back and the nape of my neck and they lift and roll toward the narrow shore, they cascade toward that impossibly tight place, into the shaft of me and then down to the tip of me and they fill me there and they are held back, the tide builds and weighs forward and it is the whole great sea of me all memory all the touching and all the words and all the smells and tastes and all that I've ever seen every particle of light and I grow inside Rebecca and when I think I'll burst from my flesh and die I do not but I grow more and more and *He says you are my bride you will have life everlasting in me and there will be no one but me and you will turn away from all others and I tremble with His arms around me and the warmth of His blood spilling down me and He puts His mouth on mine and it feels cool like the water of this lake and my feet lift beneath me and I know I am about to change, my hair lifts and swims beside me as He begins to kiss my eyes as He fills every pore as the part the churches will not show touches me, the part that was naked on the cross to Mary His mother and to Mary the whore who loved Him and to all the world naked, this part of Him that really made God a man, really did, God's cock, God walked the earth and He had a cock and that was His secret part and it still is, He knows my secrets too and our two secrets rush together and whisper to each other and it's all right, we are in love and I breathe deep and deeper still as He fills me up I will not let him go* and I do not consciously see all the lovely eyes that have looked at me this way but I look into Rebecca's eyes and they are as blue as the milk from a woman's nipple and they are dilated with love and she is the only woman in the world at that moment but I am enormous now and I am minute, in the tenderest tip of me I fill the sky and I compress into a quark and in both I leap with unshaped memories, with the eyes of all the women in the world, all the women I've embraced or failed to embrace or perhaps will yet embrace, and if God is infinite it surely *must* be thus for there is no end to the secrets no end to the cosmic whisper of all the separate and beautiful souls signified in these bodies I yearn to touch and to love and I don't need to ask Rebecca to keep her eyes open to me for she does and she will not ask what is next for us and I will not ask what is next for us and in the long pale fall of light from the window I can see her and the light is part of this and the shadow of a parasailor floating past is part of this and the shadow of a bird dashing past and every word I've spoken here is part of this the fall of snow and the sparks from a train turning and a humming in the eaves and the faint jangle of a bracelet unseen and a wisp of incense smoke rising before a dead father and a lit window across a dusk-darkened yard and the cut of a rubber tree and the smell of the South China Sea and a puddle of light beneath the streets of Paris and a city of bones and a kiss before sightless eyes and black Mary Janes and a body falling through dark water and a fish plucking at a gold band for a moment and then letting go and watching the bright scrap fade beneath it and this trembling in me and these things are infinite they gather up and they are the world made and remade forever and made new with every moment more that I live, that I go out in the street and pass among the women there, and the sky and the sea and the air and the earth cling to each of the women and there is no end I fill with no ending and I rush now and I know already that I will rush again and I rush and each time there is more to the rushing and I rush and each time I come closer *and I breathe again and my body wants to thrash as it fills with water but I do not let it I take the water into me I fill my lungs with the water and I fall now fall into the dark and He holds me close and He kisses me and He enters me now in my own secret place He is fire there and He is water and I let go to Him and I fall with Him into the dark and I whisper to Him, At last* and Rebecca whispers, At last, and she feels the rush and I fall deeper into her and her eyes are on mine but now they close softly and open again, in rapture, I know, *the rapture has come and we are one flesh and we rise together* we rise and we are one flesh in that moment, *We.*

I followed Karen Granger to the edge of the tarred street and watched her bend and take the tar into her mouth and this was when I first met her and I told her my name and I despaired. But I hadn't lost my chance with her. We spent some time together that summer and I even took her to the X-ray machine and I put my arm around her. That was the first time I ever touched her, and I never touched her again. The summer was almost over and she moved away before school began and the last time I saw Karen Granger, she was riding her bike. Riding it the way many kids in our neighborhood did in 1955: following the truck around that sprayed for mosquitoes. Following in the cloud it gave off. It was soon after the sun was down and I was sitting on the front step of our house and I could smell the heavy scent of the poison and I could hear the hoarse whisper of the truck and I was ready to rise and go into the house and then I saw her. She was riding in the cloud of spray, following the truck. I could not see the russet of her hair and I could not see her eyes and she was barefoot, I think, but I could see nothing of the details of her feet. She was just a dark shape there, following some impulse in herself that I did not understand. And she turned her face to me as she passed and she waved at me and I came down off the porch and the cloud rolled softly over me and made me suddenly light-headed and I turned away. And that was that.

I do not know if Karen Granger's lungs now are whole, or if her blood is whole, or if her bones are whole. I only know that, as I stand on the beach at Puerto Vallarta and watch a parasailor glide out over the bay, in some less definable part of me, I am not.

ROBERT OLEN BUTLER is the author of six critically acclaimed novels (*The Alleys of Eden, Sun Dogs, Countrymen of Bones, On Distant Ground, Wabash,* and *The Deuce*). All six are being reissued in 1994 by Henry Holt, which also published his collection of short stories, *A Good Scent from a Strange Mountain*, winner of the 1993 Richard and Hinda Rosenthal Foundation Award from the American Academy of Arts and Letters, as well as the 1993 Pulitzer Prize for Fiction. He lives in Lake Charles, Louisiana, where he teaches creative writing at McNeese State University.